Praise for *The Index of Self-Destructive Acts*

"Ranging effortlessly from baseball statistics to insider trading, and from street-corner prophecy to Romantic poetry, Beha finds the nuance and humanity in every subject he takes up. *The Index of Self-Destructive Acts* is that increasingly rare thing: a big, ambitious novel that boldly explores contemporary life in all of its complexities and contradictions."

—ANDREW MARTIN, author of *Early Work*

"Each character is engaging and full-blooded, and Beha pushes them hard. . . . [The novel's] breadth, ambition, and command are refreshing. An admirably big-picture, multivalent family saga."

—*KIRKUS*, a starred review

"Beha's earlier work has been rightfully compared to the work of Graham Greene, and in this new novel Beha does what only Greene and a handful of other novelists have been able to accomplish: make God, belief, and doubt the stuff of serious fiction—even down to the probing dialogue of his characters."

—NICK RIPATRAZONE, The Millions

More praise for Christopher Beha

"*What Happened to Sophie Wilder* is about many things—the New York publishing world, the growing pains of post-collegiate life, the rigors of Roman Catholicism—but at its center it's a moving meditation on why and for whom we write."

—SARAH TOWERS, the *New York Times Book Review*

"Christopher Beha is one of the most talented young writers at work today."

—JESS WALTER, author of *Beautiful Ruins*

"Beha's [*Arts & Entertainments*] captures in hilarious detail the many insidious ways we rush to cheapen our own identities, and how even as our sense of self veers out of our control, we still never stop trying for some deeper meaning. A funhouse dissection of our current frailties."

—DANA SPIOTTA, author of *Innocents and Others*

"*What Happened to Sophie Wilder* is an old-fashioned literary novel in the very best sense. . . . Beha has managed to produce a book that is satisfying for anyone who reads in order to live."

—HELEN SCHULMAN, author of *This Beautiful Life*

"I tore through *Arts & Entertainments* in a single evening, riveted by Beha's satiric indictment of an appallingly recognizable celebrity culture . . . a deft, clever, and altogether too plausible novel, its last line delivering an unexpected punch that is entirely earned."

—REBECCA MEAD, author of *My Life in Middlemarch*

THE INDEX OF
SELF-DESTRUCTIVE ACTS

Published by Tin House Books, Portland, Oregon

Distributed by W. W. Norton & Company

Library of Congress Cataloging-in-Publication Data

Names: Beha, Christopher R., author.
Title: The index of self-destructive acts / Christopher Beha.
Description: Portland, Oregon : Tin House Books, [2020]
Identifiers: LCCN 2020000720 | ISBN 9781947793828 (hardcover) | ISBN 9781947793927 (ebook)
Classification: LCC PS3602.E375 I53 2020 | DDC 813/.6--dc23
LC record available at https://lccn.loc.gov/2020000720

First US Edition 2020
Printed in the USA
Interior design by Diane Chonette

www.tinhouse.com

The Index of Self-Destructive Acts

A Novel

Christopher Beha

TIN HOUSE BOOKS / Portland, Oregon

To Jim

"The Index of Self-Destructive Acts is the total number of hit batsmen, wild pitches, balks, and errors by a pitcher, per nine innings."

—BILL JAMES

The New Bill James Historical Baseball Abstract

.

"I agree that two times two is four is an excellent thing; but if we're going to start praising everything, then two times two is five is sometimes also a most charming little thing."

—FYODOR DOSTOEVSKY

Notes from Underground
(trans. Pevear & Volokhonsky)

PART ONE:

THE YOUNG MAN FROM THE PROVINCES

(April/May)

1.

What makes a life, Sam Waxworth sometimes wondered—self or circumstance?

On the day that Waxworth arrived in New York to write for the *Interviewer*, a man named Herman Nash stood on the rim of the fountain in Washington Square and announced that the world was about to end. After close biblical reading and careful calculation, Nash had settled on November 1 at 10:00 PM as the precise moment of the event he called the "Great Unveiling." (So far as Waxworth knew, no time zone had been specified; perhaps it would be an incremental apocalypse.) A tourist captured the prediction on video, and more than fifty thousand people watched it on TeeseView that week. Nash appeared at the same time the following Saturday and the one after that, by which point his audience had grown so large that it brought out the police. When he called on his listeners to prepare for a coming battle, at least one took the words literally, throwing a bottle of urine at a mounted officer, who lost control of his horse, which ran him out of the park and several blocks up Fifth. All of this was in turn recorded and posted and viewed. Soon it seemed that Armageddon was everywhere.

Waxworth wasn't one to find intimations of catastrophe in the pages of a three-thousand-year-old assemblage of myth and poetry and legal documents. Waxworth was a philosopher—not by training or occupation but, he believed, by disposition. He tried to attend to the facticity of things. The world, in Waxworth's view, was a knowable place, once you stripped away the dead tradition and wishful thinking built up over millennia of misunderstanding. For most of human history—and even today, in places—such an effort could condemn you to death. Conditions were better in Waxworth's particular moment and milieu, but absolute honesty still required a certain amount of courage. In lieu of rack and ropes, the modern skeptic faced social suspicion and familial disappointment. Faced too his own admitted desire that life should carry more meaning than the facts would bear. Which facts were these: we occupied a tiny corner of the universe, minor planet orbiting a minor star, in an even tinier corner of cosmological time. Still we wanted all of it, the sun and the moon and the firmament that held them, to be about us. This want had been bred into humanity, selected by nature, so it must have served some purpose once, but it had long outlived its usefulness, as far as Waxworth was concerned. What was needed now was to *know*.

For all that, he felt an odd admiration for Herman Nash, who'd made a prediction that could be tested against the world and, in so doing, put himself at risk of being wrong. When you stuck to interpreting the past, you could say anything. The sheer amount of available information meant that data could be arranged to support every conceivable idea. The test of knowledge was what it told you about tomorrow. Easy enough to laugh at Herman Nash, but the very things that made his prediction so inviting to mock—its combination of specificity and unlikelihood—were exactly what impressed Waxworth. Nash wasn't using the usual methods would-be prophets relied on to perpetuate their frauds: piggybacking on a reasonably likely outcome, making open-ended predictions that could be fulfilled at any time, spouting vague language that might allow him to alter his claim when the unveiling failed to occur. There was no mistaking his terms.

"He's probably a lunatic," Waxworth admitted to his editor over dinner during his second week in town. "But that's better than being a con artist."

"There's something inspiring about it when you put it that way," his editor replied.

They were eating at Temps Perdu, a neo-bistro on the Bowery. The host had seated them at a red leather banquette near the back of the room. A large mirror hung over the editor's head, and Waxworth saw himself in it, framed by distressed brick and pressed tin. In front of Waxworth waited a foie gras terrine with rhubarb compote. French yé-yé pop played softly from speakers above. They were nearly through their first bottle of red, and the editor, whose name was Max Blakeman, was attempting to order a second. It was the spring of 2009. The global economy was in a state of collapse, and Waxworth understood the magazine industry to be more completely collapsed than most, but Mario Adrian—Teeser cofounder, social media billionaire—had lately purchased the *Interviewer*, rendering the publication more or less immune from cyclical pressure. So Blakeman had explained when convincing Waxworth to move halfway across the country to write for him. This introductory dinner seemed designed to prove the point.

"It really gets to the heart of my philosophy," Waxworth said.

"You have your own philosophy?" Blakeman gave a not-quite smile. "I've always wanted one of those, but they seem like so much work to maintain."

Max Blakeman was attentive and solicitous but had a way of making this solicitous attention feel like an unearned gratuity. That Waxworth should want to impress his new boss was natural enough, but he also wanted, to a greater degree than professional self-interest could explain, to be liked. He wanted to belong in this place.

"I believe in getting things wrong."

Blakeman smiled in full, almost indulged a laugh.

"I wish you'd told me that before I hired you. I thought you were the guy who got everything right."

Waxworth was slightly uncomfortable with his recently minted reputation as a seer. He'd been working as a software engineer in Madison the previous fall, when his political projection system had correctly predicted the exact count of the electoral college vote and the outcome of every Senate, House, and gubernatorial race. Naturally he'd been pleased with the attention that had followed this feat, but there was nothing mystical in what he'd done. Quite the opposite: the numbers had been there all along for anyone who cared to look.

"Of course I don't want to be wrong all the time, but it's bound to happen eventually. In the long run everyone regresses to the mean."

"There's a philosophy," Blakeman said. "*In the long run everyone regresses to the mean.*"

"The point is, beliefs should be tested against the world. That's the scientific method. You don't just try to convince people with arguments. You don't put reality to a vote. You set up an experiment, and you predict how it will come out. If you're wrong, you modify your theory, and you start over. Little by little, you arrive at the truth."

"So this guy should be embraced for giving his ravings some rigor?"

"If anything, more people should do it."

Blakeman leaned back in appreciation.

"Why All Religious People Should Be Like Herman Nash." He looked up as though the headline floated in the air between them. "It sounds very shareable." After a pause, he clarified, "That's a good thing. Mario is big on *shareability.*"

He said the word with cheerful disgust before raising his hand, waving away further thought of the man who was paying for their meal before gesturing again to the waiter for the next bottle.

"Speaking of shareability," Blakeman continued as their glasses were refilled, "what do you think of Frank Doyle?"

"In what sense?"

"Did you ever read those old baseball books of his? *The Smell of the Grass. The Crack of the Bat.*"

"Sure I did."

In fact, the books had been a major feature of Waxworth's childhood, the reason he'd wanted to write in the first place, but he was embarrassed to mention this, given the current state of Doyle's reputation.

"How'd you like to do something on him?"

"What is there to say, at this point? That whole story is months old."

"Fair enough," Blakeman said. "We'll start with the end of the world, and see where things go from there."

Three hours later, Waxworth got off the F train at Fourth Avenue and Ninth Street. A bus that stopped nearby would get him the rest of the way home, but he wasn't sure it ran at this hour. Anyway, the spring night was cool and clear, and he was in no rush to get back to an empty apartment. While he walked, he called Lucy, who answered after four rings. He could hear the sleep in her voice, though Madison was an hour behind New York. He hadn't realized how late it was.

"Sorry to wake you," he said. "I got stuck on the train."

"That's all right," she answered. "I'm glad you called."

He wanted to tell her about everything—the restaurant, the meal, the wine, the conversation—without sounding like he'd enjoyed himself too much. Lucy still didn't understand why he'd had to move right away, instead of waiting for her school year to end. She didn't really understand why they had to move at all.

"We've already planned my first post. Just talked it out across the table. It never would have happened over email." Now he sounded defensive, relitigating a case that had already been settled in his favor. "How's everything there?"

"Jeremy bit me on the hand today." She laughed. "Nearly broke the skin."

Waxworth couldn't tell whether he was meant to laugh along or offer sincere sympathy. Lucy liked to joke about her job—she taught special ed—but it was a kind of gallows humor, and he didn't always feel entitled to share in it. He let out an ambiguous sigh.

"I miss you."

"You too," she responded. "I want to hear all about your dinner—in the morning."

After the election, Waxworth had received some offers that would have allowed them to stay in Madison. Most of the major national publications that had linked to his website throughout the campaign had tried to hire him, but they only wanted to buy his projection system and host his blog. He'd made that mistake before. He'd still been in school when he'd sold his baseball forecasting algorithm, YOUNT, to a website called the Pop-Up. They'd given him a lump sum for the code and paid him fifty dollars a week to update its results. The money had seemed like a lot at the time—enough to clear his student loans and buy an engagement ring—but when he saw what the site charged for subscriptions, he realized that he'd settled for far less than his work was worth. When he finally demanded a raise—he'd wanted enough to live on, so he could leave his job at the university, but he would have settled for a few thousand a year—the Pop-Up found someone else to do the updates. He no longer owned YOUNT, and he'd signed a noncompete that kept him from designing another sports-projection system for at least five years.

He'd been lucky to stumble from there into politics, and he meant to make the most of it. Not learning from mistakes was the one truly unforgivable sin in Waxworth's view. Max Blakeman had offered more money than anyone else, but this was only part of his appeal. While other editors talked about what readerships they could bring Waxworth, Blakeman had talked about what Waxworth would bring to his readership. The kind of people who read the *Interviewer* needed to learn how to think numerically. That was the age we were living in.

The contract paid one hundred and twenty thousand dollars for five posts a week and four long print articles to be completed over the course of the year. That last item Waxworth had insisted upon himself. Though it wasn't entirely rational—the website had a much larger audience than the weekly magazine—he wanted the validation of print, and he sensed that these longer pieces would help him get the book deal that was his ultimate goal.

For the first few months Waxworth would be the sole writer for the magazine's new data-driven blog, *Quantified World*, but after he'd established the brand he could make his own hires. What excited Waxworth most about the job was the chance to work on a team. Getting out of your own point of view was essential to good forecasting. Aggregation—the foundation of statistical thinking— had long been known simply as "the combination of observations," and that's what collaboration gave you. If Lucy didn't like New York, they could go back to Madison when his contract was up, by which point his career would be launched.

So ran the justification he'd given to her, which was accurate in its particulars but incomplete. In fact the move had been the great draw of Blakeman's offer, and Waxworth had no intention of returning to Wisconsin. He had an opportunity at greatness, and he belonged in a place worthy of his ambitions. He needed to test his ideas against the world.

For centuries, the primary limit on human knowledge had been record-keeping. We couldn't collect all the facts. Even something relatively rudimentary like YOUNT would have been impossible when Waxworth was a kid reading box scores in the paper. It depended on a publicly available database of player statistics—every meaningful event at every major and minor league game, recorded in searchable form. We were living through a revolution in counting technologies, and the world needed people who knew what to do with the numbers. Self—or circumstance? Waxworth had no time for such mystical notions as destiny or fate. Pure luck had determined that his particular skills so well suited the needs of the moment into which he'd been born. But this made it only more important that he take his chance.

There was something else, too, which couldn't be said outright. Lucy had grown up happy. She'd had a comfortable childhood in Madison, where both her parents had worked for the university, and all she'd ever wanted for herself was the same comfort. Aspiration had never played a great role in her life. Sam had grown up poor, bouncing from place to place while his mother looked for work, dreaming that things might be better. For Sam their comfortable life in Madison had felt like an achievement, but this very fact prompted the idea that there might be more. Lucy had started at a higher point, but she'd stayed where she was. She'd lived parallel to the x-axis, and she wanted now only for y to remain constant. There had been a slope to Sam's life, and it was only natural that he should extrapolate. New York, the *Interviewer*, dinner at Temps Perdu: these all seemed like suitable next points on the graph.

He looked up at the next corner and read the sign for Sigourney Street. The name was unfamiliar to him. He already knew all the cross streets near the apartment, and this wasn't one of them. He retraced his steps for ten minutes before he found the place where he'd gone wrong. It took another ten to get home from there. The smell told him when he was getting close.

Waxworth had been fairly comprehensive when designing his apartment-search algorithm. He'd limited his range of neighborhoods based on safety, vibrancy, and proximity to a feature (waterfront, public park, major cultural institution), as well as location relative to the *Interviewer*'s offices on Union Square and the school in Park Slope where Lucy would be teaching in the fall. He'd calculated distances based on mileage and average commute time. He'd scouted suitable routes for Lucy's morning run. Within these parameters, the main criterion was value, measured in square feet per dollar. One apartment in Red Hook had come out so far ahead of the others that Waxworth worried he was missing something. It wasn't especially well served by public transportation, but this didn't seem sufficient to explain the discrepancy. You could see lower Manhattan from the window. You could walk along the river. Further research suggested that the neighborhood was even a little hip. The algorithm didn't account for this attribute—such subjective preferencing was in fact just the kind of market inefficiency the thing was designed to exploit—but it wouldn't hurt when selling Lucy on the area.

He'd examined the block on TeeseView and found it slightly postindustrial but not at all menacing. The building itself was occupied on its first floor by something called Hun Lee Poultry House, its name written in English and Chinese on a green awning beside cartoon drawings of a chicken and a duck. Waxworth imagined cooking odors coming up from the kitchen, some noise from late-night pickups, but when he adjusted his calculations to account for all this, the apartment still came out on top. If the restaurant was any good, it might become an additional feature of the place.

And so it might have, if the Hun Lee Poultry House had in fact been a restaurant, rather than a wholesale distributor—a warehouse full of live, caged birds. Halfway down the block, one suffered only a mild unpleasantness, as though something run over in the street had been left to rot. As you approached the building, the smell intensified at a rate not quite exponential but certainly more than linear. In the stairwell, unaccustomed eyes would water. You could practically see the stench in the air. The urgent squawks that passed through the walls all but demanded to be anthropomorphized into pleas for release.

All this made the apartment itself quite bearable by comparison, Waxworth reflected as he finally walked in. It was on the third floor, insulated from the noise, and the smell seemed no worse there than it did a few buildings away. A box spring and mattress had been delivered on the day he arrived, and they sat in the middle of the bedroom, piled with pillows and sheets he'd bought a few days later. He knew he ought to buy a headboard or frame or whatever it was that turned a mattress and box spring into a proper bed. Lucy usually handled such details. She'd handled them for a decade now, since their junior year of college. Like so much that fell under her purview, this was easy to overlook. He was on the cusp of thirty now, but he had no baseline for an adult life in her absence, which made it hard to account for her contributions to his well-being. Waxworth tried to avoid this sort of cognitive bias, but no one could eliminate it entirely. For example, he thought as he lay down unsteadily, perhaps a bit drunker than he'd realized during the walk, he'd never considered, when deciding on the timing of this move, how difficult it would be to sleep alone.

"Late night?" the *Interviewer*'s receptionist asked as Waxworth stepped off the elevator the next morning. She'd been reading a book at her desk when he arrived, but she set it aside as though prepared for a lengthy conversation.

Her name was Emily Something. She was twenty-two or -three and notably beautiful, but not in the blonde midwestern way familiar to him. She had chin-length black hair with bangs, and her white tank top revealed a line of Gothic-type German tattooed on the inside of one pale arm. *You must change your life*, she'd said to Waxworth when she'd caught him staring at it. *Rilke*, she'd added after a moment.

"Do I look that bad?" he asked her now.

"You look just fine. But nights with Blakeman are usually late."

"So I'm learning."

She laughed eagerly, though as far as Waxworth could determine nothing funny had actually been said.

"I'll send an intern out for Advil."

"Thanks," Waxworth said.

He still wasn't used to being treated so enthusiastically by someone so obviously cooler than he was. When Blakeman first introduced them during a brief tour of the office, Waxworth had assumed her zeal was a polite show. But she was actually friendlier in the absence of their boss. Warm greetings were more or less the core of her professional responsibilities, of course, but she seemed almost flustered by his attention. Waxworth had to remind himself that he was the magazine's big new hire, that Emily's great aspiration was probably to have something like the job that he'd just started.

He walked on with no sense of where he was headed. He didn't have his own desk; no one did. The open office plan had apparently been modeled on the Teeser headquarters in Palo Alto. There were couches and armchairs, long tables where you could dock your *Interviewer*-issued laptop, a wraparound deck with an all-weather Ping-Pong table, but no assigned places and no interior walls made of anything but glass. Waxworth didn't even really need to be there— Blakeman had assured him that he could do all his writing from home—but he felt obliged to show himself, if only for Lucy's sake.

The first table after reception had no one seated at it. Waxworth settled there, plugged in his computer, and searched online for information about Herman Nash. A few of Nash's "followers" were treating the thing with irony, or as a kind of performance art, but others obviously took his prediction seriously. Someone had created a TeesePage with a countdown clock and clips of Nash's preaching. Waxworth opened a video and listened to the man's surprisingly melodic voice. He certainly looked the part—tall and thin, with white hair that shot from his head in electrified waves and the wild gray beard of a prophet of old. Waxworth could see why the performance appealed even to those with little interest in the finer points of homiletics.

"You yourselves know full well that the day of the Lord will come like a thief in the night," Nash said. "While they are saying, 'peace and safety,' destruction will come."

Waxworth thought of his mother, as he did almost any time he heard one of the Bible verses she'd made him memorize as a child. She'd been raised a midwestern Methodist but had not had much interest in religion until Sam's father left a few months after his birth. This departure she'd taken as a sign that she'd sinned against God by having a child with a man—what was worse, a Jew—whom she'd never married. She'd been born again to a rather more consuming Baptist faith, and she'd centered her life around the Lord ever after. Sam knew the story so well because she'd told it repeatedly throughout his childhood, when his father had been named only as the agent that had brought their family back to God. After Sam got to college and announced that he was an atheist, his father somehow became instead the thing that had led her son from the righteous path, though Sam had never even spoken to him.

In the seven years since Sam's wedding—which his mother had refused to attend—they'd spoken only a handful of times. Their last conversation had been so marked by mutual recriminations that it was tough to know which one of them had finally sworn off the other. Even now, he wasn't sure whether his mother knew he was in New York. Still, he was certain that she held out hope for him: her son's apostasy could only be a prelude to a deeper faith, because God had a plan, and they were all a part of it.

Waxworth had spent a great deal of his life thinking about fore-casting, and he'd come to conclude that the greatest impediment to predicting the future correctly was the belief that the world held meaning, the belief—as his mother put it—that everything happened for a reason. This was trivially true in the strictest sense that every effect had a cause, but if you expected things to cohere into a sensible story, you were apt to make events fit your preconstructed pattern, to see things as they ought to be instead of as they were. In reality events happened one way that might as easily have happened some other way, and *ought* had nothing to do with it. That was why all good forecasting was probabilistic rather than deterministic. After the fact, we told sto-ries of inevitability, but we were not characters in some book that had already been written. The future wasn't fixed, waiting somewhere for us to arrive. It was brought into being by chance, contingency, unin-tended consequences. The best we could do was work out the odds.

It's not impossible that the world will end on the first of November, Waxworth typed into his laptop. *It's just very, very unlikely. But exactly how unlikely?* From this beginning, he detoured briefly into Bayesian inference. We could not know for sure that Nash was wrong, since the world (or at least human experience of it) almost certainly would indeed end at *some* point. Instead of simply dismissing the outcome, we should assign it an initial probability. The fact that the world had not ceased to be on any of a countless number of preceding days sug-gested that we assign a rather low initial probability to its ending at a specific future time, but how much should Nash's supposed evidence move us off this prior assumption? The answer was not much, but the question itself allowed Waxworth to raise his larger point about using predictions to put knowledge to the test.

The argument was a good introduction of his working principles, and Blakeman was right: it was shareable. It became the *Interviewer*'s most Teesed story on the day it appeared as the debut post of *Quantified World*. If a quarter of the users who'd shared it on their feeds had actually opened the link first, it was read by more people than anything Waxworth had ever written before. By the next morning, a dozen responses had appeared on various outlets, and hundreds of readers had commented on the *Interviewer*'s site. One of these commenters, who called himself *Lord of the Files*, suggested that Waxworth was being satirical, offering a subtle critique of the notion that everything could be quantified. Waxworth wrote a follow-up post, explaining that everything—at least everything real—*could* be quantified. *That's precisely what makes it real*, he patiently insisted. This post too was widely shared. On Thursday Waxworth wrote a response to the responses to his response. He could have kept this up forever, but Blakeman drew a line.

"We're still establishing your position," he explained over lunch at the Union Square Cafe, down the block from the *Interviewer*'s offices. "We need to get you into as many conversations as possible. We're looking for breadth, not depth. People should feel like a story isn't over until it gets the Waxworth treatment."

Blakeman proceeded to run through a list of news items that had flared up in the previous two days. They settled on Rod Blagojevich, the Illinois governor who'd just been indicted for trying to sell the president's open Senate seat.

"Was he getting a good deal?" Blakeman wondered. "How much is a Senate seat actually worth?"

Waxworth spent the afternoon estimating the change in lifetime earnings a person could expect after a term in the Senate. He added a few other values—the concrete perks of the job, the nonmonetary value of the position's prestige—and concluded that Blagojevich could have fairly asked for around a million dollars. Writing up his results took a few more hours. Five minutes after the post went live, *Lord of the Files* submitted a long comment about how misguided the enterprise was, either missing or ignoring the fact that the whole thing was an obvious joke.

"That's the first sign that you're a real writer," Blakeman said over coffee. "When you've got readers who can be counted on to hate anything you write before they've even read it."

"You think I'm a real writer?" Waxworth asked impulsively.

Blakeman looked mildly embarrassed by the question.

"I've been thinking more about that Frank Doyle thing," he responded, as though it had been Waxworth's idea and he was just starting to come around to it. "The time seems right for a reappraisal. Doyle was a big personality in this city for a long time, and he's just disappeared. People sort of miss him, though no one wants to admit it. The guy who took his place on the *Herald*'s opinion page is so boring. At least Doyle always liked a fight. It hardly seemed to matter what side he was on."

"What's there to be quantified?" Waxworth asked. "Maybe I could predict the chances he'll get his career back, but that seems about as likely as the apocalypse, and I've already done that one."

Blakeman grimaced slightly. He seemed to be one of those people who said nearly every word in jest but expected absolute seriousness from others at unpredictable times.

"I'm not talking about *Quantified World*. I thought it could be your first print feature. I'm sure he'd give you some good quotes. If it goes well we could put it on the cover."

"You really think the story is cover-worthy?"

"I've got a great angle. The Mets are opening their new ballpark next week, and I've got two tickets right at field level. Doyle's first time at a game since his flameout. People will eat it up. Politics and baseball in one go—it should be just your thing."

"Doyle and I don't much agree on either."

Why was he so resistant to writing about the man? All of Blakeman's instincts had proven sound, and he was now offering Waxworth the cover of the magazine.

"That's the whole point. We want a little tension. Anyway, we've already got the tickets. If you don't think it will work as a longer piece, I'm sure you can get a few hundred words out of it for the blog. If nothing else, you'll get to see a game."

Before getting on the train that night, Waxworth stopped at the Union Square Barnes & Noble to look for Doyle's books. He found a single copy of *The Crack of the Bat*, the second collection of his baseball columns.

Sam had been eleven years old when his mother gave him Doyle's first collection, *The Smell of the Grass*. There was no particular occasion for the purchase, which she'd handed over, unwrapped, a look of uncertainty on her face. They didn't have a lot of money, and gifts were so rare that the book had carried a kind of aura for Sam. She took him to the local library every other week, and he always chose baseball books—*Catcher with a Glass Arm*, *The Kid from Tomkinsville*—but this was something else entirely. It was not a single long story but a bunch of shorter ones. In fact, they weren't really stories at all. More like arguments. Doyle made constant reference to names Sam didn't know, not just old ballplayers like Ducky Medwick or Hank Bauer but Carlyle, Tocqueville, Rousseau. Every other page contained unfamiliar words. When Sam asked his mother what they meant, she sent him to the dictionary, and he could tell she didn't know them either. He loved the book, and all the things he found difficult about it only made him love it more. His favorite essay was the one in which Doyle called Robin Yount an "emblem of the working class." Sam was a Brewers fan, and he worshipped Yount. Before long he could recite whole paragraphs of that essay, though he did not understand what most of them meant.

On the train, he took out *The Crack of the Bat* and started looking over it. The book included one of Doyle's most famous columns, about how growing up a Brooklyn Dodgers fan had been "training for liberalism": *It is the liberal's nature not to be disappointed by human failures but to remain hopeful. Not for us the tragic view of life. "We'll get 'em next year" is the liberal's natural rallying cry.* When Sam first read the essay in high school, he hadn't known anything about Frank Doyle's politics. He certainly hadn't known that Doyle was far more famous in most circles as a political commentator than as a baseball writer. Sam and his mother spent every Sunday morning at church, but even if they'd been otherwise unoccupied, they would never have watched the morning talk shows whose roundtable discussions so often featured Doyle. Though an author's note said that Frank Doyle was a Pulitzer-Prize-winning columnist for the New York *Herald*, Sam had never read the paper, and he'd assumed that Doyle was a sports writer.

In truth, Sam was already starting to move on from Doyle's brand of gauzy elegy by the time his mother gave him *The Crack of the Bat*. He'd discovered Bill James, the Society for American Baseball Research, and the way of thinking that James called sabermetrics. His favorite baseball book was now James's *Historical Baseball Abstract*. His second favorite was *The Baseball Encyclopedia*—a collection of pure numbers. Entire sabermetric message boards were dedicated to tearing apart Doyle's know-nothing mythologies, and Doyle in turn liked to mock the "bean counters" who tried to pin the game down and dissect it, which always meant killing it first. Doyle's third baseball book, *The Warning Track*, had come out while Sam was in college. His mother had mailed it to him in hardcover. They weren't always speaking then, and the gift recalled happier—or at least simpler—days in their relationship. He'd never even opened it, because he knew it would disappoint him, and he didn't want to feel superior to this thing that his mother had given him in a spirit of reconciliation.

The fact that Doyle had undergone a dramatic rightward shift between his second and third books made little difference to Sam, who'd had no interest in politics before meeting Lucy. When Doyle turned into a full-throated advocate for war in Iraq, he became an embarrassment to a generation of liberals—Lucy's parents among them—who'd been reading his column religiously for two decades. But Sam had given up on the man long before.

He hadn't been watching when Doyle committed his final embarrassment in the broadcast booth, but he'd seen it a few times online. It was inexcusable, of course, but Waxworth had known far longer than most that Frank Doyle was old and out of touch. He felt about the whole incident the sad, somewhat detached feeling of discovering that someone you'd known years before and would probably never have seen again had just died. It was too bad, of course, but it hardly affected him. It had become fashionable to say that Doyle's sports writing was his only redeeming work, but Waxworth felt the opposite: the real scandal wasn't Doyle's stance on stem cells or welfare reform; it was his stance on baseball.

It occurred to Waxworth suddenly that this was exactly what he would write. He would show the general reader that Doyle had been wrong for far longer than they'd ever suspected. He was not going to offer a reconsideration of the man, an opening through which he might return to public life. He was going to bury him once and for all.

2.

Just before being discharged, Eddie had switched from Ambien to zaleplon, which had fewer side effects—no blackouts, no memory loss—but got him only halfway through the night, so he was up around 4:00 now, filled with nervous energy.

In the group sessions they'd made him join in Fayetteville before they let him go home, some guys talked about the things they saw whenever they closed their eyes. The leg of a buddy taken out by an IED, the face of the insurgent who'd put them in a chair. Eddie saw nothing. This was the problem: he saw nothing, but he still *saw*. The insides of his eyelids—not black but a dark red, with lighter particles floating across—remained vividly present. It was as though he'd been on alert for so long that whatever switch in his brain was supposed to turn his eyes off had been disconnected. Once you noticed that you were still seeing in this way, it became like trying to sleep with your eyes open and all the lights on.

By five he was on the track at the reservoir. The weather was getting warm, but he wore an old St. Albert's sweat suit to approximate the feeling of jogging in his ACUs. The light gray of his hooded shirt was dark across the chest and under the arms before he'd finished his first lap. He wasn't the only one overdressed: one man wore what looked to be aluminum foil around his arms; two women ran together in surgical masks. There was an air of desperate obligation about nearly everyone out so early, as though some malignant spirit chased them all. Usually it was something from Eddie's past that pursued him, but on this morning it was the evening ahead that he wanted to escape.

He'd always dreaded his family's parties, so central to the legend of Frank and Kit Doyle. On his mandated tours of the house, his parents' friends had been as eager to return to their adult cocktail chatter as he'd been to get back to his video games. Justin and Blakeman often stayed over on those nights, but in some ways this made things worse. The guests took an avid interest in Justin, whose mere presence flattered their good intentions. They liked the fact that he didn't entirely fit. Blakeman fit perfectly, but he had an inborn ability to charm that Eddie lacked. Eddie lacked, too, the precocity of his sister, Margo, who'd recited Keats to the *Herald*'s lead book critic at eleven years old.

In theory things would be different now. He was an adult, less inclined to care what these people thought. He'd been through things unfathomable to them. Besides which, he was the party's occasion. Yet the house would be filled with all the same people, having all the same conversations. This wasn't anybody's fault. Despite persistent prompting, Eddie hadn't added any names to Kit's guest list. He'd still been in Fayetteville, waiting for his walking papers, when she'd started talking about "having something" for him. She'd ordered invitations before he got back to New York, and it seemed too late to tell her that he wasn't feeling festive. So she'd invited the regulars. Of course, they would all have been invited anyway. The real point of the party was to pretend the past eight years had never happened. He couldn't blame anyone for that, either. Who wouldn't wish those years away?

As he ran, he imagined the polite conversations ahead of him. Why did he dread them so? These people had known him all his life, appeared in his home every three or four months throughout his childhood, watched him grow up in a kind of stop-motion reel. Surely they felt sincere gratification at his safe return. Fair to say he'd faced worse threats. The real problem was that Eddie didn't want to be safely returned. He certainly didn't think his return worth celebrating.

Around the third or fourth lap, his lungs opened a bit. He brought up a warm knuckle of phlegm and spit it through the chain-link fence, watched it clear the bricks and hit the surface of the water. After 6:00, the track started to fill out with those for whom running was a form of exercise or benign discipline rather than obsession or self-harm. Eddie usually quit about that time and tried to get some more sleep before properly starting his day, but now he pressed on. He thought he might get to ten miles. He'd barely been able to run two or three before he'd enlisted, but now it didn't seem like real effort until he neared double digits.

Kit gave her familiar worried look as he passed her on his way upstairs, as though she suspected him of secretly spending the night on the streets. He showered before dropping back into bed, where he expected to sleep for an hour, be up around eight—still earlier than Margo or Frank. But the extra mileage had done its trick. He woke just a bit before noon.

He was due for lunch with Justin at one. It was supposed to help ease Eddie into things, but even this—his first time seeing his best friend since he'd gotten back—had become an occasion for anxiety. Justin was the only one other than Kit and Frank who'd visited Eddie while he was down at Fort Bragg, and they'd always gotten together when Eddie came up to New York, but they'd still hung out fewer than a dozen times in seven years. So much had changed for them both.

Justin had told him to pick any place in the city, but they'd both known they'd be eating at the Pallas Athena, a diner halfway between the Doyles' house and St. Albert's where they'd gone two or three times a week in high school. When Eddie arrived, Justin stood to take him in a hug. They slipped into the booth across from each other, and Justin opened the menu—laminated, spiral-bound, featuring more dishes than any establishment could possibly prepare well.

"Surf and turf?" he asked, with a mockery of wide-eyed eagerness.

This was an actual item on offer, six-ounce sirloin and grilled lobster tail, $29.89. Blakeman had ordered it once, probably stoned, sophomore or junior year, or possibly just threatened to—no one could remember exactly, but they'd ritually invoked the item at the beginning of every meal there ever since. Perhaps a thousand times. A teenager's joke that quickly stopped being funny but was repeated out of a kind of loyalty and eventually became funny again through the sheer power of this repetition. They no longer laughed at the joke itself but at some implied joke about the joke, maybe even a joke about this second-order joke. The menus existed solely for the sake of it. They opened them, looked longingly at glossy photos of pasta primavera and beef stroganoff, intoned the rhyming spell, and ordered the same medium cheeseburgers they always had.

Eddie laughed. He imagined trying to explain to his joes why it was funny that such a place offered surf and turf, funny to joke about ordering it.

"You're back," Justin told him.

"I'm back," he agreed.

"Thought you might never get out, after you re-upped."

"Yet here I am."

"So what now?"

Eddie told Justin about a job interview he'd had the day before, with a friend of his mother's named Evan Schroeder, the founder of something called the Schroeder Group.

"He kept calling it a 'boutique,' as though he sold lingerie on Madison Avenue. I got through the whole thing without figuring out what he actually did."

"I've met Schroeder a few times," Justin said. "I don't know what he does, either. But he makes a pile doing it. Might be worth considering."

"Well, I've got some time to figure shit out. I've still got vacation pay coming. Full captain's salary for two more months. I can probably stretch that to the end of the year, if I put off finding my own place."

It was always strange to talk about money with Justin. As kids, they'd politely danced around the fact that he was the only one without any. Now they politely danced around the fact that he had more than anyone they knew. Justin had been working for Kit when Eddie left town, doing well enough. Then he'd gone to some hedge fund and gotten shockingly rich even by the standards with which Eddie had grown up. So far as Eddie could tell, he was more or less retired now. A full career played through in less than a decade.

"How are your parents?" Justin asked.

Eddie didn't want to talk about the tribulations of Frank Doyle. He'd been glad to miss all that.

"My dad's spending a lot of time on his book since he got fired."

"And Kit?"

The tone of concern in Justin's voice surprised Eddie, who'd never worried about Kit in his life. She didn't invite emotions of this sort, at least not from her children.

"You'd probably know better than me."

"We don't talk as much since I left Q&M."

The ancient waiter arrived in his white shirt and black waistcoat that hadn't been washed since the last time Eddie was there. Nikos, Eddie thought, but they all seemed to be named Nikos.

"Two medium cheeseburgers," he said as he set down the plates.

In fact, it was impossible to get your burger cooked medium at the Pallas Athena. When you ordered it that way, it came well done, but when you ordered medium rare it came cold and red in the middle. A poorly cooked diner burger was one thing you could get in Fayetteville—or even in the Green Zone—but it was different having one here. Eddie savored his first bite.

"How's your mom?" he asked Justin through his food.

"Holding it together. I'm glad to have her in Manhattan since Dad's gone."

"I'm sorry I couldn't make the funeral."

Justin nodded in acknowledgment, his burger in both hands.

"You had a good excuse."

He said this without rancor, but the words made Eddie wonder for the first time whether anyone else from his family had gone in his absence. They probably would have mentioned it to him. He wanted to apologize on their behalf, but he went on eating in silence.

They were working their way through the last of the wide-cut fries on the plate between them when Justin said, "I have to ask."

Eddie looked up.

"Why the fuck did you do it?"

They both laughed.

"Sorry," Justin went on, "but I've been waiting years to find out."

Eddie chewed for another moment.

"I think I was just bored."

This was a Blakeman answer. Justin deserved better, but Eddie genuinely didn't know what to say. They made small talk until Nikos brought the check, which Justin paid at the register by the door. They walked outside together and headed over to Fifth, in the direction of Justin's building. He actually lived closer than the Doyles to the Athena now, closer to St. Albert's. These days he probably knew the neighborhood better than Eddie did.

Eddie hugged Justin and gave a wave to the old Irish doorman before walking on. When he got to Seventy-Fourth, he should have turned toward Madison and headed home, but he continued downtown with no destination in mind. As he walked, Justin's question ran through his head. *Why the fuck did you do it?* Was this what made the idea of the party so unsettling? All the guests would be thinking it, all asking him in their own oblique way, and he still didn't have an answer.

He'd struggled more than most of his friends deciding what to do after graduation. He'd been a sociology major, one of those disciplines that everyone said could be applied to anything, but such flexibility meant little if you had no idea what interested you. His family was rich, which made it seem less excusable to follow the path of least resistance and try to make as much money as possible as quickly as he could.

His mother, too, had grown up rich, but Quinn and Mulqueen had still been a real family firm when she'd joined, which had lent a certain romance to her decision. Women in finance were a rarity at the time, so the choice to work for her father at Q&M had taken some courage. For Eddie to go there in turn would have been completely unimaginative. Perhaps he might have done it anyway, if Kit had pushed him in that direction, but she'd told him to "follow his heart." He supposed this was meant to be liberating, but he'd taken it as a kind of indifference, especially since she all but insisted that Justin come work for her.

Eddie got a job at an advertising agency, because its combination of business and creativity seemed a mixture of his parents' work. His friends thought it was cool that he might write something that would end up on TV, but for the first year all he did was answer phones and schedule meetings. For two years after that, he edited copy for regional radio spots. When he graduated to writing his own, it felt like a great breakthrough. He was on his way into his Midtown office when the first plane struck. When he got upstairs and heard what had happened, his immediate thought was for his mother, whose own offices were just a block from the towers. It took him most of the morning to find out that she was all right. In the days that followed, he learned of the deaths of five people he knew, including a girl he'd had a crush on in college. His mother's offices had been destroyed, and their family firm had almost gone with it.

The only certainty seemed to be that things could not go on as before. Yet that was exactly what they did. Nearly everyone settled back into normalcy with surprising speed. His mother found a new home for Q&M and managed to keep it afloat. She organized a charity golf outing in memory of fallen friends. His father wrote his column as always—though he, at least, seemed animated by some sense of mission. (The term "Islamofascism" now appeared in his writing with regularity.)

Eddie's office was near Times Square, and several times a day he passed the recruiting center there. It had an old Uncle Sam poster— "I Want You"—on the door, an almost ironic touch that conflicted with the structure itself, a sleek, ultramodern metal box perched on a traffic island right below where Broadway crossed Seventh Avenue. Eddie sometimes saw tourists who'd mistaken the place for an information kiosk walk in to ask for directions. On other days, fresh-faced young men and women in starched uniforms set up tables outside, where they answered questions and handed out doughnuts. In the weeks after the towers went down, Eddie thought about enlisting. He was angry. They'd attacked his city. They'd attacked his mother. But he hadn't acted on his anger right away, and the feeling passed, like so many feelings from that time. Still, the urge rushed up on him at odd moments, mostly when the life he'd chosen seemed most trivial.

Not long after the attack, he was promoted and given an assistant, a pretty blonde named Marissa, just out of Chapel Hill. He was placed on the account of a large brewing company. His bosses were excited about the job, even more so after a senior associate experienced what everyone agreed was a stroke of genius. The man had noticed that the client's cans had a thin coat of plastic lining inside them. When asked, the client explained that all aluminum cans manufactured in the United States had this lining, which stopped the liquid within from taking on a tinny, metallic taste. *Why aren't people aware of this?* Eddie's gifted colleague wondered. How many sodas and beers did Americans drink each day without knowing that every can had this lining? Granted, the lining wasn't unique to their client, but this didn't mean the client's customers didn't benefit from it, or that they wouldn't want to be aware of the benefit. Like so much of the agency's work, it was ultimately a public service.

The agency charged Eddie with developing a few concepts. He spent a week on them before returning with his boards. He suggested that the client color the lining blue, so that it was visible when the consumer raised the can to drink. The beer, Eddie announced, had been "flavor-sealed for freshness." Strictly speaking, these words didn't mean anything, but the client loved the idea. Within a few months thousands of cans were rolling into stores with blue linings, and the words "flavor-sealed for freshness" were being spoken dozens of times a day on national radio and TV. The night after the campaign launched, half his office stayed out celebrating. Eddie's immediate superior congratulated him and told him how few people could say what he could now say: words that he'd put together were going to find their way, however briefly, into the consciousness of the age. The next morning Eddie got off the train and walked directly into the recruitment center.

The office held four cubicles, one for each service branch, but only army and navy were occupied at the time. The man in the army cubicle rose first to introduce himself. Sergeant Huntley wore blue pants with a careful crease and a short-sleeved white uniform shirt with epaulets. He was perhaps a decade older than Eddie, but he had an adolescent's burst of raspberry acne on his cheeks and chin.

"I'm interested in joining the army," Eddie told him, though this seemed a bit superfluous.

Huntley pulled two forms from a desk drawer and slipped them onto his translucent clipboard.

"I just need to ask a few basic questions to start. Do you have a criminal record?"

"No, sir," Eddie said reflexively.

"I'm not your superior officer just yet," Huntley said. He gave Eddie a forced grin before returning to the form. "Do you have a high school diploma?"

"College," Eddie said. "Cornell."

"Have you ever thought about going to graduate school?" Huntley asked. "The GI Bill applies to that, too."

"Not really."

Eddie had started to feel his hangover. He regretted his decision to walk in, but he didn't know how to extricate himself.

They worked through the rest of the questions, and Huntley told him he would be in touch once the form had been processed. The whole encounter felt a bit like walking into a bank branch to open a savings account. Eddie was already imagining how he might turn the experience into a funny story for coworkers who asked why he'd shown up an hour late.

"I'd like to add one more thing before you go." Huntley set the clipboard down on his desk. "A lot of young men and women come in here because they need a steady salary, or they need to pay for their education, or they need to get out of a bad situation at home. My first job is to tell them how the army can help with that. My second job is to assure them that they've got the goods to do it. Some guys have failed at a few other things before. They realize that if they fail at this, the repercussions could be serious. I've got to make sure they know they can succeed. They are looking for options, and they want assurance that this is a plausible one. I tell them that the army is hard—I don't lie to anyone—but that it's going to give them a network of support that they probably haven't had before. All of the chaos at home or on the streets, that's going to be replaced by order. Everything is going to be structured. They'll be told what's expected of them, and they'll be surrounded by people who want them to succeed. It works, because these people know they need the army. That's why they walked in here to begin with. They're just looking to be told that it's possible."

He sat back in his chair with a satisfied look, as though asking Eddie to acknowledge the appeal of such a pitch, to a person in such a circumstance. Eddie nodded obediently, and Huntley made a show of looking down at the form in front of him.

"I've got no idea why you walked in here. Maybe you don't know, either. You've got a good education, a good job, you live in a nice neighborhood. I'm going to take a guess and say that you grew up in a pretty well-structured, supportive family. If I'm wrong about that, please excuse my presumption. I have to make those kinds of guesses in this job. If you did grow up with a lot of disorder, I congratulate you for having pulled yourself out of it. The point is that it seems like you've got a pretty good deal going on. I don't know precisely what the army can give you. I could appeal to your better instincts and tell you that we need guys like you—well-adjusted, well-educated guys. But I don't want you to go thinking you're better than the guys who don't have the choices you've got. Here's what I'd like you to know about joining the army: it's going to be the hardest thing you ever do in your life. Maybe you thought you went through some tough stuff when you were pledging some fraternity in college. Maybe you've got buddies who think they're pretty bad because of the hours they work. Let me tell you straight up—when you're done with this, you're going to be laughing at them. When you're done with this, you're going to know that you've worked harder than all of those guys combined—and not to close some Wall Street deal. You will have risked your life in the service of something greater than yourself. You're going to know exactly what kind of man you are."

It was just another pitch, the special pitch for guys like him, with good jobs and nice lives. Why would such a person walk into a recruiting office? Because his good job and his nice life weren't enough. So you had to hit him at his vulnerable point, which was this sense of dissatisfaction. Eddie was in the pitch business himself, so he was well positioned to know all this, but knowing made no difference. The pitch worked completely. And Huntley was right: Eddie had learned exactly what kind of man he was. The question now was what to do with this knowledge.

Eventually he'd get used to being home. Learn to treat everything he read about the unfinished war as irrelevant data and his life in New York as the main event. Learn to care about his father's racist jokes and what they meant for his career. He'd shrink himself to fit his shrunken world.

He thought about his interview the day before. *I'd love to hire one of you guys*, Schroeder had said. *Most of my junior staff, they flip out over any crisis that comes along. But you guys know what a real crisis looks like.* Eddie hadn't been sure what to make of this at the time. Did the man actually mean to say that Eddie would be better at the job because he recognized how little it mattered? Not that long ago, he'd thought he'd be in the army forever. He wasn't ready to accept the idea of spending the rest of his life at some accounting firm whose motto was "Making the business world a safer place," or telling friends that he'd been getting "killed" because he'd been in the office a couple of Saturdays in a row. Why was Kit in such a hurry to get him back to work? Hadn't he earned the right to a few weeks, even a few months, of acclimating to his new reality?

Money certainly wasn't a problem, despite his talk with Justin about stretching his terminal pay. Money had never been a problem. It was even slightly comic to be counting nickels and dimes when technically he was a millionaire. But his inheritance had never seemed real to him. His parents hadn't told him about the money until he was in high school, when they'd insisted that it wasn't enough to live on. *At least not well*, Kit had clarified. One day he could buy a house with it, or pay his children's tuition, but in the meantime he ought to put it out of his mind. He'd managed pretty successfully to do just this. He'd been enlisted when the trust terminated. He'd put the money in a brokerage account, given his mother power of attorney, and tossed the monthly statements unopened. He wasn't even sure how much he had.

Halfway down Fifth, he told himself to turn around and head home. He'd already sweat through his shirt, and he'd need to shower again and change before the party. He had some time, but he didn't want to worry his mother unnecessarily. He'd left his phone at home, so she didn't have any way to get in touch. She'd probably called at least once. But he could not make himself go back. It was only three o'clock. Drinks didn't start until 6:30. Without quite deciding on it, he knew he'd continue to the bottom of Fifth, where it ended at Washington Square. He'd take the 6 uptown from Astor Place and be home before any guests arrived. If he was freshening up when the party kicked off, that would hardly ruin the night.

As he approached the square, Eddie felt a twinge of nostalgia. Blakeman had lived for years in a town house on the north end of the park, and Eddie had spent what seemed like all of his twenties at parties there. Strange to think that for most of the people at those parties life had continued on unchanged while he was gone. He'd never exactly regretted his decision, but he did sometimes imagine a shadow Eddie who hadn't walked into the recruiting office. One who'd slept off his hangover, taken a well-deserved sick day, and gone about the rest of his life. Where would that Eddie be right now? If Blakeman was any indication, he'd be in roughly the same place he'd been then, which seemed a little sad, except that Eddie had no more figured out now than this shadow Eddie did.

The park was crowded, as it always was on warm days, especially when school was still in session, but as he entered from the north Eddie saw a particularly large gathering near the fountain in the center of the square, the kind usually reserved for a homeless a cappella group or shirtless young men breakdancing. Eddie was halfway to the fountain when he heard the voice, loud enough to reach him above the clamor but projecting a warm authority. He could at first make out only this tone, not the words themselves. As he approached, the voice's source came into view in the form of a disembodied head floating on the sea of people surrounding it. The man's face—framed by a long gray beard and white hair—was covered in wrinkles and cracks and, along the forehead, momentous folds ran parallel to the gray tufts of eyebrow hanging like storm clouds in a muddy sky. There was a tragic element in this face, but also something open and hopeful, and it reminded Eddie of many he'd seen in Iraq.

"What would you change if you knew it was all going to end?" the man asked the audience. "For that is the news I am bringing you: it is all about to end. The Great Unveiling is soon upon us."

Along the crowd's periphery people stood indecisive, loosely arrayed, unsure whether this spectacle merited their full attention. Some of them held up phones to record the performance but strangely didn't seem to be watching it themselves. Eddie pushed in to where the onlookers grew more certain of their place. He stopped about ten feet away. He was still separated from the fountain by three or four rows of people, but from there he could see and hear everything. The man had come fully into view. He wore a double-breasted gray suit, and he stood on the edge of the fountain, still empty at this time of year. The suit was neatly tailored yet worn and ill-fitting, as though it had been passed down or the man had lost weight since acquiring it.

"Sons will be set against fathers," the man said. "Daughters against mothers. He is not coming to bring peace. He is coming to bring the sword."

Up close, the voice that had carried halfway across the park still didn't seem harsh, even as it spoke of impending battle. Eddie stayed to listen, though now he would certainly be late getting uptown. That hardly seemed to matter in the moment. After several more minutes, the woman next to Eddie handed something to him—a brown fedora, filled with loose dollar bills. Eddie took out his wallet, which was filled with singles and one five. He emptied it and passed the hat along. Eventually it made its way back up to the man, who almost immediately stepped down from the fountain and dissolved into his audience.

Very quickly the audience itself dissolved along with him. It stopped being a singular crowd and became again a collection of individuals. There was nothing more to see, and Eddie was expected somewhere else, but he remained a few feet from the fountain, alone.

3.

Edward had gone missing. This was a dramatic way of putting it after all they'd been through, but what else to call it?

Kit had been out for most of the afternoon, and she'd assumed he was back from lunch when she got home. She'd passed his closed door a half dozen times while getting the house ready. Finally she'd knocked to make sure he was dressed. She knew this gesture would annoy him, but she couldn't help herself. She knocked a second time before opening the door.

Her shock at the sight of his empty room was entirely out of proportion. She understood that. She'd stood in that doorway hundreds of times, looking at that room, convinced he would never come home. There was something perverse about worrying so much over him now that he was back. But she'd gotten good at worrying; it wasn't easy to stop all at once.

She wouldn't find him anywhere else in the house. When he was home, he stayed in his room. She could barely drag him out for meals. He left each morning before anyone else was awake and returned exhausted and dazed from his runs. What he did with the rest of his time, she didn't really know. She could have asked, but she didn't want to add to his troubles.

Down the hall, Margo's door was open, and she was splayed out on the rug, still pajamaed, an open book in front of her.

"Have you seen Edward?" Kit asked.

"He's not in his room?" Margo replied without taking her eyes from the page.

"If he were would I be asking?"

Why had Kit adopted such a tough tone with Margo since she'd come home? She supposed she needed to be tough with someone, and Margo seemed to be the only one who could take it at the moment.

"I haven't seen him all day."

Margo picked up a pen to underline something, a gesture obviously intended to chase Kit away.

For years, Kit had dreamed of having her whole family back under this roof. It was perhaps a predictable irony that they all communicated less now than when they'd been on opposite ends of the globe.

"Our guests will be arriving any minute," Kit said, in search of another outlet for her aggravation.

Finally Margo looked up, as though acknowledging her mother were the only way to make her leave.

"The moment the bell rings I'll put on a dress."

Kit continued upstairs to her room, where Frank sat hunched in his chair, still wet from the shower. He'd shaved that morning, but he had a light dusting of stubble on his cheeks and chin. His large belly hung over the towel wrapped loosely around his waist.

His willfulness, his refusal to take direction from anyone, had created so many problems over the years, but she couldn't stand to see his spirit drained. She had no desire to scold him into action like another one of her children.

"Shall I pick out a suit for you?"

The question enlivened him a little.

"The double-breasted navy pinstripes," he told her. "The one Gianni cut for me last spring."

Gianni was the tailor in Milan whose atelier they visited every other year. Frank had always been known for his sense of style—the bespoke suits and the tailored shirts, the patterned socks and pocket square to match every tie. A good thing he had enough of them to last, since there wouldn't be any more trips to Milan.

She left him to dress while she made one more pass through the house. Downstairs most of the caterers were lined up outside the powder room, waiting to change into their uniforms, but one stood out in the garden, still in street clothes, lazily smoking a cigarette. He started to put it out when he saw Kit coming, but she waved to say it was all right.

"I was actually hoping to bum one," she said.

She usually had a few cigarettes at these parties—it was a habit she'd never entirely given up from the days when everyone on Wall Street smoked—but only late in the evening, after several drinks. It didn't seem a good sign that she was already asking. He passed her a plastic lighter and his pack of Parliaments.

"You've got a beautiful house," he told her, as though it were an insult.

Kit took a long drag and thanked him in a tone that discouraged further conversation. He put out his butt and turned to the door, but Kit reached out to stop him.

"I'll give you ten bucks for the rest of your pack."

He fished the Parliaments back out of his pocket and handed them over.

Kit finished her cigarette alone and lit up another. She was half-way through it when the bell rang.

In the front hall, Justin and Blakeman stood waiting while Marinela hung their coats. Seeing them relieved Kit immediately. She always invited a few people to come early, since the first to show up of their own accord were never the ones you wanted, and it had seemed fitting in this case to choose Edward's closest friends.

"I'm afraid the guest of honor has gone AWOL," she said.

"He seemed in good spirits at lunch," Justin told her, sounding more worried than she was.

"I'm sure he'll be here soon," Kit responded, trying to reassure them both. "In the meantime, let's get you two something to drink."

"How's Frank holding up?" Blakeman asked as they walked to the library, with its long shelves filled with her husband's books. Kit wasn't sure what to say. In truth, Frank still hadn't recovered from what she and Margo had taken to calling the "Ballpark Incident." It was becoming less and less certain that he ever would.

"He's really throwing himself into his book. That's helped a lot."

"I want to talk to him about being profiled for the *Interviewer*. Sam Waxworth has agreed to do something."

It took a moment for Kit to place the name.

"The election oracle?"

"He's my new star writer."

"I don't remember Frank thinking much of him."

"Oh they're going to hate each other. That's the best part."

"Are you assigning some kind of hit job?"

With Blakeman, one never knew.

"I wouldn't let it turn into that. But no one will respond to a puff piece. This is going to be *a complex reassessment of Frank Doyle's legacy*. It will get people talking about him again."

"Had they *stopped* talking about me?"

They turned to find Frank in the doorway, sly smile on his face. He could still set a whole room off kilter with his arrival. How long had he waited to make this entrance? He looked impeccable, his hair neatly slicked back, his suit a perfect fit. He'd run a razor over his face in the few minutes since Kit had left him, and his cheeks were smooth and bright with their Irish flush. Margo followed quickly behind him, likewise transformed, in a short green cocktail dress, her hair pinned up.

"Does that mean you're interested?" Blakeman asked.

Kit watched Frank considering this. It didn't sound like a great idea to her, but that hardly mattered. Frank would do what Frank wanted to do.

"The election's over. Shouldn't this character go back to wherever he came from—until the midterms at least?"

"Where exactly did he come from?" Kit asked.

"That's the best part," Blakeman answered. "He's from nowhere. I mean, Michigan, or something. But he was writing blog posts on a WordPress site when I hired him."

"The young man from the provinces," Margo said.

"That's right. He's my Bel Ami. He's going to conquer the big city, starting with the Doyles."

The bell rang again, and Kit went to answer it. Her anxiety returned at the sight of Guillaume LaFarge, her husband's literary agent, but Guillaume greeted her with his usual Gallic charm, kissing her on both cheeks before giving her a lingering hug. *All those tough conversations can wait for another time*, his manner seemed to say. While she walked him down the hall, she heard the piano player begin on "The Lady Is a Tramp," and she found herself stirred with the excitement she only ever got when entertaining.

Their parties had always been major events. Once a season they'd filled two stories of the town house, spilling out back even in winter. They were talked about for weeks, written up in the *Herald*'s style section and the *Reverberator*'s society page, before the *Reverberator* became just another celebrity gossip site. They'd never depended for their charm on the kind of extravagance that had been in the news since the collapse—life-sized ice sculptures with anatomically correct genitalia, topless waiters covered in gold leaf. In lieu of decadence, they offered low-key good taste. Kit hired college kids to pass hors d'oeuvres and work the bar, someone to play standards on the baby grand in the living room. Her banking friends knew that interesting people—a few novelists and poets, perhaps a painter or playwright, along with the usual collection of journalists and media personalities—would be there. The interesting people were drawn in turn by proximity to wealth. (For painters and poets, nothing was more interesting than real money.) The latest Hollywood star to attempt Broadway might be spotted in the corner near the kitchen, talking to the cardinal.

Naturally, Kit had cancelled their Halloween party after the towers went down. Quinn and Mulqueen's three floors at 7 World Trade had been evacuated that morning. By the end of that afternoon, Kit had watched on TV as the building where she'd spent the majority of her waking adulthood collapsed. She felt lucky in the grand scheme of things—several people she knew had died that day—but finding new offices had taken months, after which she still had to fight to keep Q&M afloat. She'd imagined doing something understated once they were back on solid footing, a kind of return-to-normalcy fête, but by that time, Edward was at officer candidate school. Things would never be normal again. She was angry at her son for enlisting, angry at her husband for starting the war (as it seemed to her that he had), and angry at the old friends with the temerity to agree with her about the pointlessness of it all. When Edward went into combat, her terror and despair did not displace that anger so much as flavor it. She'd remained in this state for the better part of six years—not a mood conducive to hostessing. Even when she'd sold Q&M and formally retired, she'd refused to mark the occasion. To the old stalwarts who asked, she said that her next party would be the one welcoming Edward home for good.

When he was discharged, people she hadn't heard from in years left messages saying how happy they were for her, how worried they'd been, and they all reminded Kit of her promise. In most cases

—certainly in Kit's case—Edward was the only person they knew who'd fought, and his safe return seemed to suggest that they could finally move on. *When can we come over to celebrate?* they asked.

One advantage to stopping the parties when she had was never finding out exactly who would have kept coming. Many of her Wall Street friends probably agreed with Frank about the invasion, and anyway they weren't inclined to let political arguments dictate their social schedules. But his prominent position in the constellation of fashionable liberalism had always been part of the draw, and their most noteworthy guests wouldn't frequent the house of a man who wrote paeans to Paul Wolfowitz and toured the Green Zone with Ahmed Chalabi. Then came the Ballpark Incident and Frank's firing from the *Herald*. Each time some long-standing acquaintance rushed to disavow her husband in public, Kit had thought: *At least I'm not throwing a party.* She didn't have to give her dearest friends a test they wouldn't pass.

But whatever scruples these people had felt obliged to pretend they'd had about Frank were simply forgotten. Everyone went out of their way to tell her how much they'd missed these parties. The intervening years had conferred on them—as it had on so many things that belonged (was it really possible?) to the previous century—a retrospective sheen of poignant innocence. How odd it seemed now, to have lived in a state of nearly constant celebration. Everyone wanted a return to the days before things went off track.

In almost every other way, the timing was terrible. Edward didn't seem to have any interest in seeing people. Even before leaving school, Margo hadn't been herself for months. Frank had declared that he was finally working on the big book that weekly deadlines had kept him from all his life, and he still spent long hours in his office, but Kit suspected that he mostly spent them drinking and watching TV. The rest of the time, he wandered the house in a haze of self-pity. He called old friends seeking commiseration and tried to get them to boycott the *Herald*, an effort that only served to show how little social capital he had left. And somehow all of this was just the beginning of their problems. Only she knew the worst of it.

Perversely, that argued in favor of a celebration. Failing to mark the occasion would have amounted to an admission that her son's return had not solved the deeper faults at the heart of her family. She wanted to prove that they hadn't been defeated—by the war, by the financial collapse, by Frank's unerring talent for compounding his mistakes. Once it was clear that all their old friends meant to be there, Kit hoped that the occasion would be good for everyone. Frank flourished with an audience, and their parties had always brought out the best in him. She'd hoped to introduce Edward to some people who could put him in the way of a new job, something substantial to occupy his time. She didn't know enough about Margo's particular complaints to guess at what might help her, but at least a party would get them talking to each other again.

After the crowd leaked into a second room, she moved between the two, diligently playing hostess, until she saw Edward come in. He was still in the clothes he'd worn to lunch with Justin—khaki pants and button-down shirt, no jacket or tie—and he was sweating as though he'd been out for another run. He was an hour late for his own party, but he was there. He was safe. More than this, he looked happy. Exhilarated, even. Whatever he'd needed to do to be able to enjoy the evening was fine with her. She caught his eye from across the room, and he gave her an apologetic smile.

A few people standing near the library door cheered as he came into view, and he raised a hand almost violently, as if protecting himself from the response more than acknowledging it. He stood in that position, framed in the doorway, while the fact of his presence—and with it, presumably, the fact of his prior absence—spread through the room. Scattered clapping coalesced into full applause. The piano player, who'd been halfway through "A Foggy Day in London Town," stopped mid-verse. Everyone waited for Edward to respond, but he seemed stuck in place, willing their scrutiny to stop. The moment threatened to turn awkward until Frank crossed the room. He pulled Edward into an embrace, raised his drink, and let out a whistle. Several people tapped their glasses, though the room was already at full attention. Frank always made some kind of speech at these parties—he never wasted an audience—but they usually came later in the night. Kit was glad he was getting it out of the way while they were all sober enough.

"It's been a while since we gathered in this house," he began. "A lot has changed. I want to say first of all how nice it is to have everyone here to welcome Edward home, and how proud I am of my son. He has put his life on the line for a worthy cause."

Another cheer went up, a few glasses raised in peremptory toast. Kit could see Edward growing restless under his father's grip, and Frank seemed to consider leaving it there, which Kit knew he couldn't do.

"The meaning of this sacrifice is in no way lessened by the fact that our current commander in chief doesn't appreciate the seriousness of the fight we're engaged in. As hard as it may be for some people in this country—maybe even some people in this room—to admit, we live in a safer, freer world than the one we occupied the last time we all stood here together. Because of men and women like Edward, millions of people have been given the opportunity to choose their own political destinies for the first time. My guess is that in the coming years there will be a lot more people in that part of the world doing the same. And when history"—here he raised his voice over a murmur of cross talk—"when history renders its judgment on our actions of the past few years, this is what will matter. Not petty grievances and minor setbacks, not even more serious mistakes, but the fact that democracy is making its way from a privileged exception to a global right. My son helped make that happen."

When Frank raised his glass, every guest raised one with him. How could they not? Yet Kit wondered how many believed what he'd said. Certainly Frank believed it himself, but did Edward? Did she? It pleased Kit to see Frank showing pride in his son, but even now she couldn't pretend to treat Edward's time in the army as anything other than a terrible mistake. She didn't much care what the fighting had meant. She didn't even care whether they'd won or lost. What mattered was that her son was alive. She knew that if he'd never come back, some part of Frank would have thought it a worthwhile sacrifice, and the very idea still angered her, even with Edward right there.

Once it was clear that Frank's speaking part was done, Kit went outside for another cigarette, which she'd been putting off doing until Edward turned up. She realized how anxious she'd been only now that she felt the anxiety leaving her body with the exhale of smoke. Justin was standing with a few old friends in the back of the garden, and he broke from the group to approach.

"That was a fine performance," he said.

"He's still got it," Kit agreed.

"It's good to have everyone back here."

"We're glad to have you back."

Besides being her son's best friend, Justin had long been a kind of protégé of Kit's, but their relationship had cooled after he left Q&M to work for Dan Eisen, and they'd seen a lot less of each other while Edward was gone. She'd had the idea that he might one day take over the firm, and it was only once he was gone that she'd started thinking seriously about selling. In her most irrational moments she blamed him a little for what had come next, though she knew he'd made the sensible decision. If he'd stayed, he might be very rich, but considerably less so than he was now.

"I'm glad we all made it through."

Something about the remark struck a nerve. They hadn't made it through quite yet, and Justin might have known as much. He was one of the few people with any real sense of what had happened to her.

"Actually, we're in some real trouble," she said.

She was trying not to sound too dramatic, but as she spoke the full force of it hit her.

"I'm sure Frank will get it back together. Blakeman's profile ought to help."

"For once I'm not talking about Frank."

She watched Justin deciding what to make of this.

"I know you took a hit when UniBank went down."

He looked down awkwardly as he spoke. He probably assumed there was money somewhere else, counted her among the many unfortunates who were just a little less rich right now than they'd been a year ago.

"There's nothing left," she said. "Nothing."

She hadn't planned to tell this to anyone, not even Frank, certainly not her son's closest friend, her former acolyte, whatever Justin was to them. She couldn't say whether it was the force of the truth, the shame of having revealed it, or maybe even some level of relief at speaking it out loud that made her start to cry. She was not someone who cried, but now she couldn't stop, and beside her Justin seemed more shocked than anything else.

"Maybe I can help," he said.

She'd practically been begging for this offer, but hearing him make it embarrassed her. After the Ballpark Incident, he'd offered to provide a statement on Frank's behalf, to talk about the role the Doyles had played in his life, but Frank had refused. Anyone who knew him at all knew he wasn't a bigot, he'd said, and he wasn't going to advertise his racial bona fides to prove it. This had likely been a tactical mistake—Justin had become one of the city's most prominent black citizens, and his good word would have gone a long way—but Kit had been relieved. She didn't want to turn decades of real family feeling into something transactional.

"It's a shame I never played the game the way Eisen does. I could have used that kind of edge."

This was unfair to Justin, who was trying to be kind. Kit knew nothing about Eisen apart from the rumors that sprung up around anyone who enjoyed the kind of success he'd had over the past decade, and the fact that a few years of working for him had made Justin more money than she'd earned in her entire career.

She tried to smile as she wiped away her tears.

"I'm being dramatic," she told him. "We'll find a way to muddle through, I'm sure." She dropped her half-finished cigarette into one of the small buckets of sand set out for the purpose. "Let's think happy thoughts. This is supposed to be a party."

The moment they stepped back through the doors, Frank caught Kit's eye. She could tell he'd been waiting for her. She gave him a nod, and he leaned over to whisper in the piano player's ear. She was halfway to him before the music started.

You could spot the true regulars, because they cleared space as soon as they recognized the song: "I'm Beginning to See the Light." Frank and Kit had danced to it at nearly every one of these parties. The story of their meeting was legend by now, and you could hear people repeating it to initiates each time they danced to this song. *They'd never spoken a word when he proposed.* They met in the middle of the room just as the first verse—*I never cared much for moonlit skies*—began. Frank took her into his arms, and she was twenty again.

He held her tight, with more strength than he'd shown in months, as though trying to tell her he was back, he'd made it through. She wanted badly to believe him. When the song ended, he kissed her to scattered applause.

They stood together while the party continued its business around them. Kit allowed herself to think that these evenings would again become an unmistakable feature of the city's social landscape. In fact, she knew, they would never throw another party in this house. By the end of the year, they probably wouldn't even be living there. Behind her, two people she didn't know were laughing about that park bench preacher who was all of a sudden the talk of New York.

"Did you hear the news?" one of them asked. "The world is coming to an end in the fall."

That would be all right by me, Kit thought as she counted the time in her head. They might just hold out that long.

4.

Frank boarded the downtown 6 at Seventy-Seventh Street an hour and a half before first pitch. Ever since agreeing to go to the game, he'd been looking forward to his old routine, riding out to the park in a home white jersey and his battered, faded Mets cap with the "Ya Gotta Believe" button pinned to the brim. Not many men in his position would take the train to the game, but that's how he was. At heart he was still a Brooklyn boy. Fans on the car had sometimes approached with questions about the team's prospects that season. *Hey Doyle, do you think Piazza's through? How long is Willie going to last? Has El Duque still got something in the tank?*

When he switched to the 7 at Grand Central, almost everyone seemed to be heading to the same place, but the few people who recognized him only whispered and laughed. In Jackson Heights, a man with bright red hair and an old Keith Hernandez shirt yelled, "You got a bum deal, Doyle," which gratified Frank, until the man commenced whistling at the woman seated next to him, one of the few passengers simply suffering through her daily commute. When she stood up and walked away, the red-haired man cursed loudly. This was among the worst parts of Frank's ordeal: the kind of allies it had brought him.

Before Blakeman's offer, he hadn't planned to attend the opening of Citi Field. For the first time in four decades, he didn't have season tickets, and he hadn't been sure he'd go to the new park at all. That the great debacle had happened during the last game the Mets ever played at Shea had felt strangely fitting. His days as the team's most famous fan—a familiar fixture in his seats behind home plate, sure to appear on the jumbotron at some point during every home game, invited often into the announcing booth and twice onto the field to throw out the first pitch—were over. As if in recognition of the fact, the stadium where he'd played that role had been torn down. He knew some people found him solipsistic, but in this case the symbolism really was striking. Who could blame him for avoiding the new home they'd erected in his reputation's ruins?

What changed his mind was the prospect of facing off with this kid. Like everyone else, Frank had read Sam Waxworth's election posts. He'd seen his projections, down to the tenth of a percentage point, of a near landslide for Obama. Without mentioning Waxworth by name, Frank had even written a column—his last, as it turned out—about why those projections would be proven wrong. Just as the baseball stateheads thought they could make their judgments without scouting, without going to games and getting real human eyeballs on players in the field, the political stateheads thought they could make predictions without reporting. But polls couldn't capture a mood. For that you needed to look around a bit. The country, Frank had decided after attending several rallies, was skittish. At such moments, people opted for experience. They might like the idea of voting for a handsome, well-spoken black man, they might tell pollsters that this was what they planned to do, but in the secrecy of the voting booth they wouldn't pull that lever for someone who hadn't completed a full Senate term. The role of commander in chief required a figure who was battle-tested—"Battle Tested" was the column's head—and that meant McCain.

If Frank had been right about any of this, he sometimes thought, the fallout from his performance at that game would have passed quickly enough. Obama would have been forgotten, and insulting him in jest would have come to seem a venial sin. Frank would have earned credit for being right about the election—not to mention the war—and the *Herald* would have been forced to take him back. Instead something like the opposite had happened on every count. While the online mob was picking gleefully through the corpse of Frank's career, this kid with a calculator was getting nearly as much credit for the victory as Obama himself, as though he'd conjured the results into being, rather than just adding up and dividing other people's work.

After a bit of reflection, Frank recognized Blakeman's proposal for what it was—an opportunity to show that he was still unbroken. He finally had what the *Herald* had owed him but hadn't offered: the chance to justify himself. The numerarchy ruled everything now. It had long ago taken over his wife's world, the world of finance, convincing everyone that computer modeling could eliminate risk, an idea that had led to some of the most irrational behavior in human history and taken the whole economy down. It had half ruined the first love of his life—baseball—and now it had set its sights on the second—politics. These people were the enemy. How could he pass up the chance to spend nine innings with one of their kings?

At the next stop, the woman switched cars, and the red-haired man fell into offended silence. The rest of the ride proceeded without event. At Willets Point, Frank filed out with everyone else, then walked upstairs to see the new park for the first time. For a moment, the sight strangled him. He'd read that the facade had been built to replicate Ebbets Field, but he wasn't really prepared to walk into the great cathedral of his youth. The effect was profound, but fleeting. The copy wasn't even especially accurate, upon closer inspection, and if anyone was equipped to know the difference, it was Frank, who'd been at the last game ever played at the old park—September 24, 1957, a date etched forever in his mind. In case there could be any confusion, the logo of a financial behemoth—one of the several that had been rescued while his wife's was allowed to collapse—occupied the space where the words "Ebbets Field" should have been.

At the top of a long escalator, an usher took Frank's ticket, passed its barcode across his handheld scanner, and returned it intact. Frank missed the tear of the stub, the homely thwack now replaced by an automated beep. There was something irrevocable about that rip, which left you with an artifact that testified forever to your presence at that particular game. Each torn edge was a little different from the others, even when you arrived as a group and handed over a stack of four or five to be taken at one go. Now the fact of Frank's entrance was stored on a server somewhere in the form of zeroes and ones, but his ticket—not even a ticket, just a piece of paper from his printer at home—remained unchanged. If he were still in the business of writing elegiac baseball essays, he would have written one about that.

He bought a program and a beer before stepping through another entrance, this time entering into the open air of the park along the first-base line. He loved taking the measure of a ballpark for the first time, because every one was different—not just the seating and the concession stands but the very dimensions of the field. Of all the unfortunate ideas that the geeks had brought to the game, the worst might have been the notion that you could compare a hitter who played his home games in front of the short porch in right at Yankee Stadium and another who played in the shadow of Fenway's Green Monster in left by applying some mathematical formula that adjusted for "park effects." Like so many statistical innovations, this struck Frank as an effort to neutralize reality, sand away all the glorious particularities of life, the things that could not be captured on a spreadsheet, that could be understood only by telling stories about them.

There was still half an hour until first pitch, but the kid was already waiting at their seats. He was around Margo's age, Frank guessed. All these guys were so frighteningly young, and so sure of themselves. How much could they possibly know?

"Mr. Doyle," the kid said. "Sam Waxworth. It's good to meet you."

He stood and offered his hand. They exchanged a few words before turning to the field to watch the lineups being announced. After all the players had been named and caps tipped, a flotilla of military personnel—active duty, veterans, members of every service branch—flooded the field for the national anthem.

"We ask you all now to stand," the PA announcer intoned, "and honor the sacrifice of those who fight to preserve our freedom."

An American flag the size of a football field was unfurled on the outfield and set waving. Frank liked these moments, and not just because Eddie was among the people being implicitly honored. There weren't many places in this city where the words *sacrifice* and *freedom* were still used without irony. After the anthem was sung, a fighter jet flew over the park, drowning out the cheers.

"Don't you think this is all a bit much?" Waxworth asked as the noise faded from the air.

"Not at all," Frank answered.

"What does it say about a great democracy that it has to insist upon itself in this way? It's more appropriate for some tiny totalitarian outpost that spends its take from the state-owned mineral mine on parades and uniforms while the public starves."

"If you ask me, we could stand to do more to honor our warriors. When I was growing up, the players actually served. Pee Wee Reese—the Dodgers' captain, for godsake—spent two years in the Pacific."

"Your son was in Iraq," Waxworth said.

"Is that a question?"

Eddie's military record was just the kind of thing Frank should have wanted to discuss for a rehabilitative profile. Critics loved to point out that he'd never served in Vietnam. This wasn't his fault—though he'd been against the war at the time, he'd been too old to be at risk of getting called up, and he hadn't taken any steps to avoid it—but that distinction hardly mattered to his opponents, who'd treated him like just another run-of-the-mill chicken hawk. When Eddie went over, they'd been forced to acknowledge that he had a real stake in things, even if they didn't agree with his stance.

"It must affect how you respond to this performance."

"I've got news for you," Frank said. "What you see as just extraneous bits of jingoism are secretly the purpose of the entire event. The game exists to be a ritual in the nation's civic religion."

When the flyover was through, the crowd stayed standing to applaud as Tom Seaver—The Franchise—emerged from the bullpen. He walked slowly toward the mound, positioned himself just in front of the rubber, and threw the ceremonial first pitch, a strike to Mike Piazza. Probably the two best players to wear the team's uniform. Frank had gotten to know both over the years, but especially Seaver, who'd led the Mets to their impossible World Series win in '69, when Frank was working for Mayor Lindsay. Seaver had been the Mets' color guy in the nineties, the first to ask Frank up to the booth. Those trips had been one of the great thrills in his life for a time, until they brought everything crashing down.

"Can I buy you a beer?" Frank asked the kid, having finished his own. Margo had warned him before the game to moderate himself, but he wasn't going to let his daughter tell him how to behave, certainly not in the form of absurd euphemisms like "moderate yourself."

"Why don't I get this round?" Waxworth said. "It's on the magazine."

While the kid bought their beers and Pelfrey threw the last of his warm-ups, Frank flipped through the pages of his program to find the scorecard. He'd kept score at every game he'd attended since he was a teenager, and he'd held on to every program. The one from that last game at Ebbets Field was probably worth a few thousand dollars. Would have been worth ten times that much if he'd put it straight into cellophane instead of filling it in.

The kid handed over Frank's beer and pulled out his own program.

"You keep score?" Frank asked.

Waxworth nodded.

"For all your hatred of sabermetrics, a scorecard is a form of data entry, a kind of computer. Put differently, a computer is just an extraordinarily powerful scorecard—a way to keep track of what happened."

"Collecting data is all well and good," Frank responded. "I'm not opposed to data. What I reject is the idea that it captures everything. When you take what happens on the field and shrink it down to fit on this page, so much gets lost. That's why I add these notations—an asterisk for a great fielding play, a cross for a bit of solid contact."

"I use your notations," Waxworth said. "I have ever since I read your essay about them in *The Crack of the Bat*. That essay was what made me start keeping score in the first place."

"So you understand what I mean," Frank responded, trying not to sound overly pleased.

"But here's the thing: you're still compressing the information on to the page. You've just invented a different system for doing it."

"That's where you're wrong. The information isn't on the page. It's in my head. These notations are a prompt for my memory. That asterisk doesn't just signify a good fielding play. It calls to mind the fact that Reyes charged in and took the ball on a short hop before throwing to first off his back foot. But it only calls it to mind for someone who was there, someone who already has the image in his head."

"Which means the notations become meaningless once you're no longer around to decode them."

"That's part of the point. Not everything that happens can be saved in a database. Things are forgotten. People die. That's just the nature of life. That doesn't mean they weren't real while they lasted."

"On the other hand, the fact that you remember something a certain way doesn't mean it was ever real in the first place. You can put an asterisk next to the kind of play that makes people think Reyes is a great fielder, but I can quantify how many runs he saves over replacement in a season, and I know that he's below average, no matter how spectacular he is in your memory."

Runs saved over replacement. Even the words were ugly.

"You're taking all the beauty out of the game."

"Why do we need to tell lies about the world in order to make it beautiful? What an impoverishing idea. The sky is beautiful as the sky. We don't need to pretend there's a God in His heaven up there. Babe Ruth did some astonishing things on the field—*actually* did them. We don't need to tell fanciful stories about the time he called his shot."

Frank had been waiting for this, and he'd prepared an answer, but when he went to retrieve it, the words were just out of reach. Had the kid flustered him? He'd always commanded a kind of natural eloquence, if anything he risked the glibness that came from such fluency, but lately he'd found himself prone to bouts of inarticulateness. He was almost relieved for the distraction when Jody Gerut sent Pelfry's third pitch into the left field bleachers.

"They're starting this season off just the way they ended the last one," Waxworth said.

To Frank there seemed to be something leading in the remark.

"If you want to hear about it, you should just ask."

Waxworth was quiet, as though working up the courage to press on.

"Do you regret what you said in the booth that day?"

"Of course I regret it. They ruined me over it."

"I didn't ask whether you regret the consequences. Do you see why it was so offensive?"

"Everyone lives to take offense these days. Causing offense is the biggest favor you can do them. People ought to thank me for it."

He wasn't supposed to say such things, but they were true.

"Can't you see the danger when a man in your position spouts racist crap?"

"Don't get started on racism. I made a joke. When I was growing up—in a mixed neighborhood, by the way, unlike a lot of the progressive thought enforcers with their one black friend from the finals club—you were allowed to joke about people's differences. That was part of what made it possible for so many different people to live in the same place and get along."

"It's a different time now."

"We just elected a black president. You'd think that would be precisely the time when people could take a joke."

Waxworth seemed unsatisfied, though any real writer would be thrilled with this kind of copy. Was he expecting Frank to recant while he took dictation?

There was a break in the action on the field as the pitching coach made a trip to the mound. As always during such moments, cameras roved about the stands, training themselves on excitable fans and projecting their faces onto the jumbotron. The spectator briefly became the event. What followed was something Frank had watched with puzzlement ever since these enormous electronic scoreboards had started to appear in every arena and stadium. For most of the fans caught on camera, the thirty, forty, fifty thousand others looking up at the screen were the biggest audience they'd ever have. This incited a strange dilemma: if you looked into the lens and properly played the part of screaming celebrant, the camera would linger on the performance, but you would never see it; alternatively, if you looked up at the screen to witness your public moment, you saw only a face looking distractedly up at the screen until the camera hurried on to someone who would better inhabit the role. Most fans attempted to split the difference, shifting back and forth between the two, working themselves into a kind of frenzy as they attempted to turn quickly enough to catch themselves on the screen still looking at the camera.

Any thought at all could tell you that this was impossible, but it happened not once a season or once a game but a dozen times an inning. It was the rare human who was not, at heart, a spectator. Contrariwise the particular genius of the best ballplayers was the sense they gave that they hardly knew you were there. Without the crowd, the game had no meaning—as Wittgenstein said, *The sense of the world must lie outside the world*—but the game must proceed as though the crowd weren't there. What was needed was some recording angel, taking it all down in a book somewhere, making it all comprehensible, and you could not be both the actor and the recorder.

Over the course of his long life, Frank had mostly been a spectator but, he'd flattered himself, he'd managed sometimes to be part of the action on the field. When the camera found its way to him, as it always did, he never looked up, never needed to. He looked straight into the lens. He listened to the cheers, sometimes doffed his cap, as though he were used to being watched, which indeed he was. It was an odd irony that men like Frank—men who knew how to accept the world's attention—were called narcissists, for their talent lay precisely in not needing to look at themselves.

Of course, the camera wouldn't find him tonight, since he wasn't seated in his usual season-ticket seats. Probably it wouldn't have gone looking for him anyway. Just as well. In recent seasons, there had been a smattering of boos along with the cheers, and after what had happened, someone would probably throw a beer at him. He wanted to talk about it now, to justify himself, but the kid refused to ask. Wasn't that the whole point? Why were they there, if not to discuss what had happened last fall?

There'd been a lot riding on that game. For the second summer in a row, the Mets had faded down the stretch after building a healthy lead in the division, but they'd still had a chance at survival. If they simply won their regular season finale against the Marlins, they would make the playoffs, where their slide of the past few weeks might come to seem a test on the way to ultimate victory rather than an embarrassing collapse. This was how baseball, how sports—how life—worked: a single action could change everything that had come before it. The present couldn't actually change the past, but it could change the meaning of the past, which amounted to the same thing. That the Mets had ended the previous season with a loss at home against the very same Marlins that had eliminated them from the playoffs was the kind of symmetry that made baseball so compelling. Rarely in life were the chances for redemption so obvious and shapely. Of course, if they lost, this same symmetry would make the result that much crueler. Either way, Frank had planned to dedicate his next column to the result.

It had been a strange time to give so much attention to baseball. UniBank was fighting for its survival. Frank didn't know how much the collapse would affect them personally, but it would certainly be an emotional blow after Kit's decision to sell. No doubt it said something about Frank that he viewed these two collapses—of his favorite team on one hand and the entire global financial system on the other—as commensurate. Eddie was in Iraq for his second tour. Frank was worried about his son, but he was glad that his nation had recommitted itself to winning. After a long hard slog, the surge had worked. U.S. troops had handed Anbar Province, where Eddie had been stationed on his first go-round, over to the locals that month, and the two countries were hammering out a lasting security pact. There was a democratic government in charge of Iraq. Most of the people Frank knew and worked with didn't want to admit it, but this was what victory looked like. He was proud of the part that his family had played in that effort. It was just like the season—it didn't matter how much struggle it had taken, so long as you won out in the end.

The vendors in his section all knew him well, and they knew to find him with frequency, but on that day he waved everyone but the beer man away. Beside him Margo, his vegetarian daughter, ate a pretzel with mustard.

"Don't you want something?" she asked. "You haven't had your usual quota of peanuts and hot dogs."

"My stomach isn't sitting right," he told her, because it sounded better than saying that he was too anxious to eat, because her brother's life and her mother's livelihood depended on the Mets scoring a few goddamned runs. He'd been subject to this kind of magical thinking for as long as he could remember, and he'd learned to keep it mostly to himself.

The game was a pitcher's duel, still scoreless in the middle of the fifth when he was invited up to the booth. He hadn't expected the invitation—it was a nationally televised game, and most of the national broadcast teams didn't know Frank that well—but in this case the color man, Tim McCarver, was an old friend who'd done the local games for years before joining the national broadcast. He'd gotten the idea that it would be nice to invite Frank up to say goodbye to Shea, so they'd sent a young production assistant down to his usual seats and found him between half-innings while Margo was in the bathroom. He'd written her a note on a napkin and slipped it into her cupholder.

When he stood, the four beers—perhaps it was five—went quickly to his head, and he briefly lost his balance. The young PA asked him whether he was up for this outing.

"My leg fell asleep," Frank said. "I'll be fine in a second."

Upstairs he asked for a bottle of water and took a minute to collect his thoughts. These things were usually pretty easy. You answered some questions and made a few comments about the game as it unfolded. He'd been watching baseball for sixty years and talking on television for more than thirty, so he knew he could handle both, even after a few beers on an empty stomach.

Three minutes later, Frank was seated between McCarver and his play-by-play man, Joe Buck. After welcoming Frank to the booth, Buck asked what he thought about another Mets collapse. Frank had met Buck a few times before and never liked him much. Something smarmy about him. Frank started reciting the column he'd been composing in his head, about redemption and meaning and cruel symmetries. He'd been proud of these sentences while they remained unspoken, but when they came out they sounded awkward and a bit maudlin. He wasn't expressing himself well—he could see it in McCarver's concerned face. Meanwhile, Buck kept that same smug grin on, as if it didn't matter what Frank said.

"You've probably watched more innings of baseball at this stadium that anyone on earth," McCarver said. "You were here when the place opened. Are you going to miss Shea?"

McCarver was helping Frank out, giving him an opportunity for an easy joke at Shea's expense. The stadium was widely and openly loathed by players and fans alike.

"It's an ugly park," Frank said, more harshly than he'd intended. "I don't think anyone is going to be sorry when it's gone."

He left it there, and Buck interjected with a bit of play-by-play. Something in his tone made Frank think that Buck was enjoying this floundering. Frank imagined the two broadcast partners fighting over whether to invite Frank up, and Buck feeling vindicated now. But it wasn't too late to salvage this thing. Frank tried to collect his thoughts.

"You're a real political junkie," Buck said, as if speaking to an old man who watched cable news all night, instead of someone who appeared on it regularly. "Senator Obama is a big baseball fan, and a Chicagoan. The Cubs are going to be in the playoffs again this year. Any chance this is the year they finally break through and end the longest championship drought in sports? Perhaps we're on the verge of two historic victories?"

The whole setup was so forced. Buck looked over with that same smug grin, and Frank did his best to return it.

"Is Barack a baseball fan?" Frank asked, feigning surprise. "I didn't know they followed baseball in Kenya." That had done the job—taking the smile right off Buck's face. Frank was so pleased with the effect that he pushed on. "Maybe he learned the game while hitting coconuts out of a tree." This part didn't quite make sense, he realized. Were there even coconut trees in Africa? And perhaps it had gone slightly too far, since McCarver seemed completely at a loss as well. The pair made no effort to smooth the thing over, instead ignoring Frank for the rest of the half-inning. They didn't even thank him on-air for joining them when the last out was made and they segued into commercial. *Well,* Frank thought as he walked out of the press area, *I might not get asked into Buck's booth again, but it was worth it to see the look on his face.*

"How did it go?" Margo asked when he got back to the seats.

"The usual bullshit," Frank said.

"I hope you didn't tell them that in the booth."

"Things went fine in the booth."

She looked at him skeptically.

"What?" he asked.

"I wouldn't have let you go up there if I'd seen the condition you're in."

"What condition? I've done this a few times before."

Many people would advise him later to blame it on the drink. In his view, beers at a ball game hardly counted as drinking. He hadn't been downing Blue Label. If he was not at his best, it wasn't the beer but the nerves and the empty stomach. And anyway, he didn't think he owed some grand explanation for his behavior. He'd made a bad joke—he could admit that—but it hadn't even really been directed at Obama. It had been directed at Joe Buck, his stupid question and his pious smile. Finally, Frank refused to blame it on the drink because he knew that if he did he would have to stop drinking. There had been a time when you could just say: *I'm sorry I did that thing when I was drunk.* Now you had to say: *I have a problem and, after long consultation with my family and my religious confessor, I have committed to seeking help.* Better to leave alcohol out of the conversation entirely. He liked drinking—he especially liked drinking while watching a ball game—and he had no interest in giving it up.

He'd been back in his seat for about an inning when Margo looked down at this fancy new phone she could never put down and said, "What did you do up there, Dad?"

"What do you mean?"

"I just got a text from a friend. It's all over Teeser that you made some racist remark on national television."

"It wasn't a racist remark. This is why I'm always telling you not to waste time on this internet garbage."

"What did you say?"

Frank tried to remember exactly what he'd said. As he went back over it in his mind, he could see how it might look when taken out of context.

"Buck was being a real prick, and I was already in a lousy mood."

"What did you say?"

By now she'd found a clip of it on her phone and before he could answer she'd started playing it. He could hear his slurring, snarling voice, and he knew that it sounded bad. When she got to the end of the clip, Margo looked from her phone up to him.

"I can't believe you."

"It was a joke."

"It was offensive."

"The man's father is from Kenya. There's nothing wrong with that. It's offensive that people would assume it was an insult."

"Obama's from Hawaii, and if he *were* from Kenya, that wouldn't make him a tree-climbing monkey."

"I never said anything about monkeys." Frank was fairly certain this was true. "Do human beings not climb trees?"

She wasn't listening. She'd found another clip, recorded just a few minutes before but already floating around in the electronic ether along with the first. It was from the half-inning after he'd left the booth. McCarver was apologizing to viewers for what they'd just heard.

"Frank Doyle is an old friend of mine," he said, "but what he just said is inexcusable. Whatever your politics are, there's no place in the twenty-first century for that kind of talk. Baseball is a game that has brought people of every race together ever since Jackie Robinson broke the color line in this very city. Frank Doyle does not represent this network or this game."

"Well put, partner," Buck added.

It was ridiculous. Frank had probably written a hundred pages about Robinson over the years. He'd known the man personally. They'd eaten meals together. He was on the verge of telling this to Margo, but the look on her face stopped him. What had upset her so much? If he was being honest, what he'd said was stupid. But he'd said plenty of stupid things over the years. Provocation was part of his job. When you made it your business to test boundaries, those boundaries inevitably got crossed once in a while.

"I want to go," Margo said.

"Are you serious? It's a tie game at the end of six. The whole season is on the line."

"If you had any idea what you'd just done you'd be ready to go, too."

He considered staying to watch the rest of the game alone, but her look convinced him that this was a bad idea. So he wasn't there when the Mets gave up two runs in the next inning, when they lost the game and the entire season. He wasn't there for the somber post-game ceremony that closed the old stadium. He never saw the place again before it was demolished.

His belief that something more than one team's season was bound up in that game seemed to prove itself correct: UniBank went bust a few weeks later. McCain made a mess of the ensuing crisis, calling on Obama to suspend campaigning. He looked old and tired and scared, and he lost the election handily, just as Waxworth had predicted. Obama's first act in office, it seemed, was to snatch defeat from the jaws of victory in Iraq, withdrawing the troops that had successfully stabilized the place. Frank was relieved that Eddie was safe now, but he was home because the war had been lost. What might have been seen as a long and difficult but noble struggle looked now like a failure and a mistake. And Frank himself was a disgrace. He never got to write his column about how one moment can change the meaning of a lifetime's hard work. He had lived it instead.

He kept waiting for Waxworth to ask about it all, but the kid seemed too absorbed in the game to do his job. He wasn't much of a reporter, Frank thought again.

"How exactly did you wind up with this job?"

"Writing for the *Interviewer*?"

"I know about the election and all that. I mean, how did you get into the prophecy business?"

Waxworth took a moment, as though considering how seriously to answer.

"When I was in college, the guys on my hall had these endless bullshit sessions. Who was the greatest left-handed pitcher of all time? How many shutdown closers is one reliable starter worth? Who was a better hitter—Bonds or Ruth? These conversations went on forever, almost by design. There was so much imprecision that any case could be made. But the nice thing about baseball is that you don't have to speculate, because they keep playing more games. If a method of evaluation is any good, it ought to apply to next season just as well as to last."

Frank had heard this argument before.

"So you made predictions."

"We calculated win totals for all thirty teams. There were maybe a dozen of us. Before pitchers and catchers reported for spring training, we each put fifty bucks into an envelope, which was kept in the care of an independent observer. Whoever had the smallest total deviation would win the whole pot."

"Let me guess." Frank knew more about these things than the statheads probably appreciated. "You took the previous year's run differential, and you plugged in some numbers to account for off-season moves."

"That's a good start," the kid said, in a mildly impressed tone that bothered Frank less than it should have. "But not enough for my purposes. Bill James demonstrated the relationship between wins and run differential almost thirty years ago. Most of my friends already knew about it, or could discover it with a little research. To get a real edge, I needed to drill deeper than that. In the same way that wins can be derived from the differential between runs scored and allowed, run production and prevention can be derived from various individual statistics. But now we have the same problem over again: the stats that track best with run production—on-base and slugging percentage—aren't themselves the most predictable, because there's so much luck involved once a ball is put into play."

"So you tracked home runs, strikeouts, and walks."

Waxworth gave an approving nod.

"That's right. Then I assumed a regression to the mean on batting average for balls in play. Once I'd figured all that out, it was pretty easy to write a program that gathered these numbers and combined them to predict future value. Of course, I'm simplifying matters a little bit. I also had to project the career arcs of different player types, and a few other variables, but basically that was it. I called it the Yearly Over/Under Number Theorem."

"YOUNT," Frank said after a moment.

"A silly reverse acronym. He was my favorite player growing up. If I'd known it was going to follow me around for years, I might have given it another name, but it did its job."

"You won a few hundred bucks, and the rest is history."

"Actually, I came in second place."

"Someone had a better system?"

"Not exactly. The winner was a kid named Craig who lived on my hall. Not a particularly bright guy. That summer he'd worked on campus, checking fire extinguishers for the public safety office, and he'd given himself scurvy by eating nothing but ramen and ketchup packets."

"Sounds like tough competition."

"He had no system. He just guessed. I'd done all that work trying to remove luck from my calculations, but I hadn't removed it from the contest itself. Of course, his results wouldn't hold up for another season, but some other equally unsophisticated method would get lucky instead. My system would keep me in the top two or three year after year, but that wasn't enough. You could predict win totals for years before it produces a sample large enough to assure that the better system wins out."

Frank listened to him explain the more expansive wager he'd proposed next: predicting every significant statistical category for every single major league baseball player—somewhere around twenty thousand outputs.

"A number that big makes guessing impossible. You need an algorithm just to populate all those fields, even if it only assumes that each player will replicate his previous season. It would take a bit of work, which was why I suggested raising the stakes to two hundred and fifty dollars. By the time the season rolled around, there were two dozen paying participants. Most of them weren't even really baseball fans. They just liked the challenge of it. We had to open a group savings account, because there was too much money to keep in an envelope. The school paper wrote an article about us. I posted my YOUNT projections on a website I'd built during an early computer science class, and I updated it weekly with a running tally of each player's actual production. I kept a blog that analyzed YOUNT's performance compared to my competitors. It was pretty clear right away that I was going to win. The question was how accurate I would be. People who had nothing to do with the bet—people who didn't even go to school with us—were following along. By the end of the summer I was getting thousands of unique visitors each week. This website, the Pop-Up, started reporting the results, which drove so much traffic to my page that the university shut it down. The Pop-Up offered to host it for the rest of the season, and the next year they bought the system. In my world, that site is a huge deal."

"I'm familiar with it," Frank said. "They used to have something called the 'Frank Doyle Idiot Watch.'"

Waxworth laughed.

"Well, I didn't write that. And they kind of screwed me over in the end, so I'm not a huge fan of the place, either."

Now Frank laughed. Despite himself, he was enjoying all this. There was nothing better than watching baseball with someone who really knew it. Eddie had never loved baseball the way Frank did. He'd liked sitting in his room with his buddies, getting stoned. Margo had come to countless games with him over the years, and she actually knew quite a bit about the sport, but things were just different for a father and daughter. You weren't supposed to say that these days, but it was true. With Margo he shared poetry, but he'd always wanted to share baseball with his boy.

In the third, an odd commotion brought their attention to a spot behind home plate. A cat had found its way onto the field and was running around the on-deck circle.

"Look at that," Frank said, delighted. It might have happened just to prove his point. "That's not something that will wind up in the box score, not something that goes into your algorithm."

The kid didn't seem impressed.

"That's because it won't have any effect on the outcome."

"You don't think it's a bad omen to have a cat run onto the field during the first game at the park? You know that it was a black cat that doomed the Cubbies in 69?"

"A bad omen? Are you serious?"

"Granted, this one wasn't black. Maybe it's a good omen, then."

"So if they do well, then it will have been a good omen. If they have another collapse like the last two seasons, it will be a bad omen. And what if they just have a mediocre season?"

"Then it won't have been an omen after all."

"You don't really believe this stuff—curses and omens and jinxes and all that?"

"Why not believe in it?"

"Because it's not true. There's no evidence for it."

"Who gets to decide what counts as evidence? The cat came on the field. You and I both saw that. You say it won't have any effect on the outcome of the game, but there's no way of knowing if you just pretend it never happened."

"I don't want to pretend it didn't happen. It's fun. It's part of the game's charm. You can tell nice stories about it. I just don't want to pretend that it *means* anything. As for whether it goes in the box score—let's say we did note the cat on the field. That's easy enough to record. If it had any effect, it would be a *measurable* effect, at which point we could try to figure out some explanation for it."

"Of course, everything can get turned into a number. The Feline Quotient. Value over Replacement Pet."

Waxworth laughed at this, and after a moment Frank laughed along. He flagged down a beer man and offered to buy the next round.

Facing a full count in the bottom of the fifth, David Wright hit a three-run homer to tie it up. The team was showing some life. Then in the top of the sixth a routine out was misplayed into a three-base error. With two outs the pitcher flinched on the mound, and the umpire called a balk. It was the one call in baseball that the average fan couldn't spot—a kind of procedural error. The pitcher didn't set himself properly, which meant the runner was allowed to advance a base. The run was let in on a technicality.

"Unbelievable," Frank said. "We're going to lose this game on a balk. How many of your computer simulations would you have to run before that happened?"

"Quite a few," the kid admitted.

"Here's something that you statheads can't capture. Some teams are just star-crossed. They can't get out of their own way. I'm not saying the cat has anything to do with it. But what do you say about a pitcher who consistently beats himself? I mean, no one on the other team had to do a thing. There's no number that captures that."

"Actually there is," Waxworth said after a moment, an odd excitement in his voice. "I haven't thought about it in a long time, but Bill James developed a stat. It adds up balks, hit batsmen, wild pitches, errors—all the things a pitcher does that are entirely in his control, that don't require the batter to do anything at all. The Index of Self-Destructive Acts."

Frank laughed again in spite of himself. The very sound of it improved his mood.

"You guys are finally good for something."

It was all over quickly after that. No more runs were scored, and the Mets opened the new park with a loss, just as they'd closed the last one. As they filed out, Frank suggested they ride into the city together, but Waxworth said he was taking the bus to Brooklyn.

"Maybe we could meet again?" Frank said. "If you've got more questions for the piece."

"I'd like that," the kid told him.

On the train back into Manhattan, the mood was surprisingly low. One game in April didn't amount to much, and anyway baseball was a game of failure. The best teams lost sixty times in a season, the best hitters made outs in two-thirds of their at bats. But the way they'd done it—opening a new park by losing on a three-base error and a balk—had everyone shell-shocked. To someone like Waxworth, Frank thought, this was an outlier, a statistical anomaly to be safely discarded. But to the humble fan, who felt things in his bones he could hardly articulate, let alone justify numerically, it could only portend trouble to come.

5.

In the lobby he found his mother deep in conversation with one of the weekend doormen, an old Irishman named Hugh. They both looked up when Justin emerged from the elevator as though surprised in the middle of a social call. He was actually running ahead of schedule—it was barely eight o'clock—but Netta had probably come straight down after getting dressed, which meant they'd been chatting for more than an hour.

She'd lived in the building for six months now, and she still seemed to spend all her time with the doormen or the nannies and housekeepers who congregated by the service entrance around the corner. Justin had introduced her to some women her own age, including two recent widows. They'd all spoken politely about getting together for tea, but so far as he could tell no actual invitations had been extended. Nor did Netta's old friends ever visit, apart from the prayer circle that Jonathan brought over every other week. She seemed almost embarrassed by her living conditions.

"Be well," Hugh told her as he ushered them into the revolving door. Touching the bill of his uniform cap, he added, "Have a good day, Mr. Price."

The black Range Rover waited in front of a hydrant outside, and Tommy smiled into the rear-view as they climbed in. They headed down Fifth for half a block and turned onto the nearest brownstoned side street. The shops of Madison Avenue gave way to the long leafy sun-drenched alley of Park, and Netta lowered her window for a better look, as she often did on this drive. Justin had grown up on these streets, but his mother affected being still a stranger to them. He found something willful in this pose, given the amount of time she'd spent in the neighborhood over the years. Not to mention the fact that she'd brought him there in the first place.

His father hadn't liked the idea of applying for a place in the Bootstrappers program, but Netta had insisted on it.

"They're going to pay for the boy's education," she'd told her husband. "What's wrong with that?"

"We already pay for his education," Justin's father had replied. "Don't we pay our taxes? Where do you think the money for his school is coming from?"

The Bootstrappers provided scholarships to underprivileged but academically promising students and helped with the transition to private education. What bothered Daryl Price was the suggestion that his son was "underprivileged"—or any other polite word you wanted to use for poor. Their family was middle class. They didn't need charity to bring up their boy. Indeed, Justin had until that point been raised to understand that he had advantages most of his classmates at MS 61 didn't share. Both his parents worked, his father as a city bus driver, his mother as a secretary in an accountant's office. He'd never worried about whether he would have enough to eat or a roof over his head. But middle class was a long way from paying for Manhattan private school, which was what Netta wanted for him. She was the one who met with Justin's teachers, and she was the one who'd decided that MS 61 wasn't good enough.

There were other reasons for her insistence, ones that couldn't be spoken out loud. Both his parents knew that Justin was coming home with his nose bloodied or his shirt ripped every few days. His father sometimes suggested that the bullying would stop once Justin toughened up a little bit, but his mother understood the reason that Justin was being targeted, and she knew that this reason wasn't going away. She hadn't needed to say this out loud. She'd just held out until she'd gotten her way, as she got her way in nearly all the family's decisions.

Once Justin was accepted into the program, his mother had chosen St. Albert's from among the half dozen participating schools because it was Catholic. She wasn't Catholic herself—in fact, she was vaguely suspicious of Catholics, who had something pagan about them—but none of the ostensibly Protestant institutions had so much as mentioned the Lord in their admissions materials.

Justin had spent the next summer being prepared for the rigors of sixth grade by tutors who were former Bootstrappers themselves, mostly now enrolled at top tier colleges, a few in law or business school or in the early stages of prestigious professional careers. They tried at once to impress upon Justin how hard he would have to work and how well this effort would ultimately be rewarded. Though he'd never missed class, always studied hard and gotten good marks, they told him he was a year behind grade level in nearly every subject. It didn't seem fair that he'd been falling behind without even knowing it, while doing everything that was ever asked of him. That summer he worked as hard as he had it in him to work, and he was constantly reminded that this was just the beginning.

Near the end of August, they'd been invited to a lunch for incoming Bootstrappers, held at a townhouse in the east seventies, between Madison and Fifth. Standing outside the front door, he could see the tree-lined eastern wall of Central Park in the distance. In the first eleven years of his life, Justin had been to Manhattan a few dozen times. He'd gone on school trips to the South Street Seaport and the Empire State Building, he'd been to a Knicks game at the Garden with a church group, but he'd never been north of Penn Station, and he'd never seen Central Park. While they waited at the door, he imagined pulling off his zip-up tie, climbing the wall, and spending the afternoon running around—as he might otherwise have been doing that day in Prospect Park—instead of talking politely to strangers.

About their hosts, Justin had known nothing but their names, which he'd been trained by his mother to say with an extended hand: *Good day, Mr. Doyle, Good day, Mrs. Doyle, Thank you for having me into your home.* He could not have known the role this family would come to play in his life—or the one they'd already played. He didn't know that this Mrs. Doyle was the chair of the Bootstrappers' board, that her family's investment bank was its primary financial supporter, that her grandmother had been among St. Albert's founders. He didn't know that the tie constricting his throat at that moment had in all likelihood belonged to her son. He didn't know that this son would be his St. Albert's classmate for the next eight years and his best friend for life. He didn't even know that the Doyles had a son.

When a white woman a few years older than his mother answered the door, Justin nervously stuck out his hand and said, *Good day, Mr. Doyle, Good day, Mrs. Doyle, Thank you for having me into your home.* Kit laughed in what was clearly meant to be a friendly way, but Justin could feel his mother stiffening beside him, and he wanted to run away from that place.

Inside, he met the rest of that year's scholarship students—black and brown boys from other parts of Brooklyn, from Washington Heights and the Bronx, about to start new lives at half a dozen different private schools, their uniforms distinguishable only by the colors of their ties and the patches on their blazer pockets. The one white boy wore shorts and a light green polo shirt, and he introduced himself as Eddie before asking each of them in turn which school they'd be attending and what grade they'd be in. Justin was one of four headed to St. Albert's, but the rest were starting in seventh or eighth grade. When Justin said that he'd be in sixth, Eddie announced with excitement that they were in the same class. They talked for most of the next two hours.

Justin had thought of that first meeting often while Eddie was gone. He'd thought of all the ways the friendship that began that day had changed his life. He was so relieved to have Eddie back. It had felt strange to live in the neighborhood and not have him around. He'd wondered sometimes whether he could have stayed if something had happened to Eddie, if he hadn't come back. But where else could Justin go? This place was his home.

They turned downtown at York and headed for the Drive, where they moved quickly until traffic came to a stop just north of the bridge. Tommy swerved on to the shoulder and sped up to the off-ramp, where he pulled smoothly back into the exit lane while the cars behind them honked in disgust. Tommy drove as though they were the only people on the road who mattered, an attitude that would have been obviously obnoxious in a private citizen but somehow seemed an acceptable form of professionalism.

In the two years since Justin had hired Tommy, his duties had slowly expanded from just driving Netta around to generally taking care of her needs. She never asked for much, but Tommy had a talent for anticipating her desires and gracefully meeting them, and they seemed to have genuine affection for each other. Tommy was a middle-aged Dominican, maybe five years younger than Netta. He was one of two Hispanics on Justin's payroll, along with Fermin, who looked after the house in Bridgehampton. The rest of his staff was from the Philippines. Yoyo—her green card said Yolanda, but Justin had never heard anyone, even her children, call her anything but Yoyo—had been managing the apartment since he moved in, and she was a great evangelist for the talents of her race. Whenever Justin needed more help, she found a cousin or friend who was looking for work. Hiring this way was easier than conducting an open search, and it saved Justin certain emotional complications: he didn't want to reject candidates for their color; at the same time, he couldn't imagine having a black servant. (Of course he didn't call them "servants" to anyone but himself, but this was what they were.)

The roads in Brooklyn were clear, and they arrived at the Bible Pathway House of God well before nine, but you would have thought they were late by the way Netta jumped from the car. She made no effort to hide the fact that these church trips were the highlight of her week. Sometimes he wished she were less enthusiastic about escaping the life he'd built for her.

Justin got out behind her and watched from the sidewalk as she hurried inside. Through the open doors, he saw about a half dozen people, mostly women Netta's age or older in bright Sunday dresses and colorful, veiled hats, women who'd been going to the church all of Justin's life. Despite this sartorial radiance, the most striking shade was the turquoise of the empty pews. The space held about a hundred people, but only a handful more would be arriving before services started. It was modest but well-looked after: outside, clean brick storefront and illuminated marquee; inside, vinyl wall covering and fresh nylon carpet, laid down at the same time the pews were last painted. Some passerby who happened to look in might wonder how the place stayed open. Justin didn't have to wonder; *he* kept it open.

The Pathway had been run throughout Justin's childhood by a charismatic preacher still memorialized on the marquee as the Hon. Bishop George Peabody but known among his followers simply as Elder George. Like Netta and many of the other congregants, Elder George was Bajan. He'd testified in a booming lilt that seemed to call the very heavens down, and he'd filled the pews each Sunday, until he died of a sudden heart attack—in flagrante, the rumors went, though Netta called this "devil's chatter." Now his son was the pastor. Jonathan Peabody was earnest and enthusiastic. Unlike his father he had a college degree and a masters in divinity, and he tried to put on a good show. His two sisters provided passable music—one playing the electric organ while the other sang and shook a tambourine. But most of their father's following had moved on, or else died out, like Justin's own father, with no one to replace them.

Some of Justin's earliest memories involved playing in the back of the packed church with Jonathan and another boy, Terrance, whose mother had rivalled Netta as Elder George's most enthusiastic disciple. After Justin went off to St. Albert's, Terrance's mother moved the family to New Jersey, and Jonathan was the closest thing to a friend that Justin still had in the neighborhood. In a lengthy letter thanking Justin for his first major gift, Jonathan had encouraged him to stop in one Sunday. *You might find my preaching more tolerant than my father's in some ways,* he added. *The Word of God is unchanging, but our understanding of it sometimes has to evolve.* Justin had been almost impressed by his tact, but he hadn't taken the offer up. Apart from his father's funeral, he hadn't stepped inside the place in years.

Netta never complained about this, except to say that it seemed a waste for Justin to travel all that way just to wait outside. She and Tommy were fine making the trip to Crown Heights on their own, she said. Justin assured her that he liked coming back, which was true, though his reasons for liking it were different than hers. Netta came for familiarity; Justin came to see change. He'd put a lot of money into the neighborhood, and he wanted to witness what had come of it.

Not everything was different, of course. As he walked north from the church, Justin passed the same Chinese takeout with the order-by-number menu and the bulletproof glass, but the hair salon that had once stood next door to it was now a skate shop. At Park Place,

Justin came to their old building, where he'd grown up, where Netta had lived until he'd moved her into Manhattan, nestled against the elevated hulk of the Franklin Avenue shuttle. Beyond it, the neighborhood became more orderly, began its transition into Prospect Heights. Blakeman had always taken endless amusement from the idea that Justin had literally lived on the wrong side of the tracks, the kind of joke only Blakeman could make.

He'd been the second St. Albert's friend that Justin had made, on his first day at the school, and he owed this too to Eddie Doyle. Justin still remembered that morning vividly. His father had spent half an hour demonstrating the proper way to knot his tie before giving up and doing it himself, pulling it flush against Justin's collar. He didn't want him wearing the zip-up that the Bootstrappers had sent them.

"You'll get it eventually," he said. He held his son firmly by both shoulders and kissed his forehead. "Don't be nervous. They're all just people."

On the train into Manhattan, Justin wanted to loosen the tie, which felt hot around his neck, but he was afraid the knot would unravel at his touch, so he just fiddled at his collar until his mother slapped his hand and said, "Leave it be." Despite his father's encouragement, he'd never felt so nervous in his life, and this was just one of the conflicting emotions pulsing through him, along with relief at escaping the daily torture of MS 61; fear of what it would mean if things at St. Albert's weren't any better (namely, that he was destined never to fit in anywhere); pride at the work he'd done that summer; anxiety about the work still ahead of him; mild aggravation at the prospect of wearing a tie every day; and guilt that he alone among his classmates was getting out. Plenty of other kids—including Terrance, the only one he was sad to be leaving behind, the one who would continue to get the beatings that Justin would now escape— might have done something with this opportunity, but only Justin's parents had made it happen. At least, he told himself, he had one friend already, but he wondered whether Eddie Doyle would be so nice with other kids around.

As it happened, Eddie found him before homeroom and introduced him to Max Blakeman, along with another boy, also named Eddie. The other Eddie was a scholarship kid like Justin, though white and not a Bootstrapper. His mother worked as the school's receptionist. All three had been going to St. Albert's since kindergarten, and Justin could immediately read their long-established dynamic. The two Eddies deferred to Blakeman on nearly everything, and once it was clear that Max approved of Justin, his place in the group was secured.

When Max asked what rap he liked, Justin understood that the honest answer—he preferred the old jazz records his father played at home—would disappoint, so he told them he was down with Biggie and Scarface, which is what Terrence would have said.

"Kids here like House of Pain and all that wigger shit," Max replied.

Both Eddies giggled nervously at the word.

"What's your tag?" Max asked.

Justin did have a tag that he'd occasionally drawn in notebooks, but he'd never shown it to anyone, not even Terrance, because he had a nagging sense that it was lame. He'd certainly never tagged anything publicly, which would have been doubly dangerous in Crown Heights: if caught by the wrong kid, he would have gotten a beating from whoever owned that block; if caught by an adult, he would have gotten a beating from his father. He demonstrated on a sheet of loose leaf that Max provided—*Price IZ Right*, with the *IZ* bleeding into the capital *R*—and the boys seemed to think it was cool. More than this, they seemed to view Justin as the natural arbiter of what counted for cool in this area. Max showed off his own tag—*Opus*, in bubble letters. When Justin granted it his approval, Max celebrated by producing a Sharpie and marking up the inside of his new locker door.

Now, some kids played in the street outside his old building, as they always did on sunny weekend days. Before starting at St. Albert's, Justin had been one of these kids, at least when he wasn't in church. He'd mostly run around with Terrance while Jonathan chased after them, wanting to be included in whatever they had planned. Terrance had lived in the same building until his mother moved them to Jersey. After that Justin had never seen him again. He'd died at nineteen, in a botched liquor store robbery in Camden.

Even before Terrance was gone, it had been clear that their mothers didn't want them spending time together anymore, and after that there was little to keep Justin tied to the neighborhood. Still, he'd had no idea—neither had his parents, presumably—how little time he would spend in Crown Heights once he went off to school in Manhattan.

After classes ended on that very first day, Eddie had invited him back to his house.

"Is that allowed?" Justin had asked.

Eddie laughed.

"Of course it's allowed. Why wouldn't it be?"

Justin was expected straight home, but his mother didn't leave her office in Downtown Brooklyn until after six, which meant he could spend at least an hour with Eddie and still make it to the apartment before she did.

At the house Eddie introduced Justin to his sister, Margo, who was just in kindergarten. The three children sat in the kitchen together while Angela, the nanny, fixed them snacks. Angela was a large black woman who spoke with a light Caribbean lilt like Justin's mother, and he felt an odd mixture of pride and shame at being served by her, though she gave no sign that Justin bore any resemblance to her that the Doyle children lacked. When Margo and Eddie finished eating, they left their dirty plates and glasses at the table, something Justin could never do at home, and they rushed up the carpeted stairs to the second floor. Justin followed Eddie down the hall to a bedroom that was bigger than Justin's own and his parents' combined. It had a basketball hoop on one wall and a Ping-Pong table folded up against another. Justin would have been happy to play with either, but Eddie instead sat down cross-legged in front of the TV, turned on his Sega Genesis, and spent the next half hour beating Justin repeatedly at *NBA Jam*.

At home that night, Justin watched his parents looking at each other, trying to decide how to respond to the news of how he'd spent his afternoon. Finally, his mother said that it was all right to see friends after school, so long as he got his homework done. "We aren't sending you to this place to play arcade games," his father added.

Justin went over to the Doyles' house each of the next two days. On Thursday, Eddie had tennis lessons, so Justin spent the afternoon watching television and waiting for his mother to get home to make dinner. He'd passed countless enjoyable hours this way in the past, but now it felt boring and stifling, the apartment too small, the TV too old. He wished that he had a Sega Genesis and *NBA Jam*. If he took the next step and imagined living in a house like the one where Eddie Doyle lived, it was only in the most abstract way, as he sometimes imagined while watching a Knicks game that he was Mark Jackson feeding the ball to Patrick Ewing—more a fantasy than an aspiration.

That changed a month later, when a transit strike shut down the subway for two weeks. Justin went off to school on the morning of the contract deadline without knowing whether his father would be heading to work or the picket line. Nor did he know how he would get back to Brooklyn that night. Near the end of the day, his home-room teacher pulled him aside to say that his mother had called. He'd be staying with the Doyles until the trains started running again. He never found out exactly how this had been arranged, but he was fairly sure that it had been Kit's doing. When he and Eddie left school that afternoon, Angela was waiting outside. She brought the boys to a drugstore down the block, where she bought Justin a toothbrush and asked whether he wanted anything else. He wanted all sorts of things, but he didn't know who would be paying for them, so he just shook his head.

At dinner that night—prepared and served by Angela and eaten around the long dining table—Justin met Eddie's father for the first time. "We have some things in common," Frank Doyle said by way of introduction. Justin was flattered that the man knew enough about him to recognize any commonalities. When he asked what they were, his host responded with great enthusiasm: "Crown Heights, to begin with. I went to Brooklyn Prep, on Carroll Street. We're also the only two people at this table who weren't born rich."

"Behave yourself, Frank," Kit said, though this scolding had a bit of performance to it.

Frank thought for a moment and added, "As a matter of fact, when I was a kid, the Irish were a persecuted minority in this city, so we have that in common, too."

Kit was genuinely embarrassed now, and Eddie rolled his eyes at Justin before heading into the kitchen on the pretense of refilling his plate. Even Margo seemed to sense that something bad had happened. All of this might have been the point, because Frank looked around the table before giving Justin a conspiratorial wink. Later, one could clearly see Frank's downfall portended in this exchange—not just the obvious delight he took in making people uncomfortable, but this sense of himself, which had survived decades of plenitude, as ultimately a working-class kid from Flatbush. He didn't doubt that he was entitled to make such jokes to a twelve-year-old boy—or that Justin was on his side.

And he was right: Justin had loved the idea that this man had grown up in conditions somehow like his own. The obvious implication was that Justin might himself one day have all the things he saw around him. Such a development would be no more improbable than the reality that Frank Doyle had them now.

Justin did feel some discomfort, but it was an odd sort. So many of the people he'd met since starting at St. Albert's, children and adults alike, spoke to him with special care, as though under orders not to do anything that would mark him as different. This felt more pointed in its way than Max's asking him whether he knew anyone who'd gone to jail or Eddie's instinctive surprise that Justin wasn't good at basketball. Because he *was* different, and there was nothing wrong with that. Frank Doyle seemed entirely unafraid of this difference, and he meant to pay Justin a kind of compliment by acknowledging it. Of course, accepting this compliment required Justin to share his difference with Frank, to allow this rich white man the prerogatives of marginalization. Though he wouldn't have put it that way as a child, some part of Justin understood even then the terms of the trade, and it seemed a small price to pay. If he'd instead expressed some discomfort, he might have saved the family much trouble in the long run. Not that an adolescent visitor to his dinner table would have changed Frank's attitude—the man was fairly unchangeable—but it might have encouraged him to keep some of these thoughts to himself. Instead Justin smiled back at Frank's wink, and the form of their relationship was established forever.

Over the next eight years, until he and Eddie both left for college, Justin rarely went more than a few days without visiting that house. When you combined that time with days at school, afternoons in Central Park, teenage nights at bars on Second Avenue, the vast majority of his adolescence was spent on the Upper East Side, but it was that one dinner table conversation that planted the seed that would grow into his young life's aim. From those early days at St. Albert's well into adulthood, nearly every decision he'd made—not only what high school electives to take, what clubs to join, where to go to college and what to major in when he got there, but also how to carry himself, what to wear, what books to read—had been made with that one aim in mind. This was why he'd gone to work for Kit Doyle out of college, and it was why he'd left Kit to work for Dan Eisen: he wanted to have what the Doyles had. He wanted to live as they lived.

Justin continued to Sterling Place, where he turned east, away from the train, into the heart of Crown Heights. He approached a limestone hulk that occupied a quarter of the block. Half a century before, this building had been a residential hotel called the Denison—the name was still chiseled above the entryway—but like nearly everything in the area it had fallen into disrepair over the course of Justin's childhood and the years immediately before and after it. The Denison belonged to Justin now, in a manner of speaking: he'd created a real estate investment trust to buy the building, and he'd found a developer to convert its rooms into rental apartments. He'd still been working for Eisen at the time, but he'd done this business independently, proud to contribute to the neighborhood's resurrection.

"You expecting a profit?" his father had asked when he heard about the plan.

"My investors sure are," Justin answered.

"If you're making a profit, you're not giving back—you're taking out."

His father's economic radicalism had seemed to increase in direct proportion to Justin's success as a capitalist. At the time, Justin had responded that dismissing any project that happened to make some money for the people who'd undertaken it meant ignoring a lot of good work, but some part of him knew now that his father had been right: his backers weren't looking to improve the neighborhood for the people who already lived there; they were readying it for those to come. The newcomers had been slowed somewhat by the downturn, but they were still on their way. When Justin was a kid, you could have spent days on this block without seeing a white face that wasn't framed by sidelocks or a wig, and even these were not plentiful unless you walked east to the real Hasidic turf. Now there were white people everywhere, mostly emaciated young men and women with tattoo sleeves and ironic T-shirts, but soon enough the well-dressed couples pushing sport-utility strollers would arrive, and these families would move into places like the Denison. When they did, a group of rich white people would get richer. Justin would get richer, too, but to his father this hadn't counted for much.

Justin had unwound almost all of his major investments in the past year, but he still owned a large share in the Denison, and he still liked to come by and look at it. He continued to be proud of the place. His father would have hated seeing the kind of people the building housed, but this wasn't Justin's fault. The old neighborhood—the one his parents had been so resistant to leaving, the one to which his mother was so eager to return—didn't exist anymore, despite the survival of Han's Good Friends or the Pathway.

He walked a few more blocks, to a tall glass-front building with cut metal lettering over the door: The Daryl Price Neighborhood Center. This building held the hospice facility where Justin's father had spent the end of his life, though back then it had been called the Crown Heights Community House. When Justin had learned that his father was dying—melanoma, initially ignored by the doctors at Brooklyn Hospital, identified after it had long metastasized—his first response had been resentment. If only his parents had agreed to move when he'd first asked them, he would have taken his father to a good doctor in Manhattan who would have made the proper diagnosis while there was still something to be done about it. His second response was defiance. He dragged his father to every specialist he could find, applied for every experimental trial, went in search of foreign sources for drugs that had not been approved by the FDA. When all the experts admitted there was nothing they could do,

Justin proposed setting his father up in his apartment, where he could make him as comfortable as possible, but Daryl had opted to finish his life on Bedford Avenue.

Justin had visited several times a week, always horrified by the place's condition, though he never mentioned this. Well before his father died, he'd decided to take the place over. The center had been run by a cash-strapped charity that was happy to make a local boy with deep pockets the chair of its board. Justin had paid for the building's renovation and renamed it. It still offered the medical services from his father's time there, though they were all much improved. The youth hall had three Ping-Pong tables. The daycare center had remote monitoring and every state-of-the-art educational toy imaginable. The third floor was for adults—mostly seniors—a kind of meeting place with bingo and movie nights. The gym in the basement had breakaway rims and hosted a midnight basketball league. An endowment, also named for his father, would keep everything running in perpetuity.

His father's death had been the crisis that led Justin to close his fund, and the Price Center had been his first large-scale act of philanthropy. He was only thirty-five, but he could have spent the rest of his days giving money away and still die rich. He'd decided that this was what he'd do. Since everything happened more quickly in the modern era, it was only appropriate that the usual multigenerational cycle of wealth—one generation made the moral compromises necessary to accumulate all the money that the next lightly laundered with targeted charitable giving while spending the rest on their tasteful and cultured lifestyle—was more and more frequently playing out over a single life span, but Justin had managed to squeeze it into a matter of years.

This building with his father's name on it was a poor substitute for the man himself, but Justin felt closer to his father while standing here than he did anywhere else. Ever since the renovation had finished, the place had brought him a reliable sense of satisfaction. He always came by while his mother was in church, and he occasionally dared on these walks to think that this was his own church—a place to detach from the world, remember the dead, reflect on the meaning of life.

He'd hoped that the sight of it would alleviate the anxiety he'd been feeling for the past several days, but when he looked at the Price Center, his unease only deepened. He usually went inside to look around, make sure the place was being maintained up to his standards, but he knew he would take no pleasure in that today, and he knew exactly why: whatever intentions had been behind it, this edifice—like all of the good works he'd done in the past year—had been bought with Eisen's money.

Kit's words repeated in his head: *a shame I never played the game the way Eisen does.* She never talked about Eisen. Why had she brought him up now—years after Justin had stopped working for him, when everyone was back together in the house, trying to make things feel as they had before? Had she meant to make him feel ashamed? To make him feel that he didn't deserve to have the same kind of life that she had? He wanted to be angry with her, but he kept returning to the sight of her crying in the garden. He'd never seen her cry before. Even when Eddie left, she'd reacted in anger, not despair.

He retraced his steps to the car, which was still waiting outside the Pathway. The service wouldn't be out for at least another twenty minutes, so Justin got in the car and told Tommy to circle the block.

As they drove, he skimmed through emails on his BlackBerry. He responded to some foundation requests before opening a message from Chloe Porter, an old acquaintance who worked in investor relations at a biotech company called Celsia. When she'd written a few days earlier to ask about getting together, he'd assumed she was looking for a job—people in IR were always itching to get over to the buy side—and he'd politely declined, saying he was swamped at the moment. Now she'd responded to say how much she would appreciate it if he could somehow find the time. There was something in particular she wanted to talk about. In fact, she had lots of interesting news. Her insistence was suggestive in a way that usually put Justin off, and he was about to delete the message unanswered when he remembered that conversation with Kit.

Ever since that night, the idea that he might help the Doyles out of their hole had been following him, but he hadn't figured out what kind of help he could give. The simplest thing would have been writing a check, but Kit would never stand for that, especially now that most of his income went to his family foundation. He'd thought about finding her a job, but she could have done that easily enough herself, and if things were as bad as she'd suggested, a bit of consulting work wouldn't be enough. It couldn't hurt to see what Chloe had to say.

He was hitting send on his reply when they turned the corner. The church doors were open, and the small crowd was trickling out. Netta held on to Jonathan's arm. As Justin got out of the car, Jonathan's smile seemed to send ripples across his handsome but chubby face. He always appeared genuinely excited to see Justin, though perhaps this was just a talent for marketing. There was a shine to his shaved head, which Justin felt an odd urge to reach out and touch.

"Brother Justin," he said, "I was just telling your mother how much I'd like for you to see the new pulpit. It's a beautiful thing, a fitting place from which to preach the Word."

Justin didn't understand the significance of this pulpit, until he realized that he must have paid for it. Jonathan's appeals went directly to the Price Foundation administrator, who only informed Justin when requests exceeded twenty grand, which Jonathan's never did. This lack of ambition frustrated Justin. He'd put several million dollars into the old neighborhood, but the only money his mother ever asked him to spend on her behalf was for the church. Jonathan could have asked for a new building or a television crew or some other extravagance, but all he wanted was to keep doing the same things his father had always done. He didn't even want a salary for himself—he had a job during the week as a city social worker—and whatever went into the collection basket went to his sisters.

Going inside would have been the polite thing, but Justin had little desire to inspect a new pulpit—just a fancy table, if he understood properly.

"I'm glad to hear that," he told Jonathan. "I'd love to see it some other time."

He took his mother's arm to guide her back toward the car. He thought she might be angry about the maneuver, but she sat inside with the same ecstatic smile she always had after church. It stayed on her face until they had very nearly crossed the Manhattan Bridge.

6.

Since coming home, Margo had spent most of her time in bed, taking notes for the dissertation she was already fairly sure she would never write. That morning, she was reading *The English Poetic Tradition*, edited by R. Harvey, and when she set the book on her lap it fell immediately open to Wordsworth's "Intimations of Immortality" ode, to which she'd turned so often she'd cracked the book's spine. *But yet I know, where'er I go, / That there hath pass'd away a glory from the earth.* She remembered reading the poem for the first time with her father, who had explained without irony its picture of the child's deep, ineffable understanding of the world that is lost in the passage to adulthood, though she'd been only a child herself then, and she couldn't imagine possessing knowledge that he didn't share.

She'd grown to love this poem, but its vision still struck her as dubious. She certainly didn't want to be returned to the naive insights of childhood. Lately she worried she was destined to remain a child forever. Aspiring academics were often warned against the risks of staying students, sheltered from the realities of the world, but Margo had always laughed the notion off. Her father had taught her that engaging seriously with ideas was one of life's great adult pleasures, the opposite of childish, and she'd found this to be true. When her college friends went off to make their six-figure finance salaries at twenty-three, she didn't think them any less sheltered than she was from whatever qualified as the *real world*. But things had changed since she'd come home. In theory she spent her time doing the same thing she would have done at school: reading and thinking and writing. But something—maybe the fact that she was doing them in her childhood room—made these activities feel infantile.

She closed the book and picked up her phone to text Amy.

Bored, she wrote. *What are you doing today?*

The response was immediate: *Werk. Like everyday.*

Right, Margo returned. *Call me when ur out.*

Amy was Margo's closest friend in New York, but she was always busy at her job. Margo was used to procrastinating by texting grad school classmates, who were generally happy for distractions, but they weren't speaking to her right now. She scrolled idly through her contacts in search of other friends she might call, but none of them could meet for coffee or lunch, because they all worked. They spent their weekdays in cubicles or open-plan offices or on trading floors. If she'd called, the more direct among them might have told her that staying in bed all day was a sign of depression. Well, perhaps Margo was feeling a bit depressed. *There hath pass'd away a glory from the earth* was actually a fairly good description of her mood.

She thought she could pinpoint exactly when things had gone sour: the sixth inning of the last game ever played at Shea Stadium, when she'd watched that clip of her father in the announcer's booth. She'd long understood that getting things wrong once in a while was part of his job, and disagreeing with him was hardly a novel experience, but he'd never before embarrassed her, except in the way that all fathers embarrassed their kids. In the clip he sounded not just wrong but ugly. She knew he wasn't racist, but what he appeared to be instead—a drunken old man spouting stupid provocations to get attention—wasn't much better. He struck her now just as he had struck so many others for so long. This need not have occasioned an existential crisis, except that she'd devoted so much of her life to impressing him. What would she do if his opinion stopped mattering to her?

It sounded so banal, but she couldn't help that. When you lived with such privilege, even your crises were bound to seem self-indulgent. She had all the neuroses that came from growing up rich, plus the added neurosis that only some had: the feeling that you weren't quite entitled to your unhappiness. The Anxiety of Affluence, Richard had jokingly called it.

She closed her contacts and looked at her notes, where she came upon one that read, simply, *Turner*. She remembered now that she'd been planning to visit the Met's J. M. W. Turner exhibition, which might have some relevance to her work, such as that still was. If nothing else, it would get her outside.

She was halfway out the door when Frank called after her. She hadn't thought to worry about running into him, since he spent most of his time tucked away in his office, where he was supposedly finishing the big book he'd been working on since Margo was fourteen. She considered pretending she'd hadn't heard him. If she stopped, he might ask where she was going and decide to come along. It was the kind of thing they'd always done together, and he either hadn't noticed or had chosen to ignore the fact that she wasn't interested in doing the things they'd always done together. She turned only when she realized that he wasn't alone.

"Sam, this is my daughter, Margo," he said to the boy beside him. "Margo, this is Sam Waxworth."

The boy seemed to expect some hint of recognition at the name. When she provided none he said, "I'm here for an interview."

He was certainly dressed for an interview, Margo thought, in his khakis and white oxford button-down. Was her father hiring a research assistant?

"It's for a magazine," he added.

Then it came to her.

"You're the young man from the provinces." He looked back blankly until she laughed. "Bad joke," she said. "It's nice to meet you, Sam." She took her hand from the door to shake his politely. "I'll leave you to your subject."

"We've actually just finished," Frank told her. "Maybe you can show Sam out."

When they got to the bottom of the stoop, Margo looked the boy over more carefully, considering what to make of him now that she knew who he was. He was an inch or so taller than she was, medium build, around her age. His light brown hair was cut close and carefully combed. His narrow face had something faintly canine about it, though he wasn't unattractive. He was almost handsome in an awkward way. She noticed his wedding ring and wondered idly what kind of woman he would marry. He looked a bit lost; it was probably his first time in the neighborhood.

"Where are you headed?" she asked.

"Nowhere in particular," he said. "What about you?"

How easy it would have been to tell him she was meeting friends, direct him politely to the subway, never see him again. In a few weeks she'd read an article in which she wouldn't merit a passing mention. But at the moment she was happy for company.

"To the Met."

"I haven't been yet," he said.

"It's worth seeing," she told him. "You're welcome to come."

He hesitated before answering. He seemed likewise to be wondering exactly what to make of her.

"I should probably get to work on this profile, but I'll walk you there."

Margo was still embarrassed about her initial greeting, and to show that she did after all know who he was, she said as they walked, "I don't think I've ever spoken to an oracle before."

Sam shook his head.

"All that stuff's a little overdone," he said, though obviously pleased by the acknowledgment. "I just like to crunch numbers."

"You went fifty for fifty."

"I got lucky."

"Don't be modest."

"Modesty's not a trait I really possess," he said with a laugh. "My model was probabilistic, which means it's not supposed to be right every time. Or rather, being right doesn't mean what people think it means. If the most likely outcome always happens, then there's a problem with the model, unless I've pegged the probability at one hundred percent. The system has to be 'wrong' occasionally, if it's doing its job. I was predicting more than a hundred outcomes, most with likelihoods in the ninety-to-ninety-five-percent range. If there'd been a few cases where the second most likely thing happened instead of the first, that actually would have made my predictions more accurate, though it wouldn't have gotten the same attention. That's the trouble with elections—there aren't really enough outcomes for the law of large numbers to kick in."

He seemed to come into sharper focus as he spoke. His enthusiasm was so guileless that it could only be laughed at or urged along, and she decided on the latter.

"The law of large numbers?"

"It's a principle of probability that says that the more times you conduct an experiment, the closer the average outcome will get to the expected outcome. In other words, chance cancels out over time. If you flip five coins, they might easily all come up heads. But if you flip five million coins, you're going to get a fifty-fifty split. Predicting election outcomes every four years is more like five coin flips. You'd have to do it for a very long time before it would produce a sample large enough to assure that the better system wins out."

"On the other hand, it's not really a coin flip at all," she said. "Because the outcome actually matters."

"Do you think so? To tell the truth, I'm suspicious of how much difference elected officials make in the world. Particularly in a system where the range of choices is so narrow."

"Why do you study it, if it doesn't make a difference?"

"Well, I started with baseball, but this company that bought my model made me sign a noncompete, so I couldn't write about sports."

"Okay, but why politics?"

"I tried a few other things first. I just asked myself what else was out there to predict. Then it was the spring of 2007, the most wide-open presidential campaign of the modern era. No incumbents on either side, not even a sitting vice president, lots of candidates for both nominations, everything up for grabs. And I could see how politics was like baseball: full of mythology, bad conventional wisdom. People talk about a candidate 'looking presidential,' which is no different from an old scout who 'throws out the numbers' because a prospect passes the 'eyeball test.' Pundits make a living getting things wrong over and over again with no consequence."

"People like my father?"

She'd meant this teasingly, but he hardly seemed to notice.

"I just mean that there was lots of data floating around that no one seemed to know what to do with. National election results, exit polls for every two years, plus extensive polling leading up to every election. I decided to see what I could make of it."

"And you accidentally got everything right."

"I got lucky," he said again.

"You'll start getting some things wrong once the law of large numbers kicks in?"

They both laughed. Margo sometimes found that long stints of reading without human interaction rendered her socially inept, but she found talking with him easy. He wasn't awkward in the way she'd expected. He was probably a little arrogant, but she was used to that, even preferred it to the alternative. It felt like a long time since she'd had a real conversation, the kind that forced you to think a little bit, the kind she'd always had with her father.

The sidewalks near the museum were filled with hot dog carts, street vendors selling prints and African masks, caricaturists entreating tourists to sit for portraits. Amid the crowd, Margo spotted a few of the gray uniform skirts she had herself worn as a Melwood girl not so many years before, when she and her friends had sat on the museum steps during lunch breaks, smoking cigarettes.

"We've got a family membership," she said. "Free tickets."

They walked inside, to the front counter, where Margo handed over her card and asked for two buttons. Beyond the entrance gate sat the grand marble stairway, lined with the carved names of old donors, Margo's grandfather and great-grandfather among them. At the top of the stairs they turned left, into the Turner exhibition, where they walked in silence to a landscape that showed a medieval ruin bathed in sun.

"This is why I came," Margo said.

Sam leaned over to read the title.

"Tintern Abbey," he read. "Should that mean something to me?"

"It was a Cistercian monastery in England. Shut down during the Reformation. The ruins became a kind of tourist site. Wordsworth wrote a famous poem about it around the same time Turner did this painting. That's why I wanted to see it, for my dissertation."

"Does it match Wordsworth's description?"

"Actually, he never describes the place. I said the poem is about the abbey, but that's not exactly right. It was just written near there."

"What's it about, then?"

Margo considered this.

"It's about coming to a place at one point in your life and coming back years later. I guess it doesn't sound like much when I put it that way. It's about memory. It's about *that blessed mood, in which the heavy and the weary weight of all this unintelligible world is lighten'd.*"

He looked more carefully at the painting, as though searching for some reflection there of what Margo had just said. She'd had plentiful experience in graduate school of boys who stopped listening the moment conversation entered territory they couldn't easily dominate, and she imagined him thinking of ways to work the subject back to baseball or her father. Instead he asked, "Do *you* think the world is unintelligible?"

The question was so unexpected that Margo laughed a bit, and she noticed Sam reddening slightly in response.

"Much of the time I do. I suppose you disagree."

"I think it's a lot more intelligible than people let on. Occasionally we don't like what it's saying to us, so we pretend that the messages are indecipherable."

"Seems like someone in your line of work would have to think that."

"Fair enough," he said. "I suppose someone in your line of work would have to insist on the mystery at the heart of everything, or the endless room for interpretation."

"I'm not sure I've got a line of work."

"Aren't you writing a dissertation on Wordsworth? I assumed you were an academic."

"I say that mostly out of habit. I've sort of left school for a while."

"What happened?"

He didn't seem to have any sense that this was a tactless question. Not even her mother had asked her so directly.

"Leigh Hunt—he was a minor Romantic poet—once wrote to Coleridge to say he'd gotten a job as the secretary to a prominent politician, a common form of patronage in those days. He was encouraging Coleridge to do the same. 'Either I will be something far greater than that,' Coleridge told him, 'or I will be nothing.' That's how I feel about graduate school right now."

She'd read the Hunt quote a few days earlier in Holmes's Coleridge biography, but she hadn't thought to apply it to herself until that very moment. It sounded silly and pretentious as it left her mouth, and she waited for him to say something slightly deflating in response. Perhaps she even wanted to be deflated. But his face showed a kind of recognition instead.

"What's your far greater thing?"

Having made the initial remark, she thought she might as well go all out.

"The same thing it was for Coleridge. Not a student of poets, but the thing itself."

It had been years since she'd attempted to write a poem, let alone voiced the aspiration to be a poet. Saying it had always felt childish, like telling someone you meant to run off with the circus. This was especially true when she'd said it to people who knew her family had money. She'd always imagined that they took her to mean she was going to live off her trust fund while she thought beautiful thoughts. Graduate school had appealed to her partly because it seemed more respectable.

"To tell you the truth," Sam said, "I've never really understood poetry. When we read it in school, I always thought I was missing something. Then the teacher would explain it, and I always wondered, *If that's what it means, why don't they just say it that way?*"

"Maybe you just had bad teachers."

She meant this to sound encouraging, but he responded defensively.

"Probably," he said. "We moved around a lot, and I went to some pretty shitty schools."

"I just meant, part of the problem is the idea that you're supposed to understand a poem, rather than enjoy it. That it's a container for some message that can be extracted, that you've failed the poem somehow if you don't get that message out of it."

"If there's really nothing to get, what's the point? I prefer the idea that I'm missing something."

"Of course poems are trying to say something. But they're not riddles. They say what they say. I went to fancy private school, but I still had some bad teachers, too." Margo wasn't sure that she wanted to tell this story to a reporter who was writing about her father, but Sam wasn't acting much like a reporter. "In third grade, I had to memorize 'The Road Not Taken' for homework. I recited the poem to my father, who asked me what it meant. We'd talked in class about the importance of taking the road less traveled, not always following the crowd, but when I told him this, he asked me to recite the poem again. This time he stopped me as I went along. 'If Frost had been writing about nonconformism'—this wasn't the word my teacher used, but my father doesn't really know how to talk to children—'why would he say that *as for that, the passing there / Had worn them really about the same?*' I didn't have an answer to that. When I got to the part that went, *I shall be telling this with a sigh*, he asked, 'Do we sigh when we think about choices we're glad we've made?' We went through the whole thing like that. 'So what do you think the poem is really about?' he asked me when we were done. I told him it was about how we can't really know where our choices are going to lead us. 'Not only that,' he said, 'but we're probably going to regret those choices either way. Frost had a fundamentally tragic view of life. There is always going to be a road not taken. We only get to live once. Nothing we do is ever going to wholly satisfy us in the end.' In retrospect, I can see why this was not a lesson my teacher was especially keen to impart to a bunch of third graders."

She remembered it still so vividly. After Frank had finished talking about the poem, he'd gone to his shelf for his volume of Frost, and together they had read "After Apple-Picking." They went through it slowly, two or three times. Again he asked her what it was about.

"He's been picking apples all day," she'd said. "He's tired, and now he's falling asleep. He's starting to dream, and he's dreaming about apples, because he's been picking them so long."

"It *is* about that," her father had agreed. "But it's also about more than that."

One more time they'd read the poem, and he stopped to talk about the apple from the tree of knowledge of good and evil. He showed how something like a poem could be about the thing it was about but also about something else, something more. He made her reread the lines about how all the apples *That struck the earth, / No matter if not bruised or spiked with stubble, / Went surely to the cider-apple heap / As of no worth,* and he started telling his eight-year-old daughter about the modernists and the desire to make poetry that concerned only the things that hung from the branches above us and never touched the ground. He talked about how Frost opposed that idea by writing about things like apple picking while writing at the same time about all the tough philosophical subjects that someone like Wallace Stevens wrote about. And so it wasn't really right to say that the poem was about something other than what it pretended to be about, only that it was about many things at the same time.

"He always spoke to me like an adult," she said. "It's the only way he knows how to talk."

She and her father had stayed up late into the night—or what seemed late to her, certainly well past her childhood bedtime—reading poems and talking about them. By morning all these lines and ideas were jumbled in her head, and she was so tired that when her turn came to recite "The Road Not Taken," she'd needed prompting and wound up getting a B. Her father had found this wonderful. Another lesson! It didn't matter what grade you got. It mattered that you understood the thing. That wasn't exactly true, her mother had interjected. It was easy for a man to claim that grades didn't matter, but a woman who wanted to be successful didn't have that freedom. She wasn't given the same margin for error, and she needed to prove that she could perform. This led to a long conversation between her parents, which Margo was urged to join, though it didn't interest her.

That night she'd decided to surprise her father by memorizing "After Apple-Picking." It was longer than "The Road Not Taken" and irregular in its rhythm and rhyme scheme, so she needed most of a month to get it right, where the other poem had taken only a few days. Reciting it to him was one of the proudest moments of her life to that point.

"I memorized a poem a month after that," she told Sam. She usually picked them with her father, though sometimes she surprised him. They were often poems that he'd memorized years before, and he would listen without the words in front of him, remembering well enough to correct her or help her along. When he didn't already know the poem, he would learn it with her. His memory for quotes and lines of verse was legendary. His columns were sprinkled with them. "I did it for more than a decade. I've still got most of them banging around my head. I want my own words banging around in someone's head like that."

"Committing stuff to memory seems sort of outdated," Sam said. "Now you can just call it up on your phone any time you want."

"There's something different about having it inside you. A professor of mine, Richard Harvey, he says that when Teeser was born a thousand poems died."

Richard had never said this to her. It was her own idea. But she couldn't bear to quote herself in the manner of Richard and Frank. She tended to put any thought she was really proud of into the mouth of an older man. There was something slightly pathological about this. Perhaps it had to do with how many of her earliest ideas had been memorized with her father's help, just like poems. Her head was full of scraps, and she was never entirely sure of their origins. The safest thing was to attribute them elsewhere.

"Seems like having this stuff saved somewhere would free up our brain power for other things. People thought it was a loss when maps were invented. Now it's a loss that we've got them on our phones. Socrates thought that writing would ruin our memories."

"Yes, I've read *Phaedrus*," Margo told him.

Sam laughed.

"I haven't. I think I got that from some tech blog."

Margo laughed, too. Most of the guys she knew would have bluffed their way through something like that.

"Isn't it true, though, that we don't remember as much as those oral cultures did? That there is a capacity that we've lost?"

"You think they got the better end of the deal?"

"Probably not. But there's no way of doing that accounting without first admitting that innovations have costs. Nothing is got for nothing."

Like two fighters returning to their corners, they fell silent and turned their attention to the wall, where Turner's sharp, early landscapes had given way to the more difficult and abstract later work. They walked another minute until they stood in front of what might have been a piece of twentieth-century expressionism. *Death on the Pale Horse.* An odd memory came to Margo.

"The first thing I ever learned about Turner were his dying words: 'So I am to become a non-entity then?' My father liked to say this when he thought he was being ignored. As though we were literally killing him by paying attention to something else."

This was a terrible thing to be telling a reporter, but Frank Doyle of all people could hardly fault anyone for their lack of discretion. He had sent her out with his profiler. He must have expected them to talk about him. She regretted only that she was giving him what he wanted.

Back on the street, Margo found herself still in the mood for company. Instead of saying goodbye, she walked toward the nearest entrance to the park, and Sam followed without hesitation. They took the footpath under a bridge where a man in an unseasonable overcoat played saxophone. After another minute, they arrived at a small pond, green with algae, and beyond it the turrets of a gothic tower. She hadn't realized she'd been leading them there.

"It's a bit like Tintern Abbey," Sam said.

They stood looking out at the water.

"I visited the Lake District a few years ago, and I had the same impression, but it never occurred to me when I was growing up, reading Wordsworth and coming to this place. In high school we came here after class to smoke. That was my main experience with Central Park. Perhaps it's strange for a city kid to be so interested in the Romantic view of nature. Or maybe it makes perfect sense."

"Is that what you're not writing this dissertation about?"

"Wordsworth and Coleridge and their conceptions of the divine," she said, in what she hoped he would recognize as a mock-studious voice. It was all so impossible. Far too large a subject. Richard had encouraged it, though it was not the sort of thing that got published as a monograph or got someone a job. She almost wanted him to laugh at it. "I'm interested in Romanticism as a response to some of the problems that come along with secularism."

Sam looked mildly disgusted.

"It doesn't bring any problems as far as I can tell."

She wasn't surprised to hear this.

"Why do you think it is that every time we seem to have entered a new age of reason, there's another resurgence of fundamentalism?"

"It's a last gasp. A lot of people have invested themselves in irrationalism, and they don't want to give it up. But reason will win out eventually, because it's the thing that really works."

He spoke with more certainty than he had all afternoon. His tone of curiosity had given way to the insistent voice of the zealot.

"Don't you think there's a lot about human experience that can't be explained rationally?"

"Not really."

"Well, how about selflessness? Why does a person like my brother, living in complete comfort, put his life in danger for a cause? Setting aside whether that cause is actually worthy of his life."

"Reciprocal altruism. All of our genes benefit if we're conditioned to work together."

"Doesn't it strike you as an odd coincidence that our particular age came up with that explanation? Enlightened self-interest—rational cost-benefit analysis—produces moral behavior? Man can only possibly act as *homo economicus*? Doesn't it seem to fit a little too neatly with the prevailing order?"

"The fact that the explanation is politically convenient—or politically inconvenient, depending on your politics—doesn't mean it's wrong. You can't explain it away by positing a magic man in the sky."

"Do you honestly think that's what people are talking about when they speak of the divine? A celestial sorcerer with a long beard, looking out for the people who worship him and punishing the people who don't?"

"Have you spent much time around real believers? That's exactly what they're talking about."

"Actually, I was raised by believers. We went to church every week."

"I've read your father's writing about Catholicism. He talks about tradition and ceremony, as though going to mass were like going to a ball game. He never says anything about virgin births and the resurrection of the dead. That's not belief. It's very easy for someone with educated parents to have this nuanced academic view of faith. I know what religion really looks like in this country. It's anti-intellectual, and it's irrational. It judges people. And we'd be better off rid of it."

"Let me guess," Margo said. "You were brought up by Bible thumpers, but now you're an atheist, because you've got the courage to face up to all the tough truths that the old church ladies can't abide."

He seemed for a moment to be preparing some sharp response before saying simply, "Something like that."

"So the least sophisticated view of God you can find, that's the real one, and anything else isn't worth arguing with."

"The sophisticated view basically amounts to insisting that God exists while admitting that his existence doesn't change anything. You want to believe in that God, fine with me. For all I know, maybe there is this pulsing invisible world beneath or above or within the physical world, but if it doesn't actually *do* anything in this world, it might as well not exist. If it does do something, we ought to be able to see it, to measure it."

"We can't count it, so it doesn't count."

"Do *you* believe in God?"

"To be honest, I don't know."

Sam laughed again, but there was a hint of exasperation this time.

"You're writing a dissertation about conceptions of the divine, and you don't know whether you believe in God?"

When he put it his way, Margo could see the strangeness of it.

"That's not how it works," she told him. "We're not supposed to ask ourselves whether the world is intelligible or whether we believe in God, we're supposed to study other people's answers to those questions."

"What's the point of that? Aren't we trying to figure out the *right* answers?"

"I guess the assumption is that there aren't any right answers. There are just more or less interesting wrong ones."

Sam stopped walking. It seemed important to him that his point come across, which was another difference from the conversations at school, which were geared more toward proving you knew the material than toward changing anyone's mind.

"Let's go back to baseball for a moment. All the mythology about the game, the mystification, gets everything backward. What actually makes baseball so great is the fact that it can be talked about with such precision. There is a series of discrete actions—a pitch is thrown for a ball or a strike; the batter swings or doesn't; he makes contact or doesn't; he reaches base safely or doesn't—and these can all be isolated and recorded. For a hundred years, baseball fans like your father have admired certain players for being 'clutch'—for performing especially well in high-stakes situations. Late in games, or late in the season. During the play-offs. A huge part of baseball mythology is based around this idea. But guess what? There is no such thing as clutch. It doesn't exist. If you look at the actual numbers, no player consistently performs better in some situations than in others. Now, if you say that out loud, people like your father will complain about how not everything can be captured in numbers. But where could it be, if it's not in the numbers?"

"That's all well and good for baseball," Margo said. "But the world isn't a game. We can't stand outside of it and watch. It doesn't have rules. Not everyone is playing for the same end, and there aren't any umpires calling balls and strikes."

"That just makes things a bit harder to observe and count up. But we're getting there. We are in a golden era of quantification. I'm sure there's plenty of stuff we're still not counting correctly, but the point is that everything that really exists *could* be counted. That's what it means for something to exist. Either it's there or it's not."

"What I'm talking about *is* there. I'm not sure whether I believe in God, but I know I believe in the soul, because I know that I've got one, from experience. *Geist*, I mean: spirit, mind, whatever you want to call it. What I experience can't be recorded by anyone else, it can't be objectively verified, but I know with absolute certainty that it exists. And not just in my head. In the world. Whenever I act on a thought, I put it into the world. Feelings that your viewpoint can't explain really do move people to action. Forget selflessness. What about love?"

"That one's actually pretty easy, too. We're social animals. We survive by banding together, so these feelings of connection are hardwired into us. Not to mention the advantages for procreation and child-rearing."

"I'm not talking about connection or procreation. I'm talking about being swept away by another person, really losing control of yourself. It's so gratuitous, so far beyond anything that might be necessary for reproductive purposes. The obsessions, the lost sleep. It's capricious and self-defeating."

"The way you describe it—losing control, obsession, sleeplessness, being transported out of yourself—it sounds like a kind of mental illness. That's not my experience. We make a practical decision to pair ourselves off in mutually beneficial ways, to reproduce our genes. It seems completely explicable."

Impulsively she gestured at the wedding ring she'd first noticed an hour earlier.

"Is that how you proposed: 'I'd like to enter into a mutually beneficial nonbinding contract with you'? Haven't you ever been transported by your wife?" She'd said it because she assumed his answer would be yes. She wanted to score a point. When she saw his face, she quickly added, "I'm sorry. That's none of my business."

He shook off her apology, but he seemed unnerved.

"Maybe it's like these poems that mean two things at once. You can have these feelings while also understanding where the feelings are really coming from, the evolutionary basis for them. That doesn't mean you don't love somebody."

She could not believe she had made him defend his own marriage. She was worse than her father sometimes. Almost in compensation she said, "It's not really true that I just left school to be a great poet. I mean, it's not untrue. A lot of different things happened all at once. But mostly it was one thing. I got involved with someone. A famous professor who also happens to be my advisor."

"Don't tell me you're sleeping with Richard Harvey?"

She couldn't believe it.

"Good God, you really do have a powerful algorithm."

They both laughed. There was nothing else to do.

"I was kidding. He's probably the only literature professor I've ever heard of, and you just mentioned him a few minutes ago."

She was glad she'd told him. It had returned them to equal footing. Another hour passed before they left the park together and walked to the Fifty-Ninth Street station. When they got there, she gave him a brief hug and watched him disappear down the stairs. She considered taking the local uptown, but she felt suddenly as though she'd been caged in her house for weeks and only now finally released. She decided to walk.

7.

On the day the profile was due, Waxworth called Frank Doyle. He had a few last questions, he said, to round the thing out. He wasn't sure whether this would be taken as diligence or incompetence, but he was actually a long way from rounding out anything, and he was getting desperate.

How had this happened? After the game and the follow-up interview, he'd still had weeks to deliver a draft—an eternity compared with his other deadlines. He'd expected to get it in early. He came into the *Interviewer*'s offices nearly every day, and Blakeman brought the piece up occasionally, but mostly they discussed how the latest *Quantified World* post was doing, when the next would be ready. Waxworth hadn't been prepared for the sheer volume he was expected to produce in this job. After years of writing a few posts a week while working full-time, he'd imagined that doubling or even tripling that number would be easy enough now that he could devote himself entirely to the task. But the difference between two or three and five or six was considerable. Half his posts during the campaign had pointed without commentary to the latest poll results. Now an *Interviewer* intern was tasked with link dumps, which was supposed to make his job easier but meant instead that everything he wrote had to contain some substance.

Blakeman had offered some advice on managing this load.

"You've got one great advantage when generating ideas," he said. "That's a framework you can apply to any story that comes along. You start each morning by reading the *Herald*'s home page. People need the news, but they want to be told what to *think* about the news. If you can give them both in one place—provide enough summary of the underlying reporting that they don't have to read it, while also giving your spin—you've saved them a lot of time."

One day it was the swine flu outbreak in Mexico. Vice President Biden had warned his family not to go anywhere near an airplane, in direct contradiction of the administration's official advice. Who was right? Biden had some intuitive sense that confined spaces helped the spread of disease. Waxworth applied a dose of empiricism to this intuition. What was the average person's risk of contracting H1N1? Did air travel meaningfully change that number?

On another day Chrysler had declared bankruptcy, and the *Herald* was filled with elegies for the great days of American manufacturing. Blakeman wanted a contrarian response. *Might we be better off without factory jobs?* Waxworth wondered. *What difference does it actually make if Chrysler is owned by a foreign company?* Once you formulated these questions, writing up an answer didn't take long. There was usually a bit of basic statistics to explain in the process, so he could fill out a few paragraphs on sample variance or standard deviation.

Blakeman expected a draft by lunch four days a week. If Waxworth had written something the day before, that post would go live while he worked, and on those days he devoted his afternoon to reading through reactions. The moment anything went online, dozens of regular readers skimmed it in search of the weakest point, to which they applied their withering irony in the comments section, as though the fact that one line could be mocked was enough to undermine the entire effort, no matter how little relation this weak point had to the argument as a whole. *Lord of the Files* was always in this first round of responders, working others into maximum froth. Waxworth tried to imagine this character who'd taken such an intense dislike to his work. What did he do with the rest of his time? Before long an equally reliable band of pseudonymous defenders came to Waxworth's aid, giving no indication they'd read the post with any more care than the critics they were savaging. Waxworth spent about an hour getting through these comments and sprinkling in his own, some under his real name, the rest using various sock puppets that Blakeman had encouraged him to create.

The professional responses on other sites were generally longer than the comments but not always better written. Waxworth read through these, and he checked his Teeser hits. Once he'd taken this all in, he wrote a clarifying post, which went live in the late afternoon. Blakeman encouraged this practice but also made clear that it wasn't strictly required, by which he meant that it wouldn't count toward his quota of weekly work. While Waxworth did this, whatever he'd written that morning was fact-checked and edited. Another version arrived in his inbox around the time he left for the day. At that point, he might only have to sign off on changes or he might need to do another hour of work. The updated post was copyedited and sent to an overnight web producer, who prepared it to go live the next morning, before readers got to their desks. There could be only one topic of conversation each day, Blakeman said, and it was decided first thing. He wanted the *Interviewer* making that decision, not responding to it.

Despite all this effort, someone else often did the deciding. Then it became Waxworth's job to react. This might mean catching up on the news of an earthquake in Italy or the navy rescue of a merchant marine captured by Somali pirates, but just as often it meant that some odd artifact had briefly captured the collective imagination, and Waxworth had to spin a few hundred words of vaguely numerical analysis out of a video of a cat carrying a lizard on its back. These posts were written in under an hour and weren't subject to the same level of editing as his other work. In fact they seemed to go online the moment he submitted them, often not even proofread.

These "reaction posts" contained hasty reasoning and sometimes outright errors, which antagonistic readers spotted immediately. Such mistakes bothered Waxworth until he realized that no one at the *Interviewer* cared. Maintaining standards was simply impossible while producing at this pace. Everyone recognized the inherent tension between volume and quality, and they'd made a conscious decision to err on the side of volume. When facts were proved wrong, they were quietly corrected, which was cheaper and more efficient than hiring enough checkers to get the stuff right in the first place. When sloppy thinking was identified, the critic's own inevitable sloppiness was pounced on in return. The important thing was never to apologize.

Occasionally, Waxworth had enough time to write something that really made him proud. Such lines were inevitably the ones that Blakeman cut.

"Don't try to be a writer," he said once when Waxworth complained.

"Isn't that my job?"

"I'm not saying you're not a good writer," Blakeman clarified, which was not the same as saying that he was. "But three quarters of our readers can't tell the difference, and the rest actively prefer bad prose. They think the good stuff's pretentious. They can tell it's trying to do something more than convey the facts, but they don't have the equipment to judge whether it's succeeding, which makes them feel defensive. The one thing readers can't stand is someone getting one over on them. Just stick to what you're doing and we'll be fine. The most important thing is that Adrian's happy."

Their patron showed up at the office almost every day, but he spent most of his time playing Ping-Pong on the deck. When he wanted to speak with someone, he sent his assistant to collect that person for a game. Waxworth had played him three times now, winning about five points in all. Adrian was always full of compliments, though he never mentioned the content of the posts, and he didn't even pretend that he was reading them. He didn't have to read them, he said. Waxworth's comment rate, his most-emailed ranking, his Teeser score were all where they needed to be.

There was something nicely quantitative about it all. Knowing that there was a clear metric for success made it easier to keep working at this pace. But when it came to the profile, everything he'd learned about working felt useless. The rules were entirely different for the magazine. It was an odd paradox: the work had to be better to appear in print, though it had a fraction of the website's readership and the web was all anyone ever talked about. Perhaps the very fact that print stories couldn't be measured by their Teeser score forced people to hold them to a higher standard while also taking for granted that they didn't actually matter. Print, he'd heard Blakeman tell someone, was where quality went to die. If he'd known this in advance, he wouldn't have insisted on including these longer assignments in his contract, but he hadn't known, and now he needed to produce.

The draft was due to Blakeman on a Friday afternoon, and Waxworth planned to fly to Madison after sending it in. He set aside the weekend before the deadline. A 750-word post took him a morning to finish, so he imagined he could work up a decent try at a three-thousand-word profile in two days. He'd been building a case against Frank Doyle in his head for almost a decade. The man was so wrong about so many things. He just needed to put it all down in words, with appropriately withering sarcasm. But this felt for the moment impossible. By Sunday, he'd still done nothing.

On Monday morning, he had another *Quantified World* post to write, and he was back into the churn. On Wednesday, he asked Blakeman for an extension, and he called Lucy to cancel the trip. She was disappointed but understanding—she'd be in New York soon enough—and he was left with two solid days to work.

Early the next Saturday, he put on a pot of strong coffee whose aroma covered the smell of panicked poultry, took his laptop out, and opened the file labelled "DoylePro." He was surprised, as he had been every time he'd looked at the document, by how little was there. Procrastination had always seemed to Waxworth an obvious cognitive failure, either an inability to measure the passage of time or an overvaluing of the present relative to the future.

Something more than the daily churn or the pressure of print kept him from this work. Strange thoughts distracted him whenever he sat down to it. He thought about Margo Doyle's question: *Haven't you ever been transported by your wife?* He couldn't precisely remember his answer, which was something about poetry, about feeling one thing while knowing another, stuff he didn't believe at all. She'd gotten the better of him throughout their entire conversation, though he was sure that the truth was on his side. Now his mind went back over those hours, filling in all that he should have said.

It was true that he'd never experienced love as a kind of derangement. He'd never lost sleep or weight over Lucy, but this didn't mean there was something wrong with their relationship. Since when was it a good thing to be driven mad? *In the long run every lasting couple finds its way past passion to a stable foundation of mutual support, respect, companionship,* he told Margo. *Lucy and I simply started in this place. Perhaps that isn't romantic, but if the alternative is sleeping with your professor and dropping out of school, I know which one I'd choose.*

This was more adversarial than the situation required—not to mention anachronistic, since the information about Richard Harvey hadn't been available to him at that point in the conversation. He started over on a less aggressive footing.

Control over our passions—continence, the ancients called it—is what makes a productive civilization possible. How much of Western thought, going back to Plato, has been dedicated to overcoming our animal urges, helping reason to maintain the upper hand?

By all means control them, Margo responded. *Just know that they're there. Or have you got no passions to master?*

If asked, he'd have to admit that he'd never felt at any great risk of being tossed from his horse. It didn't seem an enviable experience. A friend in college had become obsessed with some pretty sorority girl, the kind who would never take an interest in their sort. Often he seemed angry with the girl, who barely knew him and had certainly done him no wrong. He became depressed, he drank and missed class. His grades—the one thing he had over the kind of guys such girls typically dated—plummeted. Finally, he'd been caught in a lecture hall cutting an inch off her hair. When the campus police searched his room, they found mittens full of surreptitiously snipped locks, which he'd apparently been using to gratify himself. Such compulsions were utterly foreign to Waxworth. Was he meant to feel this as some great lack? That passion had never turned him into a glove fucker?

Suppose he *were* capable of being transported? How would that suffering benefit anyone? Perhaps a few poems would get written. And what were those poems worth, balanced against all that pain? What did poems even *do*, apart from giving rich kids like Margo Doyle a way to occupy their time?

Why was he getting so angry? He was offended on Lucy's behalf by the suggestion that she wasn't capable of inspiring great passion, even in her own husband. But Margo had intended no harm. Waxworth respected the impulse to follow an idea where it led, hurt feelings be damned. She hadn't even suggested that he felt no passion for his wife. She'd just asked the question. Had he, then, betrayed Lucy somehow? Was that what kept bothering him?

He pictured this conversation in strangely vivid detail. He could see the T-shirt Margo had been wearing. He could see her pale Irish skin. He imagined telling her that he was, in fact, passionately in love with his wife. If he hadn't mentioned as much at the time, that was only because it was personal, not relevant to the conversation. But this didn't work, since it wasn't true, and he didn't believe in winning an argument by tampering with the evidence. After that, he took another approach.

There was a class of statistical questions concerned with optimal stopping—choosing the proper time to make a decision. The classic optimal stopping exercise was called the "secretary problem." A position is to be filled, and the employer has n applicants, with n being an unknown value. Each applicant is interviewed in turn, and after each interview the employer must either hire or dismiss. Applicants can be judged only on the basis of those already dismissed, which means you can't possibly be sure you're picking the best one. But it also means that dismissing the best candidate is as much of a risk as settling for someone suboptimal. The only thing you can do is develop a stopping rule that maximizes your chances and live with the result.

Picking a mate was a straightforward optimal stopping exercise. Indeed, an alternative version of the secretary problem was called the "marriage problem." He'd started dating Lucy right around the time that YOUNT had made him a campus celebrity. She was in a higher league than any girl he'd ever so much as kissed before, and somehow she wanted to be with him. He hadn't had many serious girl-friends, but he could say with certainty that she was the best applicant he'd interviewed. He enjoyed spending time with her. He liked her family. He respected her intention to spend her life helping kids with developmental disabilities. She was pretty and thin and her love for running suggested she was likely to stay that way. He'd sold himself at a market peak, and he'd never had a reason to regret the decision.

Margo would doubtless respond with some vague notion about the one perfect person out there for each of us. Love was not about making your best decision with imperfect information; it was about waiting for destiny to deliver that person to your door. Like many calls to keep faith in the absence of evidence, he explained to imaginary Margo, this notion had caused all sorts of unnecessary suffering. A simple look around was enough to show that most people never met their one perfect match. Even when they did, that was no guarantee of happiness. Sam's mother had felt great, life-altering passion for his father, and she'd spent the rest of her life regretting it. More than regretting it, she'd displaced this passion for his absent father on to an even more reliably absent God. Such feelings were an illness from which Sam had been inoculated in childhood. Did this mean that he didn't deserve to be happy? That he wasn't entitled to a comfortable and supportive relationship? Did everyone have to live their lives in the grip of the most extreme emotions?

Waxworth refined this speech over much of the day until it was, so far as he was concerned, unanswerable, and indeed the Margo of his imagination had no answer for it. Instead she responded by stepping closer to him, so close they were very nearly touching, and saying in a whisper, *Do you really think you're immune?*

He needed to stop thinking about Margo Doyle. He was supposed to be writing about her father. He stood from the table and poured himself another cup of coffee. On the kitchen counter sat all of Doyle's books. He picked up *The Smell of the Grass*, the first of the baseball books, and he lay down in bed to read a few essays, hoping this would clear his head.

Reading the introduction, he was returned, with the kind of involuntary insistence that Doyle himself referred to in those pages as Proustian, to his childhood. He'd taken the book to bed each evening while waiting for his mother to get home. This was when they were living in an apartment complex in Janesville, and his mother was working at Mercyhealth. She was rarely home before he was put in bed by the woman from next door who came over to watch him at night. As soon as his bedroom door was closed, he'd turn his bedside light back on and read while Betty—his mother had told Sam to call her Miss Creston, but she always said she wanted to be called Betty—sat in the living room with a glass of wine, pretending not to notice. He tried to wait up for his mother, but he usually fell asleep with the light still on, and the brush of her lips against his forehead would stir him. When he opened his eyes she would smile but try to look sorry. "I didn't mean to wake you," she'd say, though he sometimes thought she put a bit of extra pressure behind her kiss to do just that, so they had a chance to talk for a little while before she tucked him back in. They would say their prayers together before she left him to sleep.

Occasionally she climbed beside him in bed, and he was filled with a great sense of well-being. The anger and anxiety that followed him through the day at school and even into his dreams briefly lost their grip. How isolated he had felt all through childhood. He'd forgotten this feeling since meeting Lucy and becoming part of her family, but it had come to him a few times since he'd been alone in New York. (Perhaps he ought to tell this to Margo?)

Sometimes he pretended to be asleep just to see the look on his mother's face as she woke him up, but this carried some risk. If she'd invited Betty to stay for a glass of wine, she'd take just a moment to confirm that he was asleep before turning out his light. If his eyes were closed, he would know what had happened only by the sound of his door clicking shut. He'd lie there, trying to stop himself from going out into the living room. He always gave in eventually. Betty and his mother would set their glasses down and squeeze him between them in a hug.

Once—he'd forgotten this completely—an older man sat on the couch in Betty's place, and he got a look of horror at the sight of Sam, as though he'd been warned that the house was haunted but hadn't quite believed he'd be brought face-to-face with the ghost. He quickly recovered and turned friendly, introducing himself as Dr. Lamott and trying awkwardly for a minute to make conversation.

"Samuel," his mother said, "you need to go back to bed."

"It's all right," Dr. Lamott broke in. "I should be going anyway."

"You don't need to go," his mother insisted, but Dr. Lamott was already standing and walking back to the door.

"It's late," he said. "We've both got to be in early tomorrow. I don't know what we were thinking."

He said this right in front of Sam, as though he were an infant or an idiot, rather than an eleven-year-old boy of better than average intelligence. The man was gone before Sam or his mother could say another word. Sam was relieved, and he expected his mother to be, too. They could return to his room, and she could put him properly to bed. Instead she turned to him in anger.

"What's the matter with you?" she asked.

He didn't know what to say.

"I couldn't sleep."

"Can't I have even the slightest bit of a life? Can't I have one night that's just for me?"

She was crying, her tears working their way through the makeup Sam had not noticed until that moment that she was wearing. She looked ugly. If Sam had been Dr. Lamott, he would have left, too. The thought startled him into tears of his own. He wanted to apologize, but he couldn't apologize for a thought he hadn't spoken out loud, and he didn't want her to think he was apologizing for interrupting her, because he wasn't sorry for that. So he said nothing, and his speechless sobs made her angrier.

"Go to bed," she told him.

When he didn't turn, she said it again, and he couldn't bear to hear it a third time, so he hurried out of the room, sure that she would come in after him and that everything would be all right. But he had to be awake for that to happen, so he started reading *The*

Smell of the Grass. She never came, and he finally fell asleep. In his dream they were a family together. Frank Doyle was his father, and he was taking Sam to see the Mets. Doc Gooden was pitching, and Strawberry hit one out with that long sweeping swing that looked like no one else's in the game. The beauty of that swing was something Sam's mother could never understand, but Frank Doyle understood it, and that meant that he understood Sam. Was this why he couldn't bear to tell the truth about Doyle? So many times in his childhood—Christ, how had he ever forgotten?—he'd longed to go to a ball game with that man.

Do you really think you're immune? Margo asked again in the same voice, and as she did she began to undress him. They were both naked, in a bed that was also a kind of cage. The chickens of Hun Lee Poultry House pecked at the bars. Sam tried to scare them away, but they had become the pale horse from the painting at the museum. Max Blakeman was Death riding on it. Margo reached down to guide Sam inside of her, and just as she did he was transformed into his father. Moving beneath him, Margo Doyle was his father. The pale horse, his father. His father, the chickens and the bars of the cage keeping his father out, or keeping Sam in.

He woke with a shudder just as the sticky dampness filled his boxer shorts. He sat up, knocking Doyle's book to the floor.

This was all rather confusing at first, but Waxworth quickly sorted matters out. He'd been in New York for a little over a month. At home, he and Lucy had sex once or twice a week—not a bad number, he wanted to tell Margo—and his body was used to this schedule. He'd had a simple physiological urge, no more fraught or meaningful than hunger or the need to piss. If he'd abstained from urination for a month, he would have suffered the same result: a wet bed. In order to fit this biological event into the flow of his dreaming consciousness, his mind had taken an image close to hand, someone he'd been thinking about that day for unrelated reasons. The rest of the strangeness—the chickens and the horse from the painting— made it all the more obvious that Margo's presence shouldn't be taken to mean anything. The bit about his father was admittedly more puzzling. In the dream he hadn't actually been transformed physically, he'd just understood with dream certainty that he was no longer himself, that he was his father instead. He didn't even know what the man looked like in the waking world. Well, human psychology was a strange thing. Waxworth had never denied the fact. Quite the opposite: it was because of our capacity for the irrational that we needed to rely on data whenever we could. His contention was not that humans were fundamentally reasonable but that reason was our best bet for understanding the world. There was nothing wrong with the occasional bizarre fantasy. The problem was taking these things seriously. The Freudian idea of dreams as hermetic texts that could be unlocked to reveal our true feelings had no more empirical basis than the necromancer's idea that dreams could tell the future. He'd made the point many times to Lucy, who'd studied psychology at school.

He decided to take the afternoon off, get the Doyles out of his head for a few hours, start fresh the next day. On Sunday morning he recommitted to getting his draft done, clearing this family from his life entirely, and at noon he called Frank to say that he had more questions to ask. He expected Frank to be annoyed by the intrusion, but instead he seemed happy, as though they spoke often.

"Why don't you come over now?" he asked. "I was about to start watching the game."

It hadn't occurred to Waxworth that he might get asked over. Just getting up there would take an hour, and he'd have to stay long enough to justify the trip. He could see all the time he'd set aside for work slipping away. But he could hardly refuse, after calling and asking to speak.

Standing at the Doyles' front door, Waxworth imagined Margo on the other side. He wasn't sure that he even wanted to see her again. What difference would it make? He couldn't have his scripted conversation while they stood in the foyer or she led him wherever her father was waiting. Still, he felt an anticipatory rush as the lock turned, and a slight disappointment when Frank opened the door.

"Come in, my boy," Frank said, as though he had some access to Sam's childhood fantasies and was lightly mocking them. "The game is just getting interesting."

They'd conducted their earlier interview in a library on the first floor, but now Frank led him upstairs to a kind of office or den, where an open cabinet revealed a large flat-screen TV. Beside the cabinet was a bar.

"Can I fix you a drink?" Frank asked.

"Just water would be fine."

Frank poured himself what looked to be scotch from a crystal decanter, and he brought it to the couch along with Waxworth's water. He sat down and turned his attention to the game. The Mets were playing the Pirates, down two to four in the bottom of the fourth, and Carlos Delgado was on second.

"Liván's looked a little shaky," Frank said, "but this offense can put some runs up."

As though to prove his point, David Wright hit a single to drive Delgado in. By the end of the inning the Mets had taken the lead. Frank muted the TV as it went to commercial. Now was the time for Waxworth to ask whatever he meant to ask.

"So you've been working on a book?"

It was the closest thing to a question he'd prepared. He realized that readers would want to know what Frank was doing with himself in his time of exile.

"It's almost done," Frank said. "It's been nice to have this time."

"Can you tell me about it?"

"Never discuss a work in progress," Frank said. "That's a solid piece of advice for you. It seeps away when you talk about it."

When the game came back on, Frank unmuted the TV. Waxworth was relieved that they didn't have to continue this conversation. What could Frank possibly say that would be enough? What Waxworth really wanted was to be told what to write, but you couldn't say this to the subject of the piece. It was a relief to realize that Doyle didn't expect to be asked anything. He seemed to find Waxworth's presence in his house totally natural. They were just watching a game together, trading small talk about what happened on the field.

At the end of the next half inning, Frank stood to refresh his drink. He repeated this act almost every inning, making no effort to disguise the frequency of these trips. The drinks didn't have much effect—he kept up the same fluent chatter throughout—until the top of the seventh, when quite abruptly he tipped back his head and started to snore. A light nudge provoked no response. A second, harder one sent Frank's head from the pillow down to the arm of the couch, where it settled comfortably as his snoring grew more regular.

Waxworth had already stayed longer than intended. Every minute spent on this couch was a minute not spent getting something on the page. But he couldn't just leave. What if Doyle woke up to find that he'd disappeared with no explanation? At the seventh-inning stretch, the players stood for "God Bless America." Waxworth turned up the volume slightly, hoping to rouse Frank. When this did nothing, he resigned himself to staying through the end of the game.

The bottom of the seventh was just underway when Margo stuck her head into the room.

"Can you turn the volume down?" she said in a sharp voice.

Waxworth stood from the couch defensively. He'd built her up in his mind into a grand antagonist, and he had to remind himself that they'd left on perfectly good terms.

"Sorry," he said.

"What are you doing here?" Margo asked. He took this at first as an accusation, but it seemed rather a simple expression of curiosity. She gestured toward the couch. "I thought he was alone."

"I needed to talk with your father for the article, but he nodded off."

Margo looked over the scene again.

"He's usually out for a few hours in the afternoon. I wouldn't bother waiting for him."

The thing that he'd wanted—permission to leave—had been granted now, but he hesitated until Margo turned to go.

Downstairs, they stood for a moment face-to-face at the top of the stoop. She looked in most ways as he'd been picturing her since they'd last seen each other, but somehow he'd forgotten her angular beauty. All the speeches he'd practiced seemed suddenly ridiculous. She probably didn't even remember the question he'd been obsessing over. He no longer felt the impulse to defend his marriage. He felt instead the simple urge to spend more time with Margo Doyle.

"Good luck with your article," she said before closing the door behind him.

He was halfway down the block when he heard her voice and turned to see her hurrying after him.

"I have to ask you something."

Despite himself, he prepared to hear her say: *Do you really think you're immune?*

"What is it?"

"Are you going to write about that?"

Still stuck in their dream conversation, he had a hard time giving her words a sensible context.

"About what?"

"My father drinking himself to sleep in the middle of the afternoon."

She sounded resentful that she should have to make herself explicit. In her description it seemed worse than it had at the time. He could see that a good journalist would absolutely put it in the piece.

"I've already more or less written everything. I just came to get one more quote."

"So you won't mention it?"

Without hesitation he answered, "I promise."

That seemed to be all she'd wanted, but she stayed, as though her demand had created a debt that she had to discharge.

"Where are you headed?"

"To the train. I've got to get home and get this story done."

"I'll walk you there."

They went a block in silence before he spoke.

"You seem to care more than your father does about what people think of him."

"Off the record?" Margo asked.

It hadn't occurred to him that any of their conversations would be on the record. They'd just been talking.

"Like I said, the article's already written."

"Of course I care what people think of him. He's my father. I'll be the first to admit that what he said was bad. I was at the park that day, and I was so horrified I made him leave in the middle of the last game of the season. He likes to drink, and he likes to joke, and he likes to be provocative. That doesn't mean his life should be over."

"His life is hardly over because he doesn't have a column in the paper and a weekly TV appearance."

"It feels that way to him."

"So why won't he just apologize?"

"I suppose he thinks that after decades of weighing in on every controversial issue, he shouldn't have to explain himself to anyone. I know it would be easier if he'd just submit to the process of ritual self-flagellation. He probably thinks he's above it. He doesn't want the spectacle of a redemption narrative when he doesn't think he's done anything wrong. For thirty years he's had an audience whenever he had an idea about anything."

"Which means he's entitled to one forever?"

"He's not entitled to anything in particular. But he's given a lot to this job. The job, I mean, of being a public figure, an opinion maker. It isn't as easy as people think."

"I'm starting to realize that." He'd meant this to sound sympathetic, but he worried that it might sound arrogant. "Not that I'm in your father's league, of course, but even working at the *Interviewer* for a few weeks has made me understand his position better. My job is to have a strong opinion every day, sometimes about things I'd never given a thought before that morning. The more provocative I am, the more contrarian, the better. I'm sure there's a line somewhere, but I won't know where it is until I hit it."

"Imagine having that job your whole life. It's inevitable that you'd say some things that look bad. The fact that it wasn't even a column that took him down, that it was just a spontaneous joke, not something he said with any foresight or intent, only makes him less willing to take it back."

Sam slowed just slightly when they approached the entrance to the station, giving Margo an opening to say goodbye, but she continued walking. He decided to get on at the next stop. He'd be stuck inside his apartment for hours while he finished this article, so he might as well get some air.

"It's nice to be out," Margo said, as though answering his thoughts. "This is my favorite time of year in New York."

"It's still winter in Wisconsin now."

"In a few weeks it gets miserable."

"Excellent timing—just when my wife gets here."

Introducing Lucy into the conversation felt like a small act of loyalty.

"Everyone who can leaves town for the summer."

"I assume that includes you?"

She hesitated, as though she didn't want to advertise her family's wealth, though it seemed too late for that.

"Bridgehampton. It's very bucolic," she said, in an almost defensive pose. "So long as you don't get a tick," she added, as if to soften the air of entitlement.

"Sounds like a terrible trade-off."

She laughed.

"I'm serious, though. Half the block has had Lyme disease at one point or another. One of our neighbors nearly died."

They didn't even slow when they passed the Sixty-Eighth Street stop. Waxworth knew by then he'd keep walking as long as Margo did. He just needed to have something sent off before he went to bed. Blakeman wouldn't be editing on Sunday night.

It was early evening by the time they arrived at the foot of the Brooklyn Bridge. Sam had seen it many times on his walks, but he'd never gotten this close. It was crowded with people—mostly tourists taking pictures of the skyline or the river, blocking the walking path so that the pedestrians had to swerve out into the bike path, where they were almost run down by speeding cyclists, who screamed at the whole parade. Despite this chaos, crossing the river on a cool spring night was an unmistakably romantic experience, and it felt strange to be doing it for the first time with someone he barely knew instead of with his wife.

From the other side of the bridge, it took another hour to get home. He waited for her to say she'd gone far enough, to flag a cab or peel off at a subway stop, but she just kept on. What would they do when they got to his building? It seemed a bit ridiculous not to ask her upstairs after she'd come all that way. But everything so far had unfolded without any intervention on his part. He wasn't ready to make something happen. When he pointed out his building, Margo had an air of anticipation—curious in an almost abstract way.

"It would be nice to see you again," he said. He laughed anxiously and added, "Off the record."

Margo took down his phone number but didn't offer hers before giving him a stiff hug and walking away. Perhaps he'd offended her. He couldn't imagine that she would ever call. Only when the moment had passed was Waxworth sure how things would have gone if he'd asked her inside. Before getting to New York, before seeing how Emily the receptionist looked at him, it would never have occurred to him that he might sleep with someone like Margo Doyle. Now it was something of a relief to realize that he'd missed his chance.

As he walked upstairs, he checked his phone for the first time since heading for Manhattan. Lucy had called three times. He was supposed to be spending this weekend with her, and instead they hadn't spoken all day. It wasn't too late to call back, but he really needed to get down to work. Did he feel some guilt that he was afraid might be discernible to her? Why would he? He had done nothing wrong. He'd gone for a walk with a source for his article. *Trying to get this thing done*, he texted her. *Will call in the morning. Love you.* He waited for a response, but nothing came, which meant she was already asleep.

He opened the file and stared at the nearly blank screen—the product of three weeks multiplied by zero. Now he had five or six hours to fill it with words. He tried to get back his feeling of outrage at all of Frank Doyle's wrongheadedness, the inspiration that had made him accept his assignment, but he couldn't generate any anger toward the man he'd left sleeping on the couch. He would not be putting the final nail into the coffin of Doyle's career.

But what to write instead? It couldn't be the great redemption narrative either. As Margo had said, that wasn't even what Frank wanted. Waxworth liked this about the man. The redemption narrative was one of the worst clichés in sports, one that sabermetrics had done a lot to destroy, and he was relieved that no one expected him to resurrect it. Suddenly he understood that he had his lede: "Frank Doyle isn't looking for redemption." From there, he would flesh out the story of Doyle's disaster—everyone knew it; you just needed a quick reminder—and write a bit about the game they'd attended together. If he needed to fill out some space, he could mention reading those baseball books as a kid. As Blakeman often told him, readers liked personal angles.

He finished just after seven in the morning. He was too tired to judge what he'd written, and he still wasn't entirely sure what the point of it all was, but he'd warned Blakeman about that from the beginning. At least he had something. Blakeman would know what to do with it now. He sent it off and got in bed. Still wired from the work, he sat up almost immediately to check his email.

Blakeman's response had arrived just a few minutes after Waxworth sent the draft. *Thanks for this*, it read. *What have you got in mind for QW?*

How could he have forgotten that he needed to write something for the web? He supposed he'd had a vague notion that they would make an exception when he had a print deadline, but he knew as well as anyone that these blog posts were his real job. He was still only weeks into the position, which was way too early to be taking the work for granted.

On the *Herald*'s home page he read a story about Arlen Specter, who'd recently switched parties, giving the Democrats the Senate majority. He sent Blakeman a short reply: *Working on something about Specter, have it to you by noon.* It should have been easy to make something out of this story. It was the kind of thing he did every day. But he was completely burnt out. He couldn't spend another minute staring at a blank screen. He remembered something he'd written back in college, before YOUNT, when his personal site had no more than a dozen readers, about Roger Clemens joining the Yankees. It was a ranking of the most significant historical turn-coats—Saul of Tarsus; Benedict Arnold; F. W. de Klerk—based on a jokey metric that accounted for delta between the two sides, frequency of cross-pollination, and value of the figure to the opposition. It wouldn't take much work to modify the post and apply it to this story. He found the thing, cut and pasted it, and worked in lines about Specter's place on the list. After that he just needed to clean up a few sentences and write a new conclusion.

It wasn't eleven yet when he sent it off, which meant he was actually early. Since he hadn't had a post up that morning, he didn't have any comments to look through, and he had the rest of the day to himself. He took a long shower and felt the exhilaration of getting everything done drain from his body. He could get in a few hours of sleep before Blakeman sent back edits on the Specter post. First he'd call Lucy. She was at work now, but he could leave a message, tell her that he'd been thinking of her and that he'd gotten the article done. He wanted her to know that the weekend hadn't been wasted.

He picked up his phone and found a new message. *This is random but having lunch in Brooklyn and thought you might want to catch up afterward.* It was followed quickly by another: *Margo, btw ;).*

When were you thinking? he texted back.

Around three?

That gave him plenty of time. He called Lucy, and when he got her voice mail he hung up without leaving a message. All that mattered was that she know that he'd called. He climbed back into bed, but suddenly he felt wide awake.

PART TWO:

THE MARRIAGE PROBLEM

(June/July)

1.

They took a bus to Atlantic Terminal and from there a train to Queens, where they changed for another train they almost missed, which was nearly full when they got on board. After walking through three cars they gave up on sitting together, and Lucy took the next empty seat they found while Sam continued looking.

As the train shook into motion, she reached into her canvas bag for her book, the long novel her mother had given her because it was set in New York, which she'd started on the flight but hadn't read since. She was still getting used to the pace of things, and she'd found it tough to make time to read.

The strange thing was that she'd never had so little to do in her life. She was a teacher, but she'd never taken a summer off before. For the past five years, she'd worked as a counselor at the day camp operated by her school in Madison, which ran through the first week in August. She'd spent the rest of that month preparing for the year, going over the files on her new students, who had idiosyncratic needs. Each year she expected the work to get easier, but every class presented its own challenge. You couldn't just rely on previous experience. Anyway, she'd liked the challenge of it, and she'd liked walking into school on the first day knowing she was prepared for anything.

Despite six years in the classroom, the only job she'd been able to find in New York on short notice was as a teaching assistant at a private school. She'd emailed her head teacher, a woman improbably named Twinkie, as soon as she was hired, suggesting that they might get together over the summer. Sounding somewhat put-upon, Twinkie had said that she'd be out of town. *We'll have plenty of time to get to know each other in the fall,* she'd concluded.

Lucy had nothing to do in the meantime. So why did she feel so overwhelmed? She'd never really been on her own before. She'd always had her parents or Sam, not to mention a few nearby friends. She felt as though she'd spent more time by herself in her first few weeks in New York than she had in her life up to that point.

Everything was harder here. Just unpacking had taken longer than she'd expected. Then she'd had to get their apartment into shape. They'd rented out their place in Madison completely furnished to a grad student couple, so they needed almost everything. For the first time since the morning of her seventeenth birthday, she didn't have a car. The apartment was a ten-minute walk from public transportation, and the famous yellow taxicabs never came to their neighborhood. She'd found a nearby IKEA that delivered, taken a bus there, and spent a full day picking out a couch, a coffee table, bookshelves, a dresser, flatware, and dishes. (How had Sam done without all these things?) Once everything arrived, setting it up took several days.

Sam had offered to help, but she'd told him she could take care of it. He was so busy with work. This had been unexpected. She'd imagined he would have lots of free time now that writing was his only job. At home he'd sometimes spent weekends or evenings on his blog posts, but she could at least sit with him, reading a book while he typed away. Now he was always in the office. She had to remind herself that this was why they'd come. It was all happening exactly as he'd said it would.

She dropped the book to the bottom of her bag and pulled out the magazine instead. A close-up of an old man's unsmiling face stared blankly at her, its expression suggesting decrepitude more than the defiance that seemed the intended effect. Underneath his jutted chin were the words FRANK DOYLE ISN'T SORRY. BY SAMUEL WAXWORTH.

Lucy still got a rush each time she looked at this cover. It seemed so much more real than anything he'd written before. She could hold it in her hands, and a copy had gone to her parents in the mail. It was there every time she went into the deli on the corner. Even after a new issue of the *Interviewer* started pushing this one off newsstands, she'd run across it a few times a day. Whenever she saw someone reading the magazine in public, she was tempted to strike up a conversation that would allow her to casually mention her last name.

She'd turned to the article so many times that her finger instinctively found the page. Another photo of Doyle, this time with his mouth turned up slightly into something more like a smirk than a full smile. Beneath the photo, a headline—"Unapologetic"—and a few descriptive sentences: *Where do you go after a lifetime of angering the Right, a decade of angering the Left, and a single moment that angered everyone? If you're Frank Doyle, you go to a ball game. Samuel Waxworth reports.*

The article had surprised her the first time she read it. She couldn't possibly put it this way to Sam, but it was better than she'd expected. She believed strongly in her husband's intelligence and his ability to explain complicated subjects, but she'd never really thought of him as a writer. She'd encouraged his blogging as a hobby, without ever expecting it to take over their lives. When the *Interviewer* first offered him this job, Lucy's biggest fear was that Sam might not be good enough. But this profile read like it belonged in these pages.

Well, he was improving, she told herself. But his writing on the web was the same as always. In fact, a few posts had carried strong echoes of his earlier work. She was probably the only person in a position to recognize these similarities, being the only person who'd read everything he ever wrote. Perhaps even Sam himself hadn't noticed. Lucy had written a paper in college about cryptomnesia—buried memories that appear in the mind as original thoughts—a phenomenon Jung had first described more than a century ago. How Sam would have scoffed if she'd suggested he might be suffering from it! He respected psychology when it aspired toward the rigor of the hard sciences, and he respected her work with children suffering from clinically diagnosed pathologies. But to Sam, Jung was a mystic and psychoanalysis a pseudoscience. Not an argument worth having.

In any case, no such echoes appeared in the profile. A different person might have written it. She was absolutely sure that certain lines—mostly jokes—hadn't come from Sam. They sounded nothing like him. She suspected that they were the work of Max Blakeman, the relentlessly ironic editor to whom Lucy had been introduced on her first day in town, when Sam proudly showed her around the *Interviewer* offices.

Perhaps that was typical. Sam had never had an editor before, and Lucy didn't really know how these things worked. But the quality of the writing wasn't the only thing she'd found surprising. He'd taken the assignment so that he could finally express all his true feelings about Frank Doyle, but he'd written instead a kind of character study—not entirely flattering, perhaps, but sympathetic. This too might have been the work of an editor. Most of Sam's disagreements with the man were a little esoteric. They had to do with matters like the tactical value of the sacrifice bunt or the intentional walk. Her own objection was straightforward by comparison: she thought that Doyle had blood on his hands.

Lucy's parents, Mitch and Joan Kelleher, were dyed-in-the-wool midwestern-university-town liberals for whom the *New York Herald* was not the local paper of a distant metropolis but a cornerstone of their daily routine, a beloved source of enlightened information and opinion, a thinking person's Baedeker to the wider world, and Frank Doyle had embodied everything that made the paper so essential to them. Lucy had many childhood memories of her father reading bits of Doyle's column aloud while drinking his morning coffee. He memorized the best lines and brought them out to end arguments with wingnut neighbors and relatives.

Such was Doyle's importance to the fabric of their lives that when he began to change they were inclined at first to explain it away. He'd always been an iconoclast, never toed the party line, that was what made him worth reading in the first place. Granted, the man had his blind spots, like any human being, but his columns were still preferable to so much of what was out there. Surely he was up to something subversive when he quoted Bob Barr approvingly in a column arguing for Clinton's impeachment? It was disappointing to read his endorsement of George W. Bush, but really what was the difference between Bush and Gore? The Kellehers were voting for Nader anyway.

Finally, these excuses hit their limit. Doyle had been advocating for Saddam Hussein's removal since the end of the first Gulf War, but so long as Clinton showed no interest in the matter this had been easy to dismiss as one of his eccentricities. After the attacks, his voice led a larger chorus singing a wounded nation into battle, and it was impossible to ignore what had become of him.

Of course Lucy had opposed the invasion from the beginning. She'd marched arm in arm with her parents at campus demonstrations and traveled with them to Chicago for the international day of protest. She was astonished at how many people on the left had twisted themselves into supporting the war. They made their arguments about the plight of women and gays in the Arab world—issues that hadn't seemed particularly urgent a few months earlier—but Lucy could see through these pretexts to an atavistic thirst for revenge, a petty desire to remind the world of American power. In their rationalizations they'd been aided by the great liberal institutions, beginning with the *Herald*—both its reporting and its opinion pages. Before long, those wingnut neighbors were quoting Frank Doyle back at Lucy's dad.

Most of the liberal hawks had since come to regret (or forget) their support for an illegal, unjust, and disastrous undertaking. The *Herald* as a whole seemed appropriately chastened about the part it had played in making the case for regime change. Only Frank Doyle stood firm. This alone should have cost him his job, long before any racial ugliness.

Lucy hadn't actually expected to read any of this in the profile. Sam wasn't really a political creature, despite his newly minted reputation as an expert in the field. He disliked the pandering, the sanctimonious rhetoric, the contortion of reasoning necessary to make sure one's own side was always in the right. At times he seemed to distrust democracy itself, which treated every opinion, even the most uninformed, as equal. Reality could not be put to a vote, he liked to say. When it came to organizing society—policing the streets, providing housing and healthcare, distributing resources to maximize both fairness and efficiency—there were right and wrong answers, and experts who knew one from the other. A sensible nation would put those people in charge and go about its business. When he'd told her his plan to build a polling algorithm, Lucy had reminded Sam of his disdain for the electoral process. "That's my biggest advantage," he'd replied. "These are all just inputs to me. That makes it so much easier to be objective."

Though Sam had marched with her on campus in protests against the war, he hadn't been passionate about the issue. His opposition, he'd explained to the other demonstrators, was based on simple math. Having estimated the likelihood that Saddam had WMDs, the likelihood that he would use them or allow them to be used against Americans, and the likely casualties that would result from such use, Sam had determined that the expected loss of American life from leaving Hussein in power was less than the expected loss that would result from his removal. These calculations made everyone a bit uneasy. Did Sam mean to say that if his numbers had come out differently he might just as easily be supporting the invasion? Of course he did. What good would his opposition be if it wasn't grounded in facts? When it came to ethics, he was a strict consequentialist. Pacifism as an absolute stance didn't make sense to him. One fellow demonstrator asked why Iraqi lives weren't included in Sam's calculations. Well, he said, he wasn't sure that Iraqi lives were the U.S. government's concern, strictly speaking. When it came time, Lucy didn't invite him on the family trip to Chicago.

But for all that, he usually wound up in the right place. Whatever calculations had been required to make him oppose the war, oppose it he had. He hadn't just predicted Obama's victory with mathematical detachment, he'd contributed to it with his vote. She didn't think she could have stayed with him otherwise. Relative indifference she could take, but she couldn't imagine sharing her life with an actual Republican.

Yet one might have written this article. The portrait was almost affectionate. Nothing in its eight glossy pages suggested that Frank Doyle had done more damage to the republic over the past decade than anyone this side of Dick Cheney. Doyle's intransigence in the face of the mess he'd helped to create was made into a character quirk. His "fall from grace"—which struck Lucy as an ugly manifestation of the country's ongoing racial insanity—was treated as a personal crisis.

Her misgivings had multiplied when the Doyles invited them for the weekend, just days after the profile hit newsstands. It felt like an obvious quid pro quo. Had Sam been corrupted so easily? But he insisted this was just how things were done. Everyone knew each other in New York; in its way, it was smaller than Madison. You couldn't help socializing with the people about whom you wrote, or writing about the people with whom you socialized. Max Blakeman, he noted by way of example, had known the Doyles all his life. To Lucy this only made it seem more sordid. If the system took such behavior for granted, maybe the system itself was corrupt.

What finally allowed her to acquiesce to the weekend was a promise she made herself: she would go, but she would be honest. Speak truth to the man, as Sam should have done. Her inbred midwestern niceness told her it was impolite to accept an invitation in order to berate the host, but her idealism, which she likewise thought of as particularly midwestern, would not let her enjoy hospitality under false pretenses. And wasn't honesty supposed to be the trait that Frank Doyle valued above all?

Once she'd allowed herself to agree to the weekend, she became increasingly excited about it. Whatever else he'd become, Frank Doyle was still a legendary figure to her, someone she could not until recently ever have imagined meeting, and she was spending the night at his house. When she and Sam went back to Madison to start a family and live their real lives, they would take this memory with them. They would speak of it decades on, as her parents still spoke of the early years of their marriage, spent in Chicago, where her father had gone to graduate school.

The train made its first stop in a town called Babylon. The rustle of passengers and the conductor's call over a grainy intercom distracted Lucy, who gave up on the magazine and stared out the window instead. She'd always thought of Long Island as an upper-crust beach getaway, but thus far she'd seen a string of working-class towns not unlike the ones you passed through while driving from Madison to Milwaukee. Presumably things became more opulent the farther out you went. If that was the case, they'd be going a long way, given what Sam had told her about the Doyles. They sped along, and the anticipated change in the landscape began. Occasional breaks in the houses revealed the bare masts of docked boats swaying like leafless trees in a winter breeze. She knew she was looking at some inlet or harbor rather than the vast Atlantic, but the sight called to mind another shamefully midwestern reason why she'd agreed to go that weekend: she wanted to see the ocean.

She was still looking out the window when Sam appeared in the aisle with their bags in hand. He was there even before the conductor announced that they were a few minutes from their stop. There was something so comforting about this. She'd missed his diligence, his great love for logistics, while they were apart.

A girl in cutoff jeans and a faded yellow polo shirt waved from the parking lot as they got off the train. With her reddish-blonde hair and flushed complexion, she bore an obvious resemblance to Frank Doyle. Lucy had never thought of the man as handsome, but this younger, feminized version of him was quite pretty.

"Look who's here," she said in greeting. "The young man from the provinces."

It sounded like a kind of insult, but Sam smiled at it.

"Margo," he said, "this is Lucy."

"I've heard so much about you," Margo told her, in a much warmer tone.

Lucy smiled and shook Margo's hand, unsure how to respond to this bit of courtesy. Sam had mentioned speaking briefly with Doyle's daughter for the piece, but Lucy couldn't imagine why they would have spoken "so much" about her. It was the sort of thing a close friend said when meeting the new flame. Margo took a bag from Sam and led them across the parking lot, to an old Jaguar that must once have been very expensive but had the appearance of a family beater. She put the bags inside and offered Lucy the front passenger seat.

They'd been driving only a few minutes when they turned down an unmarked and unpaved road on which they continued for a hundred feet or so before Lucy realized that it was the Doyles' driveway. What looked like a small house by the side of it turned out to be a two-story garage. The proper house was a little ways beyond, large but unassuming, in colonial style, with white shingles and dark green shutters. There was something almost disheveled about it—paint chipping in places, a few tiles missing from the expansive slate roof—which only added to the impressive effect, as though one naturally accrued houses in this life and couldn't be expected to care too deeply for them. Beside it was a third structure, a bit smaller than the garage, with an adjacent pool in which someone was swimming.

"That's Mom," Margo said as they got out of the car. "I wouldn't wait for a hello. She's very devoted to her laps."

Lucy watched the woman cut smoothly through the water with a feeling of kinship. Running was one of the great pleasures of Lucy's life, and she knew the joy that came from solitary exertion. When Margo's mother neared the end of the pool, she executed a flip turn that startled Lucy with its elegant precision. Lucy turned to see whether Sam was watching and found that he and Margo had continued to the house with their bags. She hurried to catch up.

"Dad's working in his study," Margo said as they walked upstairs. "Eddie is coming for the day tomorrow. He's got something he absolutely has to do in the city first, but of course he won't tell us what it is."

They walked down a long hallway, at the end of which was a room that might have been in a seaside hotel—king bed, large wooden dresser, antique writing desk, and a bay window looking out to the water.

"Come down for drinks once you're settled," Margo told them before closing the door behind her.

Lucy was leaning over the dresser, unpacking a bag, when Sam crept up behind her and put his hands on her waist. At another time in their lives, his urgency would have surprised her, but now she was almost expecting it. He'd been insatiable since she'd arrived in New York. Sometimes when he got home at night he looked ready to go before he was through the door. She'd felt pretty insatiable too, initially, but she'd assumed they would exhaust themselves and fall back into their usual routine. Instead he seemed to have become an entirely different person on this front. It must have been the excitement of this new job, in this new place.

She wasn't complaining. That passion was not among Sam's great qualities was sometimes a private disappointment to her—though it also had its advantages. She didn't have to force herself into the mood at all hours to make sure she was keeping him satisfied. She didn't fear the day when he would stop finding her sufficiently alluring and leave her for someone younger or prettier. She knew girls who took cheating men as just a part of life, but Lucy never gave the possibility a thought.

"They'll hear us."

She turned and gave him a quick kiss that might as easily have been meant to encourage him as to bring him to a halt.

"We've practically got our own wing of the house."

"Quickly," she told him. "I need to get dressed for dinner."

Downstairs, Margo sat alone on the back porch, reclined on a chaise longue, book in her hand and a full glass on the ground beside her.

"I made a pitcher of Pimm's Cup," she said as she stood to greet them again.

Lucy had spent much of the past week thinking about what to pack, and twenty minutes upstairs deciding on the navy-and-white-striped linen dress she was now wearing, but Margo was still in the shorts and shirt she'd worn to pick them up.

"That sounds great," Sam said.

While Margo poured their drinks, Lucy looked out on the yard. Sam had told her that the house was on the water, and she'd expected to see a sandy beach and the wide expanse of the ocean, but the long lawn sloped down instead to a short dock and a placid sheet of water that Lucy could see straight across to grassy land and other large houses. She felt a bit silly about her disappointment. In the distance a small motorboat disrupted the water's calm, and Lucy followed it with her eyes for a moment before realizing that it was headed straight for them.

"I think that's Justin," Margo said, as she handed Lucy her drink. "He didn't mention that he was coming over."

"Justin Price?" Sam asked. Lucy was clearly meant to know who this person was, but she couldn't remember hearing the name before.

"He probably thought Eddie would be here," Margo said. To Lucy she clarified, "He's my brother's best friend."

"Does he always travel like James Bond?"

Margo laughed.

"His place is right across the bay, but he usually drives. He must be in a dramatic mood."

The boat arrived at the dock, and Margo walked down to greet it. When Lucy saw Justin Price—a handsome black man in his thirties, dressed for a country club—she remembered why she was supposed to know the name. He was the young hedge fund genius Sam had told her about, an old friend of both the Doyle family and Sam's editor. He wore a light blue linen shirt and bright green chinos rolled up a few inches above his ankles. In one hand he held a pair of topsiders and in the other a large-brimmed straw hat. He dropped the shoes on the dock and tossed the hat jauntily onto his head, freeing his hands to tie up the boat. When he'd finished, they walked together back up to the house, where Margo introduced Sam and Lucy.

They'd had another round of drinks by the time Margo's mother appeared. She'd taken more care than her daughter over her outfit for the evening, Lucy noticed with some relief. She wore high-waisted red pants and a light blue men's shirt with the tails untucked and knotted. Lucy also noticed now that it was really Kit from whom her daughter got her beauty. She had full cheeks and large, inviting eyes. Her skin, still flushed perhaps from her swim, had a shiny smoothness. Only her elegantly graying hair suggested her age.

"Welcome, Waxworths," she said. "I'm Kit." She shook hands politely before taking Justin into a hug. "What a nice surprise," she told him. "Edward won't be here until tomorrow, but maybe you can stay over?" To Sam and Lucy she added, "My husband is on his way out," as though he were obviously the main event for which the audience needed to be prepared.

The great man himself emerged a moment later in dramatic fashion, carrying a large tray that held two plates, one piled with thick steaks dripping in marinade, the other with sliced vegetables. Between the plates was a highball glass filled with brown liquor.

"You eat meat, I hope," he said to Lucy without any introduction or preliminaries. "My daughter is a vegetarian. There is a fuzzy ethical principle at work there that I've never fully understood."

Margo barely looked over from her conversation with Justin as she said, "Adorno tells us that the holocaust begins when we walk by a slaughterhouse and say, 'They're only animals.'"

"Adorno tells us the holocaust begins when we listen to *jazz*," Frank replied with genial disgust, more to Lucy than to Margo, who had already returned her attention to her conversation. "Can you give me a hand? I'm guessing a midwestern girl like you knows her way around a grill."

He'd seemed very large while he stood in the doorway, but as they walked together, Lucy could see that they were about the same height. He had the kind of heaviness that comes with age, but she didn't think this accounted for his imposing solidity. There was an aura surrounding him, she thought, and she laughed to herself at how this explanation would have infuriated Sam.

The sun was setting by the time they arranged themselves around the long wooden table. Orange and pink light seeped out spectacularly from the water and the trees. Lucy suspected that Frank had been waiting for this striking display before letting them sit for the meal. He seemed to have a great instinct for presentation. He took the head of the table and insisted that she sit next to him.

"What did you think of your husband's profile?" he asked.

It was rather ingenious: a question about himself disguised as a question about her husband that might almost have been a question about her. She recognized a chance to test her commitment to honesty.

"He went far too easy on you."

She gave the remark the tone of a joke, and Doyle laughed eagerly.

"I couldn't agree more. He let me off the hook. He was supposed to write an index of self-destructive acts."

"Still I was very proud of him," Lucy added, unwilling to let Doyle align them together against Sam.

"For all its supposed empiricism," Doyle said, looking at her but speaking to the entire table, "your husband's method isn't very good at talking about what actually happens in the real world. It's great for making predictions about a future state that doesn't exist, but don't ask it to look back at what we all know happened and explain it. That takes interpretation. You have to be able to pass judgment. None of this phony lab-coat objectivity."

Lucy realized uneasily that Doyle was exactly right: what Sam's piece had lacked was any critical sense.

"I'd be happy to pass judgment now, if you'd like."

Doyle seemed delighted by the idea.

"Why don't you give me the rest of the meal to prove myself?"

"Sounds fair."

This exchange over, Lucy waited for someone else to take a turn in the conversation, but Doyle broke right back in, speaking directly to her.

"The problem is that you can't live probabilistically. Each of us is one of one. You have to take the leap eventually, and you have to be willing to be wrong. You can tell me there is a sixty percent chance of rain tomorrow, and, come rain or shine, you might have been right. That's fine with the weather, because there's more of it every day. But some questions we only get one shot to answer. You've got to make your commitment and live with the results."

"Like the war?" Lucy asked.

The rest of the table seemed to stiffen with a closer attention, but Frank remained unfazed.

"A perfect example," he told her. "I can punch all sorts of numbers into one of your husband's algorithms. Suppose it comes out fifty-one percent in favor of fighting? We can't go fifty-one percent to war. It's one hundred percent or nothing. If you start to take Vienna, you've got to take Vienna. Of course you can do a better job than Rumsfeld did planning for various contingencies, but that's a different matter. What you can't do is live out two different lives, go to war in one and not the other, see how it turns out, and adjust your numbers accordingly. As Kierkegaard tells us, life can only be lived forwards and understood backwards. A million different things *might* happen, but in the end only one of them will. You've just got to live with that."

In Lucy's visions of this weekend, Doyle had never actually responded to her hard truths. He had simply taken them and dissolved. In real life, he fed on disagreement. She'd been worried about being rude, but she could see that, as far as he was concerned, she was playing out the role of ideal guest. She wished there was some way to oppose him without giving him the satisfaction of that opposition.

"Perhaps you do have to commit," she said. "But you don't have to *want* to commit. You don't have to like it. And you might do it with a bit of humility. Your opponents are in the same position you are. They too have to commit, and they've done the calculations the best they can."

"You're quite right. In fact it's much worse than that. We don't just have to commit, we have to *sub*mit—to historical judgment. All sorts of people who have the luxury of not having to make this choice will feel free to evaluate it later. But I feel quite confident on that front. A year ago, the anti-war crowd considered this all a settled matter, but look at us now—we are about to have democratic elections in Iraq. If Obama doesn't screw it up, that is. A year or two from now, it could all look different."

"And another year after that, it will look different again," Sam broke in. "What moment in history is the correct vantage point from which to make these judgments? It's all so subjective. The real problem with this war is that no one actually knew what the goals were, so it's impossible to say whether it succeeded. What's the metric?"

"There is no metric," Frank said. "You statheads want formulas that will settle every argument, but these arguments can't be settled. One day you'll succeed in objectively answering every question that can be objectively answered, and we'll still be left with everything that actually matters. We'll see that the things that can't be proven are the only things worth talking about in the first place. Whereof we cannot speak, thereof we can never, ever shut up."

So it went for the rest of the meal, Frank an unending stream of talk, everyone else contributing only enough to create new occasions for his performance. It might have been insufferable, except for an added layer of knowingness—they had all played this out so many times before, and the arrival of a new audience seemed to give a freshness to the production. Lucy understood now some part of the draw these people had for Sam. Though she was suspicious of the feeling in herself, she was glad that they'd accepted this invitation. Of course, she still disagreed with Frank Doyle about everything, but she liked the rest of them, and even disagreeing with Frank Doyle had its charms.

When they'd finished eating, Kit rang a handheld buzzer that had been sitting unnoticed next to her plate, and a woman in a black-and-white uniform came out to clear the table. Growing up, Lucy had had friends with housekeepers, nannies, cleaning ladies, but she'd never had her plate cleared by a uniformed maid. It seemed a bit excessive to her. The same woman returned a moment later with a tray of cheese, and it occurred to Lucy that she'd probably prepared all the food that Frank had used as a prop while making his entrance. When the cheese was finished, they got up from the table, refreshed their drinks, and walked down to a stone firepit surrounded by Adirondack chairs. Lucy took a seat and watched Sam help Frank get the fire started.

Twenty minutes later, Lucy stood to fix another drink, but on her way up to the bar she decided she'd had too much. She wandered quietly to the dock, where she looked out at the water and tried to collect herself. She was still feeling exhilarated by her dinner table conversation. She'd argued with Frank Doyle, and he'd taken her seriously. She couldn't wait to tell her parents about it.

Thirty was too old to care so much about parental opinion, but she'd always lived under their eye. She'd attended the university where they both worked—her father as a history professor, her mother in the school of social work—and stayed on in Madison after graduation. Sam had been treated like a family member long before he and Lucy married, ever since her parents had come to understand the depths of disorder in his own home life. Lucy had practically moved back in after Sam left for New York, and when she'd finally followed him here, it was the first time she'd lived more than a few miles from her childhood home.

She heard footsteps behind her, and she watched the approaching shadow of a figure that she expected would be Sam but turned out instead to be Justin Price.

"Quite a view, isn't it?"

"We were supposed to be on the ocean," she said, a little drunk and still feeling committed to her project of ruthless honesty. "That's a silly thing to complain about, but I've never seen it before."

"I'll take you there, if you want."

"You are staying over, then?"

"I meant right now." He gestured to the boat beside them. "It's just a few minutes."

They walked back to invite the rest of the group, but no one was interested in joining them. Sam and Frank were engaged in an argument that Margo seemed to be mediating while Kit fixed herself another drink. Lucy went upstairs to change into a bathing suit, which she covered with a sweater and a pair of shorts. By the time she returned, Justin was already starting up the motor.

As they bumped along the surface, brightly lit houses punctuated the dark night sky. Lucy asked Justin which one was his, but he couldn't hear her over the wind whipping pleasantly across their faces, so she gave up and sat silently for the rest of the ride. It took a bit longer than she'd imagined, long enough that she wondered whether this had been a foolish idea. Couldn't she have waited until tomorrow? But before the feeling could solidify, they arrived at a dune that seemed to mark the waypoint between the ocean and the bay.

Justin pulled the boat out of the water a bit unsteadily, refusing Lucy's help. She realized that she was quite drunk, and she thought that Justin might be, too. She left him to his work and ran up the dune, feeling at once excited and prepared for disappointment. No emotion was less willing to appear on demand than a sense of the sublime. But when she arrived at the sand's peak and caught her first glimpse, she felt the full force of it. What was it that moved her so much? On many overcast days, the water on Lake Michigan extended to the horizon, with no sign of land on the other side, but you always knew just where the land was. Somehow it was different knowing how much farther this horizon stretched. The moon hung low, reflected in the ripples. It was a clear evening, and she could see nothing but water. It seemed impossible to believe, as she looked out, that it didn't go on forever. At most there might be some shelf somewhere, some edge of the world, from which the water poured into nothingness.

Lucy ran down the dune and into the waves, which surprised her with a chill. She stopped when the water reached her knees and turned to watch Justin roll up his pants a few more inches before walking out to join her.

"It's incredible," she said.

She walked back to dry land and took off her sweater and shorts before running in headlong. The cold surprised her anew as her chest and head submerged. She stood up, gasped, and dropped herself in again. While she floated there, Justin stripped down to his boxer shorts, revealing a slight paunch on his otherwise thin frame. He took a few steps and dove.

"I still remember the first time I came here," he said after they'd bobbed around a minute. "It was the summer after sixth grade."

"You've known the family a long time."

"Practically all my life."

"I'm sorry if this is rude, but did it bother you? What he said at that game?"

"Of course it did," Justin answered without hesitation. "Frank's been very good to me, and I want to give him the benefit of the doubt, but a lot of people I know can't afford to assume that anyone will give them the benefit of the doubt. I've spent my whole life watching what I say in different settings. It's exhausting, but I haven't had a choice. Frank doesn't think he should have to be careful. He doesn't really appreciate how hard some people have it."

"I feel that way about Sam sometimes," Lucy said. "I mean about not realizing how hard people have it." She had never articulated this before, even to herself. "In a lot of ways he's had it pretty hard himself, which may be part of it. He found a way to get through, and he expects everyone else to do the same."

This was more than she ought to be saying to a stranger. Besides which, she didn't want to talk about Frank or Sam. They seemed a long way away. She floated in silence for a few minutes. It felt as though they were doing something illicit, though everyone knew where they were. Justin was just being kind to her. If she had to guess, she'd say he was gay.

Eventually they got out and stood in the sand to dry off. The night air would have a more cutting feel on their return trip, Lucy imagined. They walked over the lip of the dune and looked down at the bare stretch of sand. Lucy only understood the significance of the sight when Justin cursed quietly beside her.

"I should have tied it to something."

He didn't seem particularly alarmed, though when Lucy looked out into the darkness of the water she didn't see the boat anywhere.

"What are we going to do?"

"I'll call someone when we get back. In the meantime, we can go down the shore to the beach road and walk back from there. It's probably three miles. It would be a lot quicker along the edge of the bay, but the walk is a little treacherous."

"That's fine with me," Lucy said, eager now to get home, afraid that Sam might start worrying about her. "I'm in good shape."

They put on their dry clothes and their shoes, and they traced the edge of the dune until the sand turned to grassy woods. It was dark amid the trees, but house lights ahead guided them. They'd been walking for about five minutes when something caught Lucy's eye. The very stillness drew her attention. Everything else in the world swayed slightly in the breeze, and the figures stood out in their unmoving calm. A mother and child by the looks of it, the child tucked between the mother's front and hind legs, both of their faces turned as though in judgment. Lucy took a step, and the deer dashed off in retreat, the sound of their leaps a withdrawing echo.

A bit farther along, the trees gave way to a manicured lawn and a large house with all its lights on. After that the walk became wooded again and they were returned to near darkness. Soon Lucy could see the Doyles' firepit, and a moment later they were in the open again. Justin hurried out ahead of her and announced their arrival, an awkward gesture so out of keeping with his earlier calm that it confounded Lucy. She saw motion ahead of them, and very slowly she realized that it was Sam and Margo, rising from a single chair.

There was no sign of Frank or Kit, who must have already gone off to bed. The four remaining souls stood facing one another. Everyone seemed ready to follow Lucy's lead.

"We had quite an adventure," she said with a smile. "The boat disappeared on us."

She laughed, and everyone else laughed along.

"Let me fix you another drink," Margo said. "It sounds like you've earned it."

"I'm going to head upstairs, actually," Lucy said. "I'm a bit worn out."

She felt suddenly exhausted, and she knew that her day of honesty was over.

2.

On Eddie's third trip downtown to see Herman Nash, the baptisms began. He'd been in the park for about twenty minutes, waiting on the outskirts of the crowd, when Nash took up his usual place on the fountain, which was full and spouting now that summer was underway. Nash always began his sermon with that brown fedora perched on the back of his head, its brim surrounding his face like a dark halo. After he'd been going for a while, he took it off and held it in front of him, crown in hand, as though using it to catch his own words as they left his mouth. He didn't make any pitch for donations before passing it around. He just sent it out into the crowd and waited for it to return.

"Every time I stand up here," he began on this morning, almost conversationally, "I see more people in front of me. Black people and white people, old people and young people, but there's one thing I know you all have in common." He paused, as though giving them a chance to determine the common thread that ran among them. "Everyone here is in *need*."

"Amen!" a woman near the front of the crowd called out.

"Plenty of people will tell you that they don't need God," Nash continued. "They don't see the *point* of Him. They don't understand what His existence explains. I've got no business with those people. They can believe whatever they want. Jesus didn't come for them. Jesus came for the poor, not the rich. Jesus came for the sick, not the well. Jesus came for the broken, not the whole. Jesus came for the losers, not the winners. Jesus didn't come to *explain* anything. He came to help the ones in need."

"I am in need, Jesus!" the same woman cried. Spontaneous interjections were common during Nash's performances, but now he stopped, as though to encourage her. She went on talking, louder than Nash himself, but after that first sentence Eddie couldn't understand a word she said. She seemed to be speaking in a foreign language, one that he didn't recognize, perhaps one not recognizable to man.

While she spoke, she pushed through the crowd toward Nash. Some people moved to protect him, but he stopped them with a wave, and they let her pass. She arrived at the fountain, where he took her into his arms as though catching something dropped from a great height. He lowered her to the water in one fluid movement and submerged her head. He left her under for a moment before pulling her out and setting her upright like a piece of fallen furniture.

"Your sins are washed away," he said, loud enough for all to hear. "Go forth and be blameless."

The woman had stopped her chattering. After collecting herself, she wandered off, appearing dazed but happy. She hardly seemed to notice the crowd giving way to let her go. Others rushed in to take her place, and the scene briefly threatened to come apart, until Nash raised his hands like a conductor calling an orchestra to attention. Everyone went still. With a few waves he encouraged them into a line.

"Whoever brings their sins to me will be baptized in these waters," he announced, as though this had been his intention all along. "Their sins too will be washed away."

They approached one by one, and Nash took them as they came, dropping them into the water and sending them along. This went on for more than an hour, but people were still waiting when Nash stepped down from the fountain with his hat in his hand. Eddie had watched it all from a distance, feeling no urge to join the line. He still wasn't sure exactly what he was doing there in the first place. Presenting himself to the man would have committed him to something. It would have meant he was looking for more than a way to pass the time.

He'd searched online for "Washington Square preacher" the morning after the party, and he'd found dozens of videos, mostly the same three or four sermons shown from different angles. The scene Eddie had come upon the day before was already online, but the screen failed to capture whatever had moved him so much at the time. Something essential was missing from the videos, leaving Eddie to wonder whether that thing had been real. He watched a few more videos and soon connected the figure in them with the stories about a man predicting the end of the world. His brief enthusiasm became embarrassing. He decided to forget about Herman Nash.

If he found himself walking the length of Fifth Avenue a week later as though he had some business downtown, arriving at Washington Square just as Nash stood up to begin his latest performance, it was partly from a lack of anything else to do. His life had been so regimented for so long, and now he had no real obligations. Reacclimating to his old life might have been enough to keep him busy, but his old life had disappeared in his absence. Every few days he called Justin to see about getting together, but Justin said he was too busy to do anything at the moment. He insisted that he wanted to see him as soon as his schedule cleared up, but he seemed to be in a hurry to get off the phone. Even at his busiest, Justin had made time for Eddie in the past, and now he was practically retired. Something had changed since the party, Eddie decided. Probably Justin had already recognized the uncomfortable truth that Eddie himself was just starting to suspect: that the person who'd been Justin Price's best friend for almost twenty years didn't exist anymore.

Margo, too, seemed constantly occupied. When Eddie first got home, she'd been around the house all the time, but now she was out every day. Kit wasn't so busy, but talking with her made Eddie anxious. She was constantly asking what Eddie planned to do next, the one question he didn't want to think about.

Frank spent long hours in his office, where he was supposedly working on his book, but each time Eddie dropped in, he found his father drinking in front of the TV. As far as Eddie could tell, the man drank himself to sleep every afternoon. Eddie kept waiting for someone to bring the problem up, but no one talked about it. Had this habit picked up after Frank's firing, or had it been going on longer than this? Had it developed so gradually that Margo and Kit didn't notice? It was strange to think that it might have been happening for years without Eddie knowing.

Twice he'd come in to find baseball on, and he'd sat down with Frank for a few innings. It had been a long time since they'd watched a game together. His father had taken Eddie to Shea half a dozen times each summer throughout his childhood, and Eddie had always been happy for the time with him. He usually knew weeks in advance when he was going to a game, but one afternoon in the fall of Eddie's sophomore year, Frank had come home from work early and called up the stairs to say he had tickets that night. Whoever he'd been planning to take—probably one of the younger editors at the *Herald*—couldn't go. They both knew Eddie was a backup plan, but Frank presented the invitation like an act of great generosity. What kid wouldn't want to go to a game with his dad?

Eddie's friends were over, and they were all quite stoned. They were often stoned in those days, at least all of them but Justin, who smoked only when he was spending the night with the Doyles, because he'd never risk being caught out of sorts by his parents. Eddie's bedroom looked out on the backyard, and they took turns leaning out the window, smoking from a little metal bowl Blakeman had bought down on St. Marks. Then they'd play Ping-Pong or video games while listening to music. They smoked as soon as they came in from school, so that they were in presentable shape by the time Eddie's parents got home.

But Frank was early, and there was no mistaking Eddie's condition. In one of those moments of terrible stoned clarity, he could see his father's thought process working out in front of him. *I won't say anything, and the kid will be back to normal by the time we get out to Queens.* Eddie knew he ought to go along, but telling his friends to go home so he could watch a ball game with his dad seemed like the hardest thing he'd been asked to do in his life.

"I've got people here," he said mildly.

Frank's face showed emotion for only an instant before coming back into stern shape.

"Of course," he said. "I'm sure your sister would love to go."

Without another word he headed down the hall to Margo's room.

Eddie was scheduled to go to a game two weeks later, but a few days before Frank announced that he'd found someone else to take.

"I know how you hate being dragged around by your old man," he said. They never went to Shea again.

This was all so typical of Frank, who did what he wanted when he wanted but could be irremediably wounded if someone else exercised the least bit of contrary will. Eddie realized that the idea that he would prefer playing video games at home to sitting at field level with his father confirmed everything that Frank already felt about his son—that he was too coddled, that he was a typical rich kid, that he had not earned his privilege as Frank had. As though these were conditions of Eddie's choosing, rather than the facts of the life that Frank himself had provided him.

At first Eddie hadn't minded the change. In truth, he found the games themselves to be long and slow and, frankly, boring. Like every boy he knew, Eddie had preferred basketball. He and Justin and Blakeman were loyal to Ewing and the Knicks when everyone else loved watching Jordan. They pretended to be John Starks and Charles Oakley when they shot hoops in the St. Albert's gym, on the blacktop of the school's courtyard, in Eddie's driveway in Bridgehampton, at the Ninety-Sixth Street courts. Among the game's advantages was the fact that you could take just a few bowl hits behind the big rock near the North Meadow and find an open hoop for a game of HORSE. You couldn't do this with baseball. If you tried to have a catch while stoned you were liable to get a hardball in the eye.

His father might well have known this reason for their preference, given the horror he showed when he discussed the subject with them. He found something perverse in the spectacle of America's young men abandoning the national pastime. *Basketball was invented in Massachusetts*, Blakeman noted one night at dinner. Unlike baseball and football, it didn't have a British predecessor. Didn't this make it the real American sport?

"That's just it," Frank had responded. "The genius of America is not about creating something *ex nihilo*"—he used such words unselfconsciously in conversations with high fifteen-year-olds—"it's about mixing the old and the new. Baseball is an old-world legacy transformed into something all our own. That's what makes it so American."

Eddie had no need to prove his patriotism at this point, and he could sit beside his father with the certain knowledge that he'd put himself through far tougher challenges than growing up lower middle class in 1950s Brooklyn. But what was any of it worth? He'd thought he might spend some time basking in Frank's approval, but now that he'd earned it, it seemed a feeble thing. For so long, he'd wanted to be worthy of this life. He'd wanted to earn his place in it, as Justin had done, rather than being the boy at the party to whom everyone must chat because his parents are the hosts. To that end, he'd gone around the world, put himself at risk, and now that he was back he couldn't see what had ever seemed worth earning. The life Eddie had lived in New York before enlisting, the life to which he was supposed to be returning now, had no meaning for him.

That was why he went out running for miles each morning, trying to exhaust himself. But it wasn't the same to be exhausted to no purpose, or exhausted only for the purpose of emptying himself. No matter how pointless the tasks the army sometimes gave you, they all fit into a larger context that had a real end. At home, every action was isolated from every other, just as every person was isolated from every other. Whatever you were doing at any time was just whatever you happened to be doing. He wanted the feeling of having all his minutes and hours bound together into something larger than himself, to feel the swell of it. He couldn't help thinking that he might find that back with Nash in the park.

On the day that Eddie finally planned to submit himself, he arrived in Washington Square at 7:00 AM. He'd come early, because the line seemed to get longer every time. Either people were going back for a second turn or there was an endlessly renewable supply of people who needed to be washed clean. The park was dotted with sleeping bags and tents and makeshift lean-tos from which campers slowly roused themselves while a small crew of uniformed police looked passively on. The campers were mostly young and white, a few with long beards or dirty dreadlocks, wearing faded T-shirts and ripped shorts that showed their tattoos, but the steady stream of people joining them included every age and race and general appearance. Many of the older ones had dressed as though for church.

A clear line ran through the general disorder up to the edge of the fountain, where Nash was expected to appear. Eddie took his place at the end of it, behind about a hundred people, all of them apparently ready to be born again. Some carried towels, others empty bottles, which they would presumably fill with water to take home, though it was just city fountain water, which could have been taken at any time. Immediately in front of Eddie stood a man with a sunken face, ravaged by drink or drugs, the sort one might expect to find spending the night in the park under any condition, though his look of attentive expectation told Eddie that he was there for the same reason as the rest of them. A circle of campers held hands and chanted, listing out sins for which they wanted forgiveness. One woman in the group had a sleeping infant wrapped against her chest. While the chanting continued, another group sang a hymn that Eddie recognized from morning chapel at St. Albert's. He hummed somewhat distractedly until a few lines came to mind. Eventually he found himself half singing along. They started another, which Eddie remembered a bit better, and he sang more confidently.

He'd told his parents that he'd be in Bridgehampton that afternoon, but he hadn't said what was keeping him in the city. He couldn't imagine admitting that he was going to be baptized. *You've already been baptized*, his mother would say for starters. Which he had, as an infant. *Baptized by whom?* his father would ask, meaning: By which sect, which entity, which institution? No answer could possibly satisfy him, least of all the honest one—not a denomination but an individual, one lately famous for predicting the apocalypse. They'd both think that Eddie had gone nuts. In fact he felt as sane as he had in a very long time.

Of course he didn't actually believe that the world was going to end in a few months. He wasn't sure that he believed anything Nash said. Eddie had never felt much of a religious impulse. His family had gone to church every Sunday throughout his childhood, at least until his grandfather died. After that they'd started spending the summer, and many weekends in the fall and spring, in Bridgehampton, where they almost never went to mass, as though it were something from which you could take a vacation. After a while they stopped going in the city, too, though his parents still spoke as though they were practicing Catholics. The church was like a club to which they'd belonged all their lives. They wished they had the time to make better use of the place, but they always paid their dues in full.

The line continued to fill up behind him, until it stretched another hundred feet. The people in back would almost certainly not have their chance that day, but they waited just in case. When Nash finally appeared, stepping up onto the fountain's lip to show himself above the crowd, some people on the outskirts cheered. Those closer to him responded instead with a quiet sharpening of attention: they'd called him into being like a memory or dream conjured to meet their deepest needs, and keeping him there required their full concentration.

"If I say, 'I will not mention his word or speak anymore in his name,'" Nash announced as he removed his hat and sent it down into the crowd, "his word is in my heart like a fire, a fire shut up in my bones. I am weary of holding it in; indeed, I cannot." He spoke in this vein for a few minutes before saying, "Bring yourselves to me, and your sins will be forgiven."

He took his time, despite all the people waiting. Each one was given a moment before being submerged. At this rate, Eddie expected to be there for more than an hour, but that was just fine with him. He was in no rush to get on the bus out east.

While he waited he tried to prepare himself, and he avoided watching what was happening ahead of him, as a kind of courtesy. There was something deeply intimate about the proceedings, something that deserved privacy.

Eddie was almost at the front of the line when a figure flashed in his peripheral vision, like a startled animal whose presence one doesn't register until it tries to escape. The man with the sunken face had grabbed Nash and pushed him under the water, as though moved by the scene to baptize the baptizer. Almost immediately Eddie understood that the man meant to keep Nash there. Some people started to scream, but no one moved. The police on the edge of the crowd stood in place, looking on passively—either they hadn't noticed that anything was wrong or didn't feel obliged to intervene.

A familiar sensation came over Eddie—the feeling of calm in the middle of chaos. Three long strides brought him to the fountain's edge, where a single swing batted the man away. The man let go as he fell, and Eddie pulled Nash from the water and took him into his arms. Now the police charged to grab the attacker while Eddie carried Nash to safety. Two officers subdued the man and put him in cuffs. The others attempted to calm the crowd, which seemed to want the ceremony to continue as though nothing had happened.

A thin stream of blood ran from a cut on Nash's forehead, pooling in the pockets of his grizzled face. His gray beard was flattened against his neck, darkened by the water, and his long hair hung limply, giving him the look of a shaggy dog caught in a storm. He also had the dumb, open smile of a dog. The person who'd commanded this great crowd seemed to have dissolved in the fountain, leaving only a shy but friendly old man. More police had arrived, and one of them asked whether Nash needed an ambulance.

Without answering, Nash pointed to where the man who'd attacked him now stood in cuffs, being questioned. "What will happen to him?"

The policeman shrugged.

"He'll probably get arraigned at some point late today or tomorrow. I'd guess he'll be charged with battery. By the look of him, he won't be posting bail, which means he'll cool off at Rikers for a while. After that, it's going to depend on what his priors look like."

"I don't want to press charges," Nash said.

The policeman sighed and shook his head.

"That's not really up to you. We'd like a statement, of course. But plenty of people saw what happened, including a bunch of cops. If you don't cooperate, he'll still get booked."

Nash ran his hands through his long, wet beard, thoughtfully pulling a knot out of it.

"If you let him go, I'll make these people leave. I can clear the park in five minutes. Without me, it will take you the rest of the morning."

The officer considered the offer before walking over to the scrum of uniforms that now surrounded the man in cuffs. He talked with one of the other cop before speaking a few words into his radio. The two walked together to the handcuffed man, who nodded solemnly at whatever they told him. When they'd finished, he responded with a few words, which seemed to be the ones they wanted to hear, because they undid the cuffs. The officer who'd spoken to Nash walked the man slowly out of the park.

While he did, Nash stood back up on the fountain, using Eddie's shoulder for support. At the sight, some people surged toward him, and the police who'd been surrounding the attacker moved in between Nash and his audience.

"What happened today happened according to a plan," Nash announced. "There will come an hour to return to this place, but right now you need to depart. Leave peacefully and reflect upon your sins in the privacy of your hearts."

He said nothing more by way of encouragement, but he passed his eyes calmly over the onlookers, who turned as though shamed by his attention. They walked in all directions toward the street. Within a few minutes the park was no more crowded than it was on an average morning. Meanwhile, Nash stayed standing with a hand on Eddie's shoulder.

When the people had mostly cleared out, the first officer returned to Nash and Eddie and took down their contact information. He asked again whether Nash needed an ambulance.

"My friend here is going to help me home," Nash said.

The officer looked briefly at Eddie before turning somewhat sternly back to Nash.

"We know you didn't mean to create a dangerous situation here, but we almost had a riot on our hands. This isn't the first time one of your performances has incited violence. If you want to do another one of these"—he struggled for the word—"*revivals*, you're going to need a permit. Otherwise we'll break the thing up and write you a citation. If you persist after that, you're going to get arrested."

The smile left Nash's face for the first time since Eddie had pulled him from the fountain. He nodded to the officer, lowered himself to the ground with Eddie's help, and began to walk. Eddie noticed a slight but definite limp that seemed to predate the morning's incident.

"I'm happy to pay for a cab," Eddie told him. The address Nash had given the officer was a high number on East Seventh Street, which Eddie guessed was four or five long crosstown blocks away.

"I'd rather walk," Nash said. He gestured at the leg and added, "It's not as bad as it looks."

They went together out the east side of the park, toward Broadway.

"That was kind," Eddie said after a while. "What you did for the man."

"Not a hair on their heads will be harmed," Nash answered.

Nash stopped often on their walk to rest and catch his breath, placing a hand on Eddie for support. When they got to his building, the elevator was broken, so Eddie helped him up four flights. When they got upstairs, Nash invited Eddie into his apartment. The door opened onto a small living room, with a couch against one wall.

"If you'll just wait a minute," he said, "I want to settle myself."

Nash walked into the bathroom and closed the door while Eddie sat down on the couch. There was a low wooden coffee table in front of him, with nothing on it but a leather-bound Bible. Beyond it was a counter that separated the room from a small kitchen area. It reminded Eddie of a joe's apartment in Fayetteville, and it struck him that it had all one really needed to get by.

After a minute or two, Nash emerged in a robe, with his long white hair pulled back into a ponytail. Eddie realized for the first time that the brown fedora had been lost in the commotion. Nash crossed the room to the far wall, where two doors stood next to each other, and he disappeared again through one of them. He returned wearing a white T-shirt and a pair of jeans. His appearance produced the intriguing but slightly disappointing effect of seeing an actor out of character.

"You live here alone?" Eddie asked.

"My niece used to share the place with me," Nash answered, gesturing at the closed second door. "She passed on to God about a year back."

"I'm sorry to hear that."

"All part of the Lord's plan." He seemed to be speaking of a condition more general than the loss of this niece. He pulled at his beard reflectively. "Did you come to be baptized today?"

Eddie felt oddly reluctant to admit the fact, though he'd obviously been standing in line. It had all seemed to make sense there in the park, while Nash wore his dark suit and his hair waved free, in a way that it didn't while Eddie sat on the man's old couch. Eddie nodded, and Nash returned to the bathroom, leaving the door open behind him. After a moment, Eddie understood that he was meant to follow. He found Nash seated on the edge of the bathtub, turning the faucet on. The shower curtain was open, and the suit hung over the curtain rod to dry. Eddie sat down beside Nash, who put a hand on his chest.

"Tell me the worst of it," Nash said.

Eddie was quite certain what the worst of it was, but he wasn't sure how to tell it.

"It happened during my second tour," he began.

He'd told himself—and his parents—that he would be doing only one stint of active duty, but he'd re-upped for another thirty-six months almost as soon as he got back from his first tour. At the time, he'd expected to stay in the army for the rest of his life. He'd thought he might be sent to Afghanistan next, but after the surge was announced, he knew he'd be going back to Iraq. His father was thrilled—they were going to do what was necessary to complete the mission—but it wasn't Eddie's job to worry about the mission. He'd been warned about this during training. The mission was determined by civilian leadership, and it was apt to change. The strategy for achieving the mission was a military matter, but it was determined above his pay grade. Eddie's job was tactics, and the job of his men was to implement them. It didn't matter whether the surge was a great act of political courage or a tragic delay of the inevitable. It just mattered that he was going back into the breach.

Everything felt different this time around. The place was so much quieter. Eddie's convoys were shot at about half a dozen times in ten months, but none of his men were injured, and they hadn't injured any locals in return. It was like a stage show compared to the serious combat he'd experienced in Fallujah two years before. This should have been a good thing. Certainly it was a good thing that none of his men had been lost. But that didn't mean that the insurgents had been defeated. It meant only that they'd decided to wait out the surge. What was the point in risking their lives, when they all knew that Eddie and his ilk would soon be gone?

On the last week of his tour, he was commanding a mounted patrol on a security sweep through Sha'ab in eastern Baghdad. This had been his primary job for most of the year, acting as a presence while the COIN teams did their door-to-door business, and this was his final outing. He was in the passenger seat of the second Humvee in the convoy. They were near the end of their loop when someone took a few shots at them. They stopped driving. Eddie opened the door and took cover behind it while he stood to clear room for his weapon. In the meantime, the shooter dropped his gun and faded into the crowd that had come out into the streets to watch them drive past. This was now the typical insurgent strategy. They would take a shot and see if they got lucky, but they weren't interested in extended firefights.

There wasn't much you could do when they slipped away like that. If you chased someone down and pulled him out of the crowd, you had to find an Iraqi police officer willing to detain him, and he'd probably be let go the moment your convoy moved on. If by some chance he was arrested, he would wind up in front of a judge on the Qaeda payroll—or one in fear for his life. So the policy was to answer with fire when they took fire and to move along when the firing stopped.

Eddie kept his weapon steady, and he didn't call for the convoy to move on. He'd lost sight of the shooter for a second, but a break in the crowd revealed him again, and Eddie got a good look. He was a kid—maybe sixteen or seventeen. He looked back at Eddie, and he had a kind of defiance, as though experience told him that he could act with impunity. Eddie's shot struck the kid in the chest and he dropped immediately. There was a panic in the crowd that had not been there when the kid was taking the shots. When Eddie gave the command to move on, there was no chatter over the radio. His crew fell back into line. He was their commanding officer, and they had all seen him go to great lengths over the previous ten months to protect them. He never asked them to do anything he didn't do first. If there was a door to kick, he was the one to kick it. If a block needed clearing out, he led the way around the corner. They knew all this. But they also knew that the kid's gun had been on the ground, and they knew that you never fired into a crowd of civilians. Eddie had broken every rule of engagement.

Five weeks later, he was back at Fort Bragg. He wasn't sure which of his men had reported the incident over his head, but he was brought in for a conversation about it almost as soon as he landed. For a few days he thought he'd be given a General or an Other Than Honorable, but in light of his overall performance and the "ambiguity" of the situation, his discharge was clean, with the understanding that he wasn't welcome to re-up.

Eddie told the story to Nash much as he'd told it to the two army therapists he'd seen after getting home. They'd talked about the stress he'd been under, the need to make quick decisions with limited information. This hadn't helped him at all. It had been the therapists' job to make him feel all right about what had happened, but he didn't think he was supposed to feel all right.

When he'd finished, Nash sat with his hands still on him, waiting for more. After a while, Eddie spoke again. What he said was not something he'd ever said to anyone before. He told Nash that throughout the quiet days of that second tour, he couldn't escape the memory of his first firefight in Fallujah, where he'd picked off five or six guys coming around a corner. He knew such a thing was supposed to haunt him, supposed to chase him all the way home, but instead he'd wanted it back. He'd felt like God, reaching down from the sky to pluck people off the face of the earth. He'd had more power than he would ever have again.

"In combat you make quick decisions under fire," he said, though he was really speaking to himself. "You have to be willing to live with your mistakes. But this wasn't a mistake. I knew exactly what I was doing. I didn't fire to protect my men. I didn't fire because I was scared. I didn't even fire because I was angry. I felt no emotion at all.

I'd been through the same experience plenty of times, and I'd never taken that shot. I fired because I'd been there all year, and I hadn't killed anyone, and I thought it might be my last chance."

Now the thing had been told. Nash looked at Eddie stoically, as though entirely indifferent to what he'd just heard.

"God's power is greater than any sin," he said. "Repent, for a new world is at hand."

All this time Nash had kept his hand on Eddie's chest, and now he abruptly dunked him into the warm water of the running bath, acting with more force than Eddie had expected. Eddie stayed under for what seemed a long time, which surprised but didn't trouble him. He knew that he could overpower Nash easily enough if it came to that, but he also knew that he wouldn't do it. He trusted Herman Nash completely. The meaning of the moment came from this trust, from the recognition that he would allow this crippled old man to suffocate him before he would resist. Just as Eddie arrived at this understanding, Nash brought him back up.

Eddie had anticipated a sense of peace coming over him, but he felt instead exhilaration, as though he'd been walking around with weights on, and now that they had been removed he had a great store of energy and strength. Nash handed Eddie a towel from the rack by the sink, and he retreated discreetly from the room while Eddie dried off his face and hair. When he'd finished, Eddie didn't go straight outside. He stayed by himself, seated on the edge of the bath, trying to catch his breath.

3.

Justin opened his eyes into agreeable disorientation, unsure what he was doing in Eddie's bed until he remembered that the Waxworths were in the guest wing. He hadn't slept in this room since before the extension was built. As boys they'd alternated nights on the bed and the floor, or else they'd just fallen asleep wherever they found themselves after staying up to all hours. Once, Justin woke to find Eddie's arm casually draped across his chest, his own head on Eddie's shoulder, and he'd stayed there, pretending to sleep, for as long as Eddie had let him. He wished he could live in that memory a moment, but he'd lost the ability to linger in bed. Even on weekends he was awake at six, ready to begin the day.

In the kitchen he made a pot of coffee. He didn't have his cell phone, so he used the Doyles' landline to report his missing dinghy, which he'd been too drunk and tired to do the night before. While he waited on hold, he looked out the window across the bay, where his own house sat partially obscured by trees. His decision to buy a place within sight of the Doyles had been a source of amusement among their friends—Blakeman had been particularly merciless—but to Justin it had felt natural. He knew and loved the area. Was he supposed to go somewhere else just to prove a point?

He was pouring himself a coffee when he heard someone on the stairs. He hurried out to the living room. Kit was a similarly early riser, and they'd spent many mornings chatting over coffee while the rest of the house slept in. He was hoping for that time now. The conversation he needed to have would take only a minute, after which he could go about the rest of his day. He'd already decided he would stick around to see Eddie. What difference would a few hours make?

Instead of Kit he found Lucy Waxworth in the living room, wearing shorts and running shoes, looking up at the framed map that hung above the couch. She startled briefly when he came through the door but smiled when she saw who it was.

"There are so many beautiful things in this house," she said, as though inviting him to share her amazement.

Justin bristled slightly at being treated as a fellow impressionable outsider rather than a member of this imposing family. He didn't want to make her feel unwelcome, but he wanted his kindness to appear to her an act of magnanimity, as it would have coming from Margo or Kit.

"I gave that to the Doyles as a fortieth-anniversary present. It's from the seventeenth century, when the area was settled."

She turned back to the thing and made a show of more careful examination.

"I don't suppose I could map a run on it?"

Her good humor made him regret his high-handed tone.

"Pretty ambitious after the night we had."

"I'm a bit compulsive. I don't feel right without a run in the morning."

Justin thought for a moment, glad to be relied on for local knowledge. He gave her directions to Mecox Road, and she was practically in a trot before she'd made it out the door. Her energy impressed him, and he admired her insistence on pushing through as though nothing had happened. He wondered how much she'd seen before he'd announced their arrival to Margo and Sam. He wasn't entirely sure what he'd seen himself.

He took his coffee out back and sat down on the porch, where he reached instinctively into his pocket before remembering again that he'd left his phone at the house. He'd had a vague idea that someone could use it later to prove he'd been here. Another bit of paranoia, like arriving by boat. That had been excessive, even melodramatic, and it had backfired completely once the thing disappeared.

The screen door slid open, and Justin tried to hide his disappointment at the sight of Sam Waxworth, who greeted him warmly and took the seat next to him. Justin still wasn't sure what to make of Waxworth. He'd spent a lot of time around serious quants, enough to know he wasn't one himself, and Sam Waxworth didn't seem to be one either. His posts never contained any math that wasn't covered in basic undergraduate statistics and probability classes. Justin had mentioned this when Blakeman had first talked about hiring the election oracle, but Blakeman had explained that the mere fact of doing math at all was enough. The *Interviewer*'s readers had been too busy with cultural studies and critical theory to take basic statistics. Being overly good with numbers might even have been a problem. Blakeman needed someone just good enough who could also write parsable prose. You could get a long way, he'd concluded, by knowing more math than the writers and writing better than the quants.

"Your profile really captured Frank," Justin said. This was true. He didn't add that Blakeman had obviously written those parts that had captured Frank the best.

"I should have spoken to you for it," Waxworth said. "You seem to know the family better than anyone."

Justin appreciated the sentiment, but he was glad he hadn't been interviewed. He'd been asked about Frank more times since the Ballpark Incident than in his whole life before then, and he was ready to be done with the question. It wasn't so bad when it came from someone like Lucy, who seemed genuinely curious to hear his thoughts, but most people raised the subject as a kind of test. Either Justin was meant to prove his loyalty by defending Frank or he was meant to prove his integrity by disavowing him. His honest answer— a man he cared about had said something hateful, which had hurt Justin to hear but hadn't made him stop caring about that man—was bound to disappoint in either case.

"You did just fine without me."

"It would still be nice to talk," Waxworth pressed on. "Maybe I could write something about you. I mean, you've made some pretty good predictions yourself, and unlike me you had skin on the line."

Justin was used to compliments like this, and he didn't take them too seriously. He'd been written up a few times in the financial press over the years, and the pieces always mentioned the fact that he'd left investment banking just before 9/11, which was seen as remarkably canny, since hedge funds like Eisen's had recovered more quickly than the banks after the attacks. No one suggested that he'd seen it coming, but people couldn't help giving him credit for the move anyway. They ascribed to him some talent for the bold choice. A few articles had made it sound as if he would otherwise have died that day, though everyone from the Q&M offices had survived. Seven years later, he'd unwound most of his own fund just a few months before the financial collapse. His charitable work had taken him off the financial pages, into the general press, where he was treated as a sort of preternatural genius, his story turned into a morality play. A self-made millionaire had raised himself from poverty and been rewarded for his decision to get up and walk away from the table. This all made good copy, particularly since it had coincided with Obama's campaign, for which Justin had hosted a fund-raiser. He was a minor avatar of the post-racial moment. Members of both parties had approached him about running for mayor when Bloomberg's term ran out, though he'd never publicly stated a political opinion in his life.

"I got pretty lucky, to be honest."

"That's probably true," Waxworth acknowledged. "But I've looked at some of the bets you made at DRE, and you really seemed to have some kind of edge. Of course that stuff's usually proprietary, but since you've quit the game, you're in an unusual position to give people an inside look at how you did it. I'd love to know."

If his tone had been different, Justin might have taken this for a threat. At the very least, he would have read into it some kind of innuendo. But it was spoken so guilelessly. Waxworth was genuinely curious to know how Justin had done it. Did he have no inkling of Eisen's reputation? Was it possible to be at once so smart and so naive?

"I'm not sure I'm ready to tell all," Justin said. "But if I change my mind I'll come straight to you."

Justin had first met Dan Eisen at one of those fund-raising galas where MDs buy tables and bring all their underlings, where everyone drinks too much and half the people don't know the name of the charity they're there to support. Late in the evening, he found himself in line at the bar with an uncomfortably overweight middle-aged man whose ill-fitting tux and skulking manner looked entirely out of place. The man asked politely what had brought Justin there. Kit had received some kind of award during dinner, and Justin somewhat drunkenly explained that he worked at her bank and also happened to be a close family friend.

"I've known her basically all my life," he said.

The man seemed interested by this, and he continued asking questions until they arrived at the front of the line, where he ordered himself a ginger ale. Before they parted ways, Justin handed over a brand new business card—he was in his fourth year at Q&M, and he'd just been promoted to associate—and raised his vodka tonic in salute.

Back at their table, Justin's one close buddy from work, another recently minted associate named Joe Ambrose, asked what he'd been discussing with Dan Eisen, which was how Justin learned that he'd been bragging about his insider status to one of the most successful hedge fund managers in the world. For the better part of a decade, Eisen had made more money than anyone else on the Street while remaining almost unknown outside the small circle that followed such things very closely. He didn't invest in fashionable restaurants or indie films. He didn't buy eight-figure Brâncuşis at auction. He didn't build Sagaponack McMansions that blighted the old money's views. His total lack of interest in the things that wealth could buy made him rather dull to the media outlets that dedicated themselves alternately to the celebration and condemnation of conspicuous consumption. He had no interest in playing guru, never went on TV to make bold predictions about where the market was headed, didn't put his name on ghostwritten books of investment advice. His quarterly reports were almost comically terse. *If you want a bedtime story,* he'd once begun a three-sentence investor letter, *read Dr. Seuss.*

Justin learned all this online in the days after their brief encounter. He also learned that Eisen didn't drink, which meant that Justin couldn't even reassure himself that his late-night boasting would be easily forgotten. In his embarrassment, he tried to forget the whole thing, so he was doubly surprised when he got an email a week later, inviting him to visit the Group DRE offices.

Eisen was like no one else Justin had ever met, a near-obese fifty-three-year-old City College grad from Bushwick, an orthodox Jew who walked around the office barefoot, in white undershirts and pressed jeans. Over lunch he asked Justin how much he knew about DRE.

"I just know you make a lot of money," Justin answered honestly.

Eisen shrugged appreciatively.

"I'm a humble stock picker. There aren't a lot of us around anymore."

Every fund was trying to get returns that were uncorrelated with market performance, but most of them did it with nontraditional investments: real estate, timber, currency arbitrage. Eisen made his money in old-fashioned equities. There was a widespread belief that the market had gotten too efficient to be beat consistently, but Eisen was disproving that.

"The market is only rational in the aggregate," he said. "On the individual level, people do stupid shit every day."

Investors overreacted to bad news. They made decisions with their emotions. A string of setbacks in some sector caused companies with strong fundamentals to be punished along with their peers. In the most extreme cases, assets could exceed market capitalization, which meant a company could be bought for less than its component parts were worth. This was transparently irrational. It amounted to accepting a ten-dollar bill in exchange for fifteen singles. Of course appearance couldn't dictate reality in the long run. Facts did win out in the end—"that's all the efficient-market hypothesis really means"—but in the meantime, the market was bound to be misunderstood by those who got stuck on the surface. There was money to be made by spotting these misunderstandings before the market corrected them. If you had enough capital to throw around, you could actually cause the correction. In which case, you were the one making the market efficient.

The philosophy behind this strategy obviously appealed to Eisen, who prided himself on being too rough around the edges for the old boys' network, and he expected it would appeal to Justin, too.

"I don't give a shit what Katherine Doyle thinks," he said pointedly after offering Justin a job. "If you're good, you're going to get paid. If you're not, you're going to get fired."

The base salary Eisen offered him was less than Justin was getting at Q&M, but a good DRE bonus was more than he'd make in a decade as an investment banker. If he did well enough, Eisen would seed a fund for him in five years, at which point seven- or eight-figure compensation might turn into nine. If he didn't do well, he would be out of a job, but this seemed a risk worth taking.

Eisen had found him at the right time: Justin was ready for a change. Kit had made clear when she gave him his first job out of college that she could only get him "into the pool," after which he would sink or swim on his own. The other junior analysts figured out pretty quickly that Justin had a prior relationship with the boss, but no one held it against him because he worked so hard. Many of them were living in the city for the first time, overwhelmed by all the opportunities. Justin was single—he intended to stay that way—and he had a handful of good friends he sometimes saw on the weekends. He didn't need to construct a social life. He simply put in more hours than the others. Everyone had known that Justin would get an offer at the end of their two-year program, and no one suggested that Kit would have to make it happen.

If anything, the ease with which he flourished at Q&M was worrying. He had great confidence in his abilities, but he was forced to admit that his competition wasn't as fierce as it might have been. After growing up in awe of the Doyles, he was shocked to realize that Q&M was in the second tier of investment banks. With his magna degree in economics from Georgetown, Justin could have gotten a first-tier offer if he'd known enough to seek one out, something he realized only after the fact. He was grateful for Kit's help, but he was starting to think that it had limited him in a way. He could never become as rich as Kit Doyle by working for her. Even if she one day passed the reins to him, as she sometimes hinted she would, the age of the family-run firm was over.

"We may be able to do a little better," she said vaguely when he told her he'd gotten an offer. "I just gave you a bump with this move to associate, and you know I can't play favorites."

"It's not about the money," Justin told her. "I need to find out if I can make it on my own."

This was meant to flatter her. For all her talk about sinking or swimming, she liked the fact that people thought of Justin as her protégé, that his success was a credit to her. Even if he went on to do great things somewhere else, it would always be known that she'd given him his start.

"Who have you been talking to?" she asked, clearly expecting to hear the name of another bank.

Her expression changed when he mentioned Eisen. It was common enough for young analysts to want hedge fund jobs, which were the quickest route to making extravagant amounts of money, but she obviously expected Justin to have other priorities.

"You've got to be careful with guys like that," she said. "They've got sharp elbows. I don't know if you're ready to play the game that rough."

As hard as it was to believe now, Justin hadn't known Eisen's reputation at the time. There might have been some whispers, particularly up at Kit's level, but they hadn't made their way into general circulation. Kit's reference to "sharp elbows" struck Justin as simple snobbery, perhaps with a hint of genteel anti-Semitism. She was making the very mistake that Eisen had warned him about—judging the unpolished surface instead of the truth at the core. He didn't tell her this, and she made no more suggestions of the sort when he announced a week later that he was accepting Eisen's offer, but he'd always sensed that he'd disappointed her. The fact that she never said as much—she never mentioned Eisen again until that night at the party—only confirmed the depth of that disappointment.

At the end of his first year at DRE, Justin received a big enough bonus to justify his decision, but he accepted it more in the way of encouragement than reward. The job was a grind, and his work was solid but unspectacular. He found the market pretty efficient after all. You had to do a lot of research, go down a lot of blind alleys, to identify where it was getting something wrong, and the corrections usually weren't that big. If you picked your spots and minimized your losses along the way, you could do a point or two better than an index, which was enough at least to keep the job. He didn't expect the same large bonus his second year, but he was astonished when Eisen told him that he wouldn't be getting one at all.

"I thought I was doing pretty well," he said.

"You get a salary for doing pretty well," Eisen answered. "You get a bonus for doing better than pretty well."

"I'm working my ass off."

Even as Justin said this, he knew it was a mistake. Eisen didn't care about effort or process or intentions. He cared about results.

"Maybe you need some help."

For a moment Justin thought he was being offered an assistant.

"I would appreciate that."

"Not from me," Eisen clarified with a disgusted laugh. "I thought you were a popular guy. Don't you have some friends who could help you out?"

Dan Eisen was perhaps the most direct man Justin had ever met, and now he was talking in riddles.

"What do you mean?" Justin asked.

"I thought you had lots of friends. I thought Kit Doyle was your fucking den mother or something. Maybe I was wrong about that. If you don't have friends, you might think about finding some. They might give you the help you need."

Eisen explained what he meant by a "friend," how a real one differed from some random schmuck with a tip. People tried to give you tips almost constantly in this business. Most of the time the difficulty was getting out of their way. A few made surprisingly blunt offers— they had something valuable, and they wanted to know what you would give them for it—but many didn't have any clear idea of what they were doing or what they wanted in return. Maybe it was enough to feel important or to be in good with someone important. Some just started talking after a few drinks, seemingly without premeditation. Their eagerness to violate whatever minor fiduciary trust had been placed in them seemed almost pathological. They couldn't stand to let secrets go to waste. Eisen told him to be wary of such people, who were apt to be as sloppy with everyone else as they were with you. What you wanted in this game was a real friend, someone who had as much to lose as you did, and so could be trusted.

Justin nodded uneasily at the end of this speech, and he waited for Eisen to dismiss him.

"Do you think you're too good for the work we do here?" Eisen asked abruptly.

"Of course not," Justin said.

"Are you afraid that Kit Doyle wouldn't approve? Is that the problem?"

This time Justin didn't answer, so Eisen went on: "Let me tell you something. It's very easy to stay on the high road when you were born up there. But that road was built by people who got plenty dirty in the process. They didn't have a name for what we do when Kit Doyle's father and grandfather were doing it. They just called it 'business.' It happened in the locker room at some racquet club where Jews and blacks need not apply. It's only when people like you and me showed up that they all decided the game had rules. 'Fair play' is just another word for pulling the ladder up behind you. Meanwhile all these so-called clean shops give their favored clients first crack at the IPO they're putting together, or they pump up stocks they know are pieces of shit because they need to get them off their books, and they have the balls to question the way I run things here? Fuck them. Are you with me, Price?"

"I'm with you."

"All right. Go out there and get to work."

Justin stood up and started walking to the door. After he'd taken a few steps, Eisen called him back.

"You want to keep your hands clean in this business, buy a fucking pair of gloves. You want to stay pure, join a monastery. You understand?"

"I understand," Justin told him, and he walked out the door.

The conversation had saddened him, though perhaps not for the right reasons. He'd been sold a vision of the world, one in which those who could see the facts as they really were could succeed, regardless of where they came from or how they looked. All he'd wanted when he came to DRE was the chance to compete on a level playing field. But Eisen was telling him that this *was* the level playing field, and Justin knew that in some sense Eisen was right. He'd always found something canny, even calculated, about Eisen's lack of polish, and now he saw how it made the refinement of others look suspicious, a self-serving put-on. He thought of Kit's remarks about Eisen's sharp elbows and the rough way he played the game. Instead of feeling that Kit had been vindicated, he thought she'd only confirmed Eisen's point. That afternoon, he emailed Joe Ambrose, who was still at Q&M, and invited him out for a drink. A year later, his total compensation cracked eight figures for the first time.

When Kit finally appeared, she was already in hostess mode, taking breakfast orders, which she relayed to Marinela before going to rouse Margo and Frank so they could all eat together. In the meantime, Lucy returned from her run, and Justin could see the whole morning slipping away in front of him. After they ate, they would lounge on the lawn or by the pool until Eddie arrived, and it would be impossible to get Kit alone without attracting attention.

Marinela reappeared in the doorway as they were finishing breakfast, and Justin saw his chance.

"Mrs. Doyle," she said. "It's Edward on the phone."

Justin waited a minute before causally following Kit inside. Nearly every room had a phone, but Marinela would have answered in the kitchen, and he guessed that this was where Kit had taken the call. He stood near the door, ready to catch her as she came back out. When she did, she walked by as though she didn't see him at all, so he reached out awkwardly for her.

"Apparently he's not coming out today," she said. "But he won't explain why. You'd think he'd want to spend some time with his family."

"This must be a tough adjustment for him," Justin answered.

He wanted to tell her that Eddie was fine, but he had no idea whether this was true. He'd been avoiding Eddie since the party, out of an abundance of caution.

"He sounded pretty worked up," Kit told him.

She half turned toward the door, though Justin's hand was still resting on her arm.

"So long as I've got you here," he said. "I wanted to mention something."

"What is it?"

"I had a drink the other night with an old friend of mine."

Kit turned back toward him, recognizing that whatever he had to say would take more than a moment. As briefly as possible, he recounted his evening with Chloe Porter.

They'd barely sat down when Chloe mentioned that she'd been thinking about leaving Celsia, and she'd wondered whether Justin had any advice. Not that things weren't going well, she'd been quick to add. In fact, it was a very exciting time at the company.

"Is that right?" Justin had asked, in a tone of mild curiosity.

"Very exciting," she stressed.

"I'm surprised to hear it, given how tough the market is right now."

"In fact, there's a big announcement coming. But you'll have to read about that in a few weeks."

She took a long sip of wine. Justin didn't want to play this game, but she obviously intended to make him.

"Your email came at a good time," he said. "My fund is basically shut down, but Eisen is looking to make a few hires, and I'd be happy to put in a word. They'd be lucky to speak to someone with your experience in biotech."

They talked about different opportunities while they finished the bottle, and Justin kept everything appropriately vague. After he'd ordered a second, he pressed her about this big announcement. She made a brief show of reluctance before giving up everything.

"The Randolphs"—this was the family that owned the controlling shares of Celsia, the founder's grandchildren—"have decided to move forward as a closely held. In the current environment, with capital all dried up and investors feeling so skittish, they think they're better off not having to worry about the market. The board is going to be approving a major stock buyback at the next meeting. The votes are lined up. I'm already drafting the press materials. Too bad they enlisted me for that," she added, in case Justin had missed the significance of any of this. "I could have made a killing, but they've put a buy freeze on insiders."

As Justin recounted all this to Kit, he left out the way he'd coaxed the information from Chloe and any suggestion that he'd gone to meet her for the purpose of gathering it. An old friend had committed a drunken indiscretion. When he'd finished, Kit looked blankly at him, as though confused by the anecdote.

"Maybe we can talk about it some other time?"

"I'm only mentioning it now because the board is meeting at the end of the month."

Kit flinched, and her pale cheeks showed a blush.

"And you thought I might want to know before then?"

She raised her voice as she spoke, but she looked more embarrassed than anything else.

"I thought it couldn't hurt," Justin said.

"We all have our ups and downs in this business. I'm sorry I gave you the idea that we were that hard up."

Justin wanted to say more, to explain himself somehow, but Marinela interrupted them on her way in from clearing the table, and Kit pulled herself from Justin's grip. He followed her outside, where Frank was holding court, expounding on the designated hitter rule as an example of Marxist alienation from holistic labor. Justin had heard this theory before, but everything old became new again when Frank had a fresh audience. The Waxworths seemed suitably impressed, though Margo was retreating with her book to the pool. Justin followed her around the side of the house but continued past the pool, toward the front lawn.

He stood for a moment looking back at everyone, briefly moved—these moments had become more and more rare over the years, though they never stopped entirely—by the improbable fact that he'd wound up in this place. He continued on and soon arrived at the freestanding garage that stood a few hundred feet from the house. The garage had an attic space that was mostly used for storage by the gardener, where Justin and Eddie had sometimes gone to smoke stale cigarettes they hid away from year to year. In high school, Blakeman would come over from his family's place in Sag Harbor with a bag of pot, and they would smoke a joint there before going back outside to hit tennis balls or shoot hoops. Long before any of them had their licenses, they took turns driving the old Jaguar up and down the driveway. During the school year, Justin was always so careful to stay out of trouble, acutely aware that the consequences were different for him than they were for his friends. But here he'd felt he could do anything they did. Those unsupervised summer days were probably the happiest of his life.

When Eddie had invited him for the first time at the end of sixth grade, Justin hadn't thought that spending three weeks in

Bridgehampton would be possible, but his mother had been relieved to have him out of the city and under a watchful eye. Only after he arrived did Justin discover that Frank and Kit stayed out only on weekends. They returned to Manhattan each Sunday afternoon, leaving the children under Angela's watch. She was mostly concerned with Margo, which meant that until Frank and Kit returned on Friday night, the boys had less supervision than Justin would have had at home, where at least the woman from downstairs checked on him a few times a day while his parents were at work. Concealing this fact from his mother seemed like a kind of favor to her, since it made everyone's lives so much easier if he stayed there. He came home safely at the end of the month, and she was happy to let him go back the next summer. He'd spent some time at the house—not always weeks, but always more than a few days—every summer since.

The Doyles' generosity, their eagerness to treat him as part of the family, had often puzzled him. What had he done to deserve it? Sometimes a cynical voice told him that Kit and Frank felt guilty about leaving their children unattended for so much of the summer. Having Justin there assuaged this guilt twice over—Eddie had a companion, while the family was doing a good deed for a scholarship kid. Perhaps there was something to this, but so what if there was? Plenty of people in the Doyles' position didn't even feel this guilt. The family's ideal of noblesse oblige was easy to mock, but the alternative wasn't a world without great wealth; it was a world where the wealthy felt no obligations.

They had given him a lot over the years, and they'd asked for only one thing in return: he had to want to be like them. In his aspiration, he had to confirm their view of their way of life—above all, the view that they were something other than just rich, that they were better than people like Dan Eisen. Was this part of why he'd chosen this means of helping Kit? It had seemed there were no other options, but was that really true? Did some part of him want to prove that when push came to shove she would play the game the same way he and Eisen played it?

The wooden stairs were missing boards on two steps, which he skipped on his way up. The dirty windows didn't catch the morning sun, and the attic space was dusty and dark. Justin stood still while his eyes adjusted. He hadn't been up there in years. By the looks of it no one else had either. He could almost see himself and Eddie, laid out on the floor, looking up at the cobwebs in the rafters. On one such stoned afternoon, after Blakeman had driven home, Justin had kissed Eddie.

He'd been thinking of doing it for years, always knowing it was impossible, until finally not doing it felt even more impossible. It was the first time he'd tried such a thing since the adolescent fumbling with Terrance that had caused them both so many problems. He and Terrance had kissed perhaps a dozen times, touched each other maybe three or four. They'd been too young even to get off; they'd just liked the feel of each other's hands. They'd never exactly been caught, and Justin still wasn't sure how word had gotten out, but it had, first to other kids at MS 61, who began to beat them both, then to Pastor George, and from there to their mothers, after which they couldn't see each other again.

"You're getting a clean slate now," his mother had said when he'd gotten accepted to St. Albert's, and though she didn't elaborate they'd both known what she meant. He'd promised himself he wouldn't try anything like that again, but by the time he'd kissed Eddie in the garage, he knew his nature wouldn't change.

For just a moment, Eddie had seemed to kiss him back, perhaps still deciding what he thought of the thing, or maybe just being kind. Then he'd stopped.

"I don't like it," he'd said.

There was nothing judgmental in his voice. He was just saying it wasn't for him. Somehow that had made it all so much worse, because Justin hadn't been experimenting to see how it felt. He wanted Eddie to love him the way he loved Eddie. Justin had cried—as he was crying now, standing in that dusty room—and Eddie had put his arm around him, comforting his best friend with a gesture that was also the drawing of a line. Later Justin suspected that Eddie had even provoked him into acting, in order to put an end to his hints, to tell him outright that he wasn't interested.

In college he'd had a few boyfriends, usually guys like himself who were neither exactly out nor exactly in, but things could only get so serious if you weren't willing to tell your family or even most of your friends. Only a few people besides Eddie knew for sure. Blakeman knew, though Justin had never told him and he was fairly sure Eddie hadn't either. Blakeman just knew these sorts of things. Occasionally he was referred to in the press as a "bachelor," which seemed to have a knowing spin to it, but he wasn't famous enough for anyone to bother outing him. He went online every once in a while. He'd spend the occasional night at a guy's place, but never have one over. Would he want more than this if he could have it? Perhaps staying in the closet was just a convenient way to avoid admitting that he was still in love with his best friend.

He was sorry that Eddie wouldn't be coming out that day, but his disappointment felt somehow unearned, since he hadn't come for Eddie's sake. He walked down the stairs and stepped back into the sunlight. He turned toward the Doyles' house and, beyond the bay, his own, just out of view. He thought of his boat, floating out there or perhaps already run aground on some neighbor's lawn. Now he needed to find a way home.

4.

"Did I win?" Amy asked as soon as she picked up the phone.

Margo stood outside the Candy Kitchen on Main Street, waiting for the bus back to New York.

"I'm not actually sure."

Inviting Sam and Lucy out to Bridgehampton had been Amy's idea. When Margo suggested the possibility to her mother, she hadn't expected Kit to follow up on it, and she certainly hadn't expected Sam to accept. Margo had had no desire to meet Sam's wife, and she couldn't imagine why he would want to bring the two of them together. She'd taken the decision as further evidence that Sam thought their friendship was entirely innocent. Amy had a different interpretation. Sam needed to see Margo so badly that he would even involve his wife. She'd bet Margo a lunch that something would happen that weekend.

"How can you still not be sure?"

Margo gave her a brief rundown of the day—the Waxworths' arrival, Justin's surprise appearance, Lucy's game sparring with Frank, the usual descent to the firepit for after-dinner drinks.

"So we're all sitting there, and Justin decides to take Lucy off on some adventure, as though I'd enlisted his help. Five minutes later, my parents go to bed. Without any intervention, we're sitting there alone."

Sam had hardly reacted when Margo moved into the empty chair beside him.

"My father was happy with the profile," she told him. "He would never say that himself, but I could tell."

"I'm glad to hear it," he said. "Though I'm not sure I'm supposed to admit that."

"How did you feel about it?"

Sam looked into the fire and squinted thoughtfully.

"I can't really tell. Getting into print was supposed to be the big goal, the gold standard. But I can spend two or three hours on a web post and generate a day of conversation. By that metric, a piece you spend weeks writing should be talked about for a year. Instead, it gets the same day's attention that everything else does. If that's all anything gets right now, the extra effort seems a bit pointless. I put in twenty times the work for the same number of Teeser shares."

"Aren't there other reasons to write?"

"The money's better in print, if that's what you mean. But it's not twenty times better. Anyway, I'm on contract."

"I don't mean money. Don't you get satisfaction out of doing your job well?"

"Sure I do. Teeser shares just happen to be the measure of how well my job is done."

"That may be Mario Adrian's measure, but is it yours?"

"He's my boss. By definition, his measure of how I do my job is the one that counts."

"There isn't any larger goal besides pleasing your boss?"

"A book deal, I guess, but lately I'm not even sure about that. I'd probably work for three years and get the same one day of attention."

"I'm not talking about attention or money or approval. What about aspiring to some kind of greatness—for the sake of greatness itself?"

Why was she asking this question? It was the kind of thing Richard would ask in his most self-important moments. Did she even care whether Sam Waxworth wanted to be great?

"I honestly don't know what that word means. When we say that a ballplayer was great, we mean that he was a historical outlier in his ability to help his team score runs, or to stop the other team from scoring. There's a context that gives his performance a purpose, and we can measure how well he did with that context in mind. It's nice when he does it with a little bit of style or grace, like DiMaggio or Mays, but ultimately the goal isn't to look good; it's to outscore the other team. In the game I'm playing right now, the goal is to get shared. I do want to be great at that. If I get another job somewhere, I might have a different goal, and I'll try to be great at that, too. But there is no abstract quality called 'greatness.'"

"There isn't any larger purpose to it all?"

Sam laughed.

"You sound like your father. Baseball is a wonderful game. It's endlessly interesting. The pace bores a lot of people, but to me it allows for real attention. There is a level of strategy that isn't possible in faster-paced sports. At the same time, there are still moments of great spontaneous beauty. The sheer difficulty of it—the skill involved in throwing a ball ninety-five miles an hour and hitting a target six feet six inches away with exact precision, and the skill involved in swinging a round bat and hitting that ball—these things are a joy to watch. I love the game. I'd wager I love it every bit as much as your father does. But what does baseball mean? The answer is: nothing. It's a game, a fun way to pass the time. To your father that isn't enough. Baseball can't just be enjoyable; it has to be *significant*. If baseball—or poetry, or whatever— gives you pleasure, that's great. It doesn't need to mean something on top of that."

"So poetry's just a game, too?"

"That's a great compliment coming from me. I love games."

"But if none of it means anything, what's the point?"

"Isn't the point just to keep us entertained?"

"To pass the time until we die."

"You make it sound like a bad thing. If that's all we've got, we might as well enjoy it."

"And politics—just a game, too?"

He seemed to struggle briefly with this.

"Some of the things that interest me about politics are gamelike, I'll admit. But politics is different, because it has a real, measurable effect on the material conditions of people's lives."

"So that's what actually matters—material conditions."

"For most people. Maybe that's hard for you to believe, because you've never had to worry about them, but it's tough to make a life for yourself if you're always worried about your next meal."

"But all those lives must be games, too? Something to be enjoyed—or not—until they're over?"

"What's the alternative? The world behind the world? And what's behind that? If that world gives this one meaning, what gives that one meaning? I know where that eternal regression ends—with a great father figure waving his hands in the sky to make it all matter. If that's my other option, I'll go with life's a game."

That's when she moved from her seat to his lap.

"Well, if it's just a game," she said, before she started kissing him.

What had come over her? She'd been a bit drunk, but she couldn't blame it on that. Perhaps the audacity was part of the appeal. There was an element of danger, but danger of an artificial kind, since nothing was really being risked. They'd be able to see the boat returning long before they'd be visible from the water. She hadn't done it with any foresight, and she hadn't known as she did it how he would respond. She still didn't exactly know, since it was all over before it began.

"As soon as I moved into action," she told Amy, "I heard a voice calling my name. It was Justin coming out of the woods."

By the time Lucy followed Justin into view, Margo was already up from the chair. She felt not what she imagined she ought to feel—embarrassment and, possibly, remorse—but frustration, and anger at these agents of her frustration. Why had they returned from the wrong direction? Had the whole outing been an elaborate trap? Lucy hardly seemed capable of such subterfuge, and Justin wouldn't knowingly be a party to it, but Margo couldn't quite believe the story of the lost boat as Justin explained it to her. She looked at Sam, who seemed only confused, as though she had truly shocked him. To her they had been heading toward this point for a long time, but apparently it hadn't seemed that way to him.

"I still don't know where we stand."

She told Amy about the rest of the weekend, how they'd all just pretended that nothing had happened. She hadn't been alone with Sam again before he and Lucy left on Sunday afternoon.

"So what are you going to do now?" Amy asked.

"I don't know. I was hoping you could help with that."

Margo and Amy had been best friends since first grade. They'd gone to Melwood together for twelve years, and they'd stayed nearly as close after Amy went off to Middlebury and Margo to Yale. In many ways, Margo was a different person with Amy than she was with her college and grad school friends, with whom she shared intellectual pursuits and sensibilities, not personal history and milieu.

It wasn't that she regressed to some earlier iteration of herself. She'd always been a different person with Amy, which was precisely what made spending time with her so comforting. They had no shared interests anymore, they'd both lost touch with most of their other Melwood friends, and they had almost nothing to do with each other's adult lives, except as spectators. They discussed their problems as though recapping episodes of a long-running show that they both loved but only one of them still followed closely.

They talked about their jobs, their parents, but more than any-thing they talked about guys. Their friendship, Margo sometimes thought, would barely pass the Bechdel test. She'd called Amy on her way home from her first meeting with Sam. At the time, she hadn't known that she'd ever see this boy again, but their tour through the Met was the most interesting thing that had happened to her since she'd come home. When Amy suggested after their second meeting that Margo text Sam the next day and claim to be in his neighbor-hood for lunch, Margo had taken her advice, as she usually did on such matters, though she hadn't really known where she wanted any of this to go. Not only was he married, but he wasn't really her type. If anything, this had been part of his appeal; it meant that nothing would get too complicated. She wanted to pass some time while she figured her life out, not to get stuck in another trap from which she would need violently to extricate herself.

So long as Lucy was in Madison, it had been possible to treat this all as harmless fun. Sam was killing time until his wife arrived, she was recovering from her disaster with Richard, and they both needed some distraction. She liked the fact that their relationship had a built-in expiration date. She wasn't sure exactly when she realized that this fiction could no longer be maintained, but when she did it only confirmed what Amy had been telling her all along. In Amy's view, you didn't spend several afternoons a week walking around aimlessly with a person you didn't want to fuck, no matter how good the conversation.

When Lucy did finally arrive, Margo waited for the inevitable slackening of tension between them. Sam would stop calling, take more time to return her texts; eventually they would stop seeing each other entirely. Either that or some crisis would force the issue. The one possibility she hadn't anticipated was that things would just con-tinue as they'd been. Sam didn't seem to see any problem with leav-ing his wife at home in a strange city while he wandered for hours with another girl. They'd chosen to keep seeing each other when the natural course of things had put a stop to it. It couldn't continue this way forever—at some point they would both have to go on with their real lives—but she didn't see how it would end. At least now, something had definitively happened.

"My bus is here," she said before Amy could deliver any more guidance.

She got off the Jitney at Seventy-Seventh Street and walked home. There was nothing really bringing her back to New York, no reason she couldn't have stayed out east with her parents, except that she couldn't quite bear the peculiar decadence of spending three weeks sitting by the pool. Days of nothing but *chaise longueurs*. If she was going to waste her time, she would do it in slightly less luxury.

Stepping inside the house, she almost tripped over a green army-issue duffel in the front hall. She was still looking down at it when Eddie appeared with a second, smaller, bag. Had he been called back up? She wasn't even sure whether that was still possible.

"We were expecting you this weekend," she said. "Justin came over."

"He didn't tell me he was coming," Eddie answered.

This seemed strange to Margo, but she didn't press the point.

"What's all this?" she asked, waving at his bags.

"I'm moving out."

"What happened?"

He laughed.

"Nothing happened. I'm thirty-five years old. Do I need a reason to move out of my parents' house? You might consider it yourself one of these days."

"But why right now, when everyone's gone? Are you running away from us?"

"An opportunity came up, a place on the Lower East Side, and I needed to jump on it right away."

He slung the small bag over his shoulder and picked up the large duffel with his other hand. There was a grace to his movements that Margo had never noticed before. He stood as though at attention before dropping both bags again and reaching out to take her in a hug. When he'd gone, Margo closed the door behind him and turned back to face the empty house.

Now she wished she'd stayed out east. Her parents would be there for the rest of the month, and Marinela would stay with them until she took her annual trip home to Latvia. It always gave her an eerie feeling to be alone in this house. The place had usually been so crowded throughout her childhood, and even when the rest of the family was gone, there had been someone paid to look after her. Though an empty house might have its uses, she thought idly, if she ever saw Sam again.

She went upstairs to unpack her bag and put her clothes away. When she'd finished, she opened Richard's anthology and flipped through the pages, looking as much at her old notes and underlinings as at the poems themselves. She'd been through the book so many times that even snippets brought with them entire continents of feeling, but she could view them only from a distance, like some Cortés staring in awe at a shoreline she was destined never to reach. Reading poetry—reading it *properly*—required more attention than she seemed to possess at the moment. She didn't have the resources for a proper encounter. Wordsworth had saved Mill by when he'd grown weary of the world. Where did one turn after growing weary of Wordsworth?

Her father had bought her this anthology around the time they'd started memorizing poems together. Margo hadn't immediately connected the editor credited on its enormous cover with her parents' friend of that name. He didn't stick out in any way from the other adults who crowded her house every few months. But at their next big party, Frank had sent her to get the book from her room to be inscribed, and he'd encouraged her to recite something for Dr. Harvey. Gradually Margo came to understand that this man was something of a celebrity within a world she had vague ideas of one day inhabiting, just as her parents were celebrities in theirs.

"Margo has started writing poetry," Kit had told Richard at another one of those nights. Margo was in high school by then, and she'd been horrified. She knew that she hadn't yet written anything that Richard Harvey would recognize as poetry. But he'd been kind about her ambitions, taken them seriously, and this had given her a chance to let him know that she'd read a few of his books. In response, he'd given her his email address and invited her to send him some of her work.

Of course he was only being polite—she had been taught at an early age to recognize adult politeness and not to impose on it—but she'd emailed when applying to college the next year, and he'd taken her for lunch at the university where he taught. Though she'd decided on Yale, they'd kept in touch throughout her undergraduate years. He came to New Haven for a conference when she was a senior and invited her to the dinner that followed, where she sat between him and various junior professors, postgrad fellows, and graduate students desperate for his attention. Among these was Margo's boyfriend, Greg, whom she'd met when he TA'ed her Modernism class. (Margo had never in her life dated a boy her own age.) At the end of dinner, Richard told Margo that she absolutely had to come study with him next year, though she hadn't mentioned any plans to apply to graduate schools.

"If you reject me a second time," he said, "I won't ever recover."

The amorous implications were barely subtextual, but Greg made sure to bring them fully to the surface when they got back to his apartment that night. He trusted that Margo knew of Richard Harvey's reputation for romantic entanglements with his students. (*Romantic Entanglements* was the title of Richard's groundbreaking study of Shelley; the kind of men Margo dated were never too jealous to hit on the proper allusion.) In fact, Margo did know of this reputation—she was fairly sure that her own undergraduate thesis advisor, an associate professor in her midthirties, had been entangled with Richard around the time that Margo was first making conversation with him in her parents' back garden—but she didn't think of herself as eligible for such attention. Greg was being absurd; Richard was closer to a father figure than an object of desire.

How she would come to regret this line of defense! She'd been in graduate school for several years before she did, indeed, find herself entangled, and when word reached Greg, now tenure tracked at a second-tier land grant university in a right-angled Midwestern state, he'd had the remark carefully preserved and ready to hand, along with his own marginal gloss, viz: *Perhaps it's your father you really want to fuck.* It was designed to hurt and briefly had, before Margo dismissed it as pseudo-Freudian rubbish. She didn't think of her father when she thought of Richard; she thought, well, of Richard, with his tobacco-thickened baritone and his dramatic gray-black mane, his distracted air and the way he had, just when you thought he was paying no attention at all, of introducing some clarification or distinction into the conversation that proved he had been attending to every word you said.

But she remembered Greg's remark when she got back to campus after the Ballpark Incident and discovered that her loss of faith in her father had somehow translated into a loss of interest in Richard Harvey. She'd gone to lunch with him the day after she got back, and he seemed utterly transformed. Margo understood it was just her perception of him that had changed, but this only made the alteration more disturbing. They didn't mention her father's downfall. It was possible Richard knew nothing about it. He was proudly apolitical—his interest was in the permanent things—and he studiously avoided the corners of the media where Frank was then being vivisected. But throughout that meal, all she could see when she looked at Richard was Frank. Richard was solicitous, he was kind, he was interested, but he was another old man who wanted to be impressed by her. Another old man she could no longer take seriously.

Their arrangement was sufficiently vague that she could put him off for a while without any grand explanation, which is what she did after that lunch. When she told him she wasn't feeling well, he wished her a speedy recovery and invited her to dinner after Thanksgiving. She accepted this invitation, mostly because turning him down felt like too much work. The intervening weeks passed very strangely. Her days lacked all texture, and without it there was no way to get any grip on them. They simply slipped past. She felt as she imagined the devoutly religious feel when they have suddenly lost faith. She was like an actress wandering a stage set, waiting for the production to begin. All of the elements for a world were there, except whatever extra thing made that world a reality.

By the night of the dinner, her feelings hadn't changed, and she decided to use the evening to break things off with him. She was prepared for him to be wounded, but she was equally prepared for him to be relieved. She thought he was probably nearly ready for his next entanglement. He might even have planned this dinner as a kind of farewell, in which case she need do nothing but listen and pretend a certain amount of brave disappointment. She was prepared for nearly anything but what actually happened: he asked her to marry him.

"You're joking," she'd told him.

"Not in the slightest."

"You hardly know me."

"I've known you all your life."

"Don't put it that way, like you were grooming me in my pubescence. It creeps me out."

"I just meant, my dear, that I recognized your precocious mind long ago. Obviously the physical attraction came much later." He took a deep breath. "You should know that I've never done this before. I'm truly in love, and I want to spend what's left of my life with you."

She was too shocked even to attempt talking him out of this strange notion, and so she agreed instead to spend some time with it and give him an answer after the holiday. She spent most of the winter break composing an emailed response. She knew she ought to tell him in person, but he would interrupt, contradict, attempt to move her from her spots. She didn't have the strength to resist. She worked very hard at capturing the right tone. She loved him too, in her way. His offer was not without its appeal. Certainly it was flattering. But she had no idea how she wanted to spend the rest of her life. She wasn't sure she was going to get her degree. She wasn't even entirely sure she still cared about poetry. He would get over all this soon enough. No doubt he'd had his heart broken before, and he'd survived. If not, well, he had broken plenty in his time. Perhaps he was due. (This last was meant to sound not cold but irreverent. She refused to take too seriously the desperate dance of an aging satyr. If she didn't stay light on her feet, she was apt to get trampled.)

The day before classes resumed, she hit send, and he appeared that night in the entryway of her apartment building. It was a mile and a half from campus, not a place that famous professors visited lightly. She'd been reading by the window, and she'd watched with some shock as he approached, the long dress coat that no grad student would ever wear pulled tightly around him. She worried that he might spot her, but he had no idea which window was hers: he'd never come to visit her before. She watched him take his phone from his coat pocket and call her, and she silenced her own phone before it rang. He hung up, and he yelled in the courtyard until she came down. He did this quite enthusiastically, as though a willingness to make a fool of himself would count in his favor. For two hours they stood in the snow, talking things out. She thought they'd come to an understanding by the time he left, but all that work was apparently undone overnight, for in the morning the emails began. He sent five the first day, ten the next. All variations on a theme. He was a tattered coat upon a stick, she his singing school. She was treating his life as triviality. Her cunt and consciousness had taken permanent residence in his soul. The fourth email of the third day—the most insistent, most graphic, most deranged to that point—she decided to forward to the chair of the English department. As she started to write his address, her email auto-completed the department list, which had somewhere on the order of eight hundred recipients—students and faculty, interested alums, and some number of local residents who audited classes and regularly attended department events.

Margo looked at the email address and imagined hitting send. She told herself it had been a terrible mistake, a technological cautionary tale. An astonishing bit of carelessness. She hadn't meant Richard any harm, she'd just wanted to be left alone. She would never have forwarded the email to this address on purpose. If there were only some way to unsend it, she would give anything to make it happen, but the past could not be rewritten. She savored briefly this delicious regret over something she hadn't even done, and just when it started going stale in her mouth, she clicked send. The instant she did, she heard Greg's words, with a new twist to them: *Perhaps it's your father you really want to fuck.*

Two days later she was called into a meeting with the chair of the department, the dean of the graduate school, and a woman who was introduced only by name but whom Margo understood to be a Title IX compliance officer of some kind. This woman, clearly in charge of the proceedings, asked whether Margo wanted to lodge a complaint against Richard Harvey. Everyone in the room understood how much trouble Margo could cause them all, but Margo also understood the trouble she would be given in return. Besides, she wasn't even angry at Richard.

"Not at all," Margo said. "We had a consensual relationship that ended badly, but nothing that requires intervention. I'm sorry for the bother that email caused."

Her attitude was received by all parties with obvious relief. Now the department chair spoke, beginning in a conciliatory tone.

"Your apology is appreciated," he said. "Since you raised the matter, I might as well note that the bother caused has indeed been considerable. I'm glad you don't mean to create any more of it. To that end, it hardly seems practical for you and Professor Harvey both to remain on campus for the time being. Needless to say, Professor Harvey's abrupt departure would be far more disruptive to the department as a whole, so I'm proposing that you take this semester off."

She couldn't believe what she was hearing. It seemed too late to say that Richard had been harassing her, to bring up the dozen other emails she'd received from him that week, to mention the fact that at least three quarters of the people in the room already knew: that she was just the latest of dozens of students Richard had fucked.

"I'm getting punished for this?"

"This is not a punishment," the untitled woman rushed to put in. "It is simply a proposed solution to a delicate situation. You will not be penalized in any way for dropping your teaching credits."

Margo should have been furious at the injustice of it all, but she was relieved instead. She'd somehow been granted the thing she'd been looking for: some room to breathe. So she came home—more like a man flying from something that he dreads than one who sought the thing he loved.

She'd told herself that she would treat the time as a kind of course release, get a few chapters drafted. But she'd hardly done any relevant reading since then, and she was slowly coming to realize that academic life held no appeal for her. Perhaps it never had. She hadn't really considered going to graduate school until Richard brought it up—insisted on it, actually—and even then she hadn't been sold, until she'd mentioned the possibility to her mother, who'd said that her trust might cover her tuition.

"I thought I couldn't have that money until I was older?" Margo had said.

"Not the principal," Kit explained, "but Grable might let you use some of the income."

Ted Grable was an old family lawyer and the trustee named in her grandfather's will. When Margo met with him, he confirmed that income from the trust could be spent on her "education, health, and welfare." Tuition certainly qualified, he said. So long as she was enrolled, the trust might cover living expenses, too. Naturally, this had made the decision easier.

Once she'd enrolled, Richard had made a future in academia seem inevitable. She was a reader of genius. She was destined for a life of the mind. This had been nice to hear, but it became harder to believe once she knew that he'd wanted to fuck her all along. So what was the alternative?

On their second or third walk together, she'd explained all this to Sam. Having already admitted why she'd left school, she found that the rest of it came naturally.

"Do you really need a graduate degree to be a poet?" he'd asked.

How could she tell him at this point that it had been years since she'd written poetry? She'd filled old marble notebooks with verse as a schoolgirl, but she'd given that up long ago—in fact, right around the time that her mother had told Richard that she was a poet. It had been a private habit, and it had not survived this outing. If she were to write now, she wouldn't know how to begin.

"You need a degree to teach."

"Do you want to teach?

"What if I'm not good enough to be a poet?"

Sam laughed, not unkindly.

"I'm afraid I'm not in a position to judge that."

She appreciated this admission. It was true, of course. Although he was theoretically a writer by profession, Sam was the least literary man Margo had ever taken up. This was part of what made her feelings for him so confusing.

He listened in a different way than the other men Margo knew. It wasn't a matter of courtesy or good breeding. His empiricism committed him to gathering evidence before he could proceed. Whatever synthesis went on could happen only after the data was in hand. Men like Richard and her father used ideas rather than facts as their raw materials. They were interested in testing their notions against hers, arguing them out. They listened, but mostly they were listening for a point they could pick up and make their own. Attentive but impatient, they waited with arms outstretched for her to pass the conversational baton. This approach had its excitements, but there was also something tyrannical about it. If it brought you places where you could never arrive on your own, they weren't always the places you'd set out to go. Sometimes they weren't even in the right direction. These men were capable of surprising Margo in stimulating ways, but they refused ever to be surprised by her. They could be indulgently amused, they could be impressed, they could admire her precocity, but they could not admit that she'd had an idea that hadn't occurred to them long before.

Sam seemed constantly surprised. And he offered up all the facts of his own life without any apparent concern for what impression they made. He told her about his mother, his absent father, the childhood hours he'd spent reading her father's books. He talked about his work for the *Interviewer*, about the response his latest piece was getting or his idea for the next one. She wasn't sure when these things got written, unless he never slept. She'd stay up talking with him well into the night, and she'd wake to see his new post already making the rounds on Teeser.

They went to a lot of restaurants. They ate meals, downed coffee, but they were almost never truly alone. They avoided even the most incidental physical contact. No matter how passionate their conversation became, they conducted it as though through some protective barrier.

One day they ate lunch at an order-by-number Chinese food joint on Second Avenue, and Margo had laughed when the fortune cookies arrived.

"Maybe this ought to be your business," she said. "Probabilistic fortunes."

Sam opened his cookie, looked at the paper inside and said, "In fifty-seven percent of simulations, true happiness lies in wisdom."

Margo opened her own.

"There is a one-in-three chance that you are about to embark on a great adventure."

They both laughed again, but when Sam tossed his fortune onto his styrofoam plate to be thrown out along with his sesame chicken, Margo discreetly tucked hers into her pocket. She still had the fortune now, in the bottom drawer of the dresser in her room, the drawer that held her old poetry notebooks and various bits of memorabilia from her life. Her tendency to save such things was another habit held in common with her father, though where she had just one drawer he had entire file cabinets filled with programs and scorecards.

She closed Richard's anthology and went to that drawer. She pulled out the fortune and she smiled, looking at it. She could see now that she had allowed herself to start liking Sam more than she'd realized. She would be sorry if it turned out that she had succeeded in putting this thing to an end.

But so it seemed that she had, for she didn't hear from him in the days that followed. More than anything, she didn't want to fall back into the state she'd been in on the day she'd met him for the first time. She didn't want to spend all her time lying in bed or on her floor, flipping through pages. She tried as often as possible to get out of the house. At night, she caught up with friends she should have been seeing since she got home. For three straight days she took the bus across town to catch the Satyajit Ray retrospective at Lincoln Center. On the third day—a week and a half after her return—she came out of a screening of *Charulata* to find a text from Sam: *Are you around tomorrow afternoon?*

As if they'd still been seeing each other nearly every day. Something perverse in her wanted to tell him she was busy. Did he think it would be that easy to strike things back up?

Sure, she wrote instead. *Why don't you come over to the house?*

In all the time they'd spent together, she'd never asked him to the house. He'd been inside only to see Frank. He couldn't know that they would be alone there, but he knew it was big enough to afford them the kind of privacy they'd so carefully avoided. There could no longer be any question about where things stood. His wife had caught her sitting on his lap, kissing him, and he was texting about getting together. Knowing Sam, he'd fully considered the implications of all this. He wouldn't have contacted her without doing his calculations first. Perhaps he'd been crunching numbers all week.

He rang the bell at three o'clock, and she took her time letting him in. She walked him to the kitchen, where she grabbed two beers to take into the library. They sat beside each other on the couch, sipping from their bottles.

"Sorry I haven't been in touch," he said.

"I know you've been very busy. Especially since Lucy got to town."

She added this almost like an afterthought, as though it had only just occurred to her that Lucy's arrival bore any relation to the matter.

"I've been thinking a lot about what happened."

Margo wanted nothing less than to talk things out. She didn't want the situation measured, measured, weighed, divided. She had acted, and now an answering action was called for on his part.

"I really don't know what came over me," she said.

"Of course I wanted it to happen," he responded abruptly. "For the past few months, you've been all I can think about. But Lucy was so far away, and I was seeing so much of you. Plus all this other excitement in my life—the move, my job—got mixed up with you in my mind. How could I be sure about anything? I realized I needed to wait for her to get here, and give her the same chance. Otherwise it wouldn't be fair."

Was he saying what she thought he was saying? It wouldn't have been *fair* to cheat on his wife if he'd done it with insufficient information?

"Now you've given her enough of a chance?"

"Probably not," he admitted. "But after last weekend, I realized it wasn't going to work. Lucy can tell there's something wrong. I can't concentrate enough to write. We have to figure something out."

Margo had a sudden, terrible vision of where this would end.

"I don't want you to leave her," she said. "That's the last thing I need in my life."

"Of course not," Sam answered, more quickly than she would have liked. "But there's got to be some other way. Can't we just go back to how we were before?"

He must have known that this was impossible. Why couldn't he just say, *We shouldn't be doing this, but I can't control myself*? Or just act without saying anything at all? Because he didn't believe in losing control. Whatever was done had to be done for reasons. There had to be a logic to it.

If she was going to be Vronsky, she would be Vronsky. It was her job to make the move. At least this time, she thought, she didn't have to worry about being interrupted. He looked surprised, even panicked, when she turned to kiss him, but after a moment he kissed her back. They stayed on the couch for several minutes, her hands around his neck, his arm draped across her shoulders. There was something almost chaste about it. Finally, she started to unbutton his shirt, and that's when she heard her mother's voice from down the hall.

5.

Frank woke that morning with a feeling of great possibility. The day stretched out in front of him, open and inviting, and he was ready to get to work. The fog he'd been in for the past few months—he could admit now that this was what it was—seemed on the verge of lifting.

They weren't usually out for an extended stay this early in the summer, but Kit had suggested a change of scenery. They might as well take advantage of the fact that they no longer had jobs keeping them in the city all week, she'd said. She'd been careful not to say that they were no longer *working*. She understood that Frank still had his work to do. In fact, part of her argument was that he would get it done more easily out east. He generally preferred writing in New York—country living made him anxious—but he could see that she'd been right.

He thought on mornings like this of that old Lindsay slogan: *He is fresh and everyone else is tired.* Whenever he had a heavy load of work to do, as he did now, he reminded himself of the excitement of those days. He'd been the mayor's youngest advisor, hired right out of graduate school. He'd switched parties along with his boss, and he'd helped to run his campaign for the Democratic presidential nomination. The loss had not been good for the mayor, but it had made of Frank a sort of figure. On this foundation the rest of his career had been built.

Downstairs, Kit was eating breakfast over a copy of the *Herald*, which she must have sent Marinela to buy in town. They'd cancelled their subscription, but the paper was too much a part of her daily routine to give up. Even Frank couldn't help taking an occasional look, though he stayed far away from the opinion pages. He poured himself a cup of coffee from the pot on the table, lightly kissed Kit's forehead, and headed toward his office.

"Don't you want something to eat?" she called after him.

After all these years, he still preferred being with her to anything else, but he couldn't afford that indulgence now. If he sat down, he wouldn't get up for another hour at least. The whole morning would slip away in comfortable conversation. Too many days had been lost. That had been one advantage to the long hours Kit used to keep at Q&M—they had left him with nothing to do but work.

"I can hold out for lunch."

"Bring something with you," she insisted, so he returned to take a banana from the bowl on the table.

A short hallway connected the main house to the east wing, which they'd built in the winter of '94. That summer a player strike had cancelled the baseball season, and Frank had used the extra time to put together some notes for the book that he'd long thought would cap off his career. This was before the Left had soured on him, at the height of his influence, and there had been considerable competition for the proposal. The *Herald* had always paid well, his collections had sold in decent numbers, but the advance Guillaume had secured from Gilroy Brothers had been the most he'd earned in his life, even accounting for the fact that it would be paid over several years. Almost as soon as the first check cleared, they were breaking ground on the extension. This was Kit's way: she was always very careful with the profits from Q&M, but any time some windfall came along to supplement their usual income, she had a ready idea for what to do with it. She brimmed with plans. It had been the same with the house itself, which they'd bought a decade earlier, after her father died. For all his wild success, Tommy Quinn had not left them an extravagant amount. Most of his money had been tied up in the firm, where Kit had felt obliged to keep it, to advance the family legacy. He had given large gifts to various cultural groups and Catholic charities, and he'd established trust funds for his grandchildren. Kit herself had come into a few million dollars, enough in those days to buy a house on the water in Bridgehampton, which she seemed to have already decided on before the estate was settled. She'd been talking about expanding to include another bedroom ever since Justin started spending summers with them. Once Frank's advance was earmarked for the construction, she added his new office to the plan.

Every time he stepped into this room he took a certain pride in knowing that he'd paid for it himself. In general Frank held himself slightly aloof from money matters. Of course, he was well aware that Kit was the family's real earner—a good reason, perhaps, to hold himself aloof—but he didn't know much beyond that. He'd written dozens of columns about the federal deficit, about monetary policy, about entitlements and discretionary spending, but he couldn't say much about his own household's bottom line. He was free to act superior to such quotidian details because he trusted Kit to manage them.

The office had large casement windows that looked out on the sloping lawn and down to the water beyond. On nice days, he could swing them open to let the bay breeze sweep through while he wrote. A table of reclaimed wood held the desktop computer he'd bought when moving into the space. His kids laughed at this fifteen-year-old relic, but it served his purposes well. He used his computer to write. He had no interest in Teeser or the other sites his editors had constantly asked him to try. He spent a little time on the internet, but he'd always had research assistants to track down a needed quote or supporting fact. He no longer had this institutional perk, but he still had his memory, and he had the books that spilled from the room's two walls of shelves onto the floor, the windowsill, the couch.

Much of this was overflow from his office in New York, though there were some duplicates. He kept copies of his own collections, which he liked to inscribe as gifts to weekend guests. He couldn't work anywhere without *Democracy in America*, *The Prince*, *Reflections on the Revolution in France*, and a few other well-thumbed standbys—several in editions for which he'd written the introductions. He needed poetry, too, and for this he kept the old anthology Richard had edited. Finally there were scores of bound galleys, advance reader copies, and finished books sent to him by publicists, editors, and friends desperate for a blurb or an appearance in his column or perhaps a brief mention on TV. He started perhaps one in ten of these, and he persisted past page two in a similar fraction of those he started, but he kept the rest, partly out of guilt and partly out of the certainty that the moment he threw one away he would find himself in desperate need of facts about public schools on Indian reservations or the history of the Army Corps of Engineers.

Though he'd always treated this steady stream of unsolicited books as a kind of imposition, he'd been deeply unnerved to watch the flow from respectable publishers diminish to a trickle after his firing. Even worse was what had replaced it: self-published tracts expounding apocalyptic racial theories or calling for armed insurrection. These days, he didn't open a package if the postmark wasn't from midtown Manhattan.

The computer took a few minutes to whir into life. On it were about a dozen files, each labeled "book" with a number ranging from one to fourteen. This was fitting in a way, since it was tough to pin down exactly what book he was writing. He'd pitched the thing during Clinton's first term as a study of American political life after the Cold War. The question he'd hoped to consider was whether, in the absence of any serious external threat, the liberal order offered its people enough beyond prosperity to earn their allegiance. He'd already missed his deadline when the towers went down, after which he'd reconceived the project. Now the book would be about whether the liberal order could motivate its people for the kind of fight this threat required. At Guillaume's suggestion, he'd sent a two-page update to Gilroy, which seemed to satisfy them, though Frank wasn't sure that anyone there had read it. The editor who'd bought the book had long since left the house.

It would take a little while to work through the drafts to see what he had. He clicked on one at random and found it completely blank. The next one he opened had a few thousand words, and he read through them slowly. It was good, he thought. Quite good, in fact. But when he came to a line from Kojève ("Human life is a comedy—one must play it seriously"), he realized that he'd repurposed it years ago—not just the quote, but everything in the document—for a column about the Lewinsky scandal. He closed the file and opened another. It took about half an hour of working through these iterations before he gave up, created a new one, and labelled it "book15."

How was it possible that he was starting from scratch? Since selling the proposal, he'd taken every August off from his column and spent the month in this room. Over fifteen years, this should have been enough to add up to a book, given his usual habits. Writing had always come easily to him. The strongest idea and its most elegant expression arrived at once, hand in hand, as soon as they were called upon. In thirty years of thrice-weekly columns, he'd missed perhaps five deadlines. His colleagues envied his ability to produce work under any conditions. He could spend a night out at some gala with Kit, drink three scotches, and come home to write a thousand words of clean copy without loosening his black tie.

Perhaps he would have been better off with a little less fluency, because he'd never developed the habit of working when it wasn't going well, and for some reason the book never seemed to go at all. What was the thing even about? One could write the occasional column about nothing, but you couldn't do that for an entire book. He always ended the summer with twenty or thirty new pages, but when he returned to the *Herald* at the start of September it was hard not to make more immediate use out of them. Some insight from Rousseau or Kołakowski, some haunting line from Pascal or Thomas Browne, or even one of his own bits of felicitous phrasing would strike him as perfectly applicable to the Terri Schiavo case or the Harriet Miers nomination. It felt wasted, sitting there on his computer. He cannibalized slowly over the course of the year, until the carcass was picked dry, leaving him each summer to start fresh.

He could have quit the *Herald* at any time and dedicated himself to the book, but he'd liked his comfortable life too much. Finally the decision had been made for him, and it seemed to be too late. Looking back now, he saw that he'd simply lacked the nerve for greatness. He'd always laughed when his writer friends spoke about artistic courage, and he'd scoffed at the few right-wingers who'd commended his own brave apostasy. That was a lot of nonsense. To write a book in the United States did not require bravery. Babel and Mandelstam had been brave. Rushdie was brave, perhaps. But Mailer, stepping into the ring for twelve rounds with Tolstoy, was not brave. Frank had been in Sarajevo for the siege. He'd gone to Baghdad during the first Gulf War and Kosovo during the bombings. In the past six years he'd made three trips to Afghanistan and four to Iraq. He'd allowed himself to think that something approaching bravery had been involved in these adventures, but he could see now that when it came to his work he'd never really risked anything, apart from offending a few cocktail party companions.

Wind shook the windows and Frank sat for a minute looking out at the lawn. This view had proven a kind of curse over the years, a constant distraction, especially when his family was out there. It wasn't so much the temptation to look at them as the idea that they could look in at him. What he was usually doing on this side of the glass—pacing around, leafing at random through the same half dozen books, talking to himself—didn't look much like work, but that's what it was. Being watched brought on a self-consciousness about his apparent lack of production, which in turn made him genuinely unproductive. But the lawn was empty today, and a low fog obscured any view of the water.

If he could just put the right first word down, everything would progress from there. That word was sitting, ripe on the branch, waiting to be plucked and pressed to the page. Why couldn't he get at it? This problem had become more and more common. He had been known all his life for his prodigious memory. He had hundreds of poems by heart, long passages of his favorite books, entire Shakespeare plays. Sometimes his column would recount decades-old conversations, with offhand statements in quotes. People joked about this, he knew, but he was always sure he'd gotten the details right. Nothing was ever lost to him.

Yet these days he had trouble accessing the most basic information. The other morning he'd had a problem with his shoes. One of the strings used to tie them up had snapped in his hand. He asked Marinela to buy him a new set, and he couldn't convey to her what he wanted. Her English was imperfect, miscommunication not uncommon, but he'd never before felt himself to be the source of the confusion. He told her that he needed a new shoe tie. A new tie-up. He'd broken his shoe-tie-up. She looked at him blankly until he went to his room, picked up the offending shoe, and brought it down to her. Without a moment's hesitation Marinela had responded, "You need new laces, Mr. Doyle? I can get them for you."

A drink sometimes helped at such moments to dislodge the offending word. His office in the city had a bar, but here he'd have to walk back to the main part of the house, where Kit might spot him with a bottle in his hand. She wouldn't say anything about it—she never had in forty years; rather late to start—but it would sour the rest of his morning. The clock on his desk read nine. He would have a glass of wine with lunch and fix something stronger for the afternoon. The question was how to get through the next four hours.

A light knock woke him from his sleep on the couch. He sat up and let out a startled bark that he hoped could not be heard on the other side of the door.

"Can you stand to take a break?" Kit asked from out in the hall. "Lunch is ready."

She was always careful not to come inside without an invitation.

"I'll be there in a minute," he called back. "I just want to finish my thought."

He heard her withdrawing footsteps and stood to collect himself. How long had he been asleep? At some point he'd pulled down a volume of Montaigne, searching for a line from "On the Education of Children," and he'd read a few pages before setting the book on his chest. It had fallen off him while he slept, and now it sat splayed open on the floor. He picked it up and returned it to the shelf before walking to the dining room.

Marinela had made them grilled salmon and a salad, which sat on the table along with a pitcher of ice water.

"Would you like some wine?" Frank asked Kit.

She declined, but he brought back two glasses and a bottle of white Rioja from the fridge. He poured a half glass for Kit and a full glass for himself, and he took a long, slow sip while she began to eat.

"It's been nice out here this week," she said.

She'd offered some variation on this banal remark to begin nearly every meal for the past five days. It was beginning to irritate him, though he could hardly blame her for lacking things to talk about. They usually spoke of the day's news over meals, but for the first time in his adult life Frank wasn't following the news. They'd long ago placed a mutual moratorium on discussing work, and they'd already run several times through Kit's maternal worry over the kids, who Frank thought seemed to be doing just fine.

"I want to make good use of the place while we can," she added now.

This seemed excessively ominous.

"Are we really that close to the end?"

"Not the end of our lives, but maybe the end of our lives in this house. I've been thinking it might make sense to downsize a little bit."

"Downsize?"

Frank hated when she used this business-world jargon that she didn't even seem to recognize as jargon.

"Sell the house, get something smaller."

"I'm familiar with the term. I'm just surprised to hear you suggest it."

"We spent all morning on opposite ends of the house. Do we really need all this space?"

"Building the extension was your idea."

"That was fifteen years ago, Frank. We've gotten a lot of good use out of it, but we're in a different moment of our lives."

Frank pushed his food around his plate and took another sip of wine.

"Edward just got back. Margo's home from school. It seems like a strange time to be 'downsizing.'"

"If we look north of the highway, we can find something with just as much room for half of what we'd get for this place."

"So it's not actually about the size of the house?"

Now Kit took her first sip of wine, which freed Frank to finish his glass.

"It might take a little pressure off."

"I didn't know we were under any pressure."

"We don't need to be overly dramatic about it. These are the kinds of things people do when they get to be our age. They retire. They move to a smaller place."

"I haven't retired," Frank said, more loudly than he'd intended. "I worked all morning."

"The point is that neither of us is drawing a regular salary." She returned her attention to her food, and Frank thought the conversation might be over. But after a bit she resumed. "So long as we're on the subject, if we sold the house, we might use some of the money to pay back your advance."

"Is that what this is all about?"

It had now been four months since Guillaume had given them the news from Gilroy Brothers. They had barely spoken of it since, and somehow Frank had managed to put the whole thing out of his mind. He'd said at the time that they should fight, but Guillaume had advised that they would need something he could plausibly call an acceptable manuscript. Frank had told him he'd have it in a few more months, and they'd left the conversation there.

"It's a lot of money they want."

Frank didn't know what to say. Indeed it was a lot of money, but he couldn't imagine it was more than they could afford.

"Have you lost faith in me, too?"

Kit's wide, beautiful brow, still smooth with the appearance of youth, now wrinkled itself in distress.

"I have total faith in you. The book will get written, and it will be great. Which is all the more reason to pay them off, so you can take the time you need and not feel this pressure. Once it's done, there will be dozens of places lining up to publish it."

Frank reached to pour himself another glass, but he found the bottle empty. He stood from the table with his plate in his hand.

"I should get back to work."

"Aren't you going to eat a little bit?"

Frank looked down at his full plate.

"I can't afford to waste any time. If I don't get a chapter finished today, we might wind up in the poorhouse."

In the kitchen he filled a highball glass with ice and found his bottle of rye. After a moment of hesitation, he took the bottle with him. If Kit didn't like it, she would have to live with it. He prepared a defensive posture, but when he passed back through the dining room on his way to the extension, she was gone. She'd left her empty plate on the table for Marinela to clear.

Rain had started up during lunch, and the fog had lifted. Frank stood by his office windows and watched the downpour bombard the bay. He took a long sip and tried to calm himself. Why had that conversation upset him so much? Did he even care whether they sold the house? He'd never shared Kit's great love for the place. It had been her idea to buy it, her idea to renovate, her idea to spend more time there now. Perhaps that was it: this was her place, and she wouldn't get rid of it unless there was a real problem.

He couldn't believe that Gilroy Brothers were serious about getting the money back. Granted, the book was late. When he'd first submitted the proposal, he'd asked for five years, but he hadn't thought he would need that long. After all, he had nearly a dozen books to his name already. But those weren't really books, just collections of his columns. They hadn't even been written, exactly. They'd accrued over time. So writing a real book was taking longer than he'd expected. But no one had seemed bothered by the fact. They hadn't checked in on him more than once a year. They hadn't made any suggestion that he might be taking too long. It wasn't some magical date on the calendar that had passed. It was just that Frank's stock had collapsed, and they wanted their investment back.

Was this her escape plan? Sell the house, clear his debts, buy him off? Could she leave him, after all these years, at his lowest moment? He had alienated them from all their friends. He had lost his job and his reputation. It stood to reason that she would want out. With Edward home and Margo grown up, there was nothing left to bind her to him. But she had been the one thing he could trust absolutely for forty years, and he couldn't stop trusting her now. Better to believe the ground would open up and swallow him.

Frank had been prone lately to bouts of paranoia, which got worse when he drank, and knowing as much did nothing to control the flow of his thoughts. These flights of suspicion were not an attractive habit, but who wouldn't be paranoid in his shoes? Everyone he'd thought was on his side—his paper, his publisher, his TV producer—had abandoned him, first chance. Enemies he hadn't even known existed had combed the *Herald*'s archives, picking over decades of work, pulling out all the lines that served their purpose. More than a thousand columns were whittled down to half a dozen, and those became all that mattered. Not even entire columns, but offending paragraphs. In the seventies he'd written approvingly of the Moynihan Report and decried the pathological breakdown of the black family. He'd blamed that breakdown on a host of causes, including racist government policy, but this part of his argument was conveniently left out. In the eighties he'd questioned whether affirmative action had outlived its usefulness, whether it might sensibly be replaced by a class-based system. In the aftermath to the Tawana Brawley case, he'd called Al Sharpton a "hustler," a characterization that still struck him as sound. Later he'd written a column about 2 Live Crew and the culture of permissiveness that forced young blacks to grow up without fathers. The social media swarm had landed with particularly gleeful ferocity on a line about the "propulsive, aphrodisiac rhythms of rap music."

There was no context given to any of this, no acknowledgment that the columns were a product of their time, or that they had been intended to be controversial. They were expressions of strong opinions, designed to start conversations. Provocation had been part of his job as a public intellectual. He hadn't even always meant what he was saying, not entirely. The important part was making people think. Anyone who did his kind of work—at least, anyone who did it well—could be raked over the coals in this way. If you hadn't written half a dozen offensive columns over the course of thirty-five years, you hadn't done your job. Had he gone too far at times? Perhaps. One could not properly test the line without occasionally crossing it.

No one would admit it, but it was really all about the war. He'd hardly been the only person at the *Herald* to advocate for regime change. Half the op-ed page had endorsed the invasion, their rationales running from preemptive defense to human rights. The paper's own front-page reporting—on WMDs, on Baathist ideology, on the lurid sadism of Uday and Qusay—offered ammunition for every possible argument. But Frank's support had been notably full-throated where others' had been caveat-laden. None of this more-in-sorrow-than-in-anger shit. Removing Saddam had seemed to Frank not the best in a range of bad options, but an exciting opportunity. He envisioned a domino effect that might lead the entire Arab world to democracy. He still didn't think that outcome out of reach, though he was the first to admit that things had not gone according to plan. He was as frustrated as anyone—more, perhaps, since he had so much riding on success—by the administration's mistakes, beginning with Rumsfeld's refusal to deploy enough troops to secure the country after Saddam's fall and running through to Bremer's decision to disband the army and de-Baathify the government. But for all that, Frank couldn't bring himself to regret that the monster was gone.

His colleagues had been quick to recant the moment things got tough, which was predictable since their support had been so shallow all along. Many hadn't given the international order a bit of thought between the end of the Cold War and September 10, 2001.

The few exceptions were long disposed to believe the worst about the projection of American power. Frank had been born in '39—he would turn seventy in the fall—and he'd been one of the few people left on the *Herald*'s staff who remembered V-E Day. His Irish immigrant mother had taken him to throw ticker tape as General Eisenhower marched down Broadway. His memories of Roosevelt were less vivid, but the man had lived on in his house after death as a kind of tutelary spirit. Frank believed in the Four Freedoms, and he believed the whole world was entitled to them. America had made some mistakes, but the baby boomers for whom Vietnam was the sum total of foreign policy history were dangerously myopic.

It was a sign of this myopia that a Roosevelt Democrat could get branded a neocon. He'd spent time with such men, he'd quoted them in his columns, but Frank was not one of them. He was a liberal, had always been a liberal, since his Lindsay days. Not a radical, but a *liberal*. He'd disliked the New Left nearly as much as he had Nixon. He'd believed in civil rights, but not in violence. He'd gone with Lindsay to Harlem on the night that Martin Luther King was shot, and he'd helped prevent rioting. He'd been against the war, but he didn't think occupying buildings over Cambodia would solve anything. He believed in the democratic process. He'd been a liberal Republican when such things still existed, but he had no interest in returning in that direction. It had been a Democrat, Scoop Jackson, who'd introduced Frank to Richard Perle, and Perle who'd introduced him to Wolfowitz. Frank hadn't given up on his party. His party had given up on liberalism. They didn't even use the word anymore. They said instead that they were "progressives," as if any movement into the future was necessarily better than the status quo.

The Left had an illiberal streak that no one seemed willing to talk about, and Frank could see it in his colleagues' reaction when he refused to join in the rending of garments over advocating invasion. By the time the surge was being discussed, he was a lone voice in favor of keeping faith. Some simply underplayed their earlier position, pretending to a consistency of viewpoint that might have been easily falsified by anyone who cared enough to do it. Others made what seemed to Frank a spectacle out of their self-flagellation. Roger Meaney—the paper's longtime managing editor and one of Frank's closest friends for a quarter century—had said at his retirement that the *Herald*'s part in the lead-up to war would haunt him for the rest of his life. (Frank happened to know that Roger had done a few things on business junkets that ought to take precedence in the haunting department.) In such an environment, Frank was a thrice-weekly reminder of the paper's past sins. Finally he'd given them an opening to do something about it.

He might have survived anyway, if he'd been a different man. A few days after the game, he was called in to see his new editor, who'd just been promoted after his real editor, Ken Calder—another friend from the paper's old guard—accepted a buyout. The new guy's name was Rob Lott, and he was about Eddie's age but looked quite a bit younger. He was short and so skinny that it didn't seem possible that he could find adult clothes two sizes too small for him, yet that's all he seemed to wear. He kept a day's worth of stubble on his face at all times, which Frank imagined was meant to make him look older but had the opposite effect, as it grew in patches and drew attention to the islands of bare baby skin on his jaw. Lott wanted him to apologize. Not just apologize, but write a column about his history with the black community. Justify the ways of Doyle to man. Write about the time he'd spent with Jackie Robinson. About his work with New York's black community under Lindsay. Maybe something about the Bootstrappers and his relationship with Justin Price. He'd written about all of this before— why wasn't anyone quoting those columns?—but he was supposed to draw them together now and append an apology.

"That sounds a little forced," Frank had said.

"This isn't an optional exercise," Lott replied, trying on a tough guy tone.

"Just suspend me for a few columns. I could use the time off."
Lott looked surprised.

"You're going to be suspended either way, Frank. This is about
keeping your job."

Frank couldn't believe that they would fire their most famous
writer for refusing to write a bullshit mea culpa enumerating all his
works of racial beneficence. *By the time I'm done*, he'd thought as he
stormed out of Lott's office, *you'll be apologizing to me to save your
own job*. He was more than prepared to go over Lott's head, but when
he got there, he found not old friends, drinking buddies, sympathetic protégés, but a rather confused and confusing corporate
bureaucracy. All his strongest supporters had left the paper when the
buyouts began. He couldn't even figure out precisely who Lott's boss
was. Everyone he spoke to said it was out of their purview, and the
paper's new hierarchy was so byzantine that they might all have been
right. There was no authority to whom he could appeal. It was a different paper from the one where he'd worked all his life, and somehow he hadn't noticed the change.

So he'd gone back to Lott's office and told him he would do it.

"I'm glad to hear it," Lott said. "There's one other thing, though.
We'd like you to stop drinking."

Perhaps this had been part of the plan all along and would have
been mentioned in the first meeting had Frank not stormed out, but
it seemed more like a sadistic turn of the knife. Lott had all the power
now, and no intention of wielding it magnanimously. He must have
known that Frank had been looking around for someone in a position to overrule him, and he must have known that Frank's return
meant that his search had failed. He must also have known that this
additional condition would be unacceptable, because this time he
didn't look surprised when Frank walked out.

Thank God there's still TV, Frank had thought initially. He'd been
appearing at least one Sunday a month on some morning show or

another for the better part of three decades, but for the moment he had nothing on the schedule. At first he thought it was a simple mis-communication. A *Herald* publicist had handled all his bookings in the past. The producers probably didn't know whom to call to get him on. So he called them himself.

"We'd love to have you back on eventually," they all said in different words.

"What do you mean, eventually?"

"Once you've settled back in after whatever apology tour the *Herald* makes you do. In fact, we'll have you on now if you want to start the apology tour with us."

"There's no apology tour. I have nothing to apologize for except making a bad joke."

"The *Herald* must want you to do something before they take you back."

"I'm not going back."

That was the end of TV. He did have some options—the most right wing of talk radio outlets, websites that ran headlines like "Rome Burns While Negro Fiddles." Frank had always been proud to have the very best enemies. What troubled him now were the sorts of people who thought he was a friend.

He took another sip of his rye, and as he felt the burn run down his throat he told himself that the trade had been worth it. All his life Frank had been known as a drinker. Not a drunk—he could generally hold himself together in public—but a man who liked to drink. It was part of his charm. Generations of journalists had stories of drinking their first scotch with Frank Doyle. After the Ballpark Incident, there had been a different kind of talk about all this. Old anecdotes that had once seemed funny resurfaced as examples of drunken misbehavior. Videos emerged of television appearances in which he'd exhibited various levels of inebriation. This had been common in that era, when studios kept full bars in the green room.

On any given panel, he was rarely the drunkest one. But no one wanted to hear that.

It was true that he sometimes drank too much, but this could be said about most men he knew. It was a hazard of the profession, life spent seated at the desk. He had his own ways of dealing with it. If he knew the glass he was pouring should be his last, he would hide the rest of the bottle, tuck it away behind some books on a shelf. He didn't need to submit to some therapeutic regime, take some phony accounting.

When he looked around now, more than anything what he saw baffled him. None of the frameworks he had used to sort things out in the past seemed relevant to the task at hand. He did not even see how he could make something coherent out of this bafflement. So he'd been defeated. But the forces that had taken him down might not be so happy to see whatever came after him.

Frank felt exhausted, and he wanted to sleep, but he couldn't allow Kit to find him passed out on the couch. He wouldn't let her wake him and drag him up to bed, all the while working over her plans to get rid of him. She needed to know that he could still do a day's work. He would have to wake himself up a little.

When he stepped outside and felt the cold stone on his feet he realized he wasn't wearing shoes. It was too late to go back for them, and his bare feet would feel nice in the wet grass. He was a little unsteady, and he needed to walk carefully. He hoped that Kit would not see him. She was far away now. Separate ends, as she'd said. The rain was coming down harder than he'd expected, and soon after stepping out he knew he had to find himself some cover. *An old man in a wet month*, he thought and laughed. Margo would appreciate that. He would tell it to her when he returned to New York.

He couldn't go back into the house to face his work. He stood in indecision and for a moment thought he was going to be sick. He needed to find a private place to do it. He couldn't just stand there, vomiting in the pouring rain. He walked to the edge of the lawn, where the trees started up. After a few steps, he stubbed his bare toe against a root and he felt a sharp slap of pain that seemed to jump right to the middle of his chest. He reached for his foot as though to silence the injured toe, and the world went upside down. The spinning made him sick, and now he did vomit, onto the dirt beside him. He tried to move to keep his face out of it, and he banged his head against a tree. After that he knew he wouldn't get up. *An old man, / A dull head among windy spaces.* He considered calling for help, but there was no one to hear but Kit, and he didn't want Kit to see him this way. He would have to wait until he felt better. In the meantime, he would rest. His last wish before fading off was: *Please don't let her find me here.*

6.

She'd been trying all week to talk with him about the house, gently and fruitlessly guiding their conversations to the subject, until finally she'd brought out this inanity about "downsizing," the kind of word Frank hated so much. Followed by the suggestion that they buy another place north of the highway—absurd under the circumstances. She should have just said, *We're desperate, and we need to sell.* But she couldn't pull the ground out from under him at precisely the moment when he needed some solidity.

It might have been easier if they'd been in the habit of discussing money, but he'd always trusted her on the matter. Perhaps she was afraid to admit how badly she'd failed. Above all, they couldn't talk about their financial trouble without talking about Frank's advance, and this would mean admitting to him that she knew that there was no book.

They'd learned about Gilroy's demand over one of the long lunches they had with Guillaume LaFarge three or four times a year. The lunch in question, their first confab after Frank's firing, had taken place at Jean-Georges on a snowy February day, and Guillaume had spent most of it expressing sympathetic outrage. Guillaume was an agent of the old school, a few years Frank's senior, who'd spent the first nineteen years of his life in Paris and the subsequent fifty-plus in New York but still spoke with a thick accent, in syntax that became noticeably more tortured after a few glasses of wine. Like Frank he loved to eat, drink, and talk. The two could have passed whole days telling stories. Discussing business was never a priority. They were waiting for coffee when he got around to asking where they stood with the big book. At this point, the question had the air of ritual.

"That's one thing about all this bullshit with the *Herald*," Frank told him. "The manuscript will finally have my undivided attention."

Usually this would have been enough to settle things, but now Guillaume said, "Gilroy has been calling. To have a timeline for them would be nice."

"Another year at most," Frank answered.

"Frank, they want their money back, is the truth. Six months for an acceptable manuscript, they say."

"Get me a year," Frank said, before calling over the waiter and ordering a carafe of port for dessert.

Kit had not been surprised by the call from Guillaume a few days later, but she was surprised at his tone. Missed deadlines were not her territory—so far as she knew, there had been no missed deadlines before—and she wasn't sure how seriously to take the threat.

"It's really quite dire," he told her.

He'd asked Gilroy for a year, but they wouldn't budge from six months. It was difficult to argue with this, when Frank was already more than a decade late. Likely enough they didn't even want a manuscript at this point, since that would trigger another payment on a book they no longer had any desire to publish. They couldn't rip up the contract simply because Frank had made himself toxic, but they could cancel it for a failure to deliver.

"Frank thinks we're dealing with gentlemen publishers," Guillaume said. "Times have changed. His editor reports to the board of a lumber company in Austria. He can't have a million-dollar hole in the books for work that never get done."

If he brought them some kind of manuscript, Guillaume said, they could fight over the definition of "acceptable," but in order to have that fight, they needed pages. This seemed like a manageable task. Frank had always been prolific. Surely after fifteen years he had a stack of readable prose somewhere. The problem would be getting him to give it up. In his mind he'd built the book into the thing that would secure his reputation, his one lasting monument. Nothing could live up to this expectation. She and Guillaume needed to intervene in some way. If she could get her hands on the work in progress, Guillaume would be able to tell whether it was good enough. He felt confident that it would be. It didn't have to be ready to see the light of day; it just needed to be something workable.

Guillaume made it sound so reasonable, and Kit was desperate. By the end of the conversation she'd agreed to find the manuscript. Frank would feel betrayed—Frank's capacity for such feelings was impressive—but she couldn't afford to be precious about his feelings at that moment. Once he'd gotten past his anger, he might be grateful. He'd been working for so long he could hardly be expected to see the thing objectively, and he'd been particularly battered around after the Ballpark Incident. To be told by someone whose opinion you respect that the manuscript was almost there might be a relief.

A search of his office in New York turned up nothing, but this didn't worry her. He'd done most of his work on the book over the summers in Bridgehampton. Early in the spring, she'd driven out east to open the house for the year. Entering his office without him felt like a far greater transgression than it had seemed while talking it over with Guillaume. Now she sat at his ancient computer and waited for it to boot up. Two rows of files labeled "book," with numbers appended, appeared on the desktop. This seemed promising. If they were slight variations, she could just pick one, or send the lot of them to Guillaume.

She started with "book14," on the assumption that the higher numbers superseded the rest. The document consisted of five mostly blank pages. Half an hour of clicking and reading established that there was nothing of use in the "book" files or anywhere else on the computer. Another hour rifling through filing cabinets, desk drawers, and shelves confirmed that no printed or handwritten pages were tucked away anywhere. Kit briefly allowed for the existence of an external hard drive or a flash stick somewhere, but Frank didn't even have a personal email account. If there wasn't a manuscript in this office, there wasn't a manuscript.

What was she to do with this knowledge? She couldn't tell Frank that she'd gone in search of his book, an admission—she could see it so clearly now—that he would take as a terrible failure of faith, one made so much worse by the incontrovertible evidence that a lack of faith had been entirely justified. How could he have confidently commanded Guillaume to get him another six months, when he knew that these months would make no difference? Yet she was angrier at herself for her betrayal than at Frank for his decade-long deception. She couldn't blame him for trying to delay the inevitable—wasn't this exactly what she was trying to do?

UniBank had been the sixth-largest financial institution in the country when it bought Q&M, and Kit's stake in it had amounted to roughly ninety-five million dollars. There had been some initial restrictions on her shares, but she could have cashed most of them out after a year. She'd held on because the stock was doing well— until it wasn't, at which point she'd decided to ride out the storm. If there were any truth to the rumors of a coming government bailout, she'd decided, UniBank would be back to its high in another year. As it was, the bailout came three weeks too late. Eighteen months after buying Q&M, UniBank had been liquidated, and Kit had gotten nothing. Three generations of work had evaporated in a matter of days. She couldn't think about it for long without becoming sick. She wondered whether Frank felt the same way about the book.

So long as she'd been working, his writing income had seemed a nice extra, the means of paying for added extravagances. Now that it was truly needed, it was gone. Having refused to resign from the *Herald*, he'd been fired for cause, and he'd lost his pension upon dismissal. That decision was still being litigated, mostly for reasons of principle, since whatever settlement might result would be eaten up by lawyers' fees. Kit herself hadn't drawn a salary in two years. She'd retired shortly after selling Q&M, and her severance, like the purchase itself, had been paid in stock. They could barely afford to keep up the status quo; they certainly couldn't afford to pay Gilroy a million dollars. She understood all at once that everything was about to collapse, and she couldn't think of any way to stop it.

If she'd asked Edward for the money—it would have to be Edward, since Margo's inheritance was still in trust, and Grable would never let her touch it—he'd give it to her without hesitation. But she couldn't do that. They might call it a loan, but she had no prospects for paying him back. She'd be taking her son's legacy to cover her own mistakes.

She'd returned to the city two days before his party. Even while planning it she'd understood that spending money recapturing the air of their old celebrations was a mistake, but now she recognized the full scale of this folly. She had once been able to put on her hostess's face whatever her mood, but she was out of practice, and the facade nearly cracked several times that night, before it actually *had* cracked, in front of Justin. Since he'd passed along this information about Celsia, she'd been telling herself that she hadn't even meant to ask for his help. But of course she had wanted help, and she hadn't known where else to turn.

Her instinct now was to forget about his tip, though her objections were more practical than ethical. She didn't have enough money to make it worthwhile. At most she could put a few hundred thousand in play, and the return wouldn't be enough to fix things. She'd be taking on all of the risk for minimal reward. That left her back where she'd started: she needed to talk to Frank about selling the house.

His initial response hadn't bothered her. He didn't take well to change, but he would have to get used to the idea. Rather than following him into the kitchen or waiting at the table for him to return, she'd decided to leave him to his work—or whatever he was doing in his office. She would press him further over dinner that night, perhaps finally tell him the truth about where things stood. She spent the afternoon puttering around the house, standing at windows, watching the rain pour down, waiting for Frank to reappear. She knew he liked to have a drink in the afternoon, and that he often nodded off on the couch afterward. He was always slightly embarrassed when she woke him up, but she thought he was entitled to the rest. He was about to turn seventy. He'd worked hard his whole life. It wasn't really his fault that they had nothing to show for it.

Around six, she knocked on his office door, not expecting an answer, and she let herself in. The room was a mess, windows open, rain and wind whipping around. *How could he work in such conditions?* she thought instinctively, though some part of her already understood that Frank wasn't there. Had the windows blown open after he left? When he didn't fall asleep, he usually came to find her after quitting for the day. Hours of solitude left him desperate for an audience. A brief lunchtime squabble wouldn't change that.

Kit remembered finding Edward's room empty on the evening of the party, and she felt some of the same panic come over her. Why were these men never where they were supposed to be?

She searched most of the first floor before going into the kitchen, where Marinela was working on dinner.

"Have you seen Mr. Doyle this afternoon?" Kit tried to sound casual. "He isn't in his office."

Marinela shook her head. She was about to return her attention to a pot on the stove, until she recognized the panic in Kit's face.

"You want me to help you look?"

They walked together around the second floor. Kit thought of their dinner getting cold and tried to make herself angry at Frank, which seemed better than the alternatives. After searching the rest of the house, they returned to his office, where they attempted to put things into some order. As she closed the windows, Kit realized for the first time that Frank could have gone out through them. But why would he want to be in that weather? It was getting dark now, and she found a flashlight in the front closet, which she put in the pocket of her raincoat. Marinela put on her own coat and followed Kit out the back door.

They went together down the slope of the lawn, and Kit ran the flashlight over the surface of the bay. She wasn't sure exactly what she was looking for—a bobbing body?—but she found nothing. They walked back to the house and around it to the driveway, where both cars were still parked. They walked over to the garage and briefly looked inside. Kit hadn't been in the attic space above the garage in years, but she climbed the dusty stairs now and called out Frank's name. She stood for a moment, listening to the darkness, before heading back down and continuing up the driveway. She and Marinela didn't speak, but Kit was glad for the company as they fought through the elements. When they reached the road, there was nothing to do but turn around.

Kit imagined finding Frank safe and dry in the house, a drink in his hand, wondering where she'd gone. But he wasn't there, and she was running out of places to look. She rang up her neighbors on each side, though neither family was around this week. Finally she found the number for the Southampton Town police in the thin yellow pages that sat beside the kitchen phone. She had the idea, perhaps from television, that they would tell her to wait some period of time or make her come to the station to fill out a missing persons report, but the man who answered the phone spent several minutes talking patiently through the situation before telling her he would send a car over.

While she waited, she considered the possibility that Frank had been taken. Perhaps she was trying to justify calling the police after losing track of her husband for an hour, but the idea seemed suddenly plausible. His name had been attached to a lot of fringe characters lately. The more she thought about it, the more some kind of abduction came to seem not just possible but even likely. When the two officers arrived forty minutes later and asked her to explain the situation, she almost began, "My husband has been kidnapped." Instead she told them the facts—that she'd left him to work after lunch and hadn't seen him since.

"Does your husband have a history of—wandering off?" the one who seemed to be in charge—his name was Detective Shimko; the other was Weber—asked when she was done.

Kit shook her head.

"Nothing like this has ever happened before."

She told them about the open window and tried to explain that her husband was, in his way, rather famous and lately somewhat unpopular, even hated in certain circles. But the idea of some vigilante making off with him had lost all its force now that the police were here. It didn't sound convincing even to her as the words left her mouth. Detective Shimko didn't betray any impression one way or the other; he just wrote the information down along with everything else.

"Is there anything more we should know? About his state of mind, for example?"

Kit looked briefly over at Marinela, who was watching from the kitchen doorway.

"He drinks quite a bit," she said. "I found an empty liquor bottle in his office that I think was mostly full this afternoon."

Shimko nodded tactfully.

"We're going to take a look around outside. Meanwhile, I'll put out a call to see if he's turned up in town."

It felt almost rude to be sending these men out in the rain, but they didn't seem at all hesitant. Perhaps they were happy to have something to do. She imagined the job was pretty quiet most of the time. Once they had gone, Kit considered calling the kids, but she wasn't sure what she would say. It still seemed possible that some misunderstanding had occurred, that Frank would turn up any moment with a reasonable explanation. The more people she told now, the harder it would be to pretend the whole thing had never happened.

With nothing left to do, she started to pray. She hadn't been to church in weeks—she hated summer masses in the air-conditioned gym, with most of the congregation halfway to the beach before the *missa* was *est*—and she regretted that now. She'd prayed constantly while Edward was away, not because she thought it could protect him, but because it had made her feel better, and his deployment had started her going to church again, after a lapse of many years. She imagined her father seeing his daughter become one of those people who turned to God only when they really needed something. She stood silently, pleading in her head, but after a moment she knelt down, resting her elbows on the arm of the couch. Without a word, Marinela knelt down beside her. Kit led them through a decade of the rosary, counting Hail Marys on trembling fingers.

When they'd finished, they stood without looking at each other. Something intimate had passed between them, something that had put them on equal footing, and it was difficult to know how to proceed from there.

Nearly an hour passed before Shimko returned alone and tapped on the glass.

"We've found him," he said once Kit opened the back door.

"Is he all right?"

"He's a little disoriented. He says he went for a walk and fell down. We've got an ambulance on its way. Meantime, Officer Weber is helping him back to the house. If you could get some dry clothes and a blanket, we'll try to warm him up while we wait."

Marinela went straight for the linen closet while Kit went to Frank's dresser. When they got downstairs, he was already inside, sitting on a couch in the living room, pale and wet. A large cut on his forehead was surrounded by the beginnings of a brown bruise. His whole body shook with what seemed like more than a chill. At the sight of him she started to cry. Her response obviously upset him—he was the one in their marriage prone to tears—but seeing this only made her cry more. Very quickly she lost control, and she wept in long deep sobs while everyone watched. Finally, Marinela took the clothes from her and brought them along with a blanket to the officers.

This snapped Kit back into action; she wasn't going to let these strangers undress Frank. She crossed the room, sat down beside him on the couch, and took him in her arms, kissing him lightly around the edges of the bruise. She unbuttoned his shirt while Marinela and the officers looked on.

"I fell," he told her, in the tone of a defensive child.

"That's all right," she answered. "We're going to get you cleaned up."

He was looking a bit better by the time the ambulance arrived. She wanted to ride along, but the driver suggested she take her own car so she had a way to bring him home. She wasn't sure she was in any condition to drive, but she was calmed somewhat by the idea that he would eventually be discharged. She went slowly in the rain on the winding road up to the highway. By the time she pulled into the hospital's parking lot, they'd brought Frank inside.

After an hour on an IV, he stopped shaking, and some color returned to his face. An emergency room doctor had glued up his cut and bandaged it. Kit could almost believe that he'd suffered an unfortunate accident from which he'd already recovered. Around midnight he was admitted to a room, and the nurses encouraged Kit to go home to rest. Instead she spent the night in a chair beside him, falling in and out of sleep, reaching each time she woke to find his hand, which did not come to life when she held it in her own.

In the morning the nurses explained that Frank's vitals had stabilized overnight. They expected that Kit might be able to bring him home that day. When the doctor arrived on his rounds, he asked a series of scripted questions about Frank's health. Had he noticed any vision problems? Any problems with short-term memory? Kit was surprised to hear Frank answer yes to both of these. He hadn't mentioned these things to her. As the questions continued, the doctor turned to more general matters, about his family, how he spent his days—almost cocktail party chatter. It was an area where Frank usually excelled, but now he struggled to keep up with the conversation. Kit could see he had no business going home. She wondered whether this was all a result of the fall or had started much earlier. She tried to remember the last time she'd had a serious conversation with him, and she found that she could not. It had been a few days, perhaps not since the past weekend. She had been so absorbed in dealing with their financial problems, and she'd mostly left Frank to himself.

"I think you're suffering from a thiamine deficiency," the doctor finally said, addressing Frank but looking at Kit. "That's a kind of vitamin B. This is probably what caused some of the confusion and your fall. The good news is, we can give you thiamine intravenously here at the hospital, and if you respond well you should be able to go home within another day or two. Then we'll need you to follow up with your doctor in New York."

Kit was relieved, but also a little ashamed. A vitamin deficiency? Could that really be right? Had she not been feeding her husband properly? The doctor returned Frank's charts to the foot of his bed. Before leaving he asked to speak with Kit in the hall, and she followed him just outside the door, which he pulled closed behind them.

"Is your husband an alcoholic?" he asked abruptly.

Kit had never been faced with the question so starkly before. Had her remark to the police about Frank's drinking been passed along? Or was it obvious to anyone who looked at his charts?

When the topic came up in less pointed fashion, she could admit that Frank liked to drink. After a few drinks herself, she might even call him a drunk. At times she could go so far as to say that he had a drinking "problem." But she rebelled on his behalf at this clinical term.

"He's never been diagnosed, if that's what you mean."

The doctor's face wavered slightly, as though poised between sympathy and annoyance.

"He's likely suffering from something called Wernicke's disease, which is generally the result of severe alcohol abuse."

"So what you told him in there was a lie?"

"No, that was all true. Wernicke's is caused by a vitamin deficiency, and at this stage it should respond to a thiamine drip. But in the long run the best thing your husband can do for his health is to stop drinking. Right now, I think his problems are reversible, but if he continues on this path, they could get much more serious."

It felt disloyal to listen to this without offering the rebuttal that Frank clearly would have offered in her place, but she only said, "I understand."

"Needless to say," the doctor pressed on, "this can be a difficult thing for a patient to hear. I think it would be best if you brought him back to New York for the rest of the treatments. I'll be back around in a few hours to see how he's progressing, and I can tell him to stay away from alcohol while the treatment is running its course, but I'll leave the larger conversation to you and his doctors at home."

Kit could see that he was ready to move on, but she wanted to keep him there, to delay her return to the room, where Frank would want to know what they'd been talking about. She couldn't think of anything to ask him, so finally she nodded and let him walk away. She began to prepare the outlines of a story for Frank, but back in the room, she found him asleep, with a peaceful look on his face. The diagnosis must have relieved him—not Alzheimer's or a stroke, just a problem with his diet.

She tried to imagine Frank without alcohol and found the exercise harder than it should have been. If she was being completely honest, it seemed an essential part of him. Even on the night they met, at her cousin's wedding, when he'd crossed the room to dance with her, he'd already had the ruddy cheeks and avid eyes that she would later come to associate with the intermediate stages of his inebriation. He'd spent a remarkable portion of their years together in this territory. One of Frank's signature qualities was his ability to drink steadily for hours while remaining in a state of only moderate alteration. At such times he was lucid and even elegant, if a little sentimental. She loved this Frank. A completely sober Frank Doyle wouldn't have proposed to her after two songs.

But there was always the risk that he would spill over into the next state—not a slightly modified version of his usual self but a different self entirely. A less palatable self. A bit crude, even sadistic. This was the self that could say what he'd said in that announcer's booth. Kit didn't like this Frank—no one did—but he appeared infrequently to be lived with. The fact that the real Frank so rarely remembered these times generally made it easier to pretend they'd never happened. This became difficult only at moments—like after the Ballpark Incident—when the consequences of this Frank's appearance survived him.

Somehow she'd never found any of this strange. So many of the men she'd known drank the way that Frank drank, behaved the way he did, beginning with her father, who'd been younger than Frank was now when he'd died from liver cancer. Had she been watching Frank drink himself to death all this time, just as she'd watched her father do?

A nurse came into the room carrying a clear bag of liquid, which she hung from a hook that extended from Frank's bed. She rubbed his shoulder gently, bringing him awake.

"Mr. Doyle," she said, "we're going to start your thiamine now. You might feel a warm sensation, but it shouldn't hurt at all."

Frank looked at Kit as though seeking some approval for the nurse's judgment. Kit nodded at Frank, and he gave a similar nod to the nurse, who hooked the bag to his IV and checked to see that it was dripping properly before leaving the room. Frank fell quickly back to sleep, and Kit walked down the hall to get herself a cup of coffee. She thought again about calling Edward or Margo—certainly they should know that their father was in the hospital—but she didn't know what she would say. It seemed better to wait until she got Frank home and spoke to the doctor in New York.

At least he'd been diagnosed with something reversible. He'd been given the chance to quit before it was too late. All of their other problems felt far away again, as they had while Edward was overseas. She knew it was only temporary, but she thought she might as well make the most of it.

They left the hospital two days later. On the way home, Frank announced that he would happily subject himself to more treatments at the end of the month but that, in the meantime, he still had work to do. There was nothing really wrong with him, he added. He just needed to eat a little better. By then Kit had already spoken at length to their family doctor in New York, Tom Dalton, who'd asked her to bring

Frank in as soon as he was released. Without going into further detail, Kit told Frank that he had no choice about returning to New York.

They hit the road after lunch, with Kit at the wheel. She'd always been the family driver, a fact that often surprised people. It seemed unlike Frank to give up so much control. But he found driving a mechanical task, unworthy of his attention. He wanted to talk, to gesture, to turn to face passengers in the back when a point of discussion required it. He would sooner plow into the divider than let a bit of woebegone rhetoric pass unchallenged. It was better for all involved when Kit took the wheel. Though neither of them admitted it, there was also the other matter. He didn't like having his drinking monitored, didn't want to be asked whether he was in a condition to drive. Since often enough he was in no such condition, it was easier to delegate the task as a matter of course. What lengths they'd gone to avoid acknowledging the facts they would now have to face.

"The doctor mentioned that alcohol might interfere with your treatments," she said in the car, trying to sound casual, as though he were going on a short course of antibiotics. "It probably wouldn't hurt either of us to dry out for a little while."

"He could have told me this directly," was all Frank said in response. "I'm not a child."

On the rest of the drive, he was as quiet as she could ever remember him being. By the time she pulled into their Lexington Avenue garage, he was fast asleep. He woke slowly while she took their bags from the trunk. Though he was usually quite gallant about such matters, he let her carry them the two blocks to the house. As they entered, Kit heard Margo's voice in conversation down the hall. She sent Frank upstairs, and to her relief he acquiesced, perhaps wanting to make himself more presentable. She still hadn't quite decided what she meant to tell the kids, but there was no sense waiting. She followed Margo's voice to the library, where she found her sitting on the couch with Sam Waxworth, both with the look of having been caught at something.

"What are you doing here?" Margo asked, her initial embarrassment turning quickly to exasperation.

"It's my house," Kit answered sharply.

"You were supposed to be staying in Bridgehampton all month."

Kit decided that lying about it, even just in front of this boy, would only make things seem more significant once the truth came out.

"Your father had a fall, so we came home to take him to the doctor."

The opposition fell from Margo's face.

"What happened?"

"We were out for a walk in the rain, and he slipped. It turns out he's been suffering from a kind of vitamin deficiency, but he's going to be fine."

"Where is he now?"

"He went up to our room."

Margo started toward the stairs. She seemed to have forgotten entirely about her guest.

"Let him rest for a little while," Kit said. "He'll be down for dinner, and we can talk then."

Margo stopped where she was, but she still didn't give any notice to Sam, who stood silently beside her. Kit stared him in the face until he said, "I should get back to work."

The three of them walked together to the front door.

"I hope Frank feels better," Sam said to Kit in the hall. "And thank you again for having us out the other weekend."

"Our pleasure," Kit told him. "It was especially nice to meet your lovely wife."

The remark had its desired effect: Sam blushed, nodded, and hurried out the door. Once they were alone, Margo seemed torn between explaining herself and going straight upstairs. Kit wanted to give Frank a few more minutes, but she didn't have the energy to think about what was going on between her daughter and Sam Waxworth.

"Where's Edward?" she asked.

Margo looked puzzled.

"He moved out last week."

"Was someone going to mention this to me?"

"I'd assumed he told you."

"Where has he gone?"

"I don't know exactly. You should probably ask him yourself."

Kit called Edward's cell from the house phone in the kitchen, and he answered after a few rings.

"Margo?"

"It's your mother. We came home early."

He waited a beat before saying, "I guess you were surprised to find me gone."

"That was among the things that surprised me."

"I was going to explain everything next week. It's all a bit—complicated."

Complications were multiplying at an alarming rate, Kit thought.

"Something's come up with your father. He's had a fall."

"Where is he?" Edward asked. "I'll leave right now."

"He's here at home," Kit told him. "It's not an emergency. But if you'll let me know where you're living, I'll come to you. It would be nice to see your new place."

Kit hadn't visited the Lower East Side in years, and she knew it had changed a great deal in that time. She expected to find her son ensconced in the kind of glass-walled luxury high-rise whose construction prompts protests at zoning board meetings, but what she saw when her cab pulled onto his block more or less conformed to her memories of the neighborhood. His building showed no sign of having been so much as refurbished in a generation. A handwritten sign that itself seemed several years old was taped to the dented elevator door and read, simply: BROKEN.

She walked four flights to the apartment number Edward had given her, where the door was answered by an old man with a wild beard and a fresh bruise occupying most of one side of his face, eerily reminiscent of the one Frank now had. This development had the odd effect of making Kit less rather than more confused. Clearly Edward had gotten his new address wrong, or else she had taken it down improperly. Either of these mistakes was understandable. He'd just moved, and she had a lot on her mind. A quick call would correct things, and this strange man would make a good story to lighten the mood when she arrived at his actual building a few doors or a few blocks away. She was about to apologize for the disturbance when the man said, "You must be Eddie's mother."

He graciously offered his hand and introduced himself as Herman. Without further explanation he turned back into the apartment, leaving Kit no choice but to follow. The space was small but clean and neatly furnished. A counter separated a kitchenette from the living room, and there were two doors, presumably leading to bedrooms, from one of which Edward presently emerged.

"Hi, Mom," he said a bit nervously. He came over to hug Kit. When they'd separated he gestured to the old man and said, "This is my friend Herman."

"We've met," Kit said.

Herman gave a slight bow. He seemed entirely comfortable with this awkward meeting. Perhaps he assumed that Edward had explained the situation to her. Now Kit looked him briefly over. He was rather well-dressed, in a suit that looked expensive, new, and sharply tailored, with an open-collared dress shirt underneath. Apart from the wild beard and hair, he didn't look as though he belonged in this run-down building any more than Edward did. He might have been some kind of bohemian artist. For a moment Kit considered the possibility that this man was her son's boyfriend. She'd occasionally wondered whether something was going on between Edward and Justin. That would have been fine with her, but this was really too much.

"I hope you won't take this as rude," she said, "but I need a moment alone with my son."

Herman bowed again and retreated quickly but without embarrassment through one of the bedroom doors. When he'd gone, Edward and Kit sat down together on the couch.

"This whole situation must seem pretty strange," Edward said.

"It does," Kit told him.

"I'm guessing it's not a secret that I've been having some trouble adjusting to being home. I talk with Herman about things, and it makes me feel better. It's been very good for me."

"Is he some kind of therapist?"

Edward thought a second.

"More like a minister, really."

As a believer herself, however neglectful she might be about it, Kit could hardly object if some God talk helped her son, but she'd never known him to have any interest in religion. He'd been obviously relieved when they'd stopped going regularly to mass after his grandfather's death, and so far as Kit could tell he'd never gone of his own accord.

"Most people don't live with their ministers," she noted.

"He needs someone to look after him. Anyway, it was about time I found my own place."

"We can find you a nicer place than this," Kit said. "You could even bring him along."

"I like it here. I'm used to pretty spartan accommodations, and I'm going to be a little tight on money for a while. I've decided to start

EMT training. It's going to take a few weeks, and once I find a job, it won't pay much at first."

"You have plenty of money."

"I don't want that money," Edward told her firmly. "It's hard to describe, but it feels like a kind of burden. I want to try to live without it. Maybe I'll change my mind in the future, but for now I want to forget it. Isn't that what you're always telling me to do?"

Kit had meant that he shouldn't go buy an expensive car or invest in a friend's restaurant, fritter the money away. She'd always assumed he would have a decent job and be able to make rent on a livable apartment. She might have told him all this now, but she'd been through too much over the past two days to argue with him. She needed him on her side.

"What happened with your father wasn't just a fall. The doctor at the hospital thinks he has some other issues. We're taking him in for tests tomorrow."

"Is it serious?"

"It might be."

She hadn't yet admitted this to herself, and it felt strangely calming to say it aloud. She gave Edward all the details, and he listened calmly and attentively. When she mentioned the part that drinking had played in Frank's condition, he didn't seem surprised.

"Is there anything I can do?" he asked.

"Not right now," she said, "but I'm sure there will be eventually."

"I'll come up to see you guys soon," Edward told her before walking her out.

After the neatness of the apartment, the squalid hallway surprised her anew. So long as she'd been talking with Edward inside, his arrangement had seemed natural, or at least explicable, but as she walked down the five flights of stairs she was struck again by the strangeness of it. Abstractly she understood that many people lived more or less happily in such conditions, that others would be grateful just to have an apartment like that one. But who wouldn't want better when better was available? She was broke, and shuttling between Bridgehampton and the Upper East Side; her son was rich, and crashing on an old man's couch. He had enough money to solve her problems, and he didn't even want it.

She was stepping out into the street when the solution came to her. She didn't have to take his money. She just needed to borrow it for a few days—a few weeks at most. It wouldn't solve all her problems, but she could pay off Gilroy and keep the dogs at bay. For the first time in months, she thought it still possible that everything would work out.

7.

"I think I'm coming down with something," Lucy told Sam over dinner. It was Thursday, the night they set aside each week for going out in the neighborhood, and they'd stood for forty minutes outside of Seoul Food BBQ, the tiny Korean place down the block, before being seated at one of the restaurant's five tables.

"What's wrong, exactly?"

She'd expected this question. Sam was generally happy to offer support and concern when the occasion called for them, but he liked to know precisely what he was expected to be supportively concerned about, and this usually required a preliminary round of information gathering. This was part of the reason she'd put off mentioning anything: her complaint was somewhat vague.

"I haven't been running well."

"What do you mean by that?" Sam asked, not without sympathy in his voice.

Lucy had run four or five times a week—forty minutes most weekday mornings, an hour on Saturday or Sunday—since her days on the high school cross-country team, but she didn't think of herself as obsessive about it. She cut runs short when she wasn't feeling strong, and she missed a day or two a month out of laziness. She'd never kept journals in which she dutifully recorded her splits. She preferred to run outside, but when the Wisconsin winter turned dangerous, she'd driven to the university gym and hit the treadmill, which was the only time she noted her pace or distance with any precision. Sam had given her a GPS wristwatch for her birthday one year, urging her to track her progress on some website, but she'd quietly reverted to her old Casio a few weeks later. The thing had felt heavy on her wrist, and anyway she didn't want to track her progress; she just wanted to run. Now she wished she had all the data she would have been collecting, so she could explain her problem in terms that Sam would appreciate.

Not that she was entirely without concrete evidence.

"I've been running the same route every day. Twenty minutes out and twenty back. Lately I'm not as far along when it comes time to turn, and yesterday it took almost twenty-five to get home."

"When did you notice this?" Sam asked, still in fact-finding mode.

Lucy tried to count back the days, and when she made the connection she spoke without thinking.

"After our weekend with the Doyles."

Sam looked down at his bulgogi. They hadn't talked about what had happened with Margo. Lucy still wasn't sure that anything *had* happened, but the expression now on Sam's face certainly supported the idea.

"You should see a doctor," he said.

A moment earlier she'd been trying to convince him of the seriousness of her problem, but his sudden acquiescence bothered her. What was the matter, really? She wasn't running as far as she used to, and she felt worn out when she was done. These were common runner's complaints. It was an unnatural thing to do to your body.

"It can wait until I start work."

This was the other reason she'd put off the conversation. Sam wasn't a salaried employee at the *Interviewer*, so he didn't get benefits, and they'd decided to go uncovered until Lucy's insurance kicked in at the beginning of the school year. A calculated risk, Sam had said before quitting his programming job. Neither of them had ever been seriously sick, and a month-by-month plan would cost more than a thousand dollars just for the summer.

"I'll keep an eye on things. If it gets worse, I'll see someone."

"We can afford a doctor's visit," Sam said, happily returning to logistical matters. "It will cost a few hundred bucks. We budgeted for that. You could see five doctors and we'd still come out ahead. I'll ask for a name at work."

By the next day Sam had found a name, and Lucy had an appointment within the week. Dr. Schilling was a tall, thin man of late middle age, with combed-over hair and a thick gray mustache that he played at with his tongue and tucked into the corners of his mouth while he worked. He took a few minutes to examine Lucy's legs before concluding that there were no structural problems.

"Since you aren't suffering any acute pain," he added, "I don't think you've injured herself. You might see an orthopedist for a second opinion."

Failing that, he recommended that she try aspirin after longer runs, elevate and ice her knees, and take a few days off when she felt especially sore. All of this Lucy could have read in a five-dollar running magazine.

She thanked him for his advice, but politely suggested that there might be more going on.

"I'm only thirty, I haven't logged that many miles. I'm not running marathons. There's no reason my body should be breaking down."

Schilling's tongue dabbed tentatively at his mustache.

"Is anything else bothering you?"

Her other complaints were more difficult to define, which was why she hadn't mentioned them to Sam, but she tried to enumerate them now. She felt exhausted during the day, but she couldn't sleep at night. Both of these symptoms might be effects of running less often, but others were not so easily explained. She had trouble concentrating. She often looked up after twenty minutes of reading the long novel her mother had given her to find that she'd barely registered a word for several pages. Everything felt slow, as though she were moving through something thicker than air. She'd always sprung out of bed in the morning, and now it took effort to get her eyes open.

Schilling raised both hands, as though to hold off this deluge.

"Big life transitions can cause a lot of stress. Do you have any history with anxiety or depression?"

"I know it sounds like that," Lucy said. "But I'm sure that my physical problems preceded this—malaise."

Schilling lapped again at his mustache, a bit more resolutely this time.

"Environmental change can also set off allergies, which would be consistent with some of these symptoms."

He wrote down the name of a rheumatologist and sent her off to pay her bill, which came to two hundred dollars. As she handed over her credit card, she reminded herself that Sam was making more money than he ever had, and that she'd be working again soon. Still, she imagined the proliferation of appointments and tests, each one costing at least that much. She decided that the next doctor she saw would be the last before school started.

The rheumatologist whose number Schilling had scrawled on the prescription pad was a friendly woman named Dr. Lee, not much older than Lucy. She listened while Lucy went through her complaints, and she conducted her exam, which included not just Lucy's legs but her elbows and wrists. She asked about Lucy's sexual habits, her diet, her consumption of alcohol, cigarettes, and drugs. She wanted to know whether Lucy had traveled anywhere exotic in the past six months.

"Not unless you count Wisconsin."

"Anything else I should know? Anything unusual about your lifestyle?"

Lucy thought for a moment.

"I live above a poultry warehouse."

This information seemed to raise her status in Dr. Lee's eyes.

"Have you handled any birds or come in contact with their waste?" she asked with obvious excitement.

Even Lucy's answer—so far as she knew, she hadn't touched any chickens or any chicken shit—didn't dim the doctor's enthusiasm.

"Just breathing in an enclosed space with them can put you at risk for some airborne viruses."

"I've definitely been breathing something." She tried to laugh. "The place stinks."

Lucy felt sure they'd isolated her problem. Why hadn't she thought of the birds before? She paid three hundred dollars at reception and headed a few blocks away to have blood drawn at a lab that charged her another two-fifty.

For the next few days, she searched the internet for information about communicable avian diseases. She read about bird flu, botulism, campylobacteriosis, and salmonella, but none of them matched her symptoms. She landed eventually on something called histoplasmosis, a fungal infection that caused fatigue and body aches. The disease usually went away by itself within a few months. If it didn't, antifungal pills could clear it up.

She waited for Dr. Lee's call with a hint of self-satisfaction, anticipating her diagnosis. She imagined calling Dr. Schilling to explain that her problem had been real, and that she'd solved it on her own. Instead Schilling himself called to say that her blood work was clean. He seemed to think she would be happy to hear it.

"Did they check for histoplasmosis?"

Through the phone she heard a burst of breath that might have been a frustrated laugh, followed by the sound of rustling paper.

"Dr. Lee put in for that. It came back negative, like everything else."

"So where does that leave us?"

"My guess is that you'll feel a lot better once you've settled in to your new home. In the meantime, I'd be happy to recommend a therapist."

When Lucy got off the phone, she started to cry. There was something wrong with her—something *real*—and she wanted to know what it was. She worked with therapists, she respected what they did, but her problems were not in her head. She wouldn't pay a hundred dollars a week to spend an hour pretending that her feelings about being too far from home had made her unable to run three miles without swelling up.

She would have to do her best to snap out of it. She couldn't spend any more days sitting in the apartment, waiting for Sam to get home, longing for their old life. Before the move, she'd made a plan to get to know the city that summer. She'd been excited to come to New York—she really had, though she'd been resistant to the idea at first. They would stay for only one year, which made it all the more important to get the most out of the time. They'd choose a different neighborhood each morning until the school year started. They'd take the train to the middle of it, and they'd walk around. She'd imagined undertaking all this with Sam, whom she'd thought would have much more free time than he did. The idea of doing it alone had overwhelmed her a little, though most of New York was as safe as Milwaukee or even Madison. By the time she'd felt comfortable enough with the city to explore, this creeping fatigue had begun.

Her stay in New York was ten percent through, and she hadn't seen the place at all. But she still had a month and a half before she started work. She could see a lot between now and then. She committed to following through on her plan. If it made her feel better—if her problems really did evaporate in the face of a little discipline—so much the better. If not, she'd have insurance by then, and she'd see every doctor she could until she got a proper diagnosis.

On the morning after Schilling's call, she went for her usual run. She picked up the concrete track less than a block from their apartment and followed it alongside a body of water that she would have all along taken for the East River had an online map not called it "Buttermilk Channel." The track—chosen by Sam when he was looking for apartments—brought her past loading docks, container plants, and a few gutted buildings, but she liked it well enough. She'd missed a few runs that week, and her lungs ached a bit on the return leg, but otherwise she felt strong. By the time she got home, Sam had left for the day, and she had the apartment to herself as she showered and changed.

She'd already decided where her first outing would take her. Whenever she called or emailed friends back home to catch up, they asked whether she'd been "down there" yet. Most of them used this precise euphemism, and she understood what they meant, though in fact "down there" was north of where she lived. One friend had asked when she was going to see 9/11, as if the day itself still existed in that place, waiting for visitors to take it in. She'd been surprised that Sam hadn't gone already by the time she got to New York, but he'd said there was nothing really there to see. Perhaps he was right, but she wanted to see the nothing for herself.

After waiting ten minutes for a bus, she gave up and walked half an hour to a train that she could take to the Wall Street stop. There was something talismanic about the name. She felt as though she were taking the subway to a magical land in some book. When she got out, it was exactly how it was supposed to be: a busy street, full of people in suits on their way to work, hot dog carts, men in what seemed to be African dress selling purses off sheets on the sidewalk. Steam rose from an open manhole into which workers in orange helmets were slowly descending. There were no signs saying where she should go, but Lucy found what looked like a tour group, and she followed it down a narrow side street.

As they waited at a light, a young girl pressed a folded piece of paper into Lucy's hand, and she accepted it, thinking it might contain some information about the area. She opened it to find instead a flyer in odd font with a hand-drawn border:

> *Ms. Clara Lune says: DON'T GIVE UP!! Ms. Clara seeks to help those who have BEEN CROSSED, HAVE SPELLS, CAN'T HOLD MONEY, WANT LUCK, WANT THEIR LOVED ONES BACK, HAVE MARRIAGE PROBLEMS, OR WANT TO GET RIDE OF STRANGE SICKNESS. SHE TELLS YOU ALL BEFORE YOU UTTER A WORD, SHE can bring the SPIRIT OF RELEASE and CONTROL your every affair and dealings. She reveals to you hidden secrets, evil eyes & lurking dangers that may harm you. ARE YOU SUFFERING FROM AN ILLNESS OR DISEASE THAT YOU CAN'T CURE? There is a Doctor of all doctors. WHEN YOUR CASE SEEMS HOPELESS THERE IS A REMEDY FOR YOU.*

At the bottom was an address and a map showing how to get to it from the Bleecker Street subway station, though Lucy had no idea where that was. She crumpled the flyer in her hand, but there was no trash can on the corner, so she stuffed it into her pocket as the light changed and she followed the group through the crosswalk.

After another block, the narrow street opened back up into a wide, almost midwestern sky. At first all she could see below was a crowd surrounding a chain-link fence. Though it was just an ordinary weekday, there was a crush of people already there. Lucy moved slowly through them until she arrived at the fence, which marked off the edge of the abyss. She looked down into the enormous hole. People were working down there, but what Lucy saw wasn't a construction site. She saw instead the locus of a great destructive act. The sheer size of the hole gave a horrific sense of the extent of that destruction. She thought of her friend who'd asked about "visiting 9/11," and it did seem that she was glimpsing something torn from the fabric of ordinary time.

A feeling of vertigo shook her as she looked down into it. She grabbed at the fence for balance. The sun had broken through since she'd gotten off the train, and she felt trapped in the heat. She imagined she could see the shades of all the lives that had been swallowed up in this place. She was glad she had come alone, because she couldn't possibly have told Sam what she felt in that moment—that she stood on the boundary of holy ground, in a place that had been sanctified by blood. She wasn't religious—in this she and Sam were in complete agreement—but she couldn't imagine any way to make sense of what she was seeing but with such words.

A new wave of people pushed in behind her, and she broke away from the fence, fighting through this crowd. She hurried several blocks, until she was back among the men in suits. How strange to see so many people going about their normal days so close to what she'd just seen. It seemed almost disrespectful, though many of these people had probably been there that morning, forced to take the full measure of something that had come to Lucy only as a kind of rumor.

Lucy herself had spent much of that day eight years before stoned, a fact she'd long tried to forget. She'd gone through a brief pot-smoking period during her sophomore year of college, when a group of boys in the suite upstairs in Chadbourne Hall would light up every afternoon before shuffling off to the dining hall. They'd extended an open invitation to Lucy and her roommate, Megan, who was hooking up with one of them. For the first few weeks of the semester, Lucy had joined them almost every day.

On the morning of the attacks, she'd been out for a run, and she'd returned to find her room empty, the television still on. After a few minutes of watching in confusion, she'd gone upstairs. She hadn't been looking to get high—it was ten o'clock in the morning— she just didn't want to be alone. She found Megan in tears, sitting with the boys on their long sectional couch, watching the news. Lucy had sat down beside her, and they'd hugged while one of the boys mournfully packed a bowl. Lucy could tell it was not their first of the day. When it came around to her, she'd accepted without much thought. No one would be going to class. The whole world was sitting in front of the television just as they were. After her second pull, she'd begun to feel terrified. Of course she knew they were in no real danger where they were, but she had a vivid vision of a plane falling out of the sky, landing on Chad, and ending all their lives instantaneously. That afternoon, she had gone to her parents' house, where she'd stayed for most of the next week.

Lucy felt ashamed by that response now. She realized how distant the events had been from the reality her life, how narcissistic it had been to imagine she was at risk, how childish to respond to that imagined danger by running home. She thought about Kit Doyle, who Sam had told her was evacuated from a burning building during the chaos. For the first time, Lucy could understand the madness that had come over some of the people who'd actually lived through that day. But madness still it had been. However understandable that fury, Lucy was only more certain that it had been a travesty to pile death upon death, to attempt to redeem blood with more blood.

At least now they seemed to be coming out of it. So much had ended with this election, and so much new begun. Though there were people who couldn't stand the fact that the country was moving on, those people would lose. They would be consigned to the margins, as Frank Doyle had already been. When she thought of her new president, she thought first of all about how reasonable he was. This was why all the efforts to make him seem exotic and foreign were bound to fail. How could people possibly succeed at making this model of genial rationality into someone angry, sinister, driven by subterranean forces? Or else, after eight years of a subliterate president, suggest that there was something primitive about a man who was not only obviously smart but also one of the most thoughtful ever to hold the office? Lucy had lived her whole life in a place that was almost entirely white, but she'd also grown up around midwestern university professors. Obama was the first president who seemed at all like the people she knew and loved. His defining feature in her eyes was not strangeness but precisely this familiarity. That America could elect such a man made her hopeful that the fever had broken, the madness was over. The country was almost back on solid footing.

Such were the thoughts with which she tried to calm herself as she walked uptown. Her plan had been to explore the neighborhood around the site, but there didn't seem to be much neighborhood to speak of, and anyway she wanted to escape the place. She walked quickly, without looking around. After twenty blocks or so, she felt better, and she slowed somewhat to look around. She came to a corner that looked familiar, and she realized that she'd walked these streets on the day she'd visited Sam's office. She wasn't far from there now. While she continued uptown, she called to tell him she was in the area. She got his voice mail and hung up without leaving a message. A few minutes later she got a text: *Finishing up a piece. will call in an hour.*

The timing seemed perfect. She wasn't sure exactly how far she was from the office, but she guessed she'd be there within an hour. She could take him to lunch once he'd finished whatever he was working on, or they could just walk around a little while. Why hadn't it occurred to her weeks ago to visit Sam during the day? He always seemed so busy, but he had to take breaks once in a while, and her own schedule was completely open. Now that she saw how easy it was to hop on a train and get there, she might make a habit of it.

Getting to Sam's building took less time than she'd expected, so she slowly circled Union Square before going inside. She'd walked several miles that day, on top of a shortened morning run, and she didn't feel at all worn out. Maybe Schilling was right: she'd just needed to shake herself out of her funk. She felt silly having spent almost a thousand dollars figuring that out.

Almost exactly an hour after she'd received Sam's text, she stepped off the elevator into the *Interviewer*'s offices, where the pretty young receptionist whose name she couldn't remember barely looked up from her book.

"How can I help you?" she asked.

"I'm here to see Sam Waxworth."

The girl dog-eared her page as though making a great sacrifice.

"Do you have an appointment?"

She smiled broadly, but her perfectly cut black bangs gave her expression an unnerving severity. Lucy shook her head.

"I was just in the neighborhood."

"He's not here today."

"Are you sure?"

"He's not in the office most days. He usually works from home."

Lucy resisted the impulse to get annoyed with this young girl, who was probably two months out of school and overwhelmed by answering phones.

"I'd know if he was at home," she said, trying to sound amused. "I just came from there. I'm his wife."

"Of course," the girl said, and she smiled again. "Nice to see you. I guess I don't know where he is, then."

Lucy was about to ask her to try Sam's desk when she remembered that Sam didn't have a desk. Perhaps this explained why the reception-ist didn't know that he came into the office every day. She was decid-ing what to say next when she felt her phone ringing in her pocket.

"This is him," she told the girl before answering.

"What are you up to?" Sam said brightly.

"Walking around," Lucy said. "I wound up in your neighborhood, and I was wondering whether you wanted to grab lunch."

Sam let out a long, disappointed breath.

"Today is going to be tough," he said. "I'd love to do it later in the week."

"Maybe you can just step outside to say hello?"

"Where are you?"

"At reception."

"You're at the office? I wish you'd said something."

"I thought I'd surprise you."

"The thing is," Sam said after a moment, "I'm uptown on a reporting trip."

"You told me you were finishing a piece."

"That, too. I needed to interview someone for a thing I'm doing, but when I was done I found a coffee shop where I could write. There's so much to get done in this job. I've really got to multitask." He seemed to be waiting for Lucy to respond to this. When she didn't, he went on. "I'd still love to see you, though. There's a great sushi place right around the corner on Fifteenth. I can get down there in half an hour, if you can stand to wait for me."

Lucy wanted to tell him that his story didn't make sense, but she was struck by the sight of the young receptionist looking quizzically up at her.

"I think I'm just going to head home."

"Sorry this didn't work out," Sam told her, though he sounded relieved.

"That's all right," she said. "I should have given you a heads-up."

She got on a downtown train at Union Square, but after one stop she realized that she'd accidentally taken the local, and she didn't know where she was supposed to change. Her long morning of activity had caught up with her all at once. She was too tired even to be angry at Sam. She'd been so embarrassed when she got off the phone and watched the receptionist studiously avoid eye contact. She might have been able to accept Sam's story, were it not for what the girl had said about how he usually worked from home. As far as Lucy knew, he'd gone into the office nearly every day since she'd arrived.

Perhaps she'd known all along. Maybe this was the reason she'd been so resistant to accepting the connection between her physical ailments and the emotional facts of her present life: the malaise had set in after their weekend in Bridgehampton, and she hadn't wanted to admit that anything had happened during that weekend that might cause such a thing. She should have spoken to Sam about it sooner. She'd thought often about what she'd seen there, but what was there to be said about it? If it came to that, how could she compete with Margo Doyle, who was pretty and rich and sophisticated, an indigenous inhabitant of a world that Sam so badly wanted to occupy?

These weren't the kinds of considerations she'd ever thought she would have to make with Sam. In college he'd courted her—there was really no other word for it—with such doggedness that it had become a joke among her friends. It might have been creepy if he'd been a different kind of guy, but he was so good-natured that she'd found his persistence endearing. She'd turned him down the first half dozen times he asked her out, and he'd never been bothered by it. For all his social awkwardness, he had this oddball confidence, which was entirely different from the superficial bravado of the frat boys who'd never been told no before. Rejection wounded those guys, but Sam wasn't wounded. Changing her mind became a project for him. Eventually she'd decided to give him a chance, and that chance was all it took.

She knew he wasn't cool. She knew that sometimes people looked at them together and wondered what she saw in him, but she didn't mind that. If she'd ever had doubts about him, it was that he was too comfortable. Without question she loved Sam, but she'd occasionally worried that she loved him for the wrong reasons. That dating Sam all through college and marrying him so soon after graduation were of a piece with her decision to spend her whole life within ten miles of the house where she grew up. He was something she never had to worry about. He would work for the university, she would teach, and they would spend the rest of their lives in Madison.

Immediately after pulling out of the Astor Place stop, the train shuddered to a halt. The lights inside the car flickered briefly but stayed on. After an unmoving minute in the tunnel, some passengers mumbled their displeasure. Lucy hadn't been on the subway often enough to know whether this was a common occurrence or something serious. She was brought back to her vision in front of the fence. What if something had happened? What if she was trapped in this place, and the last words she ever shared with Sam were lies that she'd been too scared to question?

She wished she had the novel she'd been trying to read all this time, so she could distract herself. It was a large hardcover, too heavy to carry around the city all day, and if she couldn't concentrate enough to read it while sitting quietly in her apartment, she couldn't imagine getting anywhere with it on a crowded train.

In her pocket she found the crumpled flyer. She flattened it out and idly read over it. *There is a Doctor of all doctors.* Lucy imagined going to see this woman, seeking a remedy for her strange sickness. She imagined how it would infuriate Sam if he ever found out, and this added to the idea's appeal. It would be a kind of revenge on him. She read back over the flyer more carefully. There was something hypnotic in the language, the odd capitalization. Something agreeably primitive. She was so engrossed that she hardly noticed the train shake back into motion. The next time she looked up, they were pulling into the next station: Bleecker Street. She folded the flyer and slipped it into her pocket. She was out on the platform just before the doors closed.

Outside, Lucy followed the hand-drawn map for ten minutes until she arrived at the address on the flyer, where she found an unwelcoming brown metal door with a row of buzzers beside it, one of which read, *Ms. Clara Lune.* When she buzzed, a voice came quickly over the intercom to ask who was there.

"I saw your flyer," Lucy said. "I wanted to talk with you."

"Third floor," the voice responded abruptly, and the door clicked unlocked.

There was an elevator inside, with a sign that read: BROKEN. On her way up the stairs, Lucy wondered what on earth she was doing there. She'd been in a kind of fugue state since leaving Sam's office, and she felt as though she'd just woken from it. If she'd done that a few minutes sooner, she might have turned around and walked back to the train, but now she had to press on. It would be rude not to appear, she thought, having already disturbed the woman. What would it cost her, apart from a bit of time and a few bucks? She thought again of how it would bother Sam. She liked the idea of having her own secret from him, some part of their life in New York that belonged just to her.

The door opened as though of its own accord to reveal a middle-aged woman of medium build, dressed in jeans and a green silk shirt. She had long black hair and olive skin that gave her an Eastern European or Mediterranean appearance. Perhaps she was an actual Gypsy, Lucy thought. The woman offered a hand and introduced herself simply as Claire. Her voice was more welcoming now than it had been over the intercom, as though she'd taken the intervening time to prepare. She spoke in fluent English with no discernible accent, and she invited Lucy into the apartment as though she were a guest, making no effort to disguise the fact that it was her home or to give the place a professional air.

A small, round table occupied the center of the living room, and half a dozen votive candles burned on top of it. The room also held a couch and a few bookshelves, but the candles were the only thing that seemed at all designed to create a sense of atmosphere. Claire sat Lucy at the table before disappearing briefly through a swinging door into another room. While she waited, Lucy heard a small dog barking in what might have been a nearby apartment or a different part of the one they were in. Claire returned with two glasses of water, and she gave Lucy one. There was courtesy but no sense of ceremony behind her actions.

"Tell Claire what's bothering you," she said as she sat down across from Lucy.

The request surprised Lucy, who'd thought that the woman was supposed to know what was bothering her without a word. She wasn't sure where to begin, so she described her physical ailments, because that was what she'd gotten used to describing. She mentioned all the things she'd been telling the doctors: she felt worn down; her joints ached and swelled; she couldn't run anymore; her brain did not always seem to be working at full capacity. She explained that these problems had started soon after she'd moved to New York. When she'd finished, she took a long sip of her water while she waited for some response. Claire reached across the table and took Lucy's hands in hers.

"Someone put a bad spirit in you," she said simply. Lucy wanted to smile, but after all, what had she expected to hear? When she didn't respond, Claire ran a finger over her wedding ring. "You moved to New York to be with your husband?"

Lucy felt a loss of breath.

"That's right," she said.

"You've been chasing him everywhere he goes, but he's been chasing someone else." Claire looked straight at Lucy, waiting for some reply, but Lucy gave her only a flinching nod. "I think you know who's given you the bad spirit," Claire said, "but I don't want you to tell me. For now we've just got to clear out a little space."

She let go of Lucy's hands, stood up from the table, and went to one of the shelves, where she took down what looked like a sparkler or an incense stick. She brought it back to the table and lit it from one of the candles. It gave off a lot of smoke and a vaguely spicy scent. Claire gave Lucy no direction or explanation, she just watched while it burned slowly in her hand. Lucy watched, too. As she did, she felt time slowing to the rhythm of the crawling flame. She was overtaken with a not unpleasant feeling of drowsiness, as though Claire had put something in the water. Part of her wanted to get up and leave, but that felt impossible while the flame still burned. Claire let it burn down to her fingers before she softly blew it out.

Their session was over. Lucy didn't know whether she'd been there for just a few minutes or the better part of an hour. They walked together to the door, and Claire looked Lucy over before opening it. Lucy prepared for some parting prescription, an action she might take to send her bad spirit away.

"Fifty dollars," Claire said finally.

Lucy realized then that Claire had been assessing how much her new client could afford. She had almost forgotten that she would need to pay. She took out her wallet and discovered that she had just a few singles with her.

"I don't suppose you'd take a credit card?"

"Ms. Clara Luna only accepts cash."

It was the first time Claire had used this stage name, and she spoke it with a hint of irony that had the odd effect of reinforcing rather than undermining her overall performance.

"I have to run out to an ATM," Lucy said. "I swear I'll come straight back. I can leave my bag here if you want."

Claire shook her head reassuringly, and she handed Lucy a card.

"Go home and see how you feel. In the morning, text the number on the flyer to make an appointment. You can pay me next time."

PART THREE:

THE LAW OF LARGE NUMBERS

(August/September)

1.

The treatment area at New York General had the beeping monitors and pumping machinery of a typical hospital room, but two large recliners in the place of beds. Since Frank was the only patient, Kit got in the habit of claiming the second recliner while the nurse hooked up his IV. They both brought books, but Frank invariably nodded off as soon as the nurse left, and Kit was too anxious to read.

Midway through Frank's last treatment, a woman with neatly cut white hair peeked through the door and asked in a low voice whether Kit wanted to join her for coffee. She was in her midseventies, and her outfit—a light blue shirt above a gray, ankle-length skirt—seemed like a kind of uniform, though she obviously wasn't a nurse. When Kit got to the door, she saw that the woman was wearing a name tag:

Sr. Mary Cronin
Pastoral Care

The nun led Kit down the hall, to a door marked "Family Lounge." Kit had come to this floor five days a week for three weeks now, but she hadn't noticed this room before. It held two couches, a small fridge, a sink, and a hanging shelf with a coffee maker, mugs, and a large jug full of coffee pods. A daytime courtroom show played on the wall-mounted television, which Sister Cronin muted before turning her attention to the coffee.

"Cream or sugar?" she asked Kit.

"Black is fine," Kit said. "No sugar." Still a bit disoriented, she added, "How did they know we were Catholic?"

The nun smiled as she handed Kit a cup.

"I serve the entire hospital community, regardless of religious background. I know you've been coming in pretty regularly for the past few weeks, and I wanted to make sure you're getting everything you need."

"He's actually done today," Kit said. "He seems to be responding to the treatments well enough."

"I'm glad to hear that," Sister Cronin replied. "But I was asking about you. These situations can be very difficult for caregivers."

Despite everything, Kit was a long way from thinking of herself as a "caregiver." The word conjured images of bedpans and wet wipes, which she'd been spared for now. A few weeks of drying out had improved Frank's condition considerably, and she'd assumed that he would recover fully, though lately he'd hit a plateau. His thiamine levels were back to normal, but his short-term memory hadn't returned. Kit had tried to tell herself that the process was just taking a little longer than anticipated, but now it seemed that someone had put her name on a list of people in need, people whose lives were going to change.

She should have been preparing for this for years—when you married a man a decade older than you, the custodial years loomed forever on the horizon—but Frank had always had so much vitality, and the change had come on so quickly. Or was it just that she hadn't been paying attention? Watching him shuffle along, she was sometimes struck by the possibility that he didn't want to get better. This was unfair, but he'd always been so stubborn. Surely, he could fight his way out of this thing if he wanted. Part of Frank had always preferred living in the past, and the present moment happened to be particularly inhospitable to him. She couldn't entirely blame him for wanting to erase his downfall, to live in a time when he was still one of the most influential men in the country, when his book would still be written someday.

"That's kind of you. I'm holding up all right."

"Have you got any children?"

Kit's coffee had cooled, and she took a long sip before answering. Had they moved on now to polite conversation, or was this part of the woman's business?

"A boy and a girl. Both adults."

"People with children sometimes tell me that caring for a failing spouse can be like caring for a newborn."

Kit laughed despite herself. She didn't have much basis for comparison. She'd had her children at a time when extended maternity leaves were not exactly smiled upon—they were one of the stated reasons women could not be relied upon in executive positions—and she'd still been in the process of proving that she could take over from her father. She'd returned to work within a week after each pregnancy.

"Are they in a position to help?" the nun asked.

"I hardly know what position they're in," Kit said. "My daughter lives with us, and she's devoted to her father. We also have a housekeeper who comes most days. She's very reliable."

"It's important that you find a little time for yourself. There are resources available for you."

Sister Cronin went on for a few minutes about support groups, therapists, home aides—all of it having quite the opposite effect of reassurance. She was trying to make Kit understand that Frank would never get better.

"I don't always do this," she said tentatively, as she finished up. "But since you mentioned you're Catholic, we might say a prayer if you'd like?"

Kit nodded, and the woman took her hand. They closed their eyes and bowed heads.

"Lord, I commend Katherine and Francis to your care," Sister Cronin began. As she went on, Kit thought she heard a light lilt that hadn't been present before. Certainly she spoke more naturally now. Kit too felt more comfortable. In the world where she'd been raised, you didn't take your problems to a therapist or a counselor or a support group. You took them to God.

She didn't mention Sister Cronin to Frank when he woke up. What would she have said? *Someone came to speak with me about caring for a failing spouse.* He still didn't seem to be failing to her. He was no infant. He wasn't incapacitated, just sick.

The next morning Kit woke early as usual and went downstairs alone. One surprising benefit of spending all day looking after Frank was that she'd come to appreciate her mornings again. With summer in full swing, she'd started spending them in the garden.

She'd always been the first one awake, well before 7:00, which had left her close to an hour to herself, even back when the kids were up early and rushing off to school. For most of her career, she'd spent the early morning on the phone, finding out how after-hours trading had gone, checking on the overseas markets, gleaning whatever other news might be relevant for the day ahead. Later, she'd set up a computer in the library with a dial-up connection. All the numbers she'd spent each morning compiling now waited in her inbox when she woke, but somehow this had only increased the frenzy of her days. With the information so easily available, there was a greater demand to do something with it.

After her retirement, she'd missed that rush. Her mornings seemed interminable. She was still up early, and she still checked email (now on her BlackBerry) almost reflexively, but most of it was junk. Responding to whatever actually merited attention took just a few minutes. Where once she'd wondered how she would meet all the coming day's demands, she began to worry instead about filling the time. Marinela arrived around 8:00, but she'd been told many times not to disturb Kit when she came in, and Kit couldn't tell her now that she'd be happy for the interruption.

When he'd still been at the paper, Frank had come down by 8:30 on most mornings. He'd gone to the *Herald* building two or three days a week. On the others, he'd sit with her for a few minutes before returning upstairs and installing himself in his office until lunch. He'd always spent more time in that room than his columns strictly required. Often enough, Kit understood, he was reading a book or talking on the phone or watching highlights of the previous night's games. This was all part of his job, as far as Frank was concerned, since almost anything he came across could find its way into his writing. Only after she'd retired and come to want his company did she start to wonder whether a morning spent in front of the television was really so essential to his process. Before then, how he spent those hours had been largely a matter of indifference to her. His work got done, and he was inevitably finished by the time she got home, often dressed for an evening out, with a glass of something waiting for her.

She'd been generally aware, when Frank handed her that first glass of wine at the end of a long day, that he'd already had a few glasses of something himself. This seemed natural to her. Wasn't he entitled to unwind after wrangling with the blank page for hours? Once she started spending her days at home and having lunch with him, she was forced to acknowledge that he was often enough having a drink before noon, that alcohol was less a reward for a long day of writing than the fuel by which the writing got done.

At least then there *was* writing getting done. The column kept appearing three times a week. The drinking was part of his process, like the long phone conversations, the time in front of the television, the browsing of half a dozen different books at once. She didn't claim to understand the strange alchemy by which hours in that room turned into words on a page, words that were read in a few million homes, in congressional offices, on Air Force One.

But it should have told her something when his hours in the office actually grew longer after his firing. He'd barely make a pass through the kitchen for coffee before going back upstairs and holing himself up. For the first few months she'd happily accepted the fiction that a book was getting written in that room. Once this illusion had been shattered, she'd had no idea what he did to pass that time, but the past month had gone a long way toward clearing the picture up—mostly what he did was drink.

How could she not have known? Or had she known, after all?

On their second day back in New York, they'd gone to see Dr. Dalton, who'd been much less delicate with Frank than Kit had expected.

"The drinking did it," he said abruptly.

Frank had nodded in a way that suggested they'd discussed the subject before, had perhaps been discussing it for years. What else had alcohol done to his body that she didn't know about?

"What do we do now?" Frank asked.

"You do these thiamine treatments, and you quit the booze. Not for a few weeks. Forever."

Frank took this rather calmly, which worried Kit, since it meant either that he didn't understand or that he understood and didn't intend to obey. After all these years, could he possibly just give it up like that? While he napped that afternoon, Kit had gone through the house and removed every bottle she could find. She didn't tell him before doing it, and she expected some complaint, but he hadn't said a word. So far as she could tell, he hadn't had a drink since. Had he been waiting for someone to intervene, to make him stop doing something he couldn't stop doing on his own? Should that have been her job all along?

Kit poured a cup of coffee, took in the *Herald* from the stoop, and brought it out back. Since Frank hardly knew the difference, she'd renewed her subscription, which for some reason she couldn't give up, though it had become a minefield that could be safely navigated only with great care. She'd always begun with the opinion page, but now she avoided that space entirely. The international news was filled with stories about the war. These were easier to read with Edward home, but still harrowing, because every casualty was someone's son or daughter. When she saw a report that three marines had been killed in a raid on some Taliban stronghold, Kit thought immediately of the three unmentioned mothers whose lives had also come to an end that day.

The national news was mostly about the economy, which reminded her of what she'd lost. On top of everything else, she couldn't stand being a spectator to this drama. The industry where she'd spent her entire life was at the center of everyone's attention, and she had no part to play, no consequential decisions to make, no panicked CEOs to reassure. She certainly wasn't fielding calls from Hank Paulson or Tim Geithner, as some of her old friends were now doing.

When you cut out foreign news, domestic news, and political opinion, there wasn't that much paper left, so she lingered over sections she'd once quickly discarded. She'd resisted following Frank's Mets for forty years, but now she worked avidly through the box scores. She pored over the Arts & Entertainments pages, giving twenty-minute chunks of her life to articles about cable crime dramas she had no plans to watch or the comebacks of supposedly legendary pop divas whose names she'd never heard before.

She was on her way inside to refill her coffee when the bell rang. At first she thought that Marinela had forgotten her key, but Marinela was on her annual trip home. Kit couldn't remember the last time someone had rung the bell unannounced at any hour, let alone this early. They got deliveries, they got meter readings, but friends didn't drop by unexpectedly. This wasn't a neighborhood where Jehovah's Witnesses or political canvassers went door to door.

The two men standing outside could have been either of these things, in their boxy dark suits, white shirts, and striped ties of slightly different pattern and color, which might once have hung beside each other on the same discount rack. Above their outfits they wore the studiously solemn expressions of professional pall-bearers. One was tall and heavyset, with neatly combed but thinning blond hair and the handsome, tired face of a movie star gone to seed. He held a trunk-sized briefcase in one hand. The other man had a black crew cut and youthful Asian features. He was short and thin. He seemed not just smaller than the first but more compact, as though he'd chosen this shape for himself with efficiency in mind. Instinctively Kit turned first to him.

"Can I help you?"

"Are you Katherine Doyle?"

His tone made clear that he already knew the answer.

"What can I do for you?"

"My name is Dan Canilang. This is my partner, Greg Donaldson. We're agents with the FBI's financial crimes unit, and we were hoping for a few minutes of your time this morning."

"What is this about?"

"I think it would be better for all of us if we spoke inside."

Kit hesitated briefly before letting the men in and leading them down the hall to the library.

"Can I get either of you a cup of coffee or a glass of water?"

"We're all right, ma'am," Canilang said. His partner had still not spoken a word.

"If you don't mind, I'll refill my own. I was just on my way when I heard you ring."

In the kitchen, Kit tried to settle herself. She'd been prepared for the possibility that she would hear from someone, but she'd thought it was unlikely. There was no real evidence against her. She'd been so pleased with her solution. Of course she could never take Edward's money, but she hadn't needed to take it. She was already the one who managed his investments. All she had to do was move him into Celsia. She'd have to explain things to him somehow when it came time to take the money she needed out, but he would hardly listen, if her previous conversations on the topic were any indication. He would happily sign anything she put in front of him, and she would be leaving him as much as he'd started with.

Most securities enforcement happened through self-reporting. When an individual made a large profit on a market-moving announcement, the compliance officers at the bank that executed the trade were supposed to notify the Financial Industry Regulatory Agency. A report to FINRA generated a referral to the SEC. In most cases, this is where the whole thing stopped, assuming the trade was even noticed and reported in the first place. The referral got filed away in some database and forgotten. If the person in question had been the subject of a previous referral or had some obvious connection to a company insider—the kind of thing that could be discovered without a subpoena or really any legwork at all—the SEC might open an investigation, which generally meant calling the target and asking for some explanation. Kit had never received one of these calls, but she knew plenty of people who had. If you traded in any real volume, the good timing on a single bet could reasonably be put down to luck, which was usually enough to satisfy the SEC.

These days Kit hardly traded at all, and since taking over Edward's account she'd kept most of it in mutual funds and ETFs, so she'd prepared a bit of a precautionary script, though she'd doubted that the amount she was dealing with would even generate a report, let alone merit a call. If it came to that, she'd been confident that her story would be enough to put the matter to rest. But she hadn't prepared for FBI agents at her door. The FBI didn't do civil enforcement, they did criminal investigations, and they expected to make cases.

Back in the library, Donaldson was seated on the couch where she'd left them, going through his briefcase. Canilang stood near one of the bookshelves with something in his hand. Looking over his shoulder, Kit saw a framed photo of Edward and Justin, taken when they were seniors at St. Albert's. Canilang replaced it on the shelf without remark and walked back to the couch while Kit sat in an armchair facing them. Donaldson pulled out an accordion file, from which he took a yellow legal pad and a small stack of loose papers. He placed the pad on his lap and passed the papers to Canilang.

"What can I help you with?" Kit asked.

"On June 23," Canilang began, reading directly from the sheet, "you executed a purchase on behalf of your son, Edward Doyle, of 44,680 shares of Celsia—stock ticker CLA—for the amount of $47 a share, a total purchase of $2,100,000. Is this correct?"

Kit waited a moment, as though going over the numbers in her head.

"That sounds right. It was definitely in that ballpark."

"One week later, Celsia's board announced a share repurchase at 150 percent of Friday's closing price, which netted your son a little more than a million dollars."

"This is all a matter of public record," Kit said. "I don't see why you needed to come to my house at this hour for confirmation of it."

"You understand why the timing would prompt some questions."

Here she fell back on what she'd prepared for the SEC.

"The company was undervalued. The fundamentals are very good, even in a tough economy like this, but the markets are skittish. I probably saw the same things the board saw when they decided to do the buyback."

"Just to be clear," Canilang said. "You had no knowledge of a potential repurchase at the time you made the trade?"

"I've been doing this for a long time. My experience is that luck tends to even out. I've certainly had some bad luck in the past few years, so maybe I was due."

"Or maybe you felt entitled to get yours back."

These were the first words Donaldson had spoken. He seemed as surprised by them as Kit and Canilang did. He had an oddly high-pitched voice for a man his size, and Kit thought this might be why he didn't generally do the talking.

"That's a nonresponsive answer," Canilang continued as though nothing had happened. "Were you aware of the buyback when you made the purchase?"

"Where would I have heard something like that? I sold my business. I'm retired."

"We'll get to where you might have heard it in a minute. In the meantime we'd like a yes or no answer."

Kit had spent a fair amount of time over the past few weeks considering what she would say if posed the question in such stark terms. She hadn't imagined being asked by a pair of FBI agents, but she didn't think this should change her calculations. They might have proof that Justin had known about the buyback, but they didn't have any proof that he'd told her anything. There had been no phone conversations, no text or email chains. Anything short of an admission from Justin would be circumstantial, and she had absolute confidence that Justin would never admit to such a thing.

"No."

A brief flicker passed over Canilang's face, almost a smile, as though this was the answer he'd wanted.

"When was the last time you spoke with Justin Price?"

"Does all of this have something to do with Justin?" She paused before going on. If she answered right away, that might be a kind of tell. She had no reason to lie, but at the last moment she'd remembered Justin's arrival on the boat. Clearly he'd meant to conceal his visit. What if he left it out when he asked? "We had a party for my son back in April, and Justin was here, along with a lot of old friends."

"April?" Canilang asked.

She realized right away that she'd made a mistake, but it seemed too late to go back.

"As far as I can remember."

Canilang looked briefly down at some notes.

"The problem is that a call was made from your Bridgehampton landline on Sunday, June 14, reporting Justin's boat missing. Later that day, your daughter drove him home."

"Of course," Kit said, probably too quickly. "He came over for dinner. We had guests that weekend, and Justin and I never really spoke. It slipped my mind that he'd been there."

"Have you ever spoken with Justin Price about Celsia?"

She wasn't sure whether she ought to sound surprised by the question. At this point it was clear enough where the conversation was headed.

"We've talked about a lot of stocks over the years. I can't say we never discussed it."

"Did Justin Price tell you about Celsia's buyback plans over the weekend of June 14, in advance of your purchase of the stock on your son's behalf?"

"I'd like to speak to my lawyer before answering any more questions."

"If you didn't do anything wrong," Donaldson broke in, "you don't need to lawyer up. If you did do something, maybe you should have spoken to your lawyer before you lied to us about it."

Perhaps they were just very good at their act, but Canilang seemed genuinely chagrined by these interruptions.

"Here's the deal," he continued with an almost friendly tone. "We know Justin Price knew about the buyback, because the person who told him was working for us. We know he came over that weekend to tell you about it. We've got you dead to rights on insider trading, and now we've got you on obstruction for lying to us about it. Not a great way to end a long and distinguished Wall Street career. But you're lucky, because we're not interested in you. I know that Price is an old family friend, so I want you to understand that we're not really interested in him, either. We're interested in Dan Eisen. We want Justin to give us Eisen, but first we need you to give us Justin." He handed over his card and waited for some response. Kit took the card without looking at it, and he went on. "I'll make this simple. Go ahead and talk to your attorney. Give him my card and tell him to call me by the end of the week. If I don't hear from him, I'm going to come back here with cameras from every network and paper I can drum up, and I'm going to wait until they're happy with the lighting before I frog-march you out of this house. If you so much as hint about this visit to Price in the meantime, there will be no deal, and I will talk with the U.S. Attorney about throwing on a second obstruction charge."

She had expected, when the heavy hand came, for it to come from Donaldson, but it had a much greater effect coming from the smaller, more controlled man, which might well have been the point. Kit slipped the card into her pocket, and she stood to show them out.

As she closed the door behind them, she thought she might collapse right there in the front hall, but when she turned back into the house, she found Margo staring at her from halfway up the stairs.

"Who was that?" she asked.

It seemed somehow appropriate that she would pick this one morning to get up at a decent hour. Kit wondered how long she'd been watching.

"Some old friends from work."

"A little early for a social call."

"It wasn't a social call. They want me to do some consulting, and they needed to talk some things over before going into the office for the day."

Margo walked the rest of the way down the stairs. As she got closer, her expression changed.

"Are you all right? You're shaking."

Kit tried to steady herself.

"Just a little worn out," she said. She looked up at Margo, who also seemed rather shaken. "How about you?"

"I haven't been sleeping well," Margo said. "But I'll be fine."

"Would you like to sit out back with me?"

"That's all right. I think I'll go for a walk."

As Kit let Margo out, her overwhelming thought was that she wanted a drink. She didn't care that it was eight o'clock in the morning. She was about to head for the bar in the library when she remembered that it was bare. She considered going out for something. Instead, she took her coffee back out to the garden and pieced together the paper, which had been scattered by the wind. She wanted everything to look normal when Frank got downstairs.

It was nearly noon by the time she had a chance to call her lawyer, who recommended a meeting with his firm's white-collar criminal-defense specialist. The words "criminal defense" seemed almost tactless to Kit, though this was exactly what she needed.

She spent that afternoon on the most exhaustive examination of the family's accounts that she'd ever attempted. She'd run through all these numbers many times over the past six months, but somehow she was hoping that they would look different now.

Everyone assumed there must be some money somewhere else, and she'd gotten so good at pretending as much that she'd almost convinced herself it was true. But her father had always believed in funneling profits back into the firm, and Kit had learned the habit from him. In her biggest earning years, she'd reinvested as much as she possibly could. What had seemed like prudence now haunted her.

Her grandfather had founded the firm with a partner, Miles Mulqueen, in 1935, after the passage of Glass-Steagall had forced the commercial bank where they'd both worked most of their lives out of the investment banking business. He'd run the place for nearly two decades—along the way buying out Mulqueen—before passing it on to his son. Tommy Quinn had started working for his dad straight out of Holy Cross, and he'd literally been carried out of his office. After Kit's mother died, his only child and his family business were all that really mattered to him.

A lot of men from his generation would have encouraged their daughters to marry the most promising young man in the office, but Tommy Quinn had instead encouraged her to come work for him. She'd started a few years after the bear market of '69, at the height of the counterculture, when Wall Street wasn't exactly a popular destination for ambitious college graduates. She'd taken over just in time for the '87 crash. Later she'd made it through the repeal of Glass-Steagall, which had forced Q&M to compete against international financial behemoths. Just as she'd established a sustainable business model for that environment, the attacks had taken their building down. Countless times over the years, the whole project could have ended in failure, but she had seen it through, and the sale to UniBank had been her reward. Now it had come to nothing.

At the time of UniBank's collapse, her remaining cash assets amounted to a little under a million dollars. She'd been spending that down ever since to keep the household running, which was more expensive than she'd ever noticed in the past. First there was Marinela's salary—Kit didn't cook or clean, and she wasn't interested in starting now. There were monthly payments on their mortgage, on their home and life and health insurance. There were everyday expenses once so trivial as to be virtually nonexistent—cable and phone and internet, groceries and gas—which she now noted carefully in the budget and made some effort to keep under control.

There were luxuries—Edward's party, expensive Christmas presents for the whole family—that she ought to have eliminated entirely but couldn't without admitting how bad things had become. A lifestyle was a difficult thing to change at this late stage, particularly when no amount of belt tightening would address the underlying problem. In the span of eight months, nine hundred thousand had become five. At this rate, they'd be completely broke in another year.

It surprised her, how quickly it went. They'd never been especially extravagant in their tastes. What they bought they tended to consume. They'd thrown their parties. They'd traveled often and done it comfortably. Frank bought books and booze and clothes. Their house they'd treated as a space for living; none of the objects in it had been acquired as investments, and none could be easily unloaded for capital now. There was no abstract expressionist indulgence on the wall that could be brought to Sotheby's. What artworks they had were mostly gifts from the artists themselves, which couldn't be sold without some embarrassment and wouldn't bring in much if they were. Their furniture, silver, jewelry, and other household items were valued for insurance purposes at $175,000, though they would have gotten a good deal less at auction.

The house itself they'd bought in '77, when many of their friends were retreating to Scarsdale and Greenwich, and its value had appreciated nearly a thousand percent over three decades, which had seemed a kind of reward for their faith in the city. But since they'd had no intention of selling, the house had also seemed a source of untapped value. After the Q&M offices were destroyed, the firm had needed an infusion of cash. The vultures were circling, the credit market tightening up, and they couldn't afford to wait for whenever the 9/11 compensation fund would get around to reimbursing them. She'd already known that she would be selling down the road— family-run investment banks were obsolete, even if there had been any family members interested in taking it over—but she didn't want to do it at a discount. Rather than pay usurious rates on a business loan, she'd taken out a four-million-dollar mortgage on the house and invested the proceeds in the firm. This had been enough to keep it afloat, and the move had been vindicated four years later, when UniBank gave her twice what they'd been offering in 2002.

After paying off the mortgage and the federal, state, and city capital gains taxes, they would be lucky to net five percent of the total sale price, which meant that selling at the high end of their estimated range would earn them less than five hundred thousand— and leave them homeless. Unless they planned to sleep in a shelter, it was actually cheaper to stay where they were.

At least they owned the house in Bridgehampton outright, and they could deduct the money they'd put into the expansion, which would make the tax bill more manageable. But the market on the East End had been hit a lot harder than Manhattan by the crash. They weren't the only ones looking to keep their heads above water by jettisoning a summer home, and the Wall Street bonuses with which down payments on such houses were usually made hadn't materialized that year. The agent Kit had asked for an appraisal had told her bluntly that she ought to wait another six months if she possibly could. The number he gave her when she'd pressed him seemed like a mistake, half of what the house next door had gotten two years before. They might clear enough to pay off Frank's advance, leaving them where they were now: a year away from broke. To put it in the kind of terms Frank liked to use, selling the house was necessary but not sufficient.

She'd already called Guillaume to tell him about Frank's condition, and he'd spoken with the people at Gilroy, claiming Frank's illness as force majeure. He thought they would accept half the advance and write off the rest, and Kit had told him that they would have it by the end of the summer. All in all, survival still seemed possible, but only if they could keep the Celsia money.

The next morning, she left Frank with Marinela and took the train to Wall Street. She hadn't spent much time in the financial district after the offices were destroyed, and she hadn't been there at all since UniBank's collapse. Returning made her think not of the many hours of her adult life she'd spent on these blocks, but of her childhood, when her father had often brought her down from their apartment on Sutton Place. The neighborhood looked more like those memories now that the towers were gone. For people just a few years younger than Kit, who'd come to work on the Street in the earlier eighties, those buildings had been forces of nature, the very definition of permanence, but after all they'd been there for only a generation. Kit had watched them go up, and she'd never liked them much.

The lawyer's office was in a building a few blocks north of Trinity Church. Upstairs, her personal attorney, Jack Mullen, was waiting to bring her into a conference room, where he introduced her to his colleague Paul Augustino, who was a few years younger than Jack and a bit slicker—a slightly more expensive suit in slightly less good taste, a college ring with a jewel in it on his right ring finger. Once they were all settled, Kit described the meeting with the agents. When Augustino asked her to give him the details of the trade and the thinking that had motivated it, Kit told him something very similar to what she'd told the agents about Celsia's value. When she'd finished, the two men looked at each other before Augustino spoke.

"Did you do it?"

The question startled Kit, who didn't answer right away.

"You don't seem to be the target here," Augustino elaborated. "If we're going to talk about a deal, I need to know what we can give them. Did you talk with Justin about the buyback before you made the trade?"

Kit looked for a moment at Jack, who shrugged as though to say this was all out of his hands.

"Yes," Kit said.

"Have you done anything else like this, with Justin or anyone else?"

"No."

"They're going to want you to tell them everything, and immunity doesn't apply to perjury. If we go in there, you need to be honest and inclusive."

"This was the only time."

"In that case, my advice is this. You write down exactly what happened, and I call this agent with a proffer. Given the circumstances, I think we can ask for transactional immunity, maybe protect you from civil enforcement. If we play it right, there's a good chance you can keep the money."

"What if I don't want to do it?"

"Everything I've heard suggests they're serious about getting Eisen. They're not going to give up on this. I'd imagine they want to do it quietly, so they can keep tightening the noose. Any deal we try to make once things are in process is going to involve a clawback, plus a hefty fine, if not a bit of prison time. There's not much sympathy for financial shenanigans at the moment. Of course, if you want to fight this thing, it's possible we'll win at trial. We can't know at this point exactly what evidence they've got, but right now it doesn't look like that strong a case, provided Justin Price doesn't flip on you first."

"He won't do that," Kit said.

This seemed to settle the matter, until Mullen spoke up.

"I feel obliged to mention that taking this through trial is going to be lengthy and expensive. Even if UniBank still existed, you made this trade as a private citizen, so it wouldn't be covered by any indemnification agreement. The cost is going to come out of your pocket, and it could get up pretty close to whatever you'd be paying in fines anyway."

Mullen knew more than most about Kit's financial situation. He was telling her that she couldn't afford to take the case to trial.

"Let me sleep on it."

It didn't seem like she had much choice. She needed the Celsia money. If she was forced to pay it back—or spend it on attorneys' fees—they'd be bankrupt.

But was this really the worst thing in the world? Plenty of people lost their money and went on with their lives. Would she take Justin down just to save her family from the poorhouse? When Jack Mullen called the next day to ask what she wanted to do, she told him she would wait for her door to be broken down.

2.

"I saw your wife today," Blakeman said, as though this were the setup to a joke.

"You were in Brooklyn?"

"Avenue C, visiting Eddie Doyle." He might have been speaking of a mutual friend, though Sam had never met Margo's brother. "She was coming out of his building as I was coming in."

Waxworth had been spending more time in the office since Lucy had dropped by unannounced, and he was sorry she hadn't tried again so long as she was in Manhattan. He felt some vindication knowing that he'd been where he was supposed to be at the time.

"Did you say hello?"

"She was gone before I made the connection. I wasn't expecting to see anyone I knew. The building's a real shithole."

"I wonder what she was doing there," Waxworth said, so far from suspecting anything that he didn't even think to bluff.

"Don't worry," Blakeman answered cheerfully. "She couldn't possibly be fucking anyone in that place. It's all menthols and *abuelas*. She was probably just buying drugs."

"Maybe it was somebody else."

"Sure," Blakeman allowed. "Could be that, too."

He walked away, and Waxworth looked back at his laptop hopefully, as though something might have appeared there while they were talking. Before spotting Blakeman, he'd been trying to get started on a post. He'd been relying too much on his old blog, and he needed to break the habit. In the process, he'd been struck all over again by how much work was expected of him. Blakeman had talked a lot about turning *Quantified World* into a multiauthored platform, but Waxworth was halfway through his contract and still the only contributor. This was what he'd wanted to discuss before their conversation was diverted to the Lower East Side.

In an effort to feel productive, he logged into one of the sock puppet accounts he'd set up at Blakeman's suggestion, and he wrote a few comments on yesterday's post. He was finishing up when Blakeman passed back through the office.

"Have you got another second?" Waxworth asked.

"What's up?" Blakeman responded.

Waxworth waited for him to take the empty seat beside him, but Blakeman just looked down expectantly.

"When might be a good time to talk about hiring?"

"Hiring?" Blakeman gave the word the sound of an exotic obscenity.

"The other writers for *Quantified World.*"

"That's actually pretty good," Blakeman said. He seemed genuinely amused.

"So now's not a good time?"

"You mean you're not kidding? There isn't going to be any hiring."

He said this as though it shouldn't have needed explaining. Had they already had this conversation? Had Margo put him in such a fog that he was forgetting things?

After Blakeman walked away again, Waxworth decided to talk with Adrian. These hires weren't in his contract, but they'd been promised, and if they weren't coming, he was owed some explanation. He walked out to the deck, but no one was there. A small puddle of rainwater had collected on one side of the Ping-Pong table, and a browned ball lay in it. On the ground beside the table was a single paddle, its rubber covering removed by the elements to reveal a cracked wooden face. Waxworth tried to think where else Adrian might be and realized that he couldn't remember the last time he'd seen him.

He walked back to reception, where Emily was looking studiously at her computer screen. It was the first time he'd seen her behind the desk without a book in her hand.

"Can you schedule a meeting with Adrian?" he asked.

"He's out of the office," she responded. "How about a phone appointment?"

"It can wait until he's back."

"I'm not sure when that will be. He's spending the summer in Palo Alto, at the Teeser compound." Emily lowered her voice before adding, "He says he can't stand the humidity, but I heard he's not coming back."

On his way back to his seat, Waxworth passed a fact-checker named Camille who'd worked on some of his posts. She gave him a friendly smile, and he stopped.

"What's going on with Adrian?" he said.

He was embarrassed that he had to ask.

"Nobody really knows," Camille answered. "I read on the *Reverberator* that his new obsession is flying cars. He's working with an engineer at Stanford on a prototype."

The checker sitting next to Camille shook his head.

"That's not right. He's running for Congress in the midterms, so he's got to spend all his time in his home district until then. He's ready to spend a hundred million on the campaign."

"He can't afford a hundred million," Camille broke in. "Tom Chen"—this was the *Interviewer*'s tech reporter—"told me Mario isn't as rich as everyone thought. He wasn't even really a Teeser cofounder, just roommates with one. He was, like, employee number six."

"Either way," the other checker said, "it's not great for us."

Over the rest of the day, Waxworth noticed how the atmosphere in the office had changed. He couldn't believe he hadn't recognized it sooner. Where it had once been a point of pride never to appear to be working, now everyone made a great show of busyness. A flyer on the announcement board noted that Tuesday afternoon beer and burritos had been suspended indefinitely.

Waxworth participated as best he could in the collective apprehension, but privately he wasn't worried. He'd be paid for another six months in any case. Still, he started thinking about what he would do when his contract expired. His goal in moving to New York had been to get a book contract, but he hadn't taken any practical steps in that direction. After his experience with the profile, he wasn't sure he even wanted to write a book, and if he'd sold one by the time the contract ended, he wouldn't have any excuse to stay at the *Interviewer*, which until that morning he'd had every expectation of doing. Now it felt a bit like keeping himself bound to a sinking ship, and a book seemed more like his best bet to stay in New York.

A dozen agents had emailed him since he'd started at the *Interviewer*, ranging from the biggest names in the business to an assistant at the Buckley Agency named Eli Elliott, who claimed to have a background in analytics.

"If you want to be represented by someone who actually understands what you're doing, give me a chance," Elliott had written him.

Waxworth had learned from his time with Blakeman that working with someone who understood the market was more important than working with someone who understood him, and he'd met for lunch with the three most famous agents on the list. Each one had mentioned the importance of finding someone with whom he felt "comfortable." But Waxworth had never been much for the eyeball test. He wasn't sure what "comfort" would even entail in this context, let alone why it should matter. Instead he'd developed a simple method for quantifying what he wanted: using all the publicly available data, he'd determined which of the agents had the most six-figure deals in the past year. The answer was a guy named John Craig at ADM Literary. He'd told Craig weeks ago that he'd made his decision, but that afternoon he sent back his signed agreement. In the email, he said that he thought he had an idea for the book. This wasn't strictly true, but he didn't think it would take him long to generate one.

Craig responded within minutes. He was excited to get down to work, he said. He wanted to schedule another meeting to talk through this idea and put a timeline together. He suggested that Waxworth write something long on the subject for the print edition of the *Interviewer*, which they could treat as a sample chapter for publishers. In the meantime, he'd already spoken with a reporter from the *Reverberator* who wanted to sit down with Sam.

Over dinner that night, he told Lucy the news.

"Just like that I'm going from profiler to profile subject," he said.

"That's great," Lucy told him.

But she sounded distracted. He'd worried that she would read too much into the news, take it to mean he was preparing for their return to Wisconsin. Instead she barely seemed to be listening.

"How was your day?" he finally asked.

"I mostly hung around the apartment," she said. "I feel so useless right now. I can't wait for the school year to start."

"You should get out and see some things," he told her. "I wish I had the freedom to do that."

"I just feel so tired all the time."

He didn't like talking about this tiredness of hers, this vague infirmity she'd conveniently contracted at the Doyles' house. His natural instinct when faced with a problem was to try to fix it, and in this case the solution seemed obvious enough—she needed a better attitude; she needed to stop feeling sorry for herself—but this wasn't something she'd be willing to hear.

Almost reflexively he said, "Blakeman thought he saw you in Manhattan today."

"I went in to do some shopping," she told him. "I totally forgot. He should have said hello."

If she'd simply denied it, he might have believed her. After all, Blakeman had met her only once, and she was easy enough to mistake for someone else. As it was, he could tell she was lying. He would have known it even if her story hadn't contradicted Blakeman's account of seeing her come out of the building. His next thought, after this realization, was that if he could spot her lies so easily, she had surely spotted his.

"What did you get?"

The question was a kind of entrapment. He should have just told her that Blakeman had seen her coming out of some ratty apartment building. Then she would have given him the truth, which was probably fairly benign. He was sure she wasn't seeing someone, and Blakeman's other suggestion was only moderately more plausible. Lucy had been an occasional pot smoker when they'd met, but so far as Sam knew she hadn't had anything stronger than a cocktail since graduation.

She took her time working over a bite of food before answering.

"Nothing, in the end. Everything is so expensive here."

He was pleased with this. Some part of him didn't want her honesty—not because he feared it, but because her lies gave him an advantage over her, or rather a tally on his side that compensated for her earlier advantage, that balanced their equation. He'd been thinking in such terms more and more since she'd come by the office. That had been the first time he'd deceived her outright about anything of consequence. He still wanted to believe that what he'd been doing with Margo was basically innocent—but if that was true, why hadn't he told her about it?

Throughout his childhood, Sam had been warned constantly about lying, one of the easiest sins to commit, as his mother described it, and thus one of the easiest ways for the devil to turn a heart. A man who lied would soon enough become a man who cheated, and a man who cheated eventually became a man who left. Sam had no idea how theologically sound this all was, but he understood the point—that he was in permanent danger of turning into his father, and that the only bulwark against this fate was faith in God. "Lie not to one another," went the verse his mother recited to him, "seeing that you have put off the old man." Only years later did he understand that this term meant simply shedding your former, sinful self, becoming someone new. As a child, he'd thought it meant that his own honesty, his own uprightness, was literally keeping his father at bay.

However successfully he'd shaken off the worldview his mother had instilled in him, Sam hadn't entirely purged this atavistic terror that the father's sins might be visited upon the son. He'd tried all his life to be good—tried to *put off the old man*—and to prove in the process that goodness did not require faith in some celestial prison guard, ready to lock you up for disobedience. He'd even taken some pride over the years in his own integrity. But before now he'd never found behaving himself all that difficult. Ethics, he thought, was mostly a matter of reason. There was something irrational about evil, the very word slightly silly in its grandiosity.

But when he'd lied to Lucy about spending time with another woman, he could not escape the fact that he'd done a bad thing. Rationally speaking, the solution was easy enough: he ought to stop seeing Margo. Several times he'd committed himself to this course, but after a few days, he found himself texting again to ask whether she was free. Sometimes she'd say she was busy with Frank, and Sam would feel a sense of relief, as though she'd saved him from himself. Still, he'd text again the next day. It was becoming harder and harder to balance this behavior with the sense that he'd *put off the old man*. So it was almost a relief to hear Lucy lie. He knew that she was a good person; he was sure of it. If she was lying to him, this meant that lying to your spouse did not necessarily make you bad.

"Next time let me know," he said. "I'll come and meet you somewhere."

"I didn't want to bother you," she told him. "You always seem so busy."

Perhaps Lucy's lie allowed him to text Margo the next morning after only an hour attempting to write at a coffee shop. They hadn't seen each other in a week, but she responded right away. By noon they were walking together along the eastern wall of Central Park while Sam described his book.

"It's going to be on the science of decision-making," he said. She was the first person he'd told the idea. "Sort of a popular introduction to game theory, combined with a self-help guide for people paralyzed by choice."

"Because you're so decisive," Margo told him.

She gave him a smile that tightened the muscles in his chest. It wasn't a particularly pleasant feeling, this tightening, and he'd been experiencing it more and more frequently in her company. He more or less knew the feeling's cause: He was trying to do something impossible. He wanted to become someone else, but to do it while staying himself. He wanted to be the person who slept with Margo Doyle while remaining the person who was faithful to Lucy. It contradicted the foundational laws of Boolean logic—namely, the law of identity (A equals A) and the law of noncontradiction (A does not equal Not A). He wasn't always sure he even enjoyed their time together. Occasionally he looked at her and felt what could only be described as a kind of repulsion. Then they parted ways, and he couldn't stop thinking about her. None of it made any sense.

"Things are difficult," he finally said.

"Making choices should be easy for an oracle."

"I never claimed to be an oracle."

"That's a relief. I'd hate to think you knew how this all turned out and just weren't telling me."

His chest tightened again. In fact, he did have a picture of the future, a clear and persistent one, though he couldn't possibly describe it to Margo or anyone else. In this vision, he and Lucy continued as they were until their year in New York was up, at which point he told her that he didn't want to go back to Madison. They fought about this, but eventually she went home without him. He was reasonably confident she wouldn't stay. She loved Madison—loved the familiarity—more than anything in the world. The fact that he'd fit so easily into her life had always been part of his appeal, he knew. Once he refused to fit, she would leave, and it wouldn't be his fault. Only after she was gone would he pursue things with Margo. In the end this would be best for everyone. Lucy belonged in Madison, and—Margo or not—he belonged in New York.

Of course, there were some problems with the scenario. None of it worked if he cheated now, which meant it required a certain amount of patience on Margo's part. But it was patience he couldn't ask her to expend, because none of it worked if he *wanted* Lucy to leave. He had to mean it when he asked her to stay in New York with him, and he had to regret it when she refused. This required not thinking about the future in the meantime, remaining in a state of unknowing, something he'd aimed all his life to avoid.

"No one can see the future," he finally said. "Because the future doesn't exist. All we can do is say what's most likely to happen."

He always tried to bring their talk away from the personal, toward the realm of ideas. Sometimes it seemed the only thing that made their conversations possible.

"Doesn't this probabilistic view conflict with your materialism?"
He knew he could trust her to follow his lead into abstraction,
which made him sometimes think that she understood where everything was headed.

"What do you mean?" he asked.

"The future might not exist, but if you throw two pool balls
together, a physicist could tell you with total certainty what they're
going to do, because they're just matter following physical laws. If
we're just matter, too, shouldn't the same go for us? Why is it only
humans whose behavior we have such a hard time predicting?"

"Two pool balls are a pretty simple system. Humans have a few
more moving parts. That doesn't mean we aren't made of matter."

"How about the weather? That's plenty complicated, and we've
gotten a lot better at predicting it. Not perfect, maybe, but we keep
improving. Think of all the complicated machinery we rely on to
act exactly as we expect, every time. Combustion engines, medical
devices. But once human agents are involved, we seem completely
helpless."

"Not helpless," he said. "I did pretty well with the election."

"A series of binary outcomes, the easiest thing in the world to
predict, and you used polling. Think about that: the only reliable
method we have to predict how people will vote is *asking them*.
Imagine if those physicists had to ask the pool balls which way they
would travel—and they could still only give us probabilities."

In these moments, when Margo was challenging him—intellec-
tually, not emotionally—his muscles loosened again. He was
reminded why he spent so much time with her. This was something
Lucy simply couldn't give him, and he felt justified seeking it someplace else.

"Physicists don't always deal in certainties. They can't predict
where subatomic particles will go. In fact, the whole idea that physical
behavior is probabilistic rather than deterministic comes from them."

"But in order for that pool ball to go the right way, all these individual things shooting off in random directions have to average out to just the right answer every time. That suggests something determined. Meanwhile, human behavior isn't any more predictable in the aggregate than it is on the individual level. If it were, we would have seen the crash coming. My mother's bank would still exist. Social scientists want so badly to believe that what they're doing is like physical science—their greatest fear is being lumped with us humanists. But it's all a lot of bullshit. They're telling stories, just like us."

Margo stopped walking, and they stood together in the shade of a Fifth Avenue elm. She looked oddly moved. It occurred to Sam that the reason she followed him so willingly into ideas was not because she likewise wanted to flee the personal but because she didn't recognize a distinction. For Margo, ideas *were* personal.

"So what's your explanation?"

"Humans have free will. There's no way to reconcile this fact with materialism. Matter doesn't have free will. Only we have the capacity to act in ways that make no sense. That's what introduces all the uncertainty into the system: humans can *swerve*."

Sam stood before his terror, heard it calling to him.

"We can swerve," he said, after a moment, and he reached out to bring her to him.

Margo seemed briefly surprised before she gave way. Each previous time they'd kissed, something had come along to interrupt them. Now he started to wonder what would come next, and the muscles in his chest tightened again. This time he thought he might like the feeling.

They separated and walked on. At the corner they waited for the light to change and kissed again. Would they just make out on the street like teenagers? What other option did they have? They couldn't go to her house, because her parents were there. They obviously couldn't go to his apartment. His heart began to beat so rapidly that he almost collapsed.

"I'm sorry," he said, struggling to get the words out. "I have to go."

On the morning of Waxworth's lunch with Matthew Penty—the reporter who was profiling him—the *Herald* ran a story claiming that Mario Adrian was shopping the *Interviewer* to prospective buyers. The timing was somehow appropriate in Waxworth's eyes: the profile would be the perfect chance to disambiguate himself from the magazine. He expected Penty to start right in with questions about the sale, but instead he asked about *Quantified World*, giving Waxworth the opportunity to speak expansively about his methods, his philosophy, his theory of knowledge.

"You've got something of a talent for encouraging online antagonists," Penty said. "What do you make of that?"

Waxworth was surprised by the idea, though he supposed it was right. He didn't think of all those online commenters taking shots at him as being real, certainly not real enough to reckon with in an interview.

"I guess some people have an irrational fear of math," Waxworth told him. "They think it takes the magic out of the world. But anything that disappears in the face of methodological precision wasn't really there in the first place."

He watched Penty scribbling this down across the table, and he imagined it appearing as the pull quote in the profile. Finally, Penty asked about Adrian, and Waxworth gave him the line he'd been preparing for a couple of days.

"I'm grateful to the magazine for the readership it's brought me, and I hope it flourishes. But I was doing what I'm doing now before I got to the *Interviewer*, and I imagine I'll still be doing it after I leave."

When the lunch was over, Waxworth wasn't sure what to do next. He didn't want to go into the office, where the entire staff would be panicking over the morning's news. Part of him wanted to see Margo, but he had committed to avoiding her. She had texted two days after their last meeting to see whether he was around, and he'd told her he was busy with his proposal. This was true, though it wouldn't have been enough to keep him away under other circumstances. She'd written back to say that he should let her know when his schedule cleared up, and he hadn't heard from her since.

Eventually he decided to head home. Though he hadn't seen Margo in almost two weeks, he hadn't been seeing any more of Lucy than usual. He was so busy on the proposal, besides which he was anxious in her presence, too, as though she might read on his face what he'd done.

The apartment was quiet when he arrived. He called out Lucy's name and got no response. He called her cell and heard it ringing in the apartment. He followed the sound to their darkened bedroom, where he hung up. Maybe she'd gone out for a run, he thought. She never liked taking her cell with her. He was about to switch on the lights when he spotted her under the covers.

She'd never taken naps before. If anything, she had excess energy, which was why she got anxious when she didn't run. She'd been complaining about fatigue for a while, but he hadn't understood that she was sleeping in the middle of the day. The fact that he hadn't known somehow struck him as tragic. At the sound of him, she started to stir, and she opened her eyes.

"Are you feeling okay?" he asked.

She sat up with a startled look.

"No, I'm not feeling okay. I've been trying to tell you that for two months."

"I didn't realize it was so bad."

"Well, it is so bad," she said.

She was slurring her words slightly, and she still looked confused, though she'd had enough time to come awake. Suddenly Sam thought about that building on the Lower East Side.

"Are you taking drugs?" he asked.

She laughed.

"Are you serious?"

"This seems unlike you."

"No, I'm not taking drugs."

"Do you just sleep all day?"

She shrugged.

"Sometimes."

"You should have told me."

"What do *you* do all day?"

At first he thought she was still confused.

"You know what I do all day. I work."

"How much time can it possibly take to cut and paste things you wrote two years ago?"

He had not expected this turn. He could hardly deny the charge, which had more truth to it than he had admitted to himself before that moment.

"You noticed?"

"Of course I noticed."

"Well, nobody else did. I've just been reworking some of my old material. It's not always easy to find a new way of saying something."

"You did a lot of it."

"I didn't mean to. I just got overwhelmed with all the work."

"What have you been *doing* all day?"

He needed to perform a careful accounting of the situation, give it what Blakeman would call the "Waxworth treatment." Admittedly there was nothing really to be quantified in this case, but numbers were not the point of his method. That's what people still didn't understand. Numbers were a means of introducing precision, avoiding emotion and wishful thinking, escaping one's narrow subjectivity. There were other ways of achieving this end. The core of the method was aggregation—the combination of viewpoints. He needed to imagine Lucy's perspective, combine that perspective with his own. Of course she suspected the truth, but he might still be able to convince her otherwise. On the other hand, she might suspect quite a bit more than the truth, and if he lied now he might never convince her how little had actually happened.

"Mostly seeing Margo Doyle."

"Every day?"

"Not every day," he said. "But nearly, I guess. We didn't do anything apart from walk around and talk."

"You just walked around?"

He could see how implausible it sounded, and he realized that he would be better off telling the truth.

"A couple of times we kissed, but nothing went any further than that."

He watched her taking this in. She seemed less surprised than faintly satisfied. She might actually have liked this knowledge better than discovering that her suspicions had been unfounded in the first place. He felt now that he'd made the right decision by telling her everything.

"You couldn't go through with it," she said.

"That's right," he answered, pleased that she'd provided these words. "I couldn't go through with it."

An almost teasing smile came over her face.

"Physically?"

The question startled him. He thought of his speeding heart on that street corner. But she seemed to mean something else.

"It didn't really get that far," he said. "It was more that I couldn't do it emotionally."

"I knew it." Her voice sounded triumphant. "I knew that if she tried something with you, it wouldn't work."

He supposed this was the best response he could possibly have gotten, but it didn't feel that way. The pleased look on her face worried him. However many times he'd told himself that she ought to treat the news as reassuring, he hadn't actually expected that she would. He'd been prepared for tears, and he wasn't sure what to do with what he was getting instead.

"Anyway, we haven't had any contact for weeks. It's not something you need to worry about."

"You have to promise that you won't lie anymore," Lucy said.

"I promise."

"There's no point," she added. "I'll always know. You're not the only one who can make predictions."

There was a tone of provocation in her voice. Sam remembered that she had a secret of her own. She seemed ready now to reveal it.

"What do you mean?"

"I've been seeing someone, too." She waited a beat before clarifying. "Not like that. She's a woman I meet to talk about my problems. Her name is Claire."

"She's a doctor?"

"Not exactly. None of the doctors have been able to help, but Claire helps. She's in touch with the world, and it lets her see things that other people can't always see."

"When you put it that way, she sounds like a psychic or something."

"Well, that's just one of the things she does."

"You're kidding."

"I know it sounds weird, but I was really desperate. Someone gave me a flyer on the street. I gave it a try, and I felt comfortable with her."

"You found her from a flyer? Lucy, these people are crooks."

"That's what I thought, too. But she has real insight into things. She's the one who told me about you and Margo, and she told me that you would feel it in your insides until you came to tell me about it."

"This is how they work. They listen to your problems and they feed them back to you. You obviously thought something was going on, and you signaled that to her, even if you don't think you did. All she did was repeat what you said in different words."

"She's the one who told me that you wouldn't be able to do it. How could I have signaled that? I didn't know it myself."

"You knew that I loved you too much to go through with it."

"But she didn't just tell me. She's the one who made that happen. I watched her do it."

He couldn't believe what he was hearing.

"Holy shit, Lucy. You think this woman put some kind of hex on me?"

Lucy took a long breath. Sam could see that she'd been preparing for this conversation a lot longer than he had.

"You talk about falsifiability, the power of predictions. Well, she predicted these things, and she was right. You just have to live with the fact that you're not the only one who can see the future."

"I never claimed to see the future. What this woman does has nothing to do with what I do. She's a scam artist."

"She told me you'd say that. She told me you would react this way."

"Because she knew that any sane person would react this way."

Lucy's lip quivered, but when she spoke next her words came calmly and clearly.

"I'm not crazy. I've been suffering, and you've been too busy with Margo Doyle to notice. She makes me feel better."

"How often do you see this person?"

"No more than once a week."

"Once a week? How much money have you given her?"

"When I told you I needed to see someone, you said we had plenty of money."

"Money for doctors, Lucy. Not a clairvoyant in Alphabet City. You need to stop."

"I won't."

There was nothing insistent in her voice. She was simply stating the facts of the matter. Sam had to proceed carefully from here.

"I know you aren't feeling well. I'm sorry that I haven't taken that seriously enough. We can find another doctor. We'll keep looking until you feel better."

"We don't need to keep looking. I've already found someone who makes me feel better. I know what you're going to say about correlation and causation, confirmation bias, placebo effect, whatever. All I know is that she helps. What difference does it make to you if I see her? Just live with it."

Maybe she was right, maybe it shouldn't have bothered him, but he couldn't stand the idea of his wife making weekly visits to a huckster.

"I can't live with it. You're going to have to choose between us."

She got up from bed so quickly he could barely react. She crossed the room to the closet and began to pack clothes into an overnight bag.

"You're really going to choose this woman over me?"

She looked up at him, and he saw for the first time the tears he'd been preparing himself for all along.

"You're the one who's making this a choice. I'm just tired of feeling sick."

He'd imagined a worst-case scenario where Lucy threw him out for a few days after she learned about Margo, but he hadn't considered the possibility that their conversation might end with him throwing her out. He should have taken back what he'd said, but she was acting with such purpose, more than he'd seen out of her in months. He was prepared to let her win, but couldn't she at least try to change his mind? She seemed to want this excuse to leave. If only she would admit that she needed him as much as he needed her, they could work everything out.

She zipped up her bag and walked past him out of the room.

"Where will you sleep?" he asked.

"I'll figure something out. I have more resources than you sometimes seem to think."

He watched her cross the living room to the front door.

"Wait," he called when she got there, but when she stopped and turned he had nothing to say. "Why don't you stay?" he finally asked. "If we have to do this, I should be the one to go."

"I'd rather it was me," she said, right before she left. "I never got used to the smell."

3.

A dozen students showed up for the course's first session, most of them in their twenties. Eddie could tell at first glance that some were military, and he felt an instinctive protectiveness. They looked like the kids who'd served under him, and they had that wary restlessness that joes often displayed when forced into a classroom. They wanted a life of action, and they could barely suppress their impatience with the weeks of tedium that were a prerequisite for that life. The only other person Eddie's age in the room was the instructor, a tall, dark-haired woman named Cathy whose outfit—crisp white button-down, navy chinos, thick black leather belt—seemed designed to be mistaken for a uniform.

"You're in this room because you want to become emergency medical technicians," she announced after introducing herself. "The first thing you need to know is that this title is a misnomer. As an EMT, everything you do must signal that there *is* no emergency. Once you've arrived on the scene, the emergency is over. That means nothing surprises you. Nothing frightens you. You move quickly, but always with purpose, never with panic. In order to do all that, you have to know everything in this book." She raised the training manual that had been sitting on the desk in front of her and flashed the cover before putting it down. "When I say that you have to know it, I don't mean store it away somewhere so you can recall it with a few moments' effort. I mean know it, like you know your mother's name. It has to be *here*." She snapped a finger on the word. "This course is designed to put it there." She let this sink in before continuing. "First I want to know a little bit about all of you."

Beside the manual on the desk sat a pile of papers, which she handed to someone in the front row, who then passed them around the room. When a sheet arrived at Eddie's desk he saw that it was a questionnaire. *Have you ever studied biology, anatomy, or any life sciences?* read the first question. *No*, Eddie wrote before moving on. *What made you choose this EMT-A qualification course?* There was only enough space for a two-line answer. After thinking a moment about various high-minded answers, he wrote: *I want to drive an ambulance.*

As soon as he'd decided to move in with Nash, he'd known he would have to find a job. He'd briefly considered calling Evan Schroeder to ask about coming in for a visit. But he didn't need that kind of money. In fact, he could do almost anything and make enough to cover groceries and rent. This reality struck him with the force of revelation. He didn't have to get a white-collar knowledge-economy job like the one he'd been doing before he enlisted. He could do something that helped people—or just something that he enjoyed. But what help could he give? What was it he enjoyed?

He wanted work that made him feel the way he'd felt pulling Nash from the fountain that day, when he'd moved without thinking, completely in the flow of things. This should have occurred to him sooner. Lots of vets became first responders. These jobs offered some of the army's excitement and camaraderie, even its sense of purpose. Eddie couldn't imagine becoming a cop—he would never again point a gun at someone—but that left plenty of other possibilities. He thought he'd make a good paramedic, but he'd need to get trained up. He'd suffered through self-aid/buddy-aid in basic, and he'd gotten a Combat Lifesaver course before deploying, half a day on dragging a body behind cover, applying a tourniquet, and calling in a 9-line. He didn't even know how to take vitals.

This program had been the best-rated online. The course would last for eight weeks, Monday through Saturday, nine to four, three hours in the morning and three in the afternoon, with an hour off for lunch. At the end of it, he'd take a certification exam, and he'd have a good shot at a job before his army salary ran out.

He filled in the rest of the questionnaire and walked it to the front of the room. He was the first one to finish, and as he returned to his seat he saw several faces tight with concentration. Here was another trait shared with his men: the inability—or perhaps, more generously, just the unwillingness—to distinguish busy work from the real thing.

They spent the rest of the first class on legal and ethical issues. The terminology—civil liability, scope of practice, standards of care—clearly bored the other students, but Eddie loved its novelty. In Iraq, he'd had immunity from any legal authority besides the army, and the only ethical imperative was obeying the chain of command. Rather than worrying Eddie, Cathy's persistent warnings about litigious patients reassured him that he was serving under a different order now.

He shopped for groceries on the way home, and he cooked dinner for himself and Nash that night, as he had every night since moving in. This was part of the enjoyable routine he had developed. His days were full and had a comforting consistency. At seven each morning, he went for a run—two or three miles, just enough to get his heart working. He no longer felt any compulsion to exhaust himself or quiet his mind. He came back to the apartment to eat breakfast with Nash before heading out for the day.

After dinner, Nash led them through a short scripture study before bed, mostly from the New Testament. He read aloud from his well-worn leather-bound Bible, offering minimal commentary. Sometimes he just repeated the words a second and third time, letting them speak for themselves. *Where is the wise? where is the scribe? where is the disputer of this world? hath not God made foolish the wisdom of this world? Because the foolishness of God is wiser than men: and the weakness of God is stronger than men.*

Very quickly it had come to seem natural that a life should be shaped this way. Eddie had been thrown into so many uncomfortable situations, far from his family, among total strangers, surrounded by people who wanted him dead. Sharing a sparse two-bedroom apartment with an eccentric old man was luxurious by comparison. He'd given up on trying to get Justin to return his calls, but he'd had a visit from Blakeman, whose steadfast refusal to be surprised by anything had made it easier to think of his situation as perfectly normal. Even the thing that should have been strangest about it—Nash's preaching—had a kind of familiarity. So much of it was already somewhere inside of Eddie. He'd thought he'd left the church behind when he went off to college, but thirteen years of Catholic school had left more traces than he'd imagined. He felt as though he were coming home, rather than embarking on an entirely new practice.

He tried to remember this when he spoke with his mother and was faced again with the possibility that he'd lost his mind. She called every few days to check in, very careful not to express concern or entreat him to change his mind, but completely unable to conceal her bafflement. She'd obviously looked Nash up, and she sometimes spoke as though she were trying delicately to reprogram Eddie.

At the time of his move, he'd planned to concoct some explanation for everything before his parents got home from Long Island, but a week later his mother was shaking Nash's hand and looking over the apartment—which was perfectly presentable—with her jaundiced eye. He could see that some part of her expected him to drop this plan and come home to help with Frank. But he'd started something, and he needed to see it through, even if he couldn't explain this need to her. Everything was proceeding with a logic visible only to him. He couldn't express it without making her live through it all. His life was like a piece of embroidery that showed an elegant pattern from one side but from the other was just a mess of knotted string. Sometimes he wanted to say: *You raised me to believe what Nash is telling me. The difference is that he actually behaves the way we'd all behave if we believed the things you claim to believe.*

Nash still preached as he always had, but he stayed away from Washington Square. To keep the police from bothering him, he picked a different corner each time he went out, and he never announced the location in advance. This limited the size of his crowds, but he gave the same impassioned performance in front of ten or fifteen people as he did to several hundred. More of his sermons were posted online, and the best of them got a hundred thousand views. It was strange to think that the quiet old man with whom Eddie shared this small apartment, a man who couldn't have afforded the place without his help, commanded that kind of attention. Nash himself seemed almost oblivious to it. So far as Eddie knew, he never went on a computer. Eddie had tried to tell him about his growing TeeseView following, but he remained desperate to have his flesh-and-blood audience back.

Eddie had bought him a suit, along with a new hat, which he passed every time he went out, though the proceeds didn't amount to much. Eddie wanted to tell him that he didn't have to worry about money anymore, but he understood why Nash might be skeptical of him. Even if he'd known what kind of money Eddie was sitting on, he couldn't expect Eddie's interest to last indefinitely.

Of course, the public's attention wouldn't last forever, either. It was already the middle of August. What would he do when the appointed hour arrived and everything kept on as it had before? His public persona rested on the power of this prediction. His minor celebrity would be over. At best, the collective consciousness would take a moment to mock him before moving on to something else.

To Eddie alone, Nash's power had a different source: what he'd done for him in that water. He didn't need to place blind faith in Nash, because the change that he'd experienced was tangible. For the first time in years—for the first time in his life, he was tempted at moments to say—he felt at peace. He would see Nash through whatever ridicule followed the first of November. He didn't intend to live with the man forever, but he could easily set up some kind of annuity or endowment to support him. But how to tell him this? Even broaching the subject meant raising the possibility that the prediction was wrong.

For the time being, Eddie concentrated all his attention on his training. He'd be certified well before October, and he would consider the question then. His course fascinated him. Eddie had always done well in school—at St. Albert's, Blakeman had nicknamed him "Bright" Eddie, in contrast to "Handsome" Eddie Hartley—but he had none of the love for abstract ideas that Frank and Margo shared. Like his mother, he preferred practical knowledge. Every day now he came home with a list of facts to memorize and, even better, a clear understanding of what these facts were for. They all fit into a scheme. In the second week, they started on human anatomy and physiology. The axial skeleton consisted of the skull, the hyoid bone, the spinal column, the sternum, and the rib cage. The skull consisted of the frontal bone, the parietal bone, the occipital bone, the temporal bone, the zygomatic bone, the nasal bone, the maxillae, and the mandible. The foramen magnum was the opening in the occipital bone where the brain connected to the spinal cord. The spinal column consisted of thirty-three vertebrae—in descending order: the cervical spine, C1 to C7; the thoracic spine, T1 to T12; the lumbar spine, L1 to L5; the sacrum, five fused vertebrae; the coccyx, four fused vertebrae. The upper airway consisted of the nose and mouth, the nasopharynx, the oropharynx, the larynx, and the epiglottis. The lower airway consisted of the trachea, carina, left and right bronchi, and the bronchioles. He put each one on an index card, and he drilled at night before going to sleep.

He'd been taking the class for almost a month—nearly the half-way point—when he came home one day and found Nash on the couch with a piece of folded paper in his hand.

"What's wrong?" Eddie asked when he saw Nash's expression.

Nash handed him the paper without a word. It was a letter from the city, saying that his application for a permit to preach in Washington Square had been denied due to safety concerns.

"You told me you could take care of this," Nash said.

For the past month, Eddie had hardly thought about this permit. When he'd sent the form off, he'd thought it a formality. It hadn't occurred to him that the request might be denied. He was reminded now that from Nash's perspective this permit was the entire reason Eddie was there.

On that first day in the apartment, he'd stepped back into the living room after drying himself off and found Nash slumped over on the couch, all the energy gone from him, as though it had been passed on to Eddie during that decisive moment in the bath.

"Are you all right?" he'd asked.

Nash had looked startled. He might have forgotten that Eddie was even there.

"Do you know anything about these city permits?"

Eddie hadn't secured any permits before, but he had experience planning promotional events from his advertising job, and he imagined it would be easy enough to figure out.

"I can help you with that," he said.

"How long do you think it would take?"

"A couple of weeks," Eddie told him.

"I can't wait a couple of weeks," Nash said, as though this might change Eddie's answer.

There would certainly be some way to expedite the process, but Eddie didn't know what it was.

"I can understand why you're eager to get back out there, but it's probably just as well that you take some time to recover."

Nash shook his head and ran his hands nervously over his still-damp beard.

"The police broke us up before I could get my hat back."

Eddie had almost offered to buy a new hat, so incidental had the prop seemed to Nash's performances, but after a moment he recognized its significance.

"Do you need money?"

"My niece was putting me up here before she passed," Nash explained. "I get a check from the government, but I spend it mostly on my pills. I had no way to pay the rent on my own, so I prayed to God for help. He told me that He would take care of me if I spread His word. I don't do it for the money. I do it for Him. All the same, I can't live without it. If I miss another month, they'll put me on the street."

Eddie was glad to hear that the problem was so easy to solve.

"I can cover your rent."

Nash didn't seem as pleased by the idea as Eddie had expected.

"What about the permit?"

"I can help with that, too," Eddie told him. "Is there anything else you need?"

Nash continued working at his beard while he considered the proposition.

"Food, I suppose." He said this as though he were not entirely certain such a thing would be necessary. "A roof over my head and bread on my plate should take care of it."

"I can pay for groceries."

"Just until the permit comes," Nash insisted. "When the police broke up our meeting, I thought—the good Lord is testing me now. But we just need faith. He brought you to me."

Eddie was pleased that he should appear to Nash as an instrument of God, and he wondered what more he could do to this end. Giving money was almost too easy. A few thousand dollars a month would make no difference to Eddie's own life. He had an image of Nash limping around a grocery store, carrying bags up those stairs, and he thought about offering to shop for him. Even this didn't seem enough.

"What if I moved in here? I'll pay the rent and keep the kitchen stocked. I'll look after you until you're recovered and your permit comes in."

It had been an impulsive offer. He knew so little about the man, and Nash knew even less about him. In fact, Nash had no way to be sure that Eddie even had the money to help, that he wasn't some lunatic who'd happened to be in the right place at the right time in the park. But such doubts didn't seem to occur to Nash, and since then Eddie had fulfilled all these promises.

Now he had to face the understanding that he'd failed.

"I'll try again," Eddie said. "I have some friends who might be able to help. I should have thought of that in the first place."

"How long will that take?"

"A few weeks, I'd guess."

"I can't wait a few weeks."

"Just let me know if you need more money."

"It isn't about the money." Nash seemed offended by the suggestion. "Not everything in this world can be bought. It's about my task. It will all be over soon, and it's my job to prepare."

Something had broken through Nash's usually placid surface, not anger but fear. Eddie had come to think of his prediction as a bit of salesmanship, a way to draw crowds and encourage donations. He had actually preferred this explanation. But there was no mistaking now that Nash believed the world was going to end.

"Are you sure about that date?" Eddie asked tentatively.

Nash looked up at him with surprise.

"You have doubts?"

"It just seems so unlikely."

"Was it likely that God should walk among us as a man? That He should give His life for us? That He should rise again after three days?"

He looked at Eddie as though he expected a response to these questions. Nash had never asked Eddie what he believed, but Eddie supposed Nash had taken the answer for granted after Eddie presented himself to be baptized.

"To be honest," Eddie said, "I'm not sure I believe that either."

Nash picked up the Bible from the table in front of them.

"If you don't have faith, what have we been doing all this time?"

Eddie tried to answer as honestly as he could.

"I believe in the message," Eddie said. "Love your enemy. Turn the other cheek. Blessed are the peacemakers."

Nash let out a dismissive puff, like air leaving a tire.

"If He didn't rise, the message means nothing. *I* am the truth, Jesus says. His message isn't in His words, it's in His Resurrection."

It occurred suddenly to Eddie that Nash might throw him out of the apartment. He hadn't secured the permit, he hadn't understood Nash's teachings, so what good was he to Nash?

"There are other ways to spread the Word," he answered impulsively.

"Like what?"

Having spoken without thinking, Eddie now considered the question.

"We could put up a billboard. Maybe do something in the subway. I used to work in advertising. I know the people who sell the space, and I know how to design the spots. It can say anything you want it to say."

"That all sounds expensive."

"Don't worry about the money." Though Nash was still visibly anxious, Eddie allowed himself a smile. "The Lord will provide."

For the next week, Eddie spent his lunch hours mapping out the Nash campaign. It would start with a billboard. He considered something on Broadway or Sixth, close to Washington Square, but he eventually settled on the space right outside their apartment. Nash would be able to see it from his bedroom window and know that his message was out in the world. The ad would include a photo of Nash, the date of his prediction, a quote of some kind, and the address of a website that Eddie would hire someone to build. The site would have videos of Nash, something more professional than the ones already floating around, which didn't capture his power. That would probably be enough to placate him. If not, Eddie would expand out from this base.

It had been a long time since he'd done anything like this, but he guessed that ten grand would pay for a billboard for the month of October, with another twenty for production costs. That wasn't much, but it was more than he had left in his army savings. For the first time since the trust had dissolved, he would have to tap his inheritance.

He called his money manager, a friendly middle-aged man named Doug Shapton, and told him to move fifty thousand dollars from his brokerage account into checking. Eddie had never asked for money from the account before, and he thought the request might worry Doug, as though it were his own savings being spent.

"Buying yourself a car?" Doug asked instead with a vicarious enthusiasm.

"Nothing like that. It's actually a kind of charitable donation."

"In that case, be sure to send me a receipt."

"It won't be deductible. It's more of an informal thing."

"Well, whatever it is, I'm glad you're making some use of the money. That's what it's for."

Eddie felt stupid asking the next question.

"How much have I actually got?"

"A little over three million. I can look up the exact number if you give me a second."

"I don't remember it being so much."

"That's better than the opposite," Doug said with a laugh.

"Wasn't it more like two something the last time we spoke?"

This time Doug's laugh had an edge of anxiety to it.

"Your mother is an aggressive investor."

Eddie hadn't even known that Kit was investing the money, at least not in anything risky enough to return nearly fifty percent in just a few months. He should have realized that she couldn't let so much capital just sit dormant.

The fifty thousand he was planning to spend on Nash seemed suddenly paltry. The man had changed his life, and Eddie was giving him one billboard in return? Once he'd designed an ad, he could put it up anywhere. Even a more ambitious plan—radio, local TV— could be done for a few hundred thousand, which would leave him well ahead of where he'd thought he was a few minutes before.

"In that case," he told Doug, "I'd like a little more."

When Nash saw the plan, he looked as happy as Eddie had ever seen him, which spurred Eddie on to more elaborate ideas. At each step, things cost slightly more than Eddie had remembered. The traditional outlets—the ones that would matter to Nash—were also the most expensive. In his old job, Eddie had put much effort into convincing clients that the splashiest buys were not necessarily the most effective, but in this case his only goal was giving Nash the feeling that he'd been heard, which meant he didn't waste any time on the kinds of things he might have recommended to a professional client with a limited budget. He went back twice for more money. After his initial enthusiasm, Doug turned hesitant.

"Of course it's yours to do what you want with, but the timing of these withdrawals is a bit odd. I mean, so soon after your investment windfall."

Eddie didn't know anything about a windfall. He only knew that he had more money than he'd thought, which seemed a point in favor of being generous with it.

"I never had anything I wanted to spend it on before."

Over the next few weeks, Eddie gave every spare hour outside of class to the campaign. He had to move quickly to get everything in place for a launch at the beginning of October. When he enlisted old professional contacts for help, he was slightly embarrassed to admit what he was working on, but the videographer and the editor he hired had both shrugged at his half-hearted explanations. *A client's a client.* He rented space on a dozen billboards throughout the city. The website would be ready to launch the day the billboards went up. Local TV and radio ads would run throughout the month. Finally, the high point: a thirty-second spot during the fourth game of the World Series, on the night of November 1, just hours before Nash's deadline. This airtime had cost Eddie nearly as much as the rest of the campaign combined, but once he thought of it he couldn't pass it up. He didn't know what would happen to Nash the next day, but he could say for certain that people would be talking about the apocalypse that night.

"How is all this getting paid for?" Nash asked.

"I'm taking care of it," Eddie said.

Nash thanked Eddie for his generosity and didn't say anything more about the matter, but the next evening he read without comment from Mark's Gospel: *It is easier for a camel to go through the eye of a needle, than for a rich man to enter into the kingdom of God.*

Eddie stayed up late that night, turning over Nash's words. He'd never told Nash how much money he had at his disposal, and he worried that this campaign had been a frivolous way to spend it. He thought that he'd been doing the right thing by leaving his inheritance untouched, but now he knew that it had been growing all this time through his mother's work. What had seemed like selflessness looked more like thrift. Ultimately he was just saving the money for later. What if the real right thing was to spend it, get it out into the world, into the hands of people who needed it more than he did—not by way of investing and waiting for returns, but by way of sheer profligacy?

Suppose he actually believed that the world was coming to an end. How absurd it would seem that he had left all that money just sitting there, when it could have been helping people, alleviating suffering. Even in the absence of a looming cosmic deadline, it seemed absurd. What was he saving it for? He could hardly imagine needing more than he had now—a place to sleep, a full fridge, a way to occupy his days that had some purpose to it. He might feel differently when he had a family, but couldn't he support one through honest labor, should that day ever come?

"What would you do if you had the kind of money I have?" he asked Nash over dinner the next night.

Nash smiled but shook his head.

"You cannot serve both God and mammon."

Eddie had anticipated an answer like this.

"But wouldn't it be easier for you to have just a little more, so you didn't need to pass that hat? Didn't need to worry over how the next month's rent would get paid? It would allow you to concentrate your attention on things that really matter."

Nash didn't say anything for a moment. He got up from the table and retrieved his Bible, in which he'd quickly found the lines he was seeking.

"Behold the fowls of the air," he read. "For they sow not, neither do they reap, nor gather into barns; yet your heavenly Father feedeth them. Are ye not much better than they? Consider the lilies of the field, how they grow; they toil not, neither do they spin: And yet I say unto you, That even Solomon in all his glory was not arrayed like one of these. Wherefore, if God so clothe the grass of the field, which today is, and tomorrow is cast into the oven, shall he not much more clothe you, O ye of little faith?"

Eddie left the matter there that night, but a few days later he brought it up again.

"If you don't want the money, you could give it away."

"Why don't you do it yourself?"

"I'm afraid I'll lose my nerve. If I put it in your name, I can still make the decisions about where it goes, but I won't be tempted to hold anything back."

"You want to give away all of it?"

Eddie hadn't gotten that far in his thinking, but once Nash said it, he knew this was right. If he kept some part back for himself as a safety net, the gesture would lose its meaning. He had to leap.

"All of it."

Reluctantly, it seemed, Nash gave way to the plan. The next day, he met Eddie during his lunch break and they set up a joint account. When that was done, Eddie called Doug to say he wanted all of his money moved there. Now Doug seemed horrified.

"The timing couldn't be worse from a tax perspective. You don't want to cash out immediately after a huge gain like this. Wait until you've got some losses to offset it."

Eddie told him to set aside enough to cover his tax liabilities, and Doug tried another tack.

"You haven't shown any interest in this portfolio before, and now you want to zero it out? What happened?"

"It's a long story," Eddie said. "But I know what I'm doing."

"I think you should talk with your mother first."

They both knew his mother would talk him out of it. Failing that, she might take legal steps to stop him. Doug was probably counting on that.

"It's none of my mother's business," Eddie said. "I don't want you mentioning this to her."

Doug acquiesced eventually, but the next steps took longer than Eddie had expected. The money was his, it should have been easy enough for him to take control of it, but countless administrative hurdles arose along the way. The transfer was finally set to go through on the day Eddie took his certification test. Even more than after the baptism, he felt unburdened that morning. At the same time, it was amazing how little difference the change would make in his day-to-day life. Soon he would have an EMT job, which would pay just enough to cover the rent and groceries, his primary expenses these days. He and Nash would continue on largely as they had before. *Behold the fowls of the air.*

During the test, he started to feel a little bit of a crash after all the excitement of the previous few days. For the first time it struck him that handing all of the money over at once might have been a mistake. Not that he wanted it for himself. He was still committed to giving it away, but this might not be the most effective means of doing that. Perhaps simply unloading all of it in one go was just as irresponsible as letting it sit there. It was another way to keep doing what he'd been doing all along—not thinking about how much he had. He ought instead to do what Justin was doing, all the hard work of figuring out where the money should go, whom it could help, work he knew perfectly well that Nash couldn't do on his own. He could easily take a few weeks before starting his job and dedicate that time to thinking about where to direct the money.

His grandfather, whom he remembered but not particularly well, had been very proud of his philanthropy, and Kit had continued this work, but to Eddie it had always seemed an extension of their job, a way to spread the Quinn & Mulqueen name. Many of the institutions they supported—museums and the opera and the Catholic

Church—didn't strike him as charities so much as expensive hob-
bies. It was fine to spend money on them, but no one should expect
to be congratulated for it. On the other hand, some of the work
they'd done had made a real impact in the world. The Bootstrappers
had changed Justin's life and dozens of others like his, and now
Justin was supporting it, changing more lives in his turn. Eddie
wanted to change lives that way. He would explain to Nash when he
got home that he'd decided to take responsibility, instead of loading
Nash with a burden he clearly didn't want. He imagined that Nash
would be relieved.

But before the test was over, he was suffering through another
round of doubts. Of course it wasn't easy to part with this much
money, even if it had existed only as an abstraction in his life up to
that point. It was natural that some part of him would rebel against
the separation, and natural too that this rebellion should take the
form not of unapologetic greed but of a sense that he could do better
with the money than anyone else. He'd done nothing good with it up
to now. Why should he be so convinced that he could start? If he
wanted to make the world a better place, he would do it in his small
way, by working at a job that helped people.

The test lasted two hours, taken on a computer that told Eddie
that he'd passed the moment he was finished. When he got out of the
testing center, he felt like celebrating. He decided to take Nash out
for an expensive lunch, his first real splurge on himself in as long as
he could remember. Considering the circumstances, he thought that
Nash would go along with it.

Usually Nash was reading the Bible on the couch when Eddie got
home, but now the living room was empty, and there was no answer
when Eddie knocked on Nash's bedroom door. It was the early afternoon, an unusual time for Eddie to be there during the week. Nash
was probably out preaching. Eddie was too restless to wait for him to
come home, so he went out looking on the corners where Nash liked

to set up shop. He spent most of the afternoon walking around the neighborhood, but there was no sign of the man.

Around five, Eddie went to the same grocery story he always stopped at on his way home. Part of him was beginning to panic a little, and he had to remind himself that he was the one who'd broken from their routine. In point of fact, he had no idea what Nash did on a typical weekday afternoon. *O ye of little faith*, he told himself.

Yet he wasn't surprised to get home and find the apartment still empty. Everything now had an air of inevitability. He made dinner as always. Before this afternoon, it had seemed they'd been living this way for years, but now that he thought of it, he'd only cooked at this stove on a few dozen previous occasions.

When dinner was ready, Eddie ate alone, though he set Nash's place beside him, as though he were a hidden prophet. He waited another hour before knocking again on Nash's bedroom door, in case he'd slipped in while Eddie was gone and been asleep all this time. When there was no answer he pushed the door open. A quick check of the closet and the drawers showed that Nash's few possessions were still in their usual place. Perhaps he was out thinking of ways to disburse the money. If Eddie was nervous about how it would get spent, how much more of a responsibility must it have seemed to Nash?

Eddie walked back into the living room and sat down on the couch. There on the table in front of him was the old leather-bound Bible from which they'd been reading each night. He picked it up with relief. If the Bible was still here, Nash would be returning eventually. A page in the book had been marked by a folded piece of paper. When Eddie turned there, he saw a verse underlined from Luke's Gospel: *Thou fool, this night thy soul shall be required of thee: then whose shall those things be, which thou hast provided?*

4.

Margo expected to find Amy in their usual spot at the Pallas Athena. They'd had breakfast there several days a week throughout high school and returned often during college vacations, almost always to the same booth near the window. They hadn't been together in the two years since Amy moved to Tribeca, but Amy had insisted on coming uptown before work that morning to give Margo notes for the day ahead. When Margo spotted her waiting outside, dressed in an outfit somewhere between pajamas and sweats—an outfit Amy would never wear to work—she thought that something must be wrong.

"Change of plans," Amy explained after giving her a hug.

She grabbed Margo by the arm and began to lead her uptown. Almost immediately Margo knew where they were headed. Ever since their Melwood days, the Sunrise Spa and Salon, referred to exclusively as the Triple S, had been Amy's preferred place to prepare for "special occasions," a term that in Amy's usage definitely applied to Margo's plans for the afternoon. Margo had passed the frosted-glass storefront thousands of times, but she'd been inside no more than half a dozen, always at Amy's instigation.

A woman at the front desk greeted them both like regulars and asked after Amy's mother, who joined Amy there several times a year for family bonding sessions. (Kit had her hair cut twice a month at an expensive hairdresser, and she got a deep-tissue massage on her first day at Elbow Beach every winter, but she would never have stepped inside a place like the Triple S.)

"I have you both signed up for the full service," the woman said, as though they were cars awaiting tune-up.

Margo wasn't really in the mood for the full service, but she didn't say this, since Amy would surely have responded that getting into the mood was the whole reason they were there.

"Don't you have to go to work?" she asked instead.

"Personal day," Amy answered. "I'm entitled."

"I wish I'd had a little notice."

"Of course you do." Amy laughed. "But if I'd told you, you would have refused."

Margo wasn't sure this was true. So far she'd followed Amy's advice pretty closely on these matters. It was Amy who'd insisted, after Margo's second effort with Sam had been interrupted by her parents, that he had to make the next move. He was too committed to the idea that this was all something happening outside his control, Amy said. Margo needed to force him to act. To Margo this made theoretical sense, but as a practical matter she'd nearly gone crazy waiting for him.

Finally he'd kissed her on Fifth Avenue, and she'd felt a great release, until he abruptly disappeared. Margo had been so agitated by the whole thing that she hadn't slept all night, and she'd come downstairs early to find her mother with those strange visitors, who should have been the first thing she mentioned to Amy the next time they spoke. Instead she'd told her only about Sam. Amy had counseled her to wait two days, text once, and leave it to him from there. The week of silence that followed mostly convinced Margo that Sam had made his decision. He'd stepped away from the abyss. She was disappointed, but not crushingly so. In fact, she was weirdly proud of him for doing the right thing. As for herself, she would spend as much of the summer with her father as possible before going back to school.

When Sam did call, he sounded almost drunk. He was agitated, and he spoke so obliquely that she didn't understand at first that he was telling her Lucy had left.

"What happened?" she asked.

"I don't really know," he said. "I told her about us," he added. They'd never before acknowledged the existence of such an entity, let alone discussed telling Lucy about it. "But that isn't what did it."

He didn't seem to know whether this change was permanent, and Margo didn't ask what his own preference on the matter would be. It seemed at first to simplify matters for them, but when Margo got off the phone she realized that everything remained rather complicated. If she'd had the house to herself, they could have gone up to her room at any time, or just fallen right into it on the floor of the library. (Margo imagined her mother finding them there.) Of course that was impossible now. She didn't want the thing to happen in his apartment, on his marriage bed. Despite Lucy's departure, it would have to be done with all the sordid trappings of adultery.

It had been Amy's idea to book a room at the Cue and invite Sam to meet her for a drink in the lobby bar. Margo still couldn't quite believe she was doing it, which is why she'd been happy to meet that morning for encouragement.

They went into a small changing room, where they both undressed and Amy stood for a moment admiring herself in the full-length mirror. Margo couldn't help admiring her, too. Amy's body was the product of considerable effort—two days a week of Pilates and two more of a South American martial art that had something vaguely cultish about it—along with a carefully calibrated diet. Everything about it had been earned, apart from the large and well-shaped breasts she'd inherited from her mother. Margo was prettier than Amy—they'd decided this together sometime around the fifth grade—and slim in a straight-lined, gamine way that was not without appeal, but she had none of Amy's shapely fullness. Amy's was a body to be presented to a married man in an expensive hotel room. Margo was built for the library. Of course she recognized the power she had over certain kinds of men, but it was a very different power than the sort that Amy wielded, and not one likely to be augmented or refined at a place like the Triple S.

Slippered and berobed, they walked out of the changing room. Margo expected their morning to begin with a massage, as it had on her other trips to the place, but Amy directed her toward a door marked "Waxing."

"Another surprise."

"Oh God," Margo said. "You know that isn't me."

"Of course it isn't. That's the whole point."

Before Margo could respond to this, she was being taken in hand by a middle-aged Russian woman who introduced herself as Anuta and led Margo through the doorway and onto a padded table. If Margo still had any illusions at this point that Anuta meant to apply her attention to Margo's brow or upper lip, they were dispelled when the woman carefully opened Margo's robe. What followed struck her almost like a tribal initiation rite, as though she were a young warrior being put through some ordeal before battle. The whole thing was deeply uncomfortable, but Margo found it appropriate that this performance of luxury should actually hurt. It spoke in some profound way to her feeling—one that could never be spoken out loud to anyone, not even Amy—that privilege was a kind of punishment.

Before starting her doctorate, she'd read more times than she could count Adorno's "For Marcel Proust," about the fate of the wealthy man who pursues a life as an artist or scholar rather than following a profession. She could practically recite the short passage whole: *The occupation with things of the mind has by now itself become "practical," a business with strict division of labor, departments, and restricted entry. The man of independent means who chooses it out of repugnance for the ignominy of earning money will not be disposed to acknowledge the fact. For this he is punished. He is not a "professional," is ranked in the competitive hierarchy as a dilettante no matter how well he knows his subject, and must, if he wants a career, show himself even more resolutely blinkered than the most inveterate specialist.*

In Adorno's time it might still have been somewhat daring to say that the life of the mind was just another bureaucratic maze. Now it amounted to stating the obvious. Professional ambition had long been the academic's dirty secret; today the dirty secret was that you just loved to read. On campus, Margo had engaged in all the mandatory despairing conversations about the state of the job market. She'd gone to every relevant conference and symposium. To say out loud that you just wanted to spend a few years discussing great books with smart people amounted to saying: *I'll be coming into some money before long, so I don't need to worry about getting on a panel at the next MLA convention.*

She'd brought this up once with Richard, who took such pride in being one of the last great generalists, who could write about Shakespeare *and* Milton *and* Shelley—and even Proust and Adorno—and be taken seriously by experts on each. She'd half wanted him to tell her what a loss to the world of scholarship her departure would have been. But Richard thought the academy—with its various politicized schools of *ressentiment* and its reflexive distrust of the canon, whose altar flame he was committed to keeping—could go to hell. (Why had he not told her this while entreating her to study with him?)

"You want to write poetry and live off family money?" he asked. "Just do it. It was good enough for Merrill. It's good enough for Fred

Seidel. If the work is truly great, it will outlast all of us, and no one will bother over the circumstances of its creation."

Margo had noted well his hypothetical construction. He could give her no assurances that the work would be great. You couldn't know in advance. You had to take the leap in ignorance. In her case, at least, being wrong wouldn't cost her much. There'd be a few lean years before her trust expired, but it would be like playacting at bohemian poverty. She would know all the time that the money was coming eventually, and she'd always have a warm bed waiting for her at home. This should have been reassuring, but it had the opposite effect: if giving up a semi-promising academic career and dedicating herself to writing had constituted a real risk, she might have been more inclined to do it. She was romantic enough to think that great art demanded great sacrifice—that one had to suffer for it—but you couldn't exactly go in search of suffering. You couldn't undergo it as a kind of game, seek it out as grist for the mill. To suffer one needed really to suffer. She'd tried to express all this to Richard. This was when he'd first made his joke about the "Anxiety of Affluence."

Not for Amy this anxiety. She'd grown up even wealthier than Margo, her father the producer of the second-rated network morning show, her mother an '80s weather girl turned lady-who-lunched, and so far as Margo could tell she felt no conflict about this good fortune whatsoever. She worked in PR for a fashion label, where she unapologetically leveraged her famous last name and wore shoes whose price exceeded her biweekly wage. If they'd met as adults, Margo would certainly have hated her, but Amy was funny and supportive and completely trustworthy and so they'd remained friends.

When Anuta had finished her work, she closed Margo's robe and backed discreetly out of the closet-sized room. A moment later, a light knock sounded on the door. Margo let out a welcoming murmur, and another middle-aged woman entered.

"I am Lyudmila." The woman smiled and extended her hands, turning them meaningfully like a sleight-of-hand man before a card trick. "I am masseuse."

"Nice to meet you," Margo said.

"Come with me."

Margo put on her slippers and sleepily followed Lyudmila out of the small room and into a slightly bigger one, which was mostly filled by two massage tables, one of which Amy already occupied.

"How did it go?" Amy asked.

"I may be out of commission for the big game," Margo told her.

"Trust me, you'll bounce back," Amy answered. "Just air it out a little."

"You like something special?" Lyudmila asked in a sharp tone that suggested mild disappointment at their lack of solemnity.

Margo wasn't sure what the special treatment would involve.

"Just the usual is fine."

This seemed to please Lyudmila, who gave Margo's back a light, almost playful slap.

"Very good. Now, you make relax."

Lyudmila's hands quickly found a knot below Margo's left shoulder blade. As they addressed themselves to it, their owner let out what might have been a sigh of superiority, as though Margo had denied the thing's existence and Lyudmila had gone in search of it anyway. Margo tensed up against the forceful throb, but as the knot resolved itself she settled comfortably under Lyudmila's touch. Beside her, Amy let out long, satisfied moans, which she exaggerated for comic effect.

"What are you thinking about?" Amy asked.

Margo hesitated to tell her the truth: "His wife."

"Oh God. That's not why we're here."

"She's nice."

"I'm sure she is," Amy told her. "She's nice, and she left."

"A week ago. She didn't divorce him."

Amy let out another loud sigh, which might have been expressing frustration at Margo or appreciation of her massage.

"How many people do you know whose college relationships ended badly?"

"A lot," Margo allowed.

"In how many cases did at least one of them cheat?"

Margo thought a moment.

"Just about all of them."

"Infidelity is a necessary part of breaking those powerful bonds of youth," Amy said, as though citing an anthropological study. "But that's just the proximate cause. These relationships aren't supposed to last."

"Lucy isn't his girlfriend. They're married."

"What difference does that really make? They don't have children. They just had some ceremony."

Perhaps she was right. They both had friends who'd been in relationships for six or seven years, who'd lived together after school, who'd been treated en bloc like married couples. In an earlier era, they certainly would have been married. But when they broke up, it wasn't a major tragedy for anyone involved. It was just something that happened. What sense did it make to bind your life forever to someone to whom you'd first been attached when still a half-formed thing? Margo's mother had done it, but that was a different time, and her father had been an adult when they met. These pairings that began when both parties were still children didn't work over the long haul. If they didn't end soon, they would almost certainly end later, under worse conditions. So Margo was acting as the agent of a process that would occur eventually in any case. Sam belonged here in New York, and Lucy belonged back in Wisconsin. She would return home, where she would meet a man more suited to her, and her real life would begin. She might even come to think that Margo had done her a great favor.

That Sam's marriage was about to end—that this separation wasn't a small bump along the way—seemed obvious to Margo. Which didn't mean she was destined to be with Sam herself. Quite the opposite. She was the proper person to affect this split precisely because she didn't have any ultimate interest in staying with him. It was so awkward having a relationship with the person you'd been cheating with. How could you ever trust his honesty, when your own partnership was forged in duplicitousness? So it seemed to Margo, though Richard had never been bothered by the fact that she'd been with someone else when she fell under his sway. In truth, he'd hardly noticed this detail. He took what he wanted and that was more or less the end of it.

"Is done," Lyudmila told her, and she gave Margo another playful slap before leaving the room.

Margo stood from the table, and she felt a sharp, exquisite pain in half a dozen divergent body parts. Amy laughed as she watched Margo struggle in the simple act of sliding back into her slippers.

The spent the rest of the morning in the main body of the salon, where Amy found the latest issue of *CelebNation* and offered a close reading of an article about some recently divorced starlet's pregnancy. Coming from anyone else, the chatter would have annoyed Margo, but from Amy it soothed. The sheer banality of it somehow turned off the spigot of Margo's thoughts. She was tempted to peruse the magazine herself, offer her own theory of the identity of the unborn child's father.

It was almost noon when they left the Triple S in their complimentary flip-flops, the paint on their fingers and toes still slightly sticky. They went to the Athena for lunch, and Margo expected when they left that they would say their goodbyes, but Amy immediately took her arm again and led her two blocks downtown to Lola's Lingerie, another storefront that Margo had passed more times than she could count, though this one she'd never been inside. A small arrow beside the door pointed to a buzzer, which Amy pressed. The woman behind the register looked up, smiled, and reached for a button beneath the counter to release the door.

As they entered, the woman smiled again and glanced quickly up at Margo's fresh blowout and down at her freshly painted toes.

"Special occasion?"

"Something like that," Margo told her.

"Let me know if I can help you with anything."

Margo nodded thanks, but Amy was already going through the racks as though she knew exactly what she was after. She started with the most outlandish items—garter belts and crotchless panties—so that when they settled on a black silk push-up and matching thong, the outfit seemed almost modest to Margo.

"He's going to be very happy with this," the woman said as she rang them up. This struck Margo as at once presumptuous and somehow reactionary, though also entirely on the mark.

"I need to go home to change," Margo told Amy when they got outside.

"No way," Amy answered. "I know what you've got at home. We can do better than that."

They walked a few more blocks to Barneys. It was excessive to be outfitting herself de novo, but as she tried the dresses on, Margo felt that it would make what happened in that hotel room possible, separate it appropriately from everything else. Whatever she wore there, she knew, she would never wear again. She decided on something fairly conservative—a knee-length cocktail dress and a pair of pumps. She didn't want to look like she was working the lobby at the Cue, and she wanted Sam to be appropriately surprised when the dress came off and he found what was waiting underneath.

The 6 train was slow getting downtown, and there was a line at reception, so she was running late by the time she got to the hotel room. She'd picked the Cue because it was a reasonable distance from his apartment and her house, but close enough to the *Interviewer*'s offices that they would have an excuse for meeting there if they were spotted by anyone they knew. The possibility of running into someone had never occurred to her when they were out walking around, and they'd spent hours in every imaginable neighborhood without such an encounter, but the stakes felt higher now. The Cue was expensive, but she'd essentially been sponging off her parents since leaving school, and Grable was still writing checks for her living expenses. Anyway, the cost added to the overall sense that they were doing this thing once to get it out of their system. If these appointments were to be a regular feature of their relationship, they would have found themselves a cheaper place.

Upstairs, she rushed a bit getting ready, but before walking out she looked herself over again in the mirror. Now that it was time to step into the role for which she'd been preparing, she wasn't sure she'd made the right choices. What would Sam think of it? She hoped he would have enough sense to dress up a little, because she would feel like a fool if he showed up in a T-shirt and jeans. When she'd emailed and asked him to meet her there, she hadn't mentioned the room, but she imagined he had some idea what was coming. They weren't in the habit of having two o'clock drinks in hotel bars. She considered taking the clothes she'd been wearing all day from where she'd stowed them in the closet and putting them back on, but she felt committed to something now, and she pressed on as though the slightest uncertainty would bring everything to a stop.

In the low light of the bar, it could have been any time of day, which made Margo feel less self-conscious. She ordered a whiskey on the rocks and drank it slowly while waiting for Sam. She felt a jolt from the first long sip, and she realized that she hadn't had a drink since her mother emptied all the booze out of the house.

So much of her drinking had been done there. She'd been allowed to drink at her parents' parties starting when she was fifteen. Around that same time, she'd started sneaking pours from her father's bar. There was something slightly perverse about this, since it depended on the knowledge that Frank could not keep track of his own intake. It was hard to imagine the house going dry for long. She supposed the blue law would be lifted once they sent her father away, as she'd become convinced that Kit meant to do ever since she'd seen those men at the house.

Margo wasn't sure who they were, but they definitely weren't old friends come to offer Kit work. Her parents' friends had haunted the house all her life, and these men didn't look a bit familiar. Nor did she believe that a pair of bankers would make a business call at seven in the morning. If they wanted to hire Kit for something, wouldn't they schedule one of those expensive lunches that had once seemed her parents' primary pastime? Margo assumed that sort of thing was still done, despite everything. She likewise assumed that the economy's collapse had not reduced the city's financial elite to wearing off-the-rack undertakers' suits.

They might have been salesmen, but what product induced salesmen to drop in at that hour? And why would Kit be considering such a purchase now? Her whole life had been put on hold since Frank's diagnosis. The only reasonable explanation was that Frank was the subject of their visit. Margo didn't want to believe that her mother was making plans, however preliminary, to put Frank away, but it would explain why the men had come early—to be sure they were gone before he woke up—and it would explain the visit's effect on Kit, who was not known for emotional displays.

Frank had always been a lot of work for everyone, and now he was a full-time project, but Kit kept insisting that he was getting better. He just needed to dry out—Margo could have told them that—and once he did, his mind would be back. Even if he never recovered, shouldn't there be some intermediate step before they carried him off? Why couldn't Kit hire someone to look after him at the house, like she had done for Margo all her life?

Maybe she should have been doing more to help. She'd been taking her father for long walks every few days, getting him out of the house and giving her mother a little time to herself, but she did this mostly for her own enjoyment. It was possible to spend hours with him without noticing anything wrong. Since he'd always been a nostalgist, it didn't seem strange that he wanted to talk about things that had happened years before she was born. His recent obsession with the last game at Ebbets Field was the sort of thing that might have been taken as a sign of dementia in anyone else but was actually quite typical of Frank, who was always stuck on something or other from the distant past. When he ran out of steam, she returned them to poetry. It was amazing how much of it was still immediately available to him. In many ways, his legendary memory was very much intact.

"*That is no country for old men,*" she'd said to him on the day he got back from Bridgehampton.

"*The young / In one another's arms,*" he'd responded without hesitation. "*Birds in the trees . . .*"

If someone had told her, as they'd stood reciting Yeats at the foot of the stairs, that her father was suffering from a kind of brain damage, she wouldn't have believed it. But when they'd finished with what was passed or passing or to come, she'd asked what had happened to him, and he'd looked at her blankly. She'd expected him to say that there was some misunderstanding, that her mother had overreacted. Instead he'd shrugged his shoulders and turned back up the stairs. He might have been embarrassed about whatever he'd been through out east, but he was usually very good at concocting his own version of otherwise embarrassing events. He seemed not to know what she was talking about.

"Did he have a stroke or something?" Margo had asked her mother.

"He's lost some short-term memory," Kit said. "I know it's unnerving, but it's only temporary. The doctors expect him to get better after these treatments. In the meantime, he's mostly still there."

This seemed to be true. Every time Margo referenced some experience they'd shared years before or alluded to a line of poetry they'd known, he picked right up on it, as though nothing had happened. This made it easy to forget his troubles, to touch casually upon something from the day or even the hour before. His expression changed then, and she could tell that he was trying to bluff, perhaps to bluff himself most of all.

Still, she enjoyed their conversations more than she had in a very long time. They talked the way they had when she was in high school. Perhaps she was a bit of a nostalgist, too, because she liked living in the past with him. It put them back on a simpler footing. The last year had been erased. She didn't need to forgive him for what he'd said—a forgiveness he would never have deigned to seek—and he didn't need to forgive her for cutting him off. It had never happened.

She was glad that he'd gotten a diagnosis, even if she wasn't sure what the diagnosis was. If there was a real problem—something that showed up on a scan—his recent behavior could be explained. He wasn't just old and out of touch; he was ill. His horrible attempt at humor in the broadcast booth had not been an expression of subconscious animus, or even the ramblings of a man past his prime. It was a symptom of a discrete pathology—one that might be fixed somehow. Could his whole rightward drift over the past decade be blamed on some neurological misfiring? Had it been the early symptoms of a drawn-out mental collapse? She felt guilty for having judged him so harshly, for having withdrawn her affection over something that had been out of his control. The fact that he'd hardly noticed this withdrawal made no difference; the intent had been there.

She was shaken from these thoughts by Sam's arrival in the bar. He was a few minutes early, wearing khaki pants, a collared shirt, and a blazer—very nearly the same outfit he'd been wearing on the day he'd come to interview Frank. She didn't get up from her stool to greet him, and he didn't seem to know quite what to do, whether to lean over and kiss her cheek or just sit down. He placed a hand awkwardly on her shoulder as he took the empty stool beside her.

"Can I get you something?" the bartender asked before either of them had spoken.

"What are you drinking?" Sam asked her.

"Whiskey," she told him, and Sam waved to say he'd take one of the same. Margo had been nursing hers, but when the bartender offered a refill she accepted it. They touched glasses and took a long sip.

"I don't usually drink hard stuff during the day," Sam said.

Margo thought instinctively of her father.

"Sometimes it's what you need."

She didn't want to be drunk for whatever came next, so she asked for the check before they were half done.

"I can get this," Sam told her.

"That's all right." Margo tried to sound at once seductive and casual. "I'll put it on my room."

"You've got a room."

"The view is spectacular, if you'd like to come have a look."

He didn't respond right away. Margo hadn't prepared herself for the possibility that he would decline. The few minutes while the waiter brought the check and she signed for it were excruciating. Finally, he nodded, and they walked together to the elevator bank.

The doors opened, and they stepped inside. She swiped her room card to send them to the twelfth floor. They were alone, but they didn't touch or even talk. Anyone watching would have thought they were strangers. Margo couldn't quite imagine what would happen next. She should have made more of an effort to visualize it, so that she would now have some model to follow. All her arrangements were like an empty vessel they needed to fill.

When they stepped inside the room and he moved for her, Margo's first sensation was relief. She didn't want to be responsible for everything. He pressed her against the sliding glass of the closet door, and she felt him coming to life. He kissed her neck and pushed a clumsy hand against her breast. With the other hand he pulled at the hem of her dress. If she wasn't careful, she thought, it would all happen right there, while they were still standing. Margo stepped free of Sam, pulled her dress back into place, and walked the rest of the way into the room. As he followed, Sam reached out to put a hand on her hip.

"Lie down," she told him when they got to the bed.

He did as she said, and she remained standing, watching him. She wasn't sure exactly what she meant to do, except slow things down. She did a few turns in place, moving her hips, while she reached behind her to unzip the dress. She had her back to him when she shrugged it off, so that she could see herself in the mirror opposite, and she could see Sam watching her. With the dress now down at her ankles, she turned to face him, and she leaned over to free her feet of the tangle of it, showing him her cleavage in the tight press of her new bra.

As she climbed next to him on the bed, she expected Sam to sit up to meet her, but he stayed where he was. She kissed him, and he returned her kiss, but he didn't run his hands over her body, which was waiting for his touch. He seemed to be paralyzed. She threw a leg over his waist and slowly unbuttoned his shirt, kissing his chest as she worked her way down. When she'd finished with the buttons she pulled the shirttails from his pants, but she couldn't get the shirt off without his help, and he still wouldn't move. She rolled off him and undid his belt. She opened his pants and pulled them down to the middle of his thighs. She found him there soft and small. Whatever she'd felt by the closet door was gone now. She took the thing in one hand and worked at it gently. When it didn't respond, she went more quickly, but it was like shaking an inanimate object, trying to will it to life. She looked up at Sam, who seemed to be in a trance.

She knew she should give him more time, but she was too worked up to stop, and she decided that it would help to act, without letting him think about it. She leaned over and took him into her mouth.

"Stop," he said, almost angrily.

With his saggy stretch of skin still between her lips, she looked up at him and saw that he was crying. She didn't know how long this had been going on. He stayed there inert in her mouth while he watched her recognize the tears, and perhaps it was something about her expression that set him off, because in another moment he was sobbing.

She released him and sat on the edge of the bed.

"I want to do it," he said, as he sat up. He pulled his pants up a little ways, but not enough to cover himself. "I definitely do, but I think my body and my mind are crossing signals."

Margo suddenly felt very exposed. She turned onto her back and lay quietly beside him. She could hear his sharp, heavy breaths, and she wanted to tell him, in Lyudmila's voice, to make relax. She couldn't sit there in this outfit and wait for him to be ready.

"I'm going to hop in the shower," she said.

While she waited for the water to warm, she examined herself in the bathroom mirror. Her expensive blowout would be ruined in another minute, but she didn't care. She looked over her new lingerie—almost three hundred dollars, and she'd never wear it again. She could see the outline of her sculpted pubic hair through the sheer underwear. She'd gained some weight since coming home, but she thought she wore it well. It added a bit of Amy-like voluptuousness to her. Though she was the only audience now, she couldn't help performing slightly while she undressed.

After a moment in the hot shower she started to touch herself. She tried to imagine how it would have been, how it might be still when she went back out into the room, but all she could picture was that sad saggy thing, so she imagined instead her own image turning in the mirror. Sam was still there, somewhere in a distant corner, but that hardly mattered. As she got off, her legs went wobbly with the force of it, and she leaned against the cold tile, shaking.

She left her underwear on the bathroom floor and put on one of the Cue's plush robes. The feeling of calm she'd spent so much of the morning trying to cultivate had finally come over her. She no longer worried about how things would go with Sam from here. In her mind, he'd become so superfluous that she wasn't even surprised to step back into the room and find him gone. She looked around briefly, but he'd left no trace of himself. As she climbed alone into bed, she could almost imagine that he'd never been there.

5.

After the Celsia deal went through, Justin took to wandering the neighborhood in the hope of running into Eddie, though he didn't know what he'd say if they crossed paths. He wanted to explain why he hadn't been returning Eddie's calls, but there wasn't much he could tell him.

He'd been increasingly paranoid since the day of the announcement. Minutes after the news ran across the bottom of the muted flat-screen mounted on his office wall, Justin had received a text from Chloe Porter: *I hope you made a killing today.*

She had to be setting him up. No one could be that stupid. He could see it so clearly, now that it was too late. She'd probably been busted for some petty malfeasance and made all sorts of promises about whom she could net if the Feds gave her a deal. Every whale she'd ever known suddenly became a close friend and occasional coconspirator. Whoever had brought her in would have combed through her contact list for connections to DRE, and this would have brought them to Justin. He was tempted to write back and say that he'd decided to sit this one out, maybe add that he didn't think she should be so cavalier about her professional responsibilities, but he resisted this urge. Better not even to acknowledge what she was talking about. If Chloe was working with the government, she already knew that he hadn't bit. She was just trying to keep the conversation going, give him a chance to slip up.

He would never have answered her first email if he'd understood at the time the heat that Eisen was under, but he'd been expelled from the inner sanctum of Wall Street gossip after closing his fund, so the rumors had taken longer to reach him than they would have a few years before. Even when they did reach him, they'd been hard to take seriously at first. Rumors had followed Eisen forever. But recently they'd turned troublingly specific, become something more than rumors. Two former colleagues each warned Justin that the other had been flipped. A third spoke of separate investigations by the U.S. Attorney's office, the state attorney general, and the SEC. Everyone who'd ever worked for Eisen was preparing to come downstairs in their bathrobes at midnight and find comic book G-men standing on their Larchmont lawns.

Even if it all passed, Eisen's days of going about his business unnoticed were definitively over. The crash had changed everything. Someone on Wall Street had to get locked up, and those in charge of making that happen seemed to have decided who it would be. That Eisen had never gone in for subprime lending, CDOs, credit default swaps, or any of the other business that had actually brought down the economy—that he was a humble stock picker, as he liked to say—made him in many ways an ideal target. His crimes were easy to understand, and prosecuting them wouldn't require admitting that regulators had been asleep at the wheel. He hadn't used complex financial engineering to outsmart supposedly sophisticated institutional investors. He was just an old-fashioned crook.

They were all crooks, of course, if Eisen was to be believed. But it was entirely in keeping with his view of the world that when the public finally demanded some reckoning, the institutional crooks would offer up someone like him rather than one of their own. This was why he'd always been so careful, and why Justin still didn't think they'd ever get to him. Some of his analysts would be at risk if they'd gotten sloppy, some of the experts they were paying for information would be vulnerable, DRE might even be subject to a civil judgment for lack of oversight, but Eisen himself would never be touched.

That still left the rest of them. The best thing Justin had going for him was the fact that he'd gotten out when he did, that he'd stopped making big trades and started giving his money away. It had been a mistake to get back in. He was sorry he'd ever agreed to meet with Chloe, but there was no connection between her and his old business, and he hadn't put any money into the stock.

He'd asked an old trader friend to find out whether Kit had gotten into Celsia, as much out of curiosity as anything else, and he'd discovered that she'd bought the stock in Eddie's name. He wasn't sure what this misdirection was meant to achieve. Perhaps she'd done it because Eddie hadn't been with them in Bridgehampton that weekend, but anyone inclined to look into the matter would see that Kit had ordered the trade.

Whatever its purpose, this added layer of complication made it impossible for Justin to call Eddie, so he was left trying to happen innocently upon him. He lingered over lunch at the Pallas Athena. He circled the reservoir at hours when Eddie usually went on runs. He spent evenings at the Second Avenue bars they used to haunt. He gave the effort up only when Blakeman told him that Eddie had moved downtown.

"He's got a pretty weird setup," Blakeman explained. "He's sharing an apartment in a run-down building with some old man he met in Washington Square."

When Justin pressed for more details, Blakeman said, "Ask him yourself. He wants to hear from you."

"I'd like to see him, too," Justin said. "Things are complicated."

Blakeman didn't ask for further explanation. He'd always kept himself carefully aloof from Justin and Eddie's emotional dramas, though he couldn't help being enlisted as an emissary from time to time, and Justin assumed Blakeman's efforts were somehow involved when he got an email from Eddie a few days later:

> J- I'm sorry we haven't been in touch. Whatever's up, I'm sure we can work it out. You might have heard I got a new place. I'd love for you to come by and see it. Things are busy during the week (new job, long story—I'll tell you about it when we see each other). You free this Sunday afternoon? —E

He wasn't sure whether to respond. More than a month had passed since the buyback, and nothing out of the ordinary had happened. Even if the Feds connected Kit's trade to his conversation with Chloe, he told himself, they couldn't make a case without his help, which he would never give. Perhaps the crisis had passed. He wrote back to accept Eddie's invitation.

When Sunday came around, Justin sent Tommy to take his mother to church. He could have gone along and been home in plenty of time, but an afternoon with his oldest friend was suddenly an occasion for which he felt the need to prepare, and he didn't want to be rushed. He went for a walk and when he got home he took a long shower. His phone was ringing when he stepped from the bathroom, but it had stopped by the time he got to it. He had a voice mail and two missed calls from Tommy.

When he called back, Tommy picked up right away.

"What's up?" Justin asked.

"Your mom fainted in church. She's all right now, but I'm taking her to Brooklyn Hospital just to be sure."

"Not the hospital," Justin cut in. He thought of it above all as the place that had killed his father, and he refused to send his mother there. "Take her to the Price Center."

On his way to the garage, he phoned the center to make sure the doctor on call would be ready for them. He climbed into the driver's seat of the Escalade, which he usually avoiding taking to Crown Heights. He was most of the way downtown when Tommy texted him.

Doctor at the P.C. ran some tests and says everything looked fine.

Do you want to drive her home? Justin wrote back. *I can turn around.*

Netta wants to wait for you here, Tommy responded after a minute.

When Justin arrived, Tommy pulled smoothly out of his spot to make way for the Escalade. Justin parked the car and crossed the street to the center. A woman walking in the opposite direction smiled at him and gave a tentative wave, as though they knew each other. Justin had already walked by before he realized that it was Lucy Waxworth. There was something so incongruous about her presence there, though the Waxworths were just the kind of people one found in the neighborhood these days. He felt bad for not returning a smile or a wave, but he couldn't do anything about it now. The sight of her had jarred him a little bit. She was an emissary from a weekend he'd hoped to consign to oblivion. She was one of only a handful of people who could say for sure that Justin had spoken to Kit that day, and here she was casually waving at him. He hurried into the lobby, where Jonathan waited with a look of beatific reassurance on his face.

"False alarm," he said enthusiastically. "Your mother forgot to eat breakfast this morning. She was singing and praising and she just started to feel a bit unwell. You know how the church gets in August. I guess the air conditioner wasn't up to the job today. She got herself overheated. A little rest and something to eat did the trick."

"How long has the air-conditioning been broken?" Justin asked. Jonathan's smile wavered momentarily.

"It's not broken exactly, just old. It's only a problem a few weekends each summer. We like to keep the doors open and the fans running."

"If you need air-conditioning to make the place inhabitable, just let me know and I'm happy to pay for it." Justin tried to keep his voice calm. "There's no need for old women to be collapsing in the heat."

"She didn't collapse, Brother Justin." The smile had returned in full to Jonathan's face. "She just felt a little unwell."

"Where is she now?"

"Up on the third floor. I told her I'd wait for you here."

Justin found his mother seated on a couch beside a large woman about her age who looked eerily familiar to him. She was obviously one of Netta's church friends, but he couldn't think why he knew her face so well. The two women were laughing comfortably, and they waved Justin over energetically. His mother looked perfectly comfortable—if anything, more animated than usual—as though she always spent her Sunday afternoons on this couch and he had been there to pick her up countless times before.

"You remember Mrs. Taylor?" she said as Justin approached.

He hadn't laid eyes on her since he was ten or eleven years old. She'd looked so familiar, he realized now, not because he remembered her face but because so much of her son was captured in it. She had the same freckled, light brown skin, the same round cheeks, the same sad eyes. She'd moved them out of the neighborhood the year after Justin went off to St. Albert's. They'd gone to Newark, where Terrance's father's family lived, so he could have his own fresh start. Justin was surprised that she'd come back after all these years, but even more surprised that his mother was sitting with her.

"Justin Price," she said, as though he were a long-lost relation. "It's been so long. And here you've become famous, with your name on the building and everything."

She said this with a hint of skepticism, as though she didn't quite believe in Justin's celebrity, or didn't think it commendable in any case.

"My father's name," Justin corrected her with a smile.

"That's right," she allowed. "He was a very good man."

"I'm sorry about Terrance," Justin said.

This sounded perfunctory, but how could he possibly express the emotion passing through him? He'd thought about Terrance almost every day during his first year at St. Albert's, when their mothers had kept them apart. He'd told himself that things must have gotten easier at school after he left, that Terrance probably liked life without Justin as much as Justin liked St. Albert's, but he'd known this wasn't so, even before they moved away. Once Terrance was gone, there was nothing Justin could do. In those days before email or cell phones, it wasn't really possible for two boys to keep in touch if their parents didn't want them to.

He'd been in college when Terrance was killed. There was a memorial at the Pathway, but Justin had been so angry (at whom, exactly? well, at everyone) that he knew he wouldn't be able to step inside. He hadn't even taken the train up from Georgetown. He'd never had a chance for any kind of goodbye. After that, it had become easier not to think of the boy at all, or to think of him as the instrument that had brought Justin his new life, rather than as someone who'd been denied the same opportunity.

"Thank you," Mrs. Taylor said. Justin watched the tears come briefly into her eyes, and then watched her control herself. "I think a lot of what he would have been like if he'd reached your age. He would have been happy to see you again."

"I would, too," Justin said.

"You'll be back here soon, I hope," Mrs. Taylor told them both while taking Netta into a hug.

Before they could leave, Netta had to do a round of the floor, saying goodbye to everyone she saw, including people Justin was quite sure she'd never met in her life. Finally they got downstairs, where Jonathan still waited in the lobby.

"Do you need a ride?" Justin asked.

"That's very kind, but there are some people I'd like to visit, so long as I'm here."

Justin wondered whether Mrs. Taylor was among them. How long had she been back in town? Had Jonathan stayed in touch with her? They'd never talked about it, but Justin imagined that Jonathan had gone to the funeral, which his father had overseen. They had made an odd triangle in their early boyhood. Jonathan had always been somewhat superfluous to Justin. He had to remind himself that Jonathan would have thought those days belonged to him as much as to them.

"Get that air-conditioning fixed," Justin said. "Send an invoice to the foundation."

"I appreciate that, Brother Justin," Jonathan answered, ignoring the imperative tone.

"It's such a shame what happened to that boy," Netta told Justin as they got into the car. "You were so close back then."

She said this without a trace of irony, and Justin wondered whether she was even still conscious of the work she'd done to keep him and Terrance apart.

"It was funny to see you two together," he said. "I don't remember you liking Mrs. Taylor so much."

"Who has time to hold on to things? At my age you stick to people when you've got a little history with them."

He wasn't sure what she was suggesting. She and Mrs. Taylor had acted coldly toward each other long before they'd gotten wind of what was happening and acted abruptly to put an end to it.

"I didn't know she'd come back to Crown Heights," he said neutrally.

"Just a few months ago. I've been seeing her in church. It's that time of life. We're all getting old."

Netta was in her late fifties and, notwithstanding whatever had happened that day, she seemed to be in perfect health.

"You've both got decades left."

"Maybe so, but I got a scare in me today. I kept thinking about how quick your father went. I was ready for them to tell me they'd found something."

"But they didn't."

Justin didn't mention what they both knew—that Brooklyn Hospital hadn't found anything the first time his father went in with a sore on his heel. They'd debrided it, bandaged it up, and sent him home with a topical ointment. He'd returned only when the growth had taken over most of his foot, by which time it was too late.

He reached over to pat her knee, and she softly stroked his wrist.

"I want to go home," she said.

"We're on our way."

"You know what I mean. Where we're going might be your home, but it's never going to be mine. Whatever time I have left, I want to spend it in my place, with my people, just like Sue Taylor."

For a moment he imagined that she might mean Barbados. That, at least, he could understand: island sun, childhood memories. But Crown Heights? She really did have decades left, in all likelihood. Wouldn't she be happier spending them in a doorman building facing Central Park, rather than a fourth-floor walk-up facing a mobile police tower?

"Let's talk about it after you've had some rest. I know it's been a tough morning."

"This isn't a bad morning speaking," Netta said more sharply. "I've tried living your way. I'm ready to go home."

Justin couldn't see the road in front of him. He thought he might have to pull over. What was it that bothered him so much? It was her life, after all. What difference did it make if she spent it in Crown Heights? He could put her up in the Denison or some other nice place, and he could make sure she was well taken care of there. Wasn't the point just for her to be happy? But there was something more at stake.

He'd started talking about getting his parents out of the neighborhood as soon as his first bonus from Eisen came in. They'd simply refused. When he'd brought up their safety, his father had been offended at once on his own behalf and that of the neighborhood. They'd lived through the riots, watched liquor stores turn to coffee shops, beauty parlors become vegan restaurants. They weren't going to start worrying about the crime rate now. Justin explained that he wasn't speaking about the usual street violence. People knew he had money, and that made them inviting targets. His father had told him he was making too much of himself. If criminals were going after rich people, wouldn't they have better luck on Fifth Avenue?

"Save that money," he'd finally said. "Don't assume it will be coming in like that forever."

Justin had been tempted to tell him what kind of numbers he was dealing in. It didn't need to keep coming in forever; he'd already made more than enough to support them all for the rest of their lives. But his father's refusal was obviously motivated by something more than thrift.

At the time, he was a couple of years short of retirement. At fifty-five his city pension would kick in, and he promised to reconsider the question then. When the apartment above Justin's came on the market, Justin bought it quietly and prepared to wait him out. The diagnosis came six months later.

Why had he still refused, even then? In death, Daryl Price had become a great mystery to his son. If he had not been the same in life, this couldn't be entirely blamed on the narcissism of youth. The man had seemed so solid, so self-sufficient, that the broad outlines of his story—the few facts that even an uninquisitive child comes to possess as a matter of course—hadn't seemed to require shading in. Daryl Price was born and raised in Wrigley Park, a place to which he referred so rarely that Justin had been a teenager before he figured out that it was not a city or a town but a neighborhood in Paterson. He'd been drafted at twenty and served in Vietnam, a period about which he'd never spoken to Justin. After the army, he'd briefly played the trumpet in a church band, which was how he'd met Netta Headley, whose own father had moved their family from Barbados to Brooklyn when she was a teenager.

For nearly thirty years he drove for the MTA, mostly the B8 from Bay Ridge to Brownsville. He worked fourteen-hour shifts, often on weekends and holidays. Justin and his mother were usually done with dinner and getting ready for bed by the time he got home. After a few words of greeting, he opened a beer, put on a record—Miles or Dizzy, Freddie Hubbard or Donald Byrd—and sat on the couch to listen while he ate. Netta sat with him, but they rarely spoke. Instead he attended to the music carefully, as though engaged in conversation with it. After he'd finished his food and opened his second beer, he called his son from his room to join them. He might ask a few questions about Justin's day, but always the music got its share of his attention. After a third beer he tended to nod off, at which point Netta would shake him gently awake and bring him to bed.

Though he wasn't a spiritual man so far as Justin could tell, he put on a jacket and tie every Sunday morning and spent his day off in church with his wife. When Justin made too much ruckus beside them, he reached down and took the soft flesh between Justin's shoulder and neck into a firm pinch, sending shivers through the boy's whole body, the closest the family came to the corporal punishment to which so many of Justin's young friends were subject. On sunny days, he set up a beach chair out on the street after services, and he sat with the other neighborhood men while they cooked on the grill and smoked cigarettes. In this way, a life had been lived. Had it been a happy life? It had never occurred to Justin to ask.

Like a would-be suitor, he'd waited only as long after his father's death as decorum demanded before broaching the subject of the move with his mother. When he did, he interpreted her continued reluctance as posthumous loyalty to her husband of thirty-six years, but as the months wore on he was forced to admit that she sincerely shared his father's feelings. She didn't think people needed all of the things the Doyles had to be happy. "What good is it to gain the world but lose your soul?" she'd said to him more than once. But she'd given in eventually, and he'd been sure she would change her mind once she moved.

He couldn't accept the idea that she simply belonged in Crown Heights in a way that she didn't belong where she was now. Did Frank Doyle ever stop to wonder whether he belonged on the Upper East Side, just because he wasn't born there? There was a black family in the White House—could there not be one on Fifth Avenue? It was only Netta's old-fashioned ideas that made her refuse to be happy there. And this refusal, by implication, suggested that Justin should not be happy there either. She'd sent him into this world, why would she not come with him? Then there was something else, too, something in him that thought: *If she goes back, it was all for nothing.* Providing her this life was part of a larger effort to make good of what he'd done. When she refused to accept this life, she was refusing him redemption.

Justin left the car for Tommy to park, and he helped his mother to her apartment. It was a few minutes after noon by the time he got back downstairs, so he texted Eddie to say he'd be late. A few hours earlier he would have hesitated before sending that text, but the morning's events had made much of his anxiety seem overblown. Still, he opted to take the subway downtown, thinking vaguely that his movements would be harder to track that way. Eddie's block was all the way east, another fifteen minutes once he got off the train, and it was after one o'clock by the time he got there.

Despite Blakeman's warning, Justin was perplexed when he arrived at the address Eddie had given him and found the kind of distressed property his REIT might have bought and refurbished. Why was it so difficult to imagine Eddie living in such a place? He'd always enjoyed staying over with Justin when they were kids, but Justin's childhood building had been in considerably better shape than this one, and in any case there was a difference between putting up with such conditions for the sake of a friend and seeking them out. Even if Eddie didn't want to spend any of the savings Justin knew he had, whatever new job was keeping him so busy must have paid enough to cover the rent on a nicer apartment. Failing that, he could have gone on living with his parents. If he was living in this apartment, he must have wanted for some reason to live in a place like this. In this way, he was more like Justin's parents than like his own.

Daryl and Netta had always loved Eddie, whatever their reservations about the rest of his family, with whom they'd had a polite but uneasy relationship. His mother had felt real gratitude toward the Doyles, and she'd often defended the family to her husband, but she'd been cold toward them ever since the publication of a business section profile in which Kit had called Justin "a second son."

It was typical of the Doyles, this assumption that being counted in their circle was such a gift that even his real family could only be flattered at his inclusion. Or maybe it was just that his actual parents, not being in the circle themselves, didn't matter enough to worry about offending. Netta had never mentioned the article to Justin. It was his father who had thrown the paper down in front of him and asked, "What's wrong with the mother you've already got?" Justin was almost glad his father hadn't been around to hear

Frank's remarks in that announcer's booth, which he would have taken as confirmation of his long-held suspicions of what lay in the man's heart. ("Some of us can't afford to just say any old stupid thing that comes into our heads" was all his mother had cared to comment on that matter.)

When Justin got to the fourth floor, Eddie was waiting for him out in the hall. He gave Justin a hug and invited him inside. Justin took a seat on the couch while Eddie poured them each a cup of coffee. He moved nervously about the apartment, and Justin thought he might be embarrassed, though the place was neatly furnished and larger than Justin had been expecting.

"Where's your roommate?" Justin asked.

"What do you mean?"

Hit tone was oddly defensive.

"Blakeman told me you were living here with some old man."

As he said it, it sounded like a bad joke, which it wouldn't have been beyond Blakeman to make up.

"Herman moved out," Eddie said. "It's a long story. I should probably find a one bedroom, but I've been too busy with work, and the rent is cheap."

"Tell me about your new job."

"I got certified as an EMT. I'm working for New York General. How are things with you?"

Before Justin could begin to answer, a knock on the door interrupted them. Eddie didn't seem surprised by the disturbance but offered no explanation for it. He opened the door without looking through the peephole, and Kit walked brusquely inside.

"I'm going to go out for a little while," Eddie said to no one in particular, like a bad actor reading from a script. "I'll leave you guys to talk."

As Eddie closed the door behind himself, Justin stood to greet Kit, who waved him back into his seat. She sat across from him, in the chair that Eddie had occupied a moment before.

"Sorry to spring this on you," she said. "I wanted to talk, and I thought it would be better to do it this way."

Justin was about to make a joke about her paranoia outdoing even his own, but the look on her face told him that it wasn't paranoia at all.

"I got a visit from the FBI," she said. "Whoever gave you that Celsia tip got flipped."

Justin didn't know how long ago this visit was, but the panic in Kit's voice sounded fresh. He should have been a bit panicked himself, but by this point the news had a nearly inevitable feel.

"I never should have trusted her."

"They know you came to see me in Bridgehampton. They know I made the purchase after that. They've got the dots lined up."

"That's all circumstantial," Justin said, trying to calm himself as much as her. "That's not real evidence."

"They're pushing pretty hard," Kit told him. "They've threatened to bust my door down and march me out on the nightly news. They told me not to talk to you, but I thought that if I could just bring you into them, you could tell them what you know, and we could make this all go away. They're not after either of us. They just want Eisen."

"There's nothing to tell on that front."

"They don't think it's possible that you worked there for years and never saw anything."

"Well, they're wrong."

"You don't owe him any loyalty."

Her tone made it clear that Justin did after all owe loyalty to someone.

"Listen to me," he told her, trying to convey a conviction he didn't actually feel. "So long as we both shut up they don't have anything."

"It's a bit more complicated than that. I made the trade in Edward's account."

"I know that," Justin said.

"He gave all the money away."

She said it like a challenge, as though daring Justin to keep up his calmly reassuring facade. If that was the intent, the revelation had its desired effect. All the time he'd spent worrying over the past few weeks, all the scenarios he'd played out in his head, had not prepared him for this possibility.

"Gave it to who?"

"This man he'd been living with."

"The one he met on the street?"

"He was some kind of religious hustler. A con man. He took Edward in."

"Where is this man now?"

"Disappeared completely. As though into thin air. Or ascended into heaven, I guess." She gave a grim smile. "For all I know, the Feds might have let him move the money to get leverage. In any case, they've got leverage now. The trade was in Edward's name, and he's helped the proceeds disappear, and they can put him away a long time."

Justin got up from the couch and took a step toward Kit, meaning to comfort her, but she got up as well and clutched her purse to herself, as though almost afraid, as a woman who looked like her might respond when a man who looked like him sat down beside her on the train. In that moment, Justin understood everything. He stopped where he was, and they stood facing each other. He looked Kit straight in the eye. She nodded almost imperceptibly before looking away.

"They just want Eisen," she repeated, as though this were a kind of command.

Justin waited before speaking again, slowly and clearly and perhaps a bit more loudly than necessary, as though addressing not Kit but whoever was on the other end of the line. He spoke about the conversation with Eisen, in which he'd asked about Justin's friends, and he explained the outlines of what happened after that.

"The system was very simple. If you had an edge, you never said where you'd gotten it. You just made your recommendation, and you said you were sure. Maybe you wrote up a report, though that hardly mattered since Eisen never read anyone's reports. You had some reason why your diligent research made you recommend shorting some drug company. If a month later that company reported that their blood pressure drug had failed at trial, that was just good luck."

As Justin said all this, he understood that it wouldn't be enough to save Eddie. He would have gladly given up Eisen, but he didn't have Eisen to give. There were probably a dozen people on the Street he could have offered instead, but only one who was big enough for the Feds' purposes, only one sacrifice that would get the Doyles safely out of this situation.

"The first time I did it was with NuTech, that chipmaker that hired Q&M to manage their IPO. Ambrose told me they were going to have to resubmit some of their filings, with lowered numbers. I shorted them, and I told Eisen to do the same. I didn't tell him why. I thought I could just do it once, get my year-end numbers where they needed to be, and leave it at that. But it was so easy. There didn't seem to be any reason not to do it again."

"You don't need to say all this," Kit broke in.

But it was difficult to stop once he'd started. In this way, it was like the behavior itself. There was no one telling you to slow down, to play it safe. There was certainly no one telling you that you'd made enough money—for the firm or for yourself. There was no such thing as enough.

He and Ambrose created an email account and left messages in the draft folder. Since the drafts were never sent, they couldn't be intercepted. When Ambrose had something Justin could use or Justin wanted Ambrose to look into something, they put the details in the folder and called the other to say, "You've got mail." Ambrose gave the account a porn name, so that anyone who stumbled across it in a registry would assume it was a spambot.

"We probably moved on half a dozen tips in that first year. I mostly paid Ambrose in gifts—expensive watches, a car—so they looked like personal expenditures. One summer I spent eighty grand on a rental in East Hampton and gave him the keys. When you sold and Ambrose went to work for UniBank, he brought in a few other people, and I sent work their way. Once I started my own fund, that was most of our delta right there."

He hadn't really admitted the extent of it even to himself.

"I've been trying to do some good with that money," he said. "But no amount of good will change where it came from."

When he'd finished telling her, Kit looked stricken, which annoyed Justin. She must have had some idea of what she would hear when she'd set this meeting up.

"Why?" she asked.

She might have been speaking about the whole scheme, or about the fact that he'd used his old Q&M contacts to do it, but Justin understood immediately that she was asking only why he'd told her. Didn't she understand, even now?

He took another step, and she backed away toward the door, holding her purse more tightly, as though he might contaminate her.

"I'm sorry," she said. "This isn't what I wanted to happen."

No doubt that was true, but it was what had had to happen. That must have been as clear to her as it was to him. He felt as if his whole life had been building toward it. He couldn't say this to her—it would sound ridiculous when spoken out loud—but he had to say something: this might be the last chance they ever had to speak to each other. But he stayed silent, and then she was gone.

6.

Lucy had no idea where she was headed or how long she'd be gone. She'd thrown a few things in a bag without really thinking. She just knew that she needed to get away from Sam. She remembered a hotel on Willoughby, not far from Borough Hall, which she'd come across when looking for a place where her parents could stay over Thanksgiving. She liked the idea of getting out of the immediate neighborhood. The walk took forty minutes, and she sweat through her shirt on the way.

"I'd like a room for the night," she told the distracted middle-aged man behind the front desk. "A nice one."

He looked briefly at his screen and nodded.

"I need a card and an ID," he said.

Lucy looked through her wallet for her old college Visa, the only credit card that she didn't share with Sam, which she handed over along with her driver's license. The man entered her information, and for the moment he was the only person on earth who could have said where she was. She couldn't remember the last time that neither Sam nor her parents had known where she'd be spending the night. The realization scared her a little, but she also felt something like relief.

All this time she'd been waiting for the day when Sam would announce that he was leaving her. She'd carried the possibility everywhere she went. This was why she'd never confronted him after going to his office: she hadn't wanted to initiate a conversation that could only end with the packing of bags. Now the thing in the world she'd most feared—the inevitable talk about Margo Doyle—had happened, and it hadn't destroyed her. Instead, she was the one who'd packed her bags. She felt as though she'd survived a near-death experience.

How could the balance of a relationship shift so dramatically? When they'd started dating, she'd had all the power. She was better looking, more popular, more adept in social situations. She hadn't been in the highest echelon of campus popularity, but she'd clearly occupied a rung above his. Her friends had thought it a kind of eccentricity that she was going out with this awkward boy, even granting the minor celebrity he'd gained for himself with the spreadsheet game that none of them quite cared enough to understand.

They'd been the first of their friends to marry, just a year out of school. She hadn't been in any hurry, but Sam had thought it silly to wait. Why would you, once you knew whom you wanted to be with? He liked having questions settled, and he needed a certain amount of stability in his life. She found this understandable, given his family history. Perhaps what he wanted was less a commitment from her than the feeling of committing to something himself. By marrying so young, he would bind himself to someone in a way that his father had never been bound to his mother or to him. This was an admittedly crude analysis on her part, which she never would have mentioned to him, but it seemed basically sound.

He'd proposed on graduation day, having used part of his Pop-Up money to buy a ring. The purchase must have seemed a counterproductive extravagance to him. Why spend thousands of dollars on a symbol of marriage that you could otherwise spend on the thing itself—on rent for their apartment, on a family vacation, on saving for the future? But the ring was by custom part of the commitment he meant to make, and he was capable of a romantic gesture when such a gesture was rationally required.

His mother, who'd been on relatively good terms with him in that last year of school, had come to graduation and congratulated them both warmly, but when she learned that they weren't planning a church wedding, she let them know that she wouldn't attend. Lucy and her parents were happy to work out a compromise. They even offered to involve a minister somehow. Nothing wrong with paying respect to family tradition, Mitch had said. Sam had refused to budge. This was their wedding, and it would represent their beliefs. If his mother couldn't live with that, it was just as well that she stayed home. He was actually glad, he insisted, that she'd clarified things this way.

With a mail-order imprimatur Lucy's mother performed a short ceremony on the Kellehers' front porch. A long reception followed in their backyard. Lucy felt somewhat guilty that her family had played such a central part in the proceedings while Sam's played none at all. *This* is *my family*, Sam assured her. *This is our family.* She was giving him so much. His only worry was that he didn't have enough to offer in return.

In those early days, people often expressed surprise when they noticed her ring. *You're so young*, they'd say. *A child bride.* But Lucy had found that she loved being a wife. She was a step ahead of her friends in life, and she felt as though she'd always be ahead. It didn't take long for others to catch up, though. The summer after they married, she and Sam went to their first wedding as guests. The following summer, they went to three. A few summers later, they went to five in the space of seven weeks. (Sam would know the name for that rate of acceleration.) At the first of these weddings, some guests had joked about how long she and Sam had made it already. The bride in all apparent sincerity solicited the wisdom of Lucy's experience. Lucy had never felt like an expert in anything before. For a period she had a kind of script worked out, which she modified for newly affianced friends.

Then one day she noticed that half her circle was married. It no longer mattered to anyone who'd gotten there first. She was twenty-nine years old, and no one was ever surprised when they noticed her ring. Instead most of the people who knew her were surprised that she didn't have kids. She was a bit surprised about this herself. She'd taught for a year before entering her master's program in special education—UW was the only place she'd applied—and she hadn't wanted to be pregnant at school. She'd decided that they would start trying after she was settled in a new job. During her second year of graduate school, the Pop-Up let Sam go, but she didn't see what difference that should make to their plans, since his writing hadn't brought in any real money. He worked as a software engineer in the university's development office, managing their donor database. He didn't love the job, but it paid well enough and gave him plenty of time to blog on his personal site, once he'd hit on politics as his new subject.

Everything looked just as Lucy had imagined it would, until she finished school and started talking to Sam about what came next. He said he wanted to wait until his writing career "took off" before thinking about kids. That his writing constituted a career, one that might even potentially "take off," had never occurred to Lucy, even while the Pop-Up was paying him. The site had bought the algorithm; his writing seemed like a hobby—something that gave him pleasure in his spare time. She encouraged him to keep at it, but she didn't think they should put their lives on hold while they waited for it to go somewhere. If she didn't say any of this to him outright, that was because they still had plenty of time. That was the great thing about getting married so young. The hard part was finding the man who would be the father of your children, and she'd already done that. She could stand to wait a few more years.

Then the most unbelievable thing had happened: his writing career *did* take off. She was proud of him, but she was also a bit unnerved. Suddenly people acted as though she'd seen something in him that others hadn't, that her reward for this foresight was a move to New York, Sam's name on the cover of magazines, literary agents emailing about book contracts, weekends in the Hamptons with Frank and Kit Doyle. But Lucy hadn't wanted any of these things. All she'd wanted was to get safely through this year and get them back to Madison, where they could continue the life she'd always imagined for them. She didn't want her husband to be the kind of person Margo Doyle might find attractive, because that would put her in competition with Margo Doyle, and she didn't think she could win.

Up in the hotel room, she pulled off her sweaty shirt and her jeans, and she put on pajamas before climbing into the king-sized bed. It felt slightly decadent to lie on clean sheets, in a spotless room, given how badly she'd let the apartment go. She wondered whether Sam had even noticed. He'd probably be perfectly happy reverting to the conditions in which he'd been living before she got to New York. The truth was that he wouldn't have that far to slide. So many things that she'd once done without thinking had become too much effort to do at all, and keeping the house in order was one.

Reading in bed before going to sleep each night was another. She'd brought the enormous novel she'd been fighting through since her flight from Madison. Having carried it all this way she felt she ought to give it a try, so she unpacked it from her bag and put it on the bedside table, but that was as close as she got to opening it.

When she woke with the lights still on, the digital clock on the table beside her read 9:56. She thought she'd drifted off for a bit, and she was motivating herself to get ready for bed when she looked again and discovered that it was 9:56 (now 9:58) AM. She'd been out for more than twelve hours. She couldn't remember the last time she'd slept this late. She was always up with Sam, though she sometimes found her way back into bed soon after he left for work.

He'd sent her a text, concerned but unapologetic: *I hope you're okay. Do you have somewhere to spend the night?* She wrote back to tell him she was staying at a hotel. She'd made a long call back home the day before, but she considered checking in with her parents, just to let them know that she was safe. She had to remind herself that they had no reason to think otherwise. Anyway, what would she have said? That Sam had been seeing another woman? This was literally true but not exactly accurate, and she didn't want to get into it with them, since she still expected to be back with Sam before long.

Nor did she want to mention her sessions with Claire, which they would have found as ridiculous as Sam did. Her parents were committed rationalists. (Her father preferred this term, since "atheist" defined a person based only on their relationship to a God that didn't exist.) If they had faith in anything, it was in the power of human reason to make the world a better place. They did not go in for superstitions of any kind. Even when they'd sent Lucy to church with her grandparents for Christmas, they'd warned her not to take anything she was told there too seriously. Lucy wasn't interested in defending Claire on these terms. She wouldn't have the energy to explain the matter properly, even if it had made perfect sense to her, but if she simply said that she'd walked out on Sam because he wanted her to stop seeing a psychic who advertised on the street, they'd say that she'd gone crazy. Perhaps they'd be right. She couldn't dismiss the possibility. It was hard to think clearly when you felt so tired all the time.

Having gone the first time as a kind of lark, she'd felt compelled to return and pay Claire what she owed. This at least was an ethical principle her parents would understand. At this second visit, Claire had lit another thin candle, but this time she'd spoken while it burned down.

"The woman's hold on your husband is very strong," she'd said. "The bad spirit she has cast on you is very strong." She smiled almost suggestively. "But Clara Lune is stronger."

The best she could do, from this distance, without meeting Lucy's husband or the woman in question, was to hold things in a kind of stasis. She would need to see Lucy every week. If she did, she could keep the powers at bay. Sam would not be able to act on his desires, but Claire herself could not make the desires go away. Similarly, she could keep Lucy from being overwhelmed by the bad spirit, but she couldn't send the spirit out of her. To truly break out of her dynamic, Lucy would need to act. She would need to become a participant in her own imaginary.

Claire often used words like this, words that seemed to have about them more of the clinic or the classroom than the occult. It occurred more than once to Lucy, as she handed over her cash at the end of a session, that she had done just what Dr. Schilling had suggested: she'd found a therapist. The difference was that Claire didn't force her to view her problems as originating from within. Lucy had been infected by something, Claire told her, something from the outside. She was at the mercy of forces beyond her understanding or command, and Claire was a kind of intimate of those forces. She couldn't exactly command them herself, couldn't simply reorder Lucy's life in a manner of her choosing, but she could direct things in subtle ways that acted in Lucy's favor. Claire didn't make any great claims about her own powers. She didn't name a source for her insights or explain their purpose. Her skill was in the treatment of certain physical materials—candles and incense and crystals— which she manipulated in careful ways. It remained unclear to Lucy whether her practice had some inborn element or represented merely a technique that could be learned with care. About her actions she spoke with authority, as someone with knowledge born of expertise, not unlike how Sam spoke about the uses of data or her father about the rise of the American labor movement, though both men would have balked at the comparison.

Lucy wished she'd had the wherewithal to explain some of it to Sam. Wasn't this what he tried to do with numbers—discern some order hidden within the mess of the world? He would have answered that an invented order was no order at all. He was trying to tease out patterns that really existed, not impose them as a coping mechanism. Where there was chaos, he was happy to name it as such. Well, maybe so, but Lucy couldn't live with chaos at the moment. Besides, Claire had unquestionably gotten some things right. She'd told Lucy that Sam wouldn't be able to go through with it—that she'd undone this particular power—and she'd told Lucy many times that it would be up to her to act in the end, which is what she'd done by walking out the door.

Of course Lucy knew that she could not go on seeing Claire forever. When she'd started, she'd told herself she would give it up at the beginning of the school year. At that point she would be too busy to make her way to the Lower East Side each Thursday and spend an hour looking at dancing flames. But there was more to it than that. She thought that things would get better when she started work.

This was still another week away, but perhaps walking out of the apartment had already given her enough control, because she realized all at once that her days with Claire were done. She could have easily walked in without an appointment that morning—she had never seen anyone else going into or coming out of the apartment—but the prospect held no appeal. Maybe she'd just wanted to have her own secret, since she knew that Sam was keeping one. Now that Sam's secret had been revealed, and hers along with it, there was no point in going on with the thing.

It was after eleven by the time Lucy got down to the lobby. She needed to check out before noon, but she didn't know where to go next. At the very least she had to find a cheaper place to stay that night. She used a computer in the hotel's business center to search for one. First she spent a few minutes on a travel site, but everything in the area was too expensive. A few youth hostels offered a bed and a locker for twenty bucks. Some friends had stayed in such places after graduation, but Lucy felt too old for that now. She went to TeeseList in search of a couch where she could crash a few nights.

She didn't know what kind of commitment she would have to make—a week? a month?—but the mere fact of looking seemed an acknowledgment that she wouldn't be back with Sam in the next day or two. How long did she plan to wait? And for what, exactly, would she be waiting? If she was waiting for Sam to admit that Claire had been right, she would be waiting forever. She wanted at once more and less than that. She wanted him to acknowledge that his life with her was his real life, that all this other business—not just Margo, but New York, the *Interviewer*, his career as a pundit—was a passing interlude. She had an idle fantasy of flying back to Madison and waiting for him there, making him choose what he really wanted, but she couldn't walk out on her job. Children with real needs were involved. She'd have to make it through the end of December at the very least, give the school time to find a replacement for the spring.

Three listings seemed like possible fits, and she replied to all of them. One of the posters answered almost immediately to tell her she could come see the place that afternoon. The apartment was three stops from Borough Hall on the 5 train, in a newly refurbished building called the Denison. Its occupants, Krista and Danielle, had graduated that spring from a New England college Lucy had never heard of before. She could tell they were worried that she was too old to live with them. Krista was from Long Island, Danielle from outside Philadelphia, and they'd been best friends all through school.

They'd decided to get an apartment together, for which their parents—"just for now"—were helping out on rent.

"So anyway," Danielle explained, "we realized that we could get a three bedroom for the amount they were giving us, which would leave us with some spending money if we rented out the third room."

"But it's really just the room we're renting," Krista added. "Not, like, the common space or anything."

"You could keep food in the fridge or whatever," Danielle allowed, "but we wouldn't want you having friends over to hang out in the living room."

"I don't have any friends," Lucy answered, in an effort to be reassuring that seemed to have the opposite effect.

"That's the saddest thing ever," Danielle said.

Suddenly to Lucy it did sound sad. She had always been surrounded by friends back in Madison, where she'd crossed paths on a nearly daily basis with girls she'd known all her life.

"What's your story and all that?" Krista asked.

"I came here from Wisconsin when my husband got a job, but I just moved out of our place."

"No shit. Was he cheating on you?"

"Not exactly." Lucy was prepared to leave it at that, but the girls looked expectantly at her, and she decided that she might as well explain. If she was going to live with them, they would find it all out soon enough; if she wasn't, it hardly mattered what she said. "I was seeing this psychic, and he wanted me to stop, and I said no. It makes me sound crazy when I put it all that way."

"No way," Krista assured her. "I'm New Age as fuck. I love all that stuff."

Lucy laughed.

"Well, it pretty much flies in the face of everything my husband believes. He's a hard numbers guy. He actually moved to New York to do data journalism."

Krista nodded blankly at the term, but Danielle's face showed a hint of recognition.

"Wait a second," she asked. "Your husband's not Samuel Waxmouth?"

"Waxworth," Lucy corrected. "But, yes." She still wasn't used to thinking of Sam as a kind of celebrity, and she felt an odd pride, though she'd just explained why she'd walked out on him. "Do you read the *Interviewer*?"

"Never," Danielle said, "but I read a lot of websites that make fun of him."

"Okay," Lucy replied.

They showed her the extra room, and while she was looking around she felt her pocket buzz. It had now been four hours since she'd responded to Sam, and she'd been expecting another message. She took out her phone and read his text: *Let me know if you want to talk.*

Let me know.

All at once it dawned on her that Sam didn't want her to come back, even if she was ready to apologize for seeing Claire. She had done him a great favor, removing herself as an obstacle. He could see Margo now without thinking he'd done anything wrong.

"If the room is available," she told the girls, "I'd like to move in tonight."

She spent the next week in mourning. She mourned the end of her marriage, the end of the life they'd shared together for a decade. She mourned too the life that had until that week stretched out in front of them, a life that had disappeared. She mourned the loss of the child they were supposed to have when they got home.

She might have gone on mourning much longer than that, but on the Wednesday after she moved into the apartment, she started work. She'd been looking forward to it for so long as the thing that would return her life to order, make some sense of things, but she felt beyond all that now. She could barely drag herself out of bed to get there. She and Twinkie—whom Lucy had for some reason imagined as middle-aged but was actually in her late twenties—had a few days of classroom setup before the kids arrived, which was a task Lucy dreaded even at the best of times, and she very nearly didn't show up on the first day.

On her way home, she stopped at a Chinese place near the apartment to pick up dinner. She got a call from Sam while she waited, but she didn't pick up. *At least he remembered my first day*, she thought. He left a voice mail, which she didn't check. After another minute, he texted: *We need to talk. I want to figure this out. I'm sorry for everything.*

What was she to make of this sudden change of tone? Maybe it was just that a week and a half without her had finally brought home all that he was missing. But she thought it more likely that something had gone wrong with Margo. She wasn't surprised. Part of her had known that Sam would stop being attractive to a girl like that once he became available. She realized with a certain disappointment that she would go back to him in the end. If he was willing to return to Madison and resume their old life, she would find a way to live with the fact that he had chosen another life first. Still, she could at least make him worry a little bit. She put her phone away without responding.

Back at the apartment, she ate in her room with her laptop open on her bed, as she'd done every night that week. When she'd finished, she got up to take a shower before going to bed.

"You weren't kidding about having no friends," Danielle said as Lucy passed through the living room. Lucy stopped in front of the couch, where the two girls were splayed out, legs entwined, passing a joint. "You just sit in bed all the time."

In fact, Lucy had been out of the apartment all day, but she didn't blame the girls for thinking otherwise, since they'd been asleep when she left in the morning and barely noticed when she came home.

"I thought you wanted me out of your way."

"Sure, but we still know you're in there."

"It's stupid depressing," Krista elaborated.

If Lucy were thrown out of the apartment for being too easy to live with, would she have the energy to find somewhere else to stay?

"I'm really sorry."

"You don't have to be *sorry*," Danielle said, emphasizing the word with a faux whine. "We're not, like, scolding you. Just hang once in a while."

"Just haaang," Krista agreed.

She pulled leisurely from the joint and waved the butt end at Lucy, who accepted it almost instinctively and took a long drag. The smell of pot smoke was a near-constant feature of the apartment, and she'd already decided to accept this offer if it ever came, but she hadn't prepared for the sharp taste in her throat, which brought with it an entire climate from the past. She held the smoke in her lungs a moment before exhaling slowly, trying not to cough. She passed the joint to Danielle and stood beside the couch, deciding whether she felt anything.

"I'm going to take a shower," she said finally.

The girls smiled complacently, as at a pleasant but somewhat hazy memory.

"Just haaang," Krista repeated to no one in particular.

Lucy felt the water run over her with an agreeable sense of detachment. She was definitively if lightly stoned for the first time in years. Her brief college pot-smoking phase had ended not long after September 11. From that day on, getting high had made her paranoid, though her visions of planes falling out of the sky and terror attacks targeting midwestern campuses had given way to more mundane suspicions. For a time she'd become convinced that everyone else in the room was sitting in judgment over her, that apparently insignificant gestures—the habit one of the boys had of playing with the bent brim of his baseball cap, Megan's frequent declarations that if she didn't have a drink of water she would absolutely die—were signals pregnant with meaning, designed to express this judgment. She'd mentioned the feeling once to Megan, who'd successfully talked her out of it, after which she'd worried that they were all thinking about the fact that she was so self-involved that she thought they all sat around judging her and signaling their judgement in their every insignificant gesture. After a while, that snake had succeeded in eating its own tail, and her anxiety had settled on her parents instead. She'd imagined them barging into the room, catching her with a ten-inch plastic bong sealed to her mouth, and expressing their grave disappointment in front of everyone before dragging her to rehab.

Since her parents lived only a mile from campus and were known to drop by without warning, this was an almost understandable worry, except that she never smoked in her own room or anywhere else they might have found her, and anyway the discovery wouldn't have bothered them much. They'd given her a dutiful drug talk when she was still in high school, focusing mostly on the evils of the trafficking trade and the kind of people one unwittingly supported by participating in it.

"Of course the real culprit here is the war on drugs," her father had said. "When you criminalize normal human behavior, you turn normal humans into criminals. Still, you've got to think of the consequences of your actions. But we trust you to make informed decisions."

"Besides, we went to college in the seventies," her mother had added. "We don't want to be hypocrites."

These enigmatic invocations of an earlier era might have excused any number of sins, but in her parents' case Lucy suspected the opposite—they never spoke in detail about the transgressions of their youth because they wanted her to believe they'd been wilder at her age than they really had. Either way, she had no good reason to fear their disappointment, let alone their wrath. Thinking about it in retrospect, Lucy could see that there was doubtless something psychologically significant about the fact that her free-floating neurochemical angst had nonetheless so insistently targeted them. Perhaps she'd wanted parents that she could rebel against.

She felt none of that paranoia now, and she didn't think it was because Mitch and Joan were halfway across the country. Probably Krista and Danielle got better pot than she'd ever had in Wisconsin. She'd certainly never gotten this high from one drag before. Perhaps if she'd smoked their stuff then, she never would have quit. Who could say how her life would be different now? Sam would not have dated a pothead, that was for sure. She hadn't covered up the fact that she used to get stoned once in a while, but she'd never told him the extent of it, and she imagined that he would have been a bit shocked—more than her parents, in any case. Reason was our greatest attribute, he thought. There was something pathological about the desire to disable it. He understood the appeal of a two-beer buzz, but he didn't even really like getting drunk at fraternity parties. That people went out of their way to impair their cognitive faculties, engaged in ridiculous behavior that they knew in advance they would regret in the morning if they even remembered it, these facts simply baffled him. Sam could be strangely puritanical about such things. She never would have told him this, but Lucy thought he'd inherited the trait from his mother, who naturally expressed her objections in different terms.

When she got out of the bathroom, she found the couch vacated and the doors to the girls' bedrooms shut, and she realized that she'd been in the shower for quite a while. It was after ten o'clock, not late by normal standards but later than she usually stayed awake these days. She was no longer high, but she felt a rare sense of well-being. Even the sight of the novel her mother had given her, still sitting half-read on her bedside table, did not trouble her easy passage into sleep.

7.

The moment Kit walked out of his building, Edward leapt from the stoop of the dilapidated brownstone across the street and ran over to her.

"How did it go?" he asked.

She should have expected him to be waiting, but she'd imagined that he would go for a walk or get himself something to eat until they called to invite him back. She wasn't ready to face him now.

"Not how I planned," she said, though he couldn't know what this meant. She could trust in his ignorance, not because he was stupid or naive, but because he would never have agreed to help if he'd suspected they were putting Justin at risk. Kit wanted to believe much the same about herself—that she would have done everything differently had she known how it would turn out—but she wasn't sure this was true. She'd practically begged Justin to save Edward, which is exactly what he'd done. Had she honestly thought they could walk some careful line, giving up everything on Eisen and nothing on him? Perhaps she had, or perhaps she hadn't cared. She hadn't thought she'd had any choice.

She couldn't get over the sense that he'd known what was happening. So why had he confessed? She'd tried to shut him up, and he'd refused to stop. He'd *wanted* to get it out.

"What do we do now?" Edward asked.

She didn't want to say any more with this thing still in her pocket. Besides which she was still furious with him, perhaps more so now that the full implications of his stupid decision were becoming clear. But he wouldn't let her alone. He followed her down the block, waiting for her to explain. Of course he'd be angry when he found out. But he hadn't had to make this choice. She had saved him from that much at least.

"Go inside and see your friend," she said.

After Edward was out of sight, she took the device from her pocket and examined it. Such a small thing to have cause so much trouble.

A week after the agents' first visit, her door had still been standing, and she'd felt as though she'd passed a test. For a time, she'd really thought she'd brought them all through. If they'd had any real evidence—not evidence that Justin had visited her house for the millionth time, but evidence of what he'd said while he was there—they would have shown it to her. They'd wanted her to believe she had no options, but she'd seen a few of these insider trading cases up close, and she had some idea of what you needed to make them stick. They didn't have enough.

They must have expected her to come running as soon as she spoke to her lawyers. In the meantime, they were watching, monitoring her phone, waiting for her to call Justin in a panic and give them both away. Perhaps they thought a woman would scare more easily, act irrationally at the first bit of tough talk. If so, they'd miscalculated. She'd survived her whole life in a world of blustering men. They'd been bluffing her, and she'd refused to blink.

Of course she'd hear from them again eventually, but they could no longer pretend they had enough evidence to put her in cuffs. You could only make that threat once. After a few more days, she allowed herself to consider the possibility that she was going to get away with it. She'd have to wait a bit longer than originally planned to take the money from Edward's account, but most of their problems could be finessed if it was there. Her family would be back on reasonably solid footing by the end of the year. She still flinched each time the front door opened, and she waited with held breath until Margo or Marinela announced herself. But that would pass in time.

On the day that all changed, she'd spent the morning in the garden, one of her last, she imagined, since the weather would be turning cold soon and they would certainly be gone from the house by the time it was warm again. Margo was with her, as she had been more frequently since her falling-out with Sam Waxworth, the details of which Kit still didn't know.

"We're lucky to have you here," Kit told her, out of nowhere. "You've been a big help with Dad."

Margo nodded.

"I'm glad I get to spend this time with him."

"I'll be sorry when you go back to school," Kit added. "But I don't want you putting your whole life on hold."

Margo laughed. "Ready to get me out of here?"

"Not at all."

"It can wait one more semester," Margo said. "Anyway, I'm getting work done here. I'm not teaching this fall, so I don't really need to be on campus at all."

"We'll probably put the house on the market when you go."

"Why?"

"We don't need all this space now that you're both grown up. And I don't want to have to chase your father up and down three floors. We'll get an apartment somewhere. Two bedrooms, so there's always a room for you."

"I'll miss this place."

"We all will," Kit said, though she felt something like relief that after all they would suffer only the usual losses of time. What would be taken from them was nothing more than what the passing days took from everyone.

That afternoon she'd gone for a walk while Margo watched Frank. She was a few blocks away when a black town car pulled up beside her and lowered its tinted front passenger side window to reveal the familiar face she'd been seeing it in her dreams. She'd almost convinced herself she wouldn't be seeing him again.

"Get in the car," Canilang said sharply.

She heard the click of the door unlocking, and reflexively she opened it to climb inside. She was alone on the back-row bench. Agent Donaldson sat in the driver's seat with sunglasses on, his face expressionless. As soon as Kit closed the door, he put the car back into gear. Kit wrapped the seat belt around herself, as though it could protect her from what was about to come.

"What the fuck kind of game are you playing?" Canilang said, looking over his shoulder at her.

He was angry, Kit thought, because their heavy-handed tactics hadn't worked. His only option was to go heavier, but she wouldn't budge.

"I'm not playing any kind of game. I was taking a walk."

"Where did the money go?"

Kit tried not to look surprised.

"It's in Edward's brokerage account."

"That account has been closed."

"That's got to be a mistake," she told them, trying not to let all her composure slip away. "I haven't touched it."

"Your son's been moving money for a month. Random increments, small enough to avoid reporting requirements. Apparently he got impatient, because the remaining balance was moved last week into a retail checking account."

"A joint account," Donaldson added.

"I didn't put my name on any joint account," Kit said.

"In your son's name and the name of Herman Nash."

She wanted to think they were lying to keep her off balance, but the very thing that made the story so absurd—the mention of Herman Nash—convinced her it was true. What the hell had Edward done?

"He's a con man," she said. "He got Edward involved in some kind of cult."

If she really believed this, why hadn't she done anything about it sooner? She should have dragged him out of that apartment the first time she'd visited. Never mind the fact that he was in his midthirties, that he had spent most of the past decade leading young men into battle, getting fired on and returning fire—he didn't know what he was doing. In truth, she'd thought the man strange but harmless, and she'd imagined that Edward would move on from this eccentricity before long.

"So you're familiar with this person?"

"He's trying to take my son's money."

"Not trying," Donaldson said. "He emptied the account as soon as the transfer went through."

"You're saying that Edward's been robbed? Why don't you do something about it? Arrest this guy."

"We'd like to do that," Canilang admitted, "but he seems to have disappeared."

"Find him," Kit said, no longer trying to control the anger in her voice. "Isn't that your job?"

Her tone didn't seem to bother Canilang, who looked at her skeptically.

"Did you tell your son about our conversation?"

"He doesn't know anything. I didn't even tell him about the trade. He never asks money questions, and he never touches that account."

She should have been more careful about what she said, but all she cared about now was protecting him.

"Well, he sure as shit has touched it now," Donaldson put in.

"He didn't touch it," Kit said, looking at the agent's infuriatingly placid face in the rearview mirror. "This man Nash did."

She considered briefly the possibility that Edward had undertaken some misguided scheme. Maybe Justin had told him about the trade, and he was trying to protect the money with Nash's help. She knew it wasn't true, but it was plausible enough that the agents might believe something of the sort.

"It doesn't really matter who touched it," Canilang told her. "It's gone, and we want it back. You're in a lot of trouble right now."

"I can get this all figured out," she said. "Just give me a day to talk to him."

When she'd arrived at Edward's apartment, the place had looked unchanged from her last visit. Even the old man's Bible sat in the same place on the coffee table.

"Where's your friend?" she asked. She wasn't trying to be coy; she just didn't know how to begin.

"He left," Edward answered in a flat tone. He seemed about to say more but just shook his head.

"With all your money."

Edward seemed to have been waiting for her to confront him on it.

"I had to force it on him," he said. "He didn't even want it."

He looked slightly abashed, as though he'd made a miscalculation that might complicate his own life but could only be of passing interest to her. How had she let things get this far? He'd spent too much time away from the real world. He was probably shell-shocked, and this Nash character had recognized as much before Kit had seen it in her own son.

"Why did you do it?"

"It didn't really feel like the money belonged to me. I never did anything to earn it. There was no good reason why I should have it instead of him, or instead of a million other people. I know it sounds strange, but I actually feel better since it happened. I think it was good for me. You always said the money wasn't really enough to change my life, so maybe it won't make a difference anyway."

She'd long thought of Edward as more like herself, but how like Frank was this impulse toward grand gestures—signing up to go off to war; giving away all your money to a man you barely knew—and the unwillingness to acknowledge how these gestures affected other people.

"Where did he go?"

For the first time since they'd started talking Edward looked truly troubled.

"I haven't heard from him since the money cleared."

"Why didn't you tell the police?"

About this he was stunningly rational: "I don't think any crime was committed. I told him to do what he wanted with it."

"As the legal custodian of the account," she said, "I need a formal record of where the money went."

She'd settled on this approach with Augustino, who wanted a sworn affidavit from Edward explaining what had happened.

"Are you going to use it against Nash somehow?"

"To be honest, I'd like to," she said. "But I think you're right. He hasn't committed any crime, so I don't think your statement could be used against him. All I want you to do is tell the truth."

When she and Augustino arrived at the FBI offices with their affidavit, she couldn't tell whether Canilang believed the story. It was stranger than she'd imagined. Two hundred thousand dollars spent on an advertising campaign? But Edward had all the records to prove it. Anyway, Canilang seemed not to care whether it was true. He had the leverage now he'd only been pretending to have before.

"Basically you've got two choices," he said. "You can get us Price, or we'll arrest your son."

"You don't have anything on Edward. He didn't do anything wrong."

"Are you kidding?" Canilang asked. "His best friend got a tip from one of our informants. On the basis of that tip, a trade was made in his account. We've got him structuring payments to avoid reporting. We could get him on about a dozen charges. He's looking at more than a decade in federal prison."

"You ought to be chasing after the guy who conned him out of four million dollars," Kit said.

"Maybe we will," Canilang answered. "Assuming that you and the rest of your family aren't planning to meet him somewhere in South America in a few months."

"You don't really believe we're working together. You know Edward's telling the truth."

"I don't need to believe it to make this case."

Now Augustino broke in. "You want Justin to get to Eisen?" he said.

"That's right," Canilang said.

"What if we get you Eisen ourselves?"

He laid out the plan that he and Kit had conceived together. Kit would plead to a false statement charge. She'd have to serve some time, but in exchange for sentencing leniency and a guarantee that no charges would be filed against Edward, she would get Justin to describe Eisen's criminal operations. If what she brought them was good enough, she'd serve no more than a couple of months. She'd pay a fine in the amount of the earnings on the trade, but the U.S. Attorney's office would work with the SEC to guarantee that no civil judgment would be made against her. Once they had whatever information she brought them, they could do what they wanted with it, apply whatever pressure was necessary to make Justin testify, but they couldn't expect any more help from her.

When Augustino was finished, they went out for a cup of coffee. They returned half an hour later, and Canilang said that they had a deal.

"You're going to have to wear a wire," he added.

She'd imagined something out of a gangster movie—a microphone sewn into the folds of her dress, a tape deck hidden in a shopping bag—but what she held now was the size of a pen and looked like one, even under close examination. You could actually write with it, as Canilang had demonstrated before handing it over.

"The expression is a bit of an anachronism," he'd explained. "There won't be any wires involved."

Now she threw the thing in a garbage can on the corner, where it came to rest on top of a grease-pocked pizzeria plate, beside an empty cigarette pack. She wanted to believe that she'd just disposed of the evidence against Justin, but she knew it was too late for that. The pen was a transmitter, not a recorder. Their entire conversation had been saved on a server somewhere in a building on Federal Plaza, a building where she was expected soon for a debriefing with Canilang and Donaldson and Augustino and the assistant U.S. Attorney who'd signed off on the idea. How long would it take them to figure out that she'd thrown the device away? They'd certainly ask her about it, but she didn't expect much trouble over its loss. After all, she'd given them more than they could have hoped; even if it wasn't exactly what they'd wanted, it was nearly as good.

The building was thirty blocks downtown, and it would take about forty-five minutes to get there if she walked, but she started heading in the opposite direction, uptown on Avenue B. Eventually they'd call to find out where she was, but she'd turned off her phone before the meeting and still hadn't turned it back on. Maybe they'd try the house and get through to Margo, who was watching Frank for the afternoon. Would they tell her why they were calling? It hardly mattered now. Margo would find out everything soon enough. She, too, would be angry with Kit. Like Frank, she wanted to live the life of the mind, and like Frank she could conveniently forget that the mind needed a body, that the body needed to be housed and clothed and fed. Kit had spent her life providing for them, and they would all judge her now.

She walked past a diner and considered stopping for something to eat. It was late afternoon, and she hadn't had a bite since leaving the house early that morning. But she didn't think she could keep any food down in her condition. On the next block she passed a bodega, and she realized that what she really wanted was a cigarette. She tried to remember the last time she'd had one, and she flashed briefly on the night of Edward's party, when she'd bought a pack from one of the catering staff. It was probably still in a drawer somewhere. She bought another pack and smoked one as she continued uptown. The taste brought on the feeling of late nights at work.

Her father had been a heavy smoker—it had helped to kill him in his late fifties—and he had taken great pleasure in the habit, as he did all his habits. Now people huddled outside of bars or office buildings to get their fix; it looked no more pleasant than taking medicine. Everything about her father's world was gone. If someone had told him that this would happen, he would hardly have believed it. Things in his time had had the feel of permanence. Kit understood as a matter of course that her world would soon disappear. The cigarette lasted her three or four blocks, and when she'd finished it she tossed the rest of the pack along with her butt. Perhaps some homeless scavenger would find it.

She walked a few more blocks, until she came to a church with its doors open to the street. People were filing in for the beginning of mass. Without thinking much about it, Kit went inside and found an empty pew near the back. Her anxiety lessened just a bit. For most of her life, she'd attended church every week, and she still felt at home whenever she entered one, though these days she hardly went. As a little girl, she'd been accompanied by her grandmother or an aunt or Mrs. Sheehy, the housekeeper with the thick brogue whom Kit had remembered when she'd heard the lilting prayer of the nun at the hospital.

Her father had certainly counted himself Catholic, but the particular devotion given to Kit's faith was entirely in honor of her mother, who died too young for Kit to have any memory of her. The surviving photos were few and strangely inconsistent—in one she looked dourly away from the camera, as though refusing to be coaxed from a private mood; in another she was laughing but shaking her head, so that she had left behind mostly a frustrating blur—and Kit had no image of the woman that she felt she could trust. But her father had spoken of his late wife in almost saintly terms, and everyone who'd known her mentioned that she'd been very devout. It was in her memory that Tommy Quinn had taken an equal interest in his grandchildren's religious education, and the whole family had continued attending mass regularly until he died. There had been no conscious decision to stop after that. They were just so busy, Kit more than anyone, and the kids had not complained. She and Frank still went on occasion, but apart from Christmas and Easter, they hadn't been as a family in years. Another legacy lost.

She kneeled down and attempted briefly to pray, but nothing came to her. She still did it reflexively, mostly as a way to relax the mind—a form of meditation. She didn't much believe in the power of prayer to act in the world. Prayer had gotten her through Edward's time away, but she didn't credit it for bringing him safely back. She couldn't think that way when so many women more devout than she had not had their prayers answered. Her father had always loved the old story about a shipwrecked man who prays to be rescued from his desert island. One by one a rowboat, a cruise ship, and a helicopter find him, and he sends each on its way, telling them that he trusts in God. Eventually, he starves to death, and when he gets to heaven he says angrily to God, "I put my faith in you." To which God replies, "Who the hell do you think sent that helicopter?"

He'd told this joke at Friendly Sons of Saint Patrick's dinners, Ancient Order of Hibernians banquets, and countless black-tie bene-fits where he was given awards. She'd heard it perhaps a hundred times throughout her childhood. When she was ten or eleven, people had found it cute or touching that he brought her everywhere as his date, but after a while they just took it as a matter of course. When friends went with Tommy Quinn to formal occasions, they expected Kit to be there. *She's the one distracts you while Tommy picks your pocket.* As she got older, some strangers had thought that she and her father were involved. She was a beautiful young woman, just the sort that a rich, single older man like Tommy Quinn might want, and she had a poise that made people think she was twenty-five when she was still eighteen. It was because she'd been expected to act as an adult when she was fourteen or fifteen years old, as she'd later expected from her own kids.

Above all, he had taken her seriously. He'd been a loving but somewhat stern father, from a generation of men who didn't expect to play any great role in the raising of their children, but he'd thrown himself impressively into the task once his wife was gone. He'd had plenty of help, and he worked very long hours, but he was present in almost all her childhood memories. It was just that these memories were not the sort most children had, because he bound her to his adult life rather than devoting himself to the life of a child. She'd known from a very young age that she wanted to go into business with him. Her father was not what anyone could call a feminist. If he'd had a son, he would never have considered for a moment that she might come to work for him. But she was all he had.

Was it any wonder that she'd been interested in older men? If it had not been for her many years of talking with adults at those din-ners, perhaps she would not have jumped so readily to dance with Frank Doyle. Had she really just wanted someone like her father? She didn't think so. What she'd wanted more than anything was a man who would support her choices and let her have her career. Frank didn't need the kind of wife that some men needed. After being raised by a busy, powerful man, she had certain expectations. She had always loved Frank's energy. Lindsay had had a slogan back in the day: *He is fresh, and everyone else is tired.* That was the way she'd always felt about Frank. He was fresh. How much of a life would she have when he was gone?

The church was half-full when a bell rang and the congregation stood for the beginning of mass. The priest emerged from the sacristy with a girl of eleven or twelve walking beside him. Such things were not allowed in her day, otherwise her father would have made her an altar server. No music played, and they headed directly up front, rather than processing down the side aisle and back up the center. The priest made the sign of the cross, and mass began. It was remarkable how quickly Kit fell back into the rhythm of it. Every time she went, she told herself that she would start attending again, and another six months would pass before she crossed the threshold. Maybe that was because she wasn't sure that it changed anything out in the world.

She could go to confession, she thought, something she hadn't done in years, even when she still went regularly to mass. She dismissed the idea. To be absolved you had to be contrite, and she didn't really think that she was. She was sorry she'd been forced to make this choice, but she couldn't say that she would choose any differently if she had it to do over again, even knowing what Justin would do. When you got down to it, Edward was her son, and Justin was not. Justin was like a son, but in that "like" rested all the difference in the world.

There was still plenty he could do to save himself. Once he knew he had no choice, he would give up on the idea of protecting Eisen. He'd be able to work out his own deal. And if it was really true that he had nothing to give them but himself? Well, he could afford to go away at this point. He'd lose a few years of his life, come out in his early forties still very rich. Edward had just spent six years at war. He couldn't go through this now. If Kit herself went in for even a few years, Frank would be gone when she got out.

She went up to the front of the church for Communion. When she came back down the center aisle, she considered continuing straight out the door. Instead she returned to her pew and kneeled. She stayed in place even after the priest and the altar girl had returned to the sacristy. She kept her head down and her eyes closed, listening to the shuffle of the departing congregation. Once the church was entirely empty, she stood and walked out.

Now was the time to call Augustino and head to the meeting that awaited her, but she continued uptown. She expected the black town car to pull up beside her at any moment and take her away, but it never happened. She was on her own. It took her almost two hours to walk all the way uptown, and she felt agreeably exhausted by the time she got home. Of course she couldn't stop now; she would have to take over from Margo and spend the rest of the day with Frank. She was happy to do it. Lately being with Frank felt a little bit like escaping into the past.

When she heard Margo screaming from upstairs, from the direction of the office, she thought immediately that something had happened to him. She dropped her purse and followed the voice. Margo was still yelling when Kit arrived in Frank's office, but he was sitting safely on the couch. Margo had the remote in her hands, and they were both watching the TV. There was a split screen, showing the Mets game on half of it, while the other half broadcast breaking news: Justin being walked out of his building in handcuffs, his head down. The half-screen cut back and forth between a camera on the ground and an aerial shot of the building, with a spotlight shining down on it. A ticker explained what they were seeing: *Justin Price, investor, philanthropist, and prominent Obama donor, arrested. Feds charging massive insider trading scheme.*

Somewhere in there, Kit thought as she watched the building on the screen, is Netta Price. It was the first time, in all of this, that she'd given the woman a thought.

"Shut it off," she said. But Margo just stood there watching. Kit crossed the room, took the remote from her daughter's hands, and turned the television off herself. Even after the screen had gone dead, there was still some sound, like a kind of aftereffect. She didn't know what to do to make it stop. After a moment, she realized that it was the whir of news helicopters, which were directly above their house. All of this was happening right around the corner. As she should have known it would: Justin practically lived with them. My God, she thought, what have I done?

PART FOUR:

HE IS FRESH, AND EVERYONE ELSE IS TIRED

(October/November)

1.

Someone had forgotten to shut the front door—probably Marinela on her way in that morning—and a brisk wind was blowing into the house as Frank came downstairs. He tried to close it, but a wooden wedge was propping it in place. The rug that should have been running the length of the entryway had been rolled up and set against a wall in the corner, beside the claw-foot umbrella stand, and a long stretch of brown kraft paper had been taped to the parquet in its place.

Frank followed the paper through the hall to the library, whose door was also wedged open. Inside, three men were taking down his books and putting them into cardboard boxes. They'd already emptied half his shelves. The men moved roughly but methodically, with great assurance and no sense that they didn't belong. They were robbing the house in broad daylight, Frank briefly thought—but even he understood that a band of thieves would not begin with the books.

Two of the men were quite large—one mostly muscle, the other fat. The third was much skinnier, even scrawny. All three were young and black, and they wore bright green sweatshirts over dark jeans. Frank wanted to ask what they were doing, but he was slightly afraid of them. He stood unmoving in the doorway until the muscular one stopped and politely waved a hand before continuing with his work.

needlessly aggressive music. Up close, the man might have been Latin rather than black, or maybe both. He wore his hair in those long, thin braids that some of the ballplayers wore these days. His green sweatshirt had the words *Strong Arm Movers* printed across the chest.

"Where do you think you're taking that?" Frank asked.

The man removed a sheet of paper from his back pocket, unfolded it, and examined it carefully. He looked at a label stuck to the top of the box and back at the paper in his hand.

"These is going into storage," he said.

Despite the cold air coming in from the open door, beads of sweat dripped from his thin braids. He reached a gloved hand to wipe them, wetting the paper in the process. He looked quizzically at the damp page before folding it and returning it to his pocket.

"No these is not," Frank said firmly. "Bring that box back into the library and put my books on the shelves, where they belong."

The man seemed slightly puzzled but otherwise unbothered by Frank's tone. He shook his head as though Frank had not understood. Without making any move toward the box he said, "I'm just supposed to put it in the truck."

"You're not putting my books in any truck," Frank said. "You're putting them back where you found them."

The man let out a long, almost amused sigh, as though they were old friends having a familiar disagreement. Frank reached down for the box, but before he'd lifted it an inch off the floor, he felt dizzy. The thing fell from his grip with a thud. He would need another approach.

"This is some mistake. You've got the wrong house."

The man took the paper back out of his pocket, unfolded it again, and passed it to Frank. He pointed at the top of the page.

"This your house?"

Frank followed the man's finger and found their address printed along with the words *ATTN: Marge Doyle*. Instinctively, Frank shouted Margo's name, and the man with the braids seemed to be fighting off the urge to laugh at the sight, which made Frank shout louder, until he heard footsteps hurrying down the stairs.

"Why are you yelling?" Margo said as she came into view.

She didn't seem at all surprised by the sight of the man standing next to him.

"Did you tell these people to pack up my books?"

Margo gave the man with the braids a nod, and he stepped aside.

"We're moving," she said. "Remember? We sold the house."

As he heard this, it sounded right to Frank, but it seemed too big a thing to have forgotten. In any case, it wasn't Margo's place to be signing off on a move. He needed to talk with Kit before things went any further.

"Where's your mother?"

"She'll be home soon," Margo said. "Let's go upstairs and let the movers do their job."

Unwilling to give up his grievance so easily, Frank gestured toward the man with the braids.

"He told me my books were going into storage."

"Just until we find a good place for them," Margo said. "The new apartment doesn't have room for everything."

"I can't work without those books."

"It's temporary. I'll make sure you have everything you need."

She gestured Frank somewhat officiously up the stairs. As he went, he heard Margo apologizing, and he stopped to watch the man pick up the box and walk it out the door.

In his office, Frank sat down while Margo turned on the TV. She clicked through a few channels before finding the highlights from last night's games, and she settled down beside him on the couch. Apparently the Yankees had played the Phillies in the World Series. It was game three, and the Yankees won, on home runs from A-Rod and Swisher. The playoffs were almost over, and Frank hadn't even noticed. Why did he keep thinking it was still summertime?

He always felt a little less grounded when the baseball season was over, so he was disturbed to discover that he hadn't seen it coming to an end. Of course the Yankees were playing in the Series, as always— *like rooting for U.S. Steel*—but he couldn't remember how things had turned out for his Metropolitans. Was that possible? On any given day since the team's founding in '62, Frank could almost certainly have told you exactly how things stood with the Mets: their record, their place in the division, how many games back they were, whom they'd played that day and whom they'd be playing tomorrow, whether at home or on the road, who was scheduled to start. It sounded like a lot of information when put that way, but it had simply been the context of his life. He'd remembered it all as he'd remembered Lear's speech on the heath, as he remembered Kit's birthday, the fact that she preferred tulips to roses. The season was so long, and the teams played almost every day, the games very easily became the rhythm of one's life, the ritual by which the passage of time could be marked. Occasionally on a trip abroad he would drop the thread of the season for a week, but only when he ventured somewhere so far flung that he couldn't find the International *Herald*, whose daily edition managed to squeeze the standings, league leaders, and every game's box score in tiny type onto a single page. The disorienting feeling of losing touch was precisely how he knew he'd entered exotic territory. In such cases, catching up on the season was how he reacclimated to American soil. This was how he felt now—as though he'd just returned home from a long foreign trip to find his whole life in disarray.

The highlights ended and the screen was filled by a logo and the words "World Series 2009." A moment before, Frank couldn't have said what year it was, but he found this realization less disturbing than the fact that he still couldn't say how the Mets had finished their season. In fact, the two failures seemed to amount to the same thing.

"I've got more packing to do," Margo said once the commercials were underway. "Please don't bother the men downstairs."

Kit would not have let her speak to him as though to a child, but he'd never been any good at discipline. The revenge of youth on age. *Why should not old men be mad?*

"When is your mother coming back?"

"Soon," was all Margo said.

"Where did she go?"

Margo opened her mouth as though to speak, but nothing came out. He wasn't trying to cause problems. He just wanted to know where his wife had gone. Why was that such a difficult question to answer?

"Right now it's just you and me," Margo finally said. "We've got to let the movers pack up the house."

As he watched her leave, Frank had a moment of terrible clarity: they were sending him away. He'd gotten old and useless—he couldn't even remember what year it was—and they wanted to be rid of him. Kit couldn't face him while she did it, so she'd left the house and sent these men for him. When they were done with the library, they would move on to his office and his bedroom. Once all his things were packed, there would be nothing left but to pack up Frank himself and put him into storage, too.

He needed a drink. It was a bit early for that, but that could be excused on such a day. He got up from the couch and crossed the room, but he found his bottles gone from the bar. The glasses and the decanter and even the ice bucket were in their proper places, but these were all useless without any booze. The men had stolen his scotch while he slept. He was about to call out to Margo, but he stopped himself. He checked the time on the cable box. It was 10:30 in the morning, and his daughter had just finished scolding him. He wasn't going to ask where his liquor bottles had gone.

They'd probably packed up the bar in the library, too. Anyway, Frank couldn't bear the idea of facing the men, especially the one with the braids, who'd conspired with his daughter to make a fool of him. He thought of getting a bottle of wine from the kitchen, but he was afraid of being caught.

Was he really going to allow himself to be imprisoned in his office? Was he just going to wait until they were ready to take him away? He needed to escape.

Starting with the library had been their fatal mistake, since all the books he truly needed were here. He turned the sound up on the television so that Margo would think he was watching if she decided to listen in, and he started to go through his shelves. Surely his three-decade-old copy of Herodotus was among the essentials. He placed it on the floor near the couch, the beginning of a pile. Thucydides perhaps he could do without. He worked his way slowly around the room, making difficult choices. Every shelf had something he wanted badly to bring along but forced himself to leave. Aeschylus, not Sophocles. Daniel Bell but not David Riesman. Not Hawthorne but Twain. Already the pile was too big. He remembered that attempt to lift the box in the hall. He'd have to be even more selective. In a way, it was a great gift to be forced to choose. This had been the problem with the big book—he'd tried to make it about everything, and instead it had been about nothing at all.

Halfway around the room, he pulled *Middlemarch* from the shelf and noticed something behind it. He had to take out the books on either side—*Adam Bede* and *Daniel Deronda*, both great but neither truly necessary—before he could be certain of what it was: a half-empty bottle of scotch. Something miraculous at work in this discovery. An earlier version of himself, one he couldn't even remember, had hid it there along the way, as though he'd known he would need it now. He pulled the bottle free and retrieved a glass from the bar. Having poured himself a drink, he sat back down on the couch and took a long sip while considering what to do next.

The TV had started showing highlights again, followed by each team's "path through the playoffs." It seems the Phillies had beaten the Dodgers in the NLCS. Frank took in this fact with the usual odd mix of emotions his old team still engendered in him, something like what he imagined a happily married man would feel when stumbling upon the woman who'd broken his heart so many years before, when he was in the full flower of youth. His first eighteen years had been devoted to the Dodgers. That wasn't easily forgotten. He didn't exactly wish for their success, but he felt a reflexive disappointment when he learned of this loss.

If the Dodgers had survived to face the Yankees, he could at least have rooted for them wholeheartedly, as he had every time the two teams had played in the World Series, even as far back as '63, when the wound was fresh, when Walter O'Malley—the great betrayer, an Irishman of all things—still owned the team, and some of the best players were Brooklyn holdovers. The Dodgers had swept that year, and a full generation had passed before the Yankees fielded another decent squad. Frank wouldn't have wanted it any other way.

He'd refused to play under the Yankee banner even in their old neighborhood stickball games. In Flatbush, only the Italians wanted to be Yankees, because of DiMaggio and Rizzuto and Berra. The Puerto Ricans wanted to be Giants, like the screwballer Rubén Gómez, and everyone else fought to be on the Dodgers. That meant Jews and Poles and Irish—most, like Frank, the first in their families born in this country—and a handful of blacks whose parents had come up from the South, making them immigrants, too, of a sort, though they were in some ways the only real Americans in the pack. For the rest of the week, they lived on their own blocks, shopped at their own stores, went to their own houses of worship, but there weren't enough of any one tribe to form a team, so on Sunday afternoons out on Ditmas Avenue, they mixed.

This bothered some of the Irish boys but not Frank. How could he possibly object to playing beside a colored kid after Pee Wee Reese put his arm around Jackie Robinson? Frank had been seven years old when Jackie broke into the league, just beginning to follow the game. It was the first year he was deemed old enough to go to the ballpark, but he almost wasn't allowed—not because of integration, but because of the Lip. That off-season the Dodgers manager, the Catholic Leo Durocher, had married a Hollywood starlet, Laraine Day, trouble being that she was still married to her first husband. So long as a bigamous adulterer was running the team, the CYO wouldn't send poor parish kids to the games. Frank would be lucky if his mother let him listen to Red Barber make the call on the radio. Spring training was already underway by the time the commissioner suspended Leo the Lip for conduct detrimental to the game. The bishop relented, and with him Nora Doyle.

A month into the season—May 23, 1947, to be exact—he went to Ebbets Field for the first time. The Dodgers beat the Phillies five to three. Jackie was three-for-four with two home runs. The man was the most beautiful thing Frank had seen in his young life, at once fierce and elegant. Beside him the other players appeared to be moving through a fog, tentative and uncertain. The Dodgers won the pennant that year. They'd gone from being a second-division team to the class of the league, and the difference was Jackie Robinson. The only appropriate ending for such a season was a World Series win, but the Yankees beat the Bums in seven games, guaranteeing Frank's lifelong enmity. From then on, he would always fight to be a Dodger on those Sunday afternoons. Failing that, he could accept being a Giant, but never a Yankee. And it wasn't Pee Wee he pictured each time he stepped to the plate. It wasn't the Duke. He imagined himself as that beautiful black man.

He knew even then that he couldn't move his body like Jackie did, but he'd tried over the years to make his mind work with that same ferocious grace. In this way, he thought he might live a kind of life of action, even if he spent it mostly sitting at a desk. The problem was that he'd dedicated so much of his life to the extraneous. He'd written a hundred columns on which party was looking better in the next midterm. What difference had it made? Now he didn't even know who was president, and he couldn't imagine how that would matter beside the things he still had in his head. He looked at the mountain of books he'd built beside the couch. Perhaps he didn't need any of them. Auerbach had written *Mimesis* from memory, after fleeing the Nazis; surely Frank could write the big book in flight from his family. It was all still there, at least for now, but he had to act soon. He was starting to slip. Like the body, the mind went eventually, and he risked turning into Willie Mays—the most graceful man who ever stepped on the diamond—wandering center field at Shea as though lost. He poured himself another drink and took the bottle with him down the hall. He hurried a bit as he passed Margo's room, but she was sitting on her bed with a notebook in her hands, so absorbed in whatever she was reading that she didn't notice him.

Upstairs he went into the walk-in closet where he'd always dressed himself in front of the full-length mirror hanging from the door. He was surprised by the stubble on his face, his long and unkempt hair. He never went out of the house without a fresh shave, but he didn't have time for that now. He looked over the row of Italian suits and the row of tailored shirts that together filled his half of the closet on two long rods, the line of shoes that filled the rack above them. These clothes he'd accrued over forty years would all be left behind. His days of cutting a figure in the world were done. He just needed to work. He put on a pair of wool slacks and a white shirt, argyle socks and brown Berluti loafers. He found an old weekend bag and packed a few more things—a clean shirt, some underwear, another pair of pants. He considered packing a sweater or a coat, but it was still summer and he would be done before it turned cold.

A small shelf by his bed contained first editions of all his books, and he couldn't resist taking a few along. They would be a kind of talisman, a reminder that the work could get done. The collections of columns about NAFTA and impeachment and the Contract with America held no interest for him, but he took copies of the baseball books. He poured another drink, put the bottle in the bag, and zipped it shut. Still light enough to carry. He stepped quietly as he passed Margo's room. She was listening to music, her back to the door, and she didn't notice him at all.

The front door was open, as though it were waiting for him. The first thing that struck him when he stepped outside was the cold. He looked up at the trees lining their block and saw the lightly oranging leaves. Summer was gone. He wasn't dressed for the weather, but it was too late to turn back. Across the street, two large black men leaned against a moving truck, smoking cigarettes and breathing heavily. They waved at Frank as though they all knew each other. It was comforting to be recognized. Probably Mets fans.

At the corner he dropped the bag and removed the bottle. He took a long slug while deciding where to go next. The answer when it came was obvious. He screwed the bottle shut but didn't return it to his bag. He walked with the bag in one hand and the bottle in the other to Fifth, where he hailed a cab downtown.

As the cab pulled into Herald Square fifteen minutes later, Frank reached to his back pant pocket and found it empty. The driver stopped outside the Herald Building, punched the meter, and looked expectantly into the rearview.

"I've forgotten my wallet," Frank said.

The driver cursed in a language unknown to Frank before turning around in his seat, leaning toward the opening in the plexiglass, and saying, as though to clarify, "Son of the bitch."

"I'm sorry," Frank said.

"Leave with me," the driver told him, pointing to the bag on Frank's lap. "You get money and bring back."

Everything Frank had left was in the bag. He couldn't trust this man with it. But there had to be something inside that he could give him. He pulled out his copy of *The Smell of the Grass*.

"This is a first edition of a book I wrote," he explained. "A famous book. If I sign it, you could probably get a few hundred dollars for it."

A mild exaggeration, but a signed first edition was certainly worth more than a cab ride. The driver didn't seem pleased with this solution, but eventually he nodded. Frank asked for a pen and opened to the title page. He considered inquiring whether the driver wanted it inscribed, but he knew the joke would be as little appreciated as the value of the book itself. He blew briefly on the signature before closing the cover and handing the book through the opening. The driver made no effort to reach for it, so after an awkward moment Frank dropped it on the front passenger seat, amid a pile of old newspapers and a roll of paper towels. He was barely on the sidewalk before the car sped away.

Inside the Herald Building, Frank walked straight to the security turnstile and waited for the guard behind the desk to press the button that would release him into the elevator bank.

"Can I help you?" the guard asked.

He must have been new, because Frank didn't recognize him, and Frank had always had a good relationship with the building staff. The head of security, an Indian named Prasad, was a die-hard Mets fan, and they'd talked on many mornings about the previous night's game. The sport was a great democratizer. Prasad followed the off-season rumor mill even more closely than Frank did, and he always knew the latest trade talk or who had the hot arm in Triple-A. Where was he now?

"Frank Doyle. I work at the newspaper."

"Do you have your access card?"

For the second time in as many minutes, Frank reached for his empty back pocket.

"I'm afraid not."

"Some other form of ID?"

Security had gotten ridiculous in the building after 9/11. There was a fine irony to that: no one who worked at the paper wanted to admit that Islamic terrorism was an existential threat, but they sure as hell wanted to protect their elevators.

"I left the house without my wallet this morning. I assure you that I write for the paper. I'm actually fairly well-known."

The man looked Frank over, letting his eyes land pointedly on the bottle that Frank now remembered was in his hand.

"Is there someone upstairs I can call? Someone who can come down here and bring you in as a guest?"

"Roger Meaney," Frank said immediately.

It would infuriate Rog to have to come downstairs in the middle of a workday to let Frank in, which is exactly why Frank had chosen him. The guard looked at his screen, typed a few letters, and turned back to Frank.

"Could you spell that for me?"

That the man had never heard of the paper's managing editor almost made the whole thing worth it. Frank could already imagine *Could you spell that for me?* being the punch line of this story when he told it to the office.

"*Mean* with an *e-y*."

The guard looked again at the screen.

"I'm afraid that name isn't coming up on our system."

"That's ridiculous," Frank said, but in that instant it came to him that Roger was no longer the managing editor. He'd retired a few years ago. Frank couldn't remember the name of his replacement.

"Try Ken Calder," he said a little more uncertainly. Before the guard had even punched in the name, Frank knew it wouldn't come up. Ken was gone, too. He'd taken a buyout. There had to be plenty of people still working at the paper who could vouch for Frank, but he couldn't remember a single one. The guard seemed about ready to escort him out.

"How about this?"

Frank put down the bottle and opened his bag, from which he retrieved *The Crack of the Bat*. Some people would have mocked his decision to bring his own books on this expedition, but so far they were proving quite useful. He flipped to the author's photo. It was more than thirty years old but still easily recognizable as him.

"Look here. That's obviously me. I'm a little older and grayer, but still. And it says right below it, 'Frank Doyle is a Pulitzer Prize–winning columnist for the *New York Herald*.'"

The guard read the words over, examined the photo, and looked back up. With his eyes still on Frank, he punched a few numbers into his desk phone.

"Can you come out and help me with something?" he said into the receiver.

A door on the other side of the lobby opened, and from it walked Prasad, who smiled at Frank as he approached. Frank smiled back with relief. He should have asked to speak with Prasad from the beginning.

"It's good to see you, Frank," Prasad told him.

"You, too," Frank responded.

"It's a shame about the team this year. We had the talent, you know, but we got bit by the injury bug. Santana, Wright. It's like we were playing under a bad omen."

"The baseball gods are fickle," Frank agreed.

"What can I help you with?"

"I left my wallet at home, and your man here is being very diligent, which we all appreciate."

Frank nodded at the guard, who looked on curiously.

"Who are you here to visit?" Prasad asked, a bit nervously.

Frank didn't know what to make of this question.

"Not visiting anyone. Just headed upstairs to do a little work."

Prasad shook his head as though disappointed by this answer.

"You know, Frank," he said, almost in a whisper. He looked around as though about to divulge a rare secret. "You don't work here anymore."

Frank wanted to laugh. Someone was playing a joke on him. It was a good one, too, but now was not the time for it.

"Sure," Frank said. "But I need to get upstairs."

"You retired about a year ago," Prasad persisted.

The expression of embarrassed pathos on his face wasn't something easily faked. But he couldn't be right. Frank would never retire. He wouldn't accept a buyout like Meaney or Calder. For starters, he didn't need the money.

"Of course, I know that," he assured Prasad anyway, unwilling to have this fight in his current state. "I happened to be in the neighborhood, and I thought I would stick my head in to see the old place."

"It's nice to see a familiar face," Prasad said, his tone a crushing mix of pity and relief. "Lots of changes here, you know."

"Listen," Frank said, "I should have done this years ago."

He took the book from where it sat on the security desk and turned to the title page. He picked up the pen from beside the sign-in sheet. This time he would inscribe it, though he was not entirely sure how Prasad spelled his name—or for that matter, whether the name was his first or last. He drew a large, dramatic *P* that trailed quickly into a scribble. Beneath it he added a note about their years of great baseball talk. He signed it and passed the book over. Prasad smiled again, and this time Frank thought he saw tears coming into his eyes. He offered Frank a hand, and they shook—so far as Frank could remember, their first physical contact in the twenty years they'd known each other. Frank turned to go, but before he got to the door Prasad called after him. Frank stopped and looked back.

"We'll get 'em next year."

Outside, a large billboard dominated the north end of Herald Square. Half of it was filled with the face of a man with a long gray beard against a dark background, the other half with large type: *What would you change if you knew it was all going to end? November 1, 2009, 10 o'clock.*

Frank wasn't sure exactly what day it was. He would have said that it was still summertime, but the chill in the air suggested October. Well, it did seem to Frank that things must be coming to an end pretty soon. He screwed open the bottle, which was nearing empty now, and he drank down the last of it. He would need to buy another. But he didn't have his wallet.

He had to find a place to work. The main branch of the public library was just a few blocks away. He'd spent many hours there over the years, for galas or speaking events, though he'd never actually worked in the library during the day. But it was one place where he wouldn't be asked for money or ID. He walked crosstown to Fifth, where the street was filled with traffic, mostly yellow cabs, and the sidewalk with tourists. At the corner he found a garbage can, and he tossed the bottle into it. That left him just his bag. Did he really need it? He opened it and took out his last remaining book, *The Warning Track*. The rest he dropped beside the bottle in the can.

What would you change if you knew it was all going to end? Suddenly Frank understood that what Prasad had said was true. Or almost true. Frank had been right that he hadn't retired. He'd been fired for some stupid thing he'd said. They'd asked him to apologize, and he'd refused to do it. There was a principle involved, but he couldn't for the life of him say what it had been. How long ago was that? He'd given his whole life to the paper, and they'd cut him loose the first chance they got. But that wasn't quite right, either. The paper had given him far more than he'd given it in return. He'd never appreciated the place, always thought of his column as a kind of obligation, something that was keeping him from his real work. It had been his real work. For better or worse, that work was over. It was too late to do anything about it.

He saw himself now with great clarity, an old man with a stubbled face, an old forgotten book in his hand, headed to the public library to rant about the work he needed to get done. There was no more work. It was too late. *What would you change?* He stood at a corner, facing a green walk sign, looking at the line of cabs waiting for the light to turn. He saw the walk sign become a blinking don't walk and then a solid one. *What would you change if you knew?* The cabs started to move. *So,* Frank thought, before stepping into the street, *I am to become a nonentity, then?*

2.

Tuesdays were her busiest at work, and that day Twinkie had called in sick, which meant that Lucy would be alone with the kids until gym, with only a half hour for lunch. This was the second time in just a few weeks that she'd had to take the lead, but she didn't really mind. In some ways, she found it easier to work alone. Though she was the assistant, she had more experience than Twinkie, kept firmer control over the students, was—to put it simply—better at the job.

She felt slightly foggy that morning, but most of the day passed uneventfully, until just after lunch. While walking the kids through a social studies segment, she got halfway into a sentence and found herself unable to get out the other end. She couldn't remember the word she'd been about to speak. When she tried to put her thought differently, the thought itself was gone. She couldn't fake her way through the sentence, because she couldn't remember what she'd already said.

Experience told her that the best tactic in moments of classroom uncertainty was pressing forward, never giving up the kids' attention. It hardly mattered what you said, so long as you kept talking. The moment you stopped, they filled the vacuum with their own talk. But she couldn't remember any words at all. She wasn't sure that she'd ever known any words. That sounds expelled from holes in our faces might stand in some way for human feelings and ideas seemed luridly bizarre. Scattered scraps of conversation passed between the children. Some boys stood from their seats. The situation readied itself for complete disrepair. Then a change in the room brought all attention back to her. How rare to have every one of these faces looking up at once. Most had expressions of benign curiosity, but in a few Lucy could see discomfort and even fear. Gradually it came to her that she was babbling, standing at the board making nonsense sounds. Now she was afraid, but she didn't know how to get back on track, or even how to make herself stop. She didn't know how long this had gone on by the time something in her brain snapped into place and she fell silent. From there she did her best to continue talking as though nothing had happened.

Half an hour later, she walked the children down to gym. After dropping them off, she went to the bathroom to throw water on her face. She wasn't sure how worried she should be. She'd suffered a few less dramatic incidents of mild aphasia since the school year's start, when words didn't arrive in proper order, when she said one thing while meaning another or found herself unable to express a simple idea. They had all occurred in the presence of other adults, who'd quickly swooped in to finish her thought, taking her hesitation for a youthful lack of poise. (Only Lucy knew the real extent of her pedagogic confidence.) These events had been unnerving in the moment, but once out of them Lucy found it hard to believe they'd even happened, and she largely forgot them until the next one arrived. If she thought about them at all, she blamed them on the pot she'd been smoking most nights, a habit she fully intended to cease as soon as she stopped living with Krista and Danielle.

This latest incident felt harder to dismiss. If it could be blamed on pot, it would demand that she stop smoking, but it seemed to point instead to the malaise of the past four months. Now that she had insurance, she could have gone to the doctor, but she didn't have time, and she didn't want to be told again that everything was in her head. Looking in the mirror, she considered the possibility that Clara Lune was interfering with her mind, punishing her for stopping their appointments.

She wondered what she would say to the children after gym, but when the time came most of them appeared already to have forgotten the incident. The world was for them an often-incomprehensible place, and life had trained them to assume that whenever they did not understand adult behavior the fault was their own. Part of Lucy wanted to acknowledge the strangeness of what she'd done, assure them that they ought to be upset by what they'd seen, as she was upset by it. Instead, she went about the rest of the day. They had another hour before dismissal, and she had half an hour of cleanup after that.

On her way out of the building, Lucy noted that another day had passed without her telling the school that she meant to leave at the end of the semester. Every morning she planned to have this conversation, and every afternoon she left without having said anything.

Sometimes she told herself that she needed to speak with Sam first. They'd seen each other only one since she'd left, but they'd spoken several times, and it was fairly clear to them both that she'd regained control of the relationship. If she'd told him that she was going back to Madison when school broke in December, he would agree to come along. It sounded like he would have his book sold by then, and he wouldn't need to stay at the *Interviewer*.

She didn't bring up Margo when they talked, and he didn't ask about Claire. They both understood that these obstacles had been cleared from their way. The only remaining barrier to their reunion was Lucy. What exactly was keeping her away? She wanted to experience some independence before returning to her old life. Perhaps she also wanted him to suffer a bit more, to even out their ledger.

If what happened next was up to her, and she wanted to get back to Madison, it stood to reason that this was what they would do. So why had she still not said anything? Eventually—perhaps around Thanksgiving—it would be too late. The decision would make itself. Perhaps that was just as well. All she was committing to, by not saying anything, was staying through the end of the school year, which was what she'd been prepared to do from the beginning. If she went back to Madison without a job, she would lose another five months of her life, probably spending it at her parents' house while she and Sam waited for the lease on their own to end.

At a bodega near the apartment, she bought a six-pack of beer to share with the girls. Upstairs, she found them sitting together on the couch, watching a video on Danielle's laptop.

"Want to get high?" Krista asked as Lucy walked in.

"Sure," Lucy said.

She took three beers from her bag and went to the kitchen to put the others in the fridge. Back in the living room, the girls had shifted slightly to make room for her.

Lucy had worried that they would regret their initial invitation to "hang," but when she'd joined them the next night, they'd acted as though she were part of their normal routine. She'd sat with them after work almost every day since.

Krista rolled and lit a joint while Lucy drank her beer. When the joint came to her, she took a single, long drag and passed it on.

"What'd you do today?" Danielle asked, as she almost always did.

"I was at work."

"Right. How was that?"

It seemed difficult to explain what had happened without making either too little of it (I lost my train of thought in the middle of class) or too much (I had some kind of psychotic break and freaked the kids out). The girls already thought she was strange.

"Long," she said. "One of the other teachers was sick, so I had to do everything on my own."

"Sucks," Krista said.

"Hard," Danielle agreed.

All three of them laughed.

Lucy liked these girls, though by any objective measure they should have infuriated her. They had a great talent for self-dramatization, got in spectacular fights over matters that seemed completely trivial to Lucy when she understood them at all. They hardly worked—Krista a few shifts a week at a coffee shop, Danielle even fewer at a bookstore in Soho—but complained constantly about their jobs, about the ridiculousness of their customers, the stupidity of their bosses, the myriad ways in which their workplaces would be improved if the world would just listen to them.

Yet they seemed despite or perhaps because of all this self-induced turmoil to be having so much fun. Even their complaints were lodged with a kind of knowing irony, as though they were a necessary part of the game being played. The primary—perhaps the sole—objective of the game was to enjoy yourself. That this attitude ran counter to every ethical principle with which Lucy had been raised was part of its appeal. So many of her college friends had moved to big cities after graduation—mostly Chicago, but also New York, San Francisco, LA—some to start graduate school or take jobs at banks or marketing firms, but many to do what Krista and Danielle seemed to be here to do: spend a few years having fun before real life began. They got jobs that let them pay the rent but gave them no real responsibilities.

When Lucy had found out that she was moving to New York, she'd emailed two old friends who as far as she knew were still living here. Megan—her old roommate, with whom she'd lost touch—had written back almost immediately to say that after six years in the city, she'd moved to Columbus, where her husband had grown up. She offered an enthusiastic list of restaurants and bars in Williamsburg and the Lower East Side. *These are probably out of date already!!* she wrote. *But it's a start. I'm so jealous of your little adventure. Have so much fun.* On one of her date nights with Sam, Lucy had taken him to a bar on Megan's list, and she had never felt so old in her life, at least not until she moved in with Krista and Danielle.

The other girl had taken more time to respond. She'd moved about a year before to Westchester, she'd written. She loved the city, but she'd wanted her kids to have a lawn. She was home with them full time, and she didn't get into Manhattan much, but she would definitely let Lucy know the next time she planned a trip. Lucy hadn't followed up, and she'd never heard from the girl again.

She'd come too late. Why hadn't she moved when she was younger? Why had she stayed all that time so close to home? She was tempted to blame Sam—he'd needed stability; he'd wanted to get married right away—but that got it reversed: she'd chosen Sam because Sam meant safety, because he'd given her an excuse to stay where she was. Married or not, they could have gone anywhere. They'd stayed in Madison because she'd wanted to stay. Even once he'd found this good job in New York, she'd wanted to stay. Why had she spent so much of her life afraid? She had learned in a child psychology class about attachment theory, in which a stable caregiver became a "secure base" from which to explore the world, but it seemed to her that the opposite had been true, that her roots had held her where she was.

"We're going to throw you a party," Danielle announced. "You need to meet some people."

"You need to meet some boys," Krista clarified.

"I'm still married," Lucy reminded them. That fact suddenly seemed very funny to her.

"You're not obligated to fellate anyone in the bathroom," Krista answered. "Just have a conversation with someone who isn't, like, a mentally challenged youth."

"You're a mentally challenged youth," Danielle told Krista.

"Plus," Krista persisted. "Nothing would drive Waxmouth crazier than looking on your TeeseStream and seeing you partying with some hot young meat."

Lucy didn't have a TeeseStream, but she knew this was beside the point. Did she *want* to drive Sam crazy? She couldn't really say.

Her life was like that now. She had no idea what she wanted, no idea what the future held, no idea where she would be even six months from now. She had never felt that way before. She was often scared but also excited. There was much about her life in these days that was difficult, but she found this difficulty stimulating, perhaps even necessary. Her life up to this point had been too easy, she thought. She hadn't meant it to be that way, hadn't realized that she was shying away from difficulty, but that was what had happened. Now, almost everything was hard. She might get dragged out to sea, the waters might swallow her alive, but she might as easily find herself having safely passed to some place entirely new, a place she'd never even imagined before.

"Sure," she said. "A party sounds cool."

Lucy's phone buzzed a few minutes later, and she knew it was her parents calling. She considered ignoring it, but she'd taken only one pull. Better to get the conversation over before she had more.

Her parents checked in every few days, but a brief conversation was usually enough to dispel any worry that might lead to tougher questions. When they asked about her job, she stressed how busy she was, which she hoped would explain why she wasn't calling them. When they asked about Sam, she said he was fine, which seemed to be more or less true. She didn't lie, merely omitted the elements necessary to the construction of an accurate picture of her life. This was better for everyone. She would likely enough be back in Madison just a few months from now with Sam in tow, and if her parents thought that he had been cheating—she wasn't even sure that he had, but it was the only conclusion the facts would support—they would never forgive him for it.

"We heard the news," her mother said when she picked up. "Why didn't you tell us?"

She supposed it was inevitable that they would find out. Sam might have called them, but she couldn't imagine why he'd want them to know. Maybe he'd told a friend back home who'd passed on word to them. She almost believed that they'd simply sensed it; their power over her felt at times that great.

"How are you holding up?" her father asked.

Her parents' habit was to sit in different rooms, on different phones, speaking to her at the same time, giving her the full stereo effect of their dinner-table chatter.

"The whole thing is pretty surreal," Lucy said.

"It's probably a big misunderstanding," her mother cut in.

Lucy let out an inarticulate affirmation. She supposed in a sense that it was.

"How is Sam?" her father asked.

What kind of question was this? Lucy understood that they thought of themselves, in relation to Sam, less as in-laws than in loco parentis, but at least in this case, she thought, their loyalties ought to be clear.

"All right, I guess."

"Well I think he's being very poorly treated," her mother said.

What had he been telling them?

"By me?" she asked.

"By the magazine."

Now Lucy was thoroughly confused. In her slightly stoned state she felt, like her students, uncertain how much of this confusion was her own fault.

"The *Interviewer*?"

"Not them," her mother said, sounding frustrated. "The other one, the one that wrote the story."

Lucy remembered the profile Sam had been so excited about.
"The *Reverberator.*"

"That's right," her mother said.

"We're sure there's a very good explanation for all of it," her father put in.

"It's a big misunderstanding," her mother repeated, more definitively this time.

There was a silence on the line while they waited for Lucy to give them the very good explanation that would clear up the misunderstanding. She pressed the phone against her thigh while she pointed to Danielle's laptop on the coffee table.

"Can you go to the *Reverberator*?" she asked the girls.

Danielle clicked a few times and the headline came up on the screen: "Quantified Swirl: Has the Algorithm King Been Double Billing?"

Lucy put the phone back to her face.

"I can't really explain right now," she said. "Like you said, it's a misunderstanding. We'll get everything straightened out soon."

"This is so exciting," Krista said as Lucy hung up the phone.

Danielle was reaching for her computer, but Lucy said, "Can I read it first?"

"Oh, right," Danielle said.

The article—what Sam had told her would be a puff piece, a profile to help sell his book—was an exposé. As she got through the first paragraphs, Lucy felt an instinctive drive to protect Sam. He needed her now more than he ever had. But she continued on with increasing incredulity. She'd known about the old posts, but there was more than that. The article said he'd been plagiarizing the *Herald*. How could he have thought he'd get away with that? Then he'd lied about it all to the journalist who was profiling him. The whole thing made him sound like an idiot, which was one thing he was not.

She finished the article and looked up at the girls. She had no idea what to say.

"That's weird about your husband," Krista said, as though it were a rumor they'd both heard days ago.

"Yeah," Lucy told her.

"Kinda cool though," Krista added. "It feels like I know a disgraced celebrity."

"Does anyone want another beer?" Lucy asked, getting up from the couch. She thought she was about to cry, and she didn't want to do it in front of the girls. She knew they would be perfectly sympathetic, but she didn't want their sympathy at the moment.

"For sure," Danielle said.

Standing alone in the kitchen, Lucy was somewhat surprised to find that her overwhelming emotion was anger. She knew exactly what had happened, why he had not been getting his work done, why he'd started cutting corners in ways completely unlike the Sam she knew. He'd dragged them across the country for his grand ambitions, and then he'd tanked it all for the first pretty girl who paid any attention to him. She drank half her beer in front of the open fridge while she pulled herself together. Then she went back into the living room.

By the end of the next day, the *Reverberator* had run almost a dozen updates to the story, most concerning their own role in uncovering Sam's transgressions. They were treating the whole thing like a mini-Watergate, with their anonymous tipster in the role of Deep Throat, and this Penty guy as Woodward and Bernstein rolled into one. The last update announced that Sam had been fired by the *Interviewer*, with quotes from Max Blakeman and Mario Adrian, expressing their disappointment and their commitment to earning back their readers' trust. The link to the *Quantified World* blog was removed from their home page. When Lucy searched their site for Sam's name, no results came up at all. His work had been entirely scrubbed.

The next day, the *Herald* ran a single short story, focused on their own role in providing the source material for Sam's thefts. A few days later, when they reported that a Russian oligarch named Dmitri Davidovitch was buying the *Interviewer*, Sam merited one mention in a rundown of Mario Adrian's rocky tenure as publisher. By this time, Lucy's parents were calling every few hours, and she'd silenced her phone. She knew she ought to call Sam, but in every article she read about his downfall, in every line, she saw the words "Margo Doyle."

So she turned her attention instead to the girls' party. She came to suspect that they'd been planning the thing for some time before they'd decided to include Lucy and make her the occasion for it. They didn't ask whether she wanted to invite anyone, which was fine, because she had no one to invite. She was getting along with the other teachers, but they were mostly married and older—older than Krista and Danielle, that was, not necessarily older than Lucy herself—and she didn't know any of them well enough to include them. She offered to pay for alcohol, and the girls eagerly accepted, buying it themselves with her card. That seemed to be the only real preparation involved.

That afternoon, Krista announced that they were going for a run, which would give them a "glow" for the night. There was a gym in the Denison's basement with a row of treadmills that faced a large flat-screen TV, where the girls liked to go sometimes when they were on one of their detoxes. A detox meant that they went one or possibly two days without drinking or getting high, though this was taken somewhat liberally—often a detox night ended with a glass of wine, which was a reward for detoxing.

"Why don't you come with us?" Danielle asked. "You never get any exercise."

Though she hadn't been on a single run since she'd started living with them, Lucy had probably logged more miles in the past year than the two of them had in their lives combined. If she'd told them that, they wouldn't have believed her, and even if they'd believed her it wouldn't have meant anything to them. To Krista and Danielle, Lucy had no past whatsoever. She had sprung up at exactly the moment she'd walked in their door looking for an apartment. All of the business about Sam was like the backstory a sitcom character was given to explain her presence in an incongruous place. It was not something an actual human being had lived through and definitely not something that infringed on their lives. This didn't bother Lucy—in fact she liked it. To her, too, the life she'd had before moving in with them—not necessarily her life in Madison but the months she'd spent with Sam in New York—had come to seem unreal.

She put on her running clothes and sneakers, which had been tucked away in her closet. The girls expressed surprised amusement at the discovery that she even had exercise clothes.

"Why don't we run outside?"

"Is that a joke?" Krista said. "It's freezing."

It was probably fifty degrees. Lucy routinely ran in single-digit weather. Part of the point of running was being out in nature. There was something depressing, even kind of wasteful, about running in place, expending energy to go nowhere, but she couldn't explain this to them.

What qualified as running for Krista and Danielle, it turned out, was setting the treadmills at 4.5 with a slight incline and watching episodes of *Hartley Ever After*, talking through the commercial breaks. When Lucy jacked her treadmill up to her usual pace of eight-minute miles, they laughed and told her to cool it. Stop making them look bad. She did stop, mostly because after a minute she realized she wasn't in good enough shape to sustain it. She set her machine at the same pace as theirs and watched the show. By the time they got back upstairs an hour later, they had barely broken a sweat.

Lucy was surprised at how young the guests looked, closer to her students' age than her own. She'd gotten used to Krista and Danielle, but a roomful of them was a different matter. Their friends all said hello to Lucy with an aggressive cheerfulness that made her think they'd been warned about the weird, depressive roommate. She reminded herself that she was good at socializing, that she'd always liked parties. Three months earlier, she'd gone toe-to-toe with Frank Doyle.

She started to feel better after her second drink. The room was mostly full by then, so she could stand in a corner without attracting too much attention. She was wondering how long she needed to stay before politely slipping off to bed when Krista approached, dragging a tall, lanky boy in a T-shirt and a pair of jean shorts. Lucy wasn't sure whether the shorts were being worn ironically.

"This is Dave," Krista said.

"Nice to meet you," Lucy told him.

"He's from the Midwest," Krista added suggestively, as though this were some kind of kink that he and Lucy shared.

"Outside Chicago," Dave explained.

"I'm from Madison."

"Cool," Dave said.

In the time it had taken to exchange these sentiments, Krista had disappeared, leaving them together.

"Do you want to dance?" Dave asked.

He was cute in a somewhat goofy way, with an overbite and crooked front teeth, giving the impression that orthodontics had not yet made their way to the wilds of suburban Illinois. Lucy nodded, and they walked a few steps toward the general mass of moving people filling up the center of the room. Dave was not a good dancer, but he was enthusiastic, which made Lucy, who was also an enthusiastic and not good dancer, feel at ease. She'd loved to dance in college, when dancing mostly meant jumping up and down in the vicinity of other people, or moving provocatively with a group of girls while boys in red and white hats watched on suspiciously, waiting for an opportunity to separate someone from the herd. Sam hated to dance, though he always submitted to one or two slow songs at weddings. It had been a long time since she'd danced with a boy as she was now dancing with Dave.

He started to work his bare leg, sweaty below his shorts, between her legs, and he was sucking on his lower lip with his crooked front teeth, which was completely disgusting but also a little bit funny. (Did he mean it to be funny?) Lucy wasn't sure what, if anything, Krista had told him about her. She was wearing her wedding ring, but it might not have occurred to a boy that age to look, or to recognize the significance of it when he noticed it. Perhaps Krista had said that Lucy was on a hiatus from her husband, which made her a good candidate for a low-pressure hookup. Lucy was absolutely sure that she wasn't going to do anything with this boy, but she was enjoying his attention.

"Do you want something to drink?" he asked when the song ended.

"Sure," she said, and he loped off through the crowd, toward a table piled with bottles and cups and bags of ice. A minute later he appeared beside her with not two but four plastic cups in his hands.

"I got us shots. You down for that?"

Lucy took two of the cups from him, one filled with ice and what might have been vodka or gin, the other half full of brown sludge. She hadn't had more than a couple of beers or a glass or two of wine in an evening since that night at the Doyles' house. She already knew that she would be a wreck the next day, but she didn't really mind. Krista and Danielle made it seem as though hungover mornings—sitting around in pajamas; watching TV; ordering bacon, egg, and cheese sandwiches from the deli on the corner; complaining how terrible you felt while laughing about what had happened the night before—were the real point of it all, that this business of the party was just a necessary preliminary. She imagined sitting with them on the couch, eating one of those breakfast sandwiches while they asked her what had happened with Dave.

"I'm down," she said.

She came awake with an arm draped over her, and she knew right away that it didn't belong to Sam, just as she knew that she wasn't in her bedroom in Madison, but she let herself believe both these things before opening her eyes and thinking about what to do next.

Beside her, Dave snored lightly. They were both fully dressed—if those shorts qualified. This was something, at least. She didn't think that anything had happened, but she couldn't be entirely sure, because she didn't remember much. The party had thinned after a while, and the remaining people had taken up the couch and the floor surrounding it while Krista rolled a joint. It had seemed fairly clear to Lucy that Dave meant to wait everyone out, and she didn't know what to do about that fact. There were still a dozen people left when she announced that she was going to sleep.

She'd been in bed for just a few minutes when the door to her room opened.

"Can I come in?" Dave had asked.

"I'm not making out with you," she'd answered. "I'm married."

"That's fine," Dave said. "We'll just sleep."

He waited for her to answer, and when she didn't he approached the bed. With every step he took, she was preparing to say no, but she never did, and then he was under the covers. At the time it had seemed weirdly innocent. He was a kind of child to her. If he tried anything, she would just make him stop. She would tell him that he had to leave. But he didn't do anything. He was asleep before her, occasionally kicking his legs like a dreaming animal. Once he was asleep, she allowed herself to enjoy the simple pleasure of having a warm body beside her through the night.

Now that feeling was gone entirely. She wanted him out of her bed, out of her brain. She pushed him, and he stirred but didn't wake, and she didn't push again, because she realized that a waking Dave would be harder to manage than a sleeping one. As it was, she could just get up, leave him there. He would find his way out eventually.

She didn't know whether Krista and Danielle would be awake yet, but she didn't want to face them. She couldn't answer their questions, couldn't even stand up to their good-natured, knowing expressions. When she sat up in bed, the first thing she saw was the novel her mother had given her, which had sat half-read on the bedside table for weeks. In search of distraction, she took it into her hands and opened to the long-marked page. She found it transformed. Someone had turned the words into illegible markings. She flipped to another page, one she'd already read, and she found the same thing. Gradually she came to understand that she was the one transformed. The marks were the same, but she couldn't make meaning of them. She flipped desperately, in search of a word she knew, something she could grasp, a foothold from which she could bring her brain back into working order. She closed the book and stood very quickly from bed.

For a moment she thought she was going to fall over. Was she having a stroke? She steadied herself by reaching out for the wall. It was very important that she not wind up back in that bed, that she not wake up Dave. If this boy she didn't know should see what was happening to her, it would become real.

The living room was in disarray, but there was no sign of the girls. She should go into their room, wake them up, ask for help. But something told her that they couldn't do anything for her now. They were just kids. Whatever help she needed she would have to find out in the world. She left the apartment without her keys, which she realized only after the door had closed behind her. She looked down the

long, clean, newly carpeted hall. The janitor was scrubbing a window
with something that gave off a strong citrus smell. Lucy thought she
might almost prefer the stench of captive animals. She considered
asking him for help, but she didn't know what to say. *Things have
stopped meaning*, she might have told him.

She walked to the elevator bank and pressed the call button. She
had to catch her breath while she waited for it. A few months before,
she was running twenty miles a week, and now she was winded from
going fifty feet down the hall. She felt a return of the dizziness that
had come over her when she got up from bed. She was about to reach
out for something when the elevator door opened. She stepped inside
and pressed the button for the lobby. She was going to go down now.
That's all she'd needed, all along. *I just needed to go down*, she told
herself, as she felt her legs wobble. She had no idea where she was
going, but she suddenly understood that she wouldn't make it there.

3.

Two men in white painters' gear hung from the billboard across the street. It was 11:00 in the morning, and they'd already covered over what had the night before been an advertisement for Teeser's dating app. While Eddie had rarely noticed the ad consciously, its absence from the scenery struck him now. He could still picture the attractive if somewhat voracious-looking middle-aged white man surrounded by cartoon thought bubbles, each filled with a different object of desire—a conspicuously beautiful young Latina, a muscled and mustached black man in leather, a coquettish girl (surely the actress must have been of age, but she looked barely in her teens) of Southeast Asian extraction. Eddie didn't remember what other creatures the bubbles had contained, but he knew by heart the slogan that had run beneath it all—*Whatever Your Pleasure, TeeseMeet's Got You Covered.*

The men slowly posted the first panel of a new ad. Somehow Eddie didn't realize what it would be until he saw the eyes. He would have recognized them immediately, even had they not had that wide expanse of wrinkled forehead above them, the fedora perched over a wild tangle of white hair. Eddie stared up at those eyes as though he might draw their attention down to his level. Since Nash's disappearance, he'd experienced an odd mix of emotion whenever he'd thought about the man. Everyone expected him to be angry, which he was, but he couldn't bring himself to regret anything. Naturally he was sorry that Nash had absconded, but he refused to blame him for the events that had transpired after he'd so successfully vanished. It was like cursing the weather or an inanimate object you'd tripped over. Like cursing God.

Looking up now, Eddie felt more than anything the desire for Nash to notice him there, absurd as that might have been. He'd intended to cancel all these buys, but Kit's lawyers—they were apparently also Eddie's—had said that this would only create complications. The theft of the Celsia gains had been a mitigating factor in Kit's deal, they'd explained. Better to leave it alone. The government might be tempted to reopen the case if the money reappeared, and they would certainly confiscate whatever Eddie recovered. At the time, Eddie had been grateful for this permission to write the whole thing off. It meant avoiding the embarrassing prospect of calling up old contacts to admit that his client had disappeared—or, worse, that there had been no client, really, that he'd been spending his own money on a campaign for the end of the world.

Perhaps it still seemed possible that Nash would reappear with some reasonable explanation. Some part of Eddie hadn't entirely given up hope. He had to keep believing in Nash, because he had to believe that he'd really been forgiven. Or else it was just easier than admitting what a terrible mistake he'd made.

For all his thought on the matter, it hadn't occurred to him until this morning what leaving his orders in place meant in practice: fifty billboards going up throughout the city at the beginning of October; dozens of radio spots and subway ads; finally, thirty seconds of national airtime during game four of the World Series, the night of the apocalypse. For the next month, Nash would be everywhere.

The noon shift was about to start when Eddie arrived at New York General. He dressed at his locker in a hurry, preparing for the eight hours ahead. He would have happily worked longer, but he'd done a double the night before—8:00 PM to 4:00 AM—and union rules didn't allow you to work more than twenty-four hours in a forty-eight-hour stretch. Within those limits, Eddie had been picking up as many shifts as he could. After a few hundred hours, he could take a test to move from EMT-Basic to EMT-Advanced, making him eligible for a fire department job, which would put him in real emergencies. It would also pay a little better; for the first time in his life, he needed the money. Fifty-hour weeks covered groceries and rent, but he was trying to save for a paramedic course.

Most of the job was scheduled rides, which the veterans referred to somewhat derisively as "skeds" and treated as glorified taxi work. When patients had to be brought to the airport to see some specialist in Boston or Minneapolis, or back to the assisted living center from which they'd come two days before, or home to die, they got a ride in a cube. The FDNY dispatched plenty of 911 calls to the hospital units, but they kept the serious stuff—multicar crashes, shootings, any situation in which medical personnel might be at risk—for themselves. About half the time you went out on an unscheduled call, you came back with an empty cube. Whatever emergency was thought to have occurred was over before you got there, and you were greeted with sheepish relief. So far, Eddie had worked a couple of heart attacks, one stroke, a few falls, and a broken ankle from a high school soccer match in Central Park. His most dramatic outing had come when a drunk woman crashed into a hydrant on Second Avenue and the police wanted someone to sign off on her condition before they took her away in cuffs.

Each cube was staffed with one paramedic and one EMT, and the hospital kept four cubes on at a time, so even when one was out there were usually at least six people sitting around, playing cards, talking shit. Eddie had been prepared for this. He knew that emergency response jobs were better understood as exercises in waiting punctuated by occasional pseudo-emergencies. Even in a war zone, the real thing was relatively rare. The challenge was staying alert through the languor, which was helped by the constant knowledge that if something serious happened—another attack, for example— the city would need all the resources it had. Even the hospital units would be right in the middle of it.

On the day the billboard went up, Eddie was paired with a paramedic named Rob, a guy about Eddie's age who'd been working for the hospital for more than a decade. It was a quiet afternoon, so there was a lot of garage time, and Eddie spent most of it listening to Rob chatter. Rob was known to be very good out on a job, but he was full of nervous energy that made it impossible for anyone to relax when they shared a shift with him. No one could tell him to shut up, because of the respect his experience commanded. Rob was one of a few New York General paramedics who'd been called downtown when the towers fell, and he sometimes brought the day up during quiet stretches, as though to remind them all of the job's real stakes. Eddie had not mentioned that his mother had been there. He was trying not to think about Kit.

They were finishing a hand of rummy when Kara walked by.

"Smoke?" she asked Eddie.

He nodded, and they walked together out the garage's back entrance, which hung over the FDR Drive and had a view of Roosevelt Island.

"What's up with you, Doyle?" Kara said when they got outside. "You don't look good today."

She was a fellow basic who'd started around the same time as Eddie, and she referred to him exclusively by his last name, which she said with an odd intimacy. After six weeks of work, she was the only colleague he considered a friend, though their interactions were mostly limited to these sessions at the back entrance. She worked regular hours, always the noon-to-eight, and he looked forward to the days when they were on together. Like most basics, she was several years younger than Eddie, and she was very pretty, though she made some effort to conceal the fact in the garage. On their first shift together, she'd asked whether he smoked, and he'd lied in order to have an excuse to step outside with her. They'd gone out for one or two on each shift they'd shared since then. After bumming from her a few times, he'd bought his first pack in years, just to offer her one.

"You don't look so great yourself."

She laughed briefly, but her face turned serious.

"What's your story, Doyle?"

She gave the words a particular inflection that he'd sometimes heard in the military, one meant to signify something like: *How did you wind up here?* It was fairly easy to identify those who didn't come from places where people enlisted as a matter of course, those who'd had other options. People who fell into this category tended to find each other, and they asked this question in much this way. Sometimes the answer was as simple as *It runs in the family,* but sometimes it was complicated. A similar dynamic prevailed in the garage. A few of the basics were in med school or considering it, or they had some other reason for doing the job on a temporary basis, but advanced EMTs and paramedics—the lifers— tended to come from the same neighborhoods in Brooklyn and Queens as the firefighters and cops they worked with every day.

"I got out of the army about six months ago. I did a couple of tours."

He knew this answer only raised more questions, but he didn't know what else to say. On previous shifts, he and Kara had exchanged notes on paramedics they'd been paired with, they'd spoken about their training and their impression of the job, but they'd never discussed their personal lives.

"This gig must be pretty low stress by comparison."

"I'm hoping for a city job once I get my EMT-A. Maybe things will get more exciting then."

"So you're in it for the long haul?"

"It feels that way."

She looked skeptical but inclined to take his reticence as a challenge. He was thinking of ways to change the subject when a bell rang above the back door, indicating that a call had come in. They tossed their half-finished smokes. Inside the garage, Rob was already behind the wheel of their cube.

"Some kid sliced his pinkie off at an after-school pumpkin-carving party," he announced while Eddie climbed into the passenger seat.

Rob always drove on the way out. Though stressful, these drives were almost fun. You could blow through reds, blare the siren, cut in and out of traffic, all without worrying about cargo in the back. He usually drove the return leg, too, unless the cargo required an IV or intubation, which Eddie wasn't yet certified to do. A lot of basics complained about paramedics who kept the easy driving for themselves, but Eddie didn't need any extra experience in emergencies.

Eight minutes out, they arrived at a doorman building in the eighties on Park.

"Can you believe this place?" Rob said in the elevator. "That's one thing about this job. You see every part of the city. After a while, nothing surprises you."

Eddie nodded quietly.

Inside the apartment, two dozen crying first graders surrounded a gaggle of parents who seemed at least as upset as their children. Some of the boys wore St. Albert's uniform blazers. Eddie remembered going to parties like this one at that age. He'd probably been to one in this very building. Angela would have brought him and gone for a walk in the park until the party was over.

A trail of blood led them to the injured boy and his mother in the kitchen. This was fairly dramatic by the standards of the job, and Eddie took some pleasure in the effect their arrival had on the pair.

He thought of what he'd been told in his course: *Once you arrive, the emergency is over.* He carefully removed the washcloth someone had used to stanch the bleeding, and Rob bandaged the tiny nub that remained. They wrapped the separated finger in gauze, and Eddie put it on ice in a cooler.

When they got downstairs, Eddie took the driver's seat without asking. The boy wouldn't need any serious attention on the way, but his mother was young and attractive, and Rob would want the job of comforting her. As Eddie pulled out into traffic and turned the siren on, he heard Rob speaking with great authority, assuring the mother that her son's digit—Rob had a taste for this kind of ersatz jargon— could easily be reattached, all but suggesting he would have done it himself had the circumstances required it.

By the time they'd deposited the boy and his mother safely in the emergency room, their shift was almost over. Eddie would be coming back to the hospital in eight hours, so he showered and dressed as quickly as possible. Outside the men's locker room, Kara was waiting for him.

"A couple of us are grabbing a beer," she said. "Any interest in joining?"

It was the first time he'd seen her out of uniform. She wore dark jeans and a gray cable-knit sweater. Her hair, which she always kept in a tight ponytail while on the job, hung loose around her face, and she was even prettier than Eddie had imagined when he'd pictured her in mufti.

"I'm picking up the four-to-noon," he said. "I'd better get home and get some sleep."

"Maybe next time?"

"Next time for sure."

It was almost nine when he got to his block with dinner in a take-out bag. Instinctively he looked up at the billboard, where the rest of

Nash's face had been filled in, along with the words: *What would you change if you knew it was all going to end?*

This time he didn't stop to contemplate. He walked straight inside and took the stairs two steps at a time up to the fifth floor. He ate on the couch before heading to his room. If he got to sleep by nine thirty, he could get in six hours before going back to work. Through the bedroom window, Nash's enormous eyes looked in at him. *What would you change if you knew it was all going to end?* Though Eddie had written the message himself, it seemed directed at him. He'd installed blackout curtains so that he could sleep in the middle of the day when his schedule required it, and he pulled them shut, leaving himself to undress in the darkness while the questioning gaze remained outside. With a bit of groping, he made his way across the room to his bed and climbed beneath the covers. In the darkness, he saw Nash's eyes. He closed his own, and Nash's were still there, looking at him as though waiting for an answer to his question.

If the world were coming to an end, Eddie thought, he would go see Justin. After his arrest, Eddie had left a long message in which he'd said he would help any way that he could. He'd even added that he was sure that Kit could do something. Of course, he'd understood that there must be some connection between the arrest and the meeting in his apartment that afternoon, but he assumed that Kit had heard rumors of an investigation and met with Justin to warn him about it. He didn't suspect that his mother had set Justin up.

When he'd learned the truth from the lawyers, he'd told them that he was ready to take the blame for everything.

"It's too late for that," said the one named Mullen, whom Eddie had met a few times before. "The Feds have the evidence they need. Nothing we do now is going to change that."

"What will happen to Justin?" he asked.

"That depends on what he's got for them," the other lawyer said. "If he can get them Eisen, his sentence will be as light as your mother's."

They had just finished explaining that Kit would plead guilty to one count of making a false statement, for which she expected three to five months. If she started serving right away, she might be home for Christmas.

"And if he can't get them Eisen?"

They had no answer for this.

Justin had called Eddie back two days later, after he'd been formally charged and released on bail.

"Tell them it was me," Eddie said. "I stole the information, made the trade, and gave the money to Nash. There was nothing you could do."

"That won't help," Justin said in the calm voice that Eddie usually found so reassuring. "The things I'm being charged with have nothing to do with that trade."

"Maybe we can get the evidence thrown out," Eddie said, though he'd already been through this with the lawyers. "I didn't know my apartment was being bugged. I didn't give my permission. Can they still use the recording in court?"

"They won't be using anything in court. I'm going to plead. It will be a lot easier for everyone, especially my mom."

"I'm sorry," Eddie told him. "I'll do whatever I can to get this fixed."

"It has been fixed," Justin said.

Eddie took this to mean that Justin had worked out a similar deal, that he'd be serving a few months. Two days later, the *Herald* reported that Justin Price planned to plead guilty to securities and wire fraud. The story ran on the front page, below the fold, and it noted that these charges each carried maximum sentences of twenty years. The paper was quick to add that his actual sentence would likely be shorter than this, but it certainly didn't suggest that he'd be home by Christmas. A week after Kit started serving her three months, Justin was sentenced to six years.

They'd spoken a fair amount since then, more than they had in a long time. Eddie always answered when Justin called, and he returned every call that he missed, but he didn't know what to say. Ever since he'd heard the news, his overwhelming feeling had been shame. He felt ashamed even though he couldn't say what he would have done differently. It had been a mistake to give his money to Nash, but only because he might have helped more people with it. The money's disappearance, not its recipient, had caused all the trouble, and Eddie still thought that giving it away had been the right thing to do. He was still glad to be free of it. Perhaps the source of his shame was the fact that he'd ever had the money at all. His shame was the war his father had sent him to fight. His shame was the people his mother had sacrificed on his behalf. His shame was the thing of which he'd once been proudest, of which he'd wanted so badly to be worthy. His family was his shame.

Eddie sat up in the darkness and shook his head, as though trying to cast off Nash's gaze. It was sometimes difficult to get to sleep right after a shift, when you were still wound up, but his work schedule had more or less resolved his insomnia. This was another reason he picked up so many shifts. He'd lately avoided taking anything to sleep, since he had to be fresh when he woke up. Now it was probably already too late. He lay back down and pulled the blanket over his head.

After that meeting with the lawyers, he'd stopped answering Kit's calls. He didn't listen to the messages she left or read her emails. Margo had begged him to come home for one last dinner before their mother went away, but he'd refused.

"She'll be home in a couple of months," he'd said.

"Not *home*," Margo had responded.

Before Kit was released, the house would be sold to pay off the lawyers' bills and her fine. Eddie wasn't sure what Margo and Frank were doing for money in the meantime, but he didn't ask, because he was in no position to help. Perhaps it was wrong to harden his heart against them all. He could have visited Kit if he'd wanted—she was in a lockup in northern Westchester—but thinking about this proximity only reminded him that in a few weeks Justin would be going to a federal prison in Indiana.

It was after midnight when he finally gave up on sleep. He turned the lights on in his room and made his way over to the window. He opened the curtains and looked out, as though to convince himself that what he saw there was just a sign—an advertisement—and not the eyes of the man himself. Eddie looked at the familiar creases in the forehead, the thick gray of the brows. Before he knew quite what he was doing, he opened the window and began to yell out.

"What do you want from me?" he screamed. "Haven't I given you enough?"

He thought it might act as a kind of release, but it brought no satisfaction, only whipped up his rage. As he continued to yell, two boys who'd been walking down the street, bounce-passing a basketball to each other, stopped to look up at him. He must have seemed crazy, but they took in his screaming with only mild curiosity. He was not the first mad man to scream wildly out a window in this neighborhood. He was still yelling when they lost interest and continued down the block.

On his way out a few hours later, he was careful not to look at the billboard, but it hardly mattered at this point, because the eyes followed him all the way to work. There was a pair on the subway platform and another in the train, hanging right above his head. They were at a bus stop on York, right around the corner from the hospital. By the time he got into the garage, he felt like he'd been chased.

After his army training, he knew that he could get through a busy double shift without sleep, but he was still relieved to have a slow morning. There were two cubes ahead of his in the lineup, and his only trip out was a sked at six, picking up a woman from a nursing home and bringing her in for surgery. Kara was on for the noon-to-eight, but she was first in the lineup that afternoon, and an early call came in. He was sent out before she was back, so they barely saw each other during their shift. While getting dressed in front of his locker, he decided that he'd go for drinks with the group that night. He wasn't on again until the next evening shift, and he was in no hurry to get back to his apartment and Nash's waiting eyes. He would have a couple of beers, take a sleeping pill as soon as he got home, pull the curtains, and pass out for twenty hours. He dressed quickly so he could catch Kara when she got out.

"Is this next time?" he asked.

"I don't really feel like hitting the bar with the guys," she said.

"Another next time, then."

Kara paused.

"Do you think we could just grab a bite, the two of us?"

They went to a diner on First Avenue, where they faced each other in a narrow booth. Eddie realized that he must look terrible—worn out, troubled—but Kara didn't seem to mind.

"So what's *your* story?" he asked.

She'd graduated from college four years before. She'd majored in economics, and she'd gotten a junior analyst job right out of school.

"Typical Wall Street bullshit," she elaborated.

He nearly asked where she'd worked, but the question could only lead down a path that ended at Kit. Perhaps she already had some inkling of the connection.

"I got canned after the collapse," she continued. "A total blessing. I hated that job, but I never would have had the guts to quit."

She'd been covering the healthcare sector at work, and she'd decided that she wanted to be a doctor. Now she was taking the post-bac premed course at Columbia while picking up shifts to make money and get some experience.

"Do you feel like a drink somewhere?" she asked when the waiter brought the check.

"I should probably get some sleep," Eddie said.

"You worked a double today," she said, and she smiled. "So I know you aren't going in early tomorrow."

After one round at a bar down the street, they took a cab to her apartment on the Upper West Side, where they kissed for a few minutes on her couch, until she got up to get them each a beer from the fridge. When Eddie woke the next morning in her bed, fully dressed, he had only the vaguest memories of her shaking him lightly awake on the couch and leading him there. She was gone, but he found a note on the bedside table: *Had to go to class. You looked like you needed the sleep. Help yourself to anything in the fridge, and call me if you want to meet up later.*

On their third date, Eddie told Kara everything. He hadn't planned to do it, but it all came out naturally after she asked about his family. When he told her, she knew exactly who they were, which made everything easier, because so much followed from that. She already knew about Frank's firing and Kit's arrest. She knew about Justin. She'd gone to hear him speak once when she was still an analyst.

Telling her about his role in Justin's arrest meant telling her about the money, which in turn meant telling her about Nash. She'd seen the ads on the subway and the bus stop near the hospital, but she couldn't believe that they were all his work.

"I put one up right across the street from my apartment," he said. "I thought it would make him happy to see it. Now it looks in at me all night while I'm trying to sleep."

"That's terrible," Kara said, but she started to laugh.

Eddie had been thinking a lot about how she would react to the story, but he'd never imagined she'd find it funny. Watching her laugh, he could see the cosmic justice to it, and he started laughing, too. It made everything slightly more manageable.

"I haven't really slept in almost a month."

"Good news," Kara said. "It's October 31. Only one night to go. After that, either the world will end, or the billboard will come down."

"I'm not sure I can make it one more night," he told her, no longer laughing.

"More good news. You've got someplace else to stay."

They were both on the noon-to-eight the next day, and they spent a lazy morning at Kara's apartment before heading in together. The few hours after they woke were the happiest Eddie had experienced since Nash's disappearance.

He was back in Rob's cube that day, and they were the first in line. They'd been on for only a few minutes when a call came in. A homeless man had thrown himself into traffic on Fifth Avenue, near the public library. He was still conscious, drunk but not seriously hurt, which was why the fire department had passed on the call.

Rob drove straight crosstown on Seventy-Second, swerving occasionally into oncoming traffic to get through red lights. Eddie listened to the siren whining above them and felt a sense of great well-being, as though he was doing what he'd been born to do. They turned down Fifth and moved quickly through traffic to Forty-Eighth, where they arrived at a wall of cars. A cop was directing traffic over to Madison, and he stepped out to open the bus lane for them. In front of them a cab was stuck half in the lane, so it was impossible to get past. Rob got on the mike to shout the cab out of his way, and it pulled up another six inches, just enough for them to get around. Once they'd shot through the bottleneck, all of Fifth opened in front of them. The only car in the street for the next twenty blocks was the cab that had hit the man. A scrum of onlookers near

it hid the man himself from view, and Eddie could see a cop struggling to keep them at bay. Most of them turned when the ambulance
emerged from the traffic. They cleared out as Rob pulled the cube
alongside the cab, stopping it in the middle of the street.

The first thing Eddie noticed as the man came into view was the
book on the ground beside him. One of his father's baseball books.
A strange thing for a homeless man to be carrying. Just as this was
sinking in, Eddie spotted the dress pants. One leg was brown with
blood, and the foot below it was twisted in an awkward direction, so
that Eddie could see the heel of it, where he read the name of an old
Italian cobbler. He was too shocked at first to say anything, and as
he brought himself under control he was stopped by an odd kind of
reticence. He looked up from the leg to the stubbled face and sunken
cheeks, and he waited for a sign of recognition, but in the eyes he saw
only the frightened expression of an injured man.

"Dad," he said.

Rob and the cop both stopped and looked at Eddie. Only Frank
failed to respond to the word.

"Fuck," the cop answered.

Eddie got down on his knees, placing himself at his father's eye
level. Frank still looked back blankly. Eddie felt suddenly embarrassed, as though the others might think he'd been lying.

"Dad," he said again.

Now Frank looked right at him.

"What?" he responded, as though a stranger had spoken his
name.

With surprising tenderness, Rob put a hand on Eddie's shoulder.
"We need to take vitals."

Eddie took his kit from his shoulder bag and went to work.
Temperature was low, pulse elevated, breathing rate slow, but none of it
dangerously. Frank was obviously in shock, and Eddie suspected that
the leg was badly broken, but they would make it to the hospital all right.

"You're going to be fine," he said.

"What would you—"

Before Frank could finish, Rob was beside them with the splint, starting to stabilize the broken leg.

"Let's get the board," Rob said when they were done.

They pulled the gurney from the back of the cube and wheeled it over. Eddie thought of his father as such a large man, and his instinct was to ask the cop for help in moving him, but as they slid the draw sheet under him Eddie realized that Frank had turned thin and fragile. They got him on the gurney and wheeled him to the cube, where Eddie put on an oxygen mask while Rob opened Frank's shirt and applied the 12-lead ECG. They loaded him inside, and Eddie climbed into the cube behind him. Rob closed the doors and walked around to the driver's seat. As the sirens went on and the cube started moving, Eddie reached out for his father's hand.

Frank looked over at him, and Eddie thought he saw a first hint of recognition. Frank tried to speak, but the flow of oxygen seemed to send the words back down his throat. He swatted in frustration at the mask until Eddie gently lifted it from his face.

"What?" Frank said again.

"Dad," Eddie told him. "It's me."

"What would you change?"

"About what?"

"What would you change?"

"I don't know what you're trying to say."

"If you knew?"

All at once it came to Eddie, and he didn't want to hear it again. As if this desire had acted in the world, the cube was filled with the urgent beeping of the ECG and the oximeter.

"What's going on back there?" Rob asked.

"He's going," Eddie yelled. For the first time in almost a decade of emergencies, he felt himself panicking. He wanted to be told what to do.

"If you knew," Frank said.

"We're almost there," Rob yelled. He looked briefly over his shoulder. "Put his fucking oxygen on."

"If you knew it was all going to," Frank said as Eddie let go of the mask, which snapped over Frank's mouth, swallowing forever the last word.

4.

He'd been completely unprepared when they came for him. Of course he'd expected it eventually, but he'd assumed he would have some time. The FBI would want to build their case, corroborate what he'd told Kit. They had no reason to imagine that he knew about the recording—if he'd known, why would he have confessed? Maybe they would tap his phone, try to get something on Eisen out of it. Later he learned that Kit had disappeared after the meeting and thrown her wire out. The Feds were worried that she'd run off to warn him, and they'd moved in before he could destroy any evidence. But he'd known none of this that night.

They'd come prepared to break their way in, but they didn't even have to knock. His apartment was the only one on his floor, and the elevator didn't stop there without a key, so he often left the front door unlocked. Once the doorman let them up, all they had to do was turn the knob. When they'd charged down the hall with their guns out, Justin honestly thought they were going to kill him. If they could do it on Eastern Parkway, why not Fifth Avenue? He'd never been so scared in his life. They surrounded him on the living room couch, and in his rush to get his hands above his head, he poured half a glass of red wine on his white shirt. Looking at the stain, he imagined he'd already been shot. They stood him up, cuffed him, and brought him downstairs.

At least his mother hadn't been forced to cower in a corner while they dragged him off. In her apartment upstairs, she would tell him later, she hadn't noticed the helicopter spotlight pouring through her park-facing windows. Hugh called up to her after Justin was walked out of the lobby, and she'd turned on the TV just in time to see the police car pull away. At the station, he asked his lawyer to tell her he'd be home the next day and explain everything. She was a strong woman, she wasn't going to collapse in a heap, but beyond that he wasn't sure how she would take it.

When he explained what he'd done, she almost seemed to have been expecting it, as though she'd known that wealth of the kind he'd acquired must always be accompanied by some crime. Perhaps this explained his parents' long-standing resistance to living with him: they hadn't wanted to be implicated.

"We didn't need all this," she said. "You didn't have to do it."

He might have told her some of the things that Eisen had told him—that things had always been done this way in their world, that the rules really existed to exclude people like them, that there was a kind of justice on their side. But this all seemed paltry when placed in the light of her implacable expression.

"I know," he said.

"All I wanted was for you to be safe."

"I'll be safe," he said. "They're going to make sure I'm sent to a place that isn't too bad. I'm telling them everything I know."

Netta wrapped her arms around him and briefly cried, but she brought herself quickly back under control.

"You've got to stay on the righteous path now," she said. "I might not be around when you get out, but I want to know that we're heading to the same place."

"You've got a lot of years left," Justin insisted. "We're going to have plenty of time together."

He really believed this. By the time he was released, she would be in her mid-sixties. But she didn't seem to need his reassurances.

"Just stay on the path from here," she said. "I want you to talk with the pastor about all this."

Justin had no desire to see Jonathan, let alone to talk with him about his life, but he would do anything to make his mother feel better. He would have preferred to meet at the church, so that he could minimize social niceties and leave when he wanted, but he didn't much feel like facing the reporters outside his building. He certainly didn't feel like leading them to Crown Heights so that they could put a picture of the Pathway on page one and speculate about the state of his soul. He agreed to a meeting at the apartment.

Jonathan arrived right on time, dressed in a black suit and a clerical collar. He'd spent many afternoons upstairs with Netta, but he'd never been down to Justin's before, and he didn't seem especially impressed by what he saw. Perhaps when he looked around he sensed only the wages of sin.

"Can I get you something?" Yoyo asked after letting him in.

Justin expected him to ask for some water, or maybe a beer.

"I'll take a whiskey on the rocks."

Jonathan sat down comfortably on the couch to wait for his drink. He'd grown into his role over the years, Justin thought. He had some of his Elder George's presence, if not his charisma, which probably could not be learned. Was he happy he'd followed in the man's footsteps? Did he worry as much as Justin did about what his father would think of the life he'd made?

Justin asked Yoyo for the same and took a seat on the other couch. He wasn't sure what would happen now. Was he supposed to make some kind of confession? He'd more or less done that when he'd said everything out loud at Eddie's apartment, and he would have to do it again when he made the sworn statement that would be used for his plea agreement. He couldn't see what would be gained by repeating it all now, and he wasn't sure how much Jonathan would understand anyway. It seemed superfluous. Hadn't God heard everything the first time?

"Brother Justin," Jonathan said. "I was hoping I'd hear from you."

"My mother wanted me to call," Justin said.

"She's a good woman," Jonathan replied. "She's proud of you."

Justin didn't like the idea of his mother talking about him with Jonathan, even to express her pride.

"I want her to be happy. She thinks I'm on the right path now, and I want that to be true. But I can't pretend to believe something I don't believe, not if being on the right path means living honestly."

"You don't have to pretend anything," Jonathan assured him. "Let's just talk. Everything that passes between us stays between us."

Their drinks arrived, and they each took a long sip before Jonathan continued.

He started telling Justin about some kind of service he wanted to hold for him. He called it a "prison wake," as though part of Justin had died and would now be memorialized. He was vague on exactly what it would entail, except that it should take place right before Justin went away and wouldn't require any declaration of faith. All Justin had to do was show up at the appointed hour and leave himself open to the experience.

"It will be a good way for the community to say goodbye," Jonathan explained, as though Justin were still part of the community, still living down the block, sitting in a pew every Sunday morning. "It might help you to know that you aren't alone, that you've got people on the outside."

"Give me some time to think about it," Justin said, though he already knew what his answer would be. He had no intention of going back into that place.

"I don't have to tell you that you're not the first brother from the neighborhood to go away. I've spent a lot of time doing prison ministry. Maybe I can give you some sense of what to expect."

Justin was headed to a minimum-security lockup as part of the deal he'd worked out by saving the government the cost of a trial. He didn't think he'd have to worry about skinheads or shower rape or whatever else Jonathan was used to hearing at Rikers prayer groups, but he was happy to fill the time.

"I'd appreciate that."

"The biggest thing people tell me about isn't the fear of violence. It isn't the gangs. It isn't the bad food or the lack of privacy. It isn't even missing people outside. I hear about a loss of dignity. I hear about despair. When you're given a number and treated as nothing but that number, it's easy to think of yourself that way. When you live in a place designed to make you feel worthless, it's easy to do just that. But you're not a number, and you're not worthless. You are a child of God."

He'd obviously made this speech before, and he was good at it, but Justin didn't think it applied all that well in his case. Perhaps Jonathan recognized the thought somehow in Justin's expression, because he sat up suddenly and looked around the room, as though he'd only just noticed where he was.

"I must sound pretty silly warning a guy with a hundred million in the bank about feeling worthless."

Justin laughed.

"A little bit," he admitted.

"Well, I've got bad news for you," Jonathan said somewhat fiercely. "Where you're going, you're no better than any other nigger with a rap sheet." Justin had never heard Jonathan say the word in the thirty-five years they'd known each other, and he was visibly struck by it. Having produced the desired effect, Jonathan leaned back with a smile. "The good news is that in the house of God, you're no worse than one, either."

"I don't believe in God," Justin said simply.

"That's all right," Jonathan answered. "God still believes in you."

He smiled again, this time a bit sheepishly, as though he knew this was a weak response but couldn't quite break himself of the habit. For a moment it seemed that they were boys again, sitting in the back of the church while Jonathan's father preached.

Maybe it was that feeling that made Justin ask, "Are you seeing a lot of Terrance's mom?"

The smile left Jonathan's face.

"I come by and visit her on my usual rounds. I think she did right by coming back."

"It must be tough for her," Justin said. "Even worse than it is for my mom."

Jonathan nodded, and it seemed that this might be the end of the conversation, until he said, "I'm sorry about everything."

Somehow Justin knew right away what he was talking about, but as though he didn't he answered, "It's a sad story."

"That's not what I mean," Jonathan told him.

"I know it's not," Justin said.

Jonathan took a long sip of his drink.

"T told me himself," he said. "Swore me to secrecy. I think I was jealous of you two. Not that I was—not like that. You were the only friends I had. Then it seemed like you had something that I couldn't share with you. I felt excluded. So I told a few kids at school. Once I saw what was happening, I told my dad, so he'd make it stop. I didn't mean for him to tell your mothers, didn't mean for them to break you up."

"It was a long time ago," Justin said.

"After Terrance died, I spent a lot time thinking that was my fault. I was the reason they left town. I always told myself that things had turned out so well for you, that I'd actually done you a favor. But now maybe you see it differently."

"I don't regret getting out of the neighborhood," Justin said. "Whatever happened after that wasn't your fault."

"You're good to say that, whether you mean it or not."

"I mean it. What happened to Terrance, that's not your fault, either."

Jonathan was crying now, not dramatically, but a few stray tears dropping down his round, quiet face.

"Before I leave," Jonathan said, "I was going to ask you to say a prayer with me. I know it's just words to you, but it won't take long."

Both men stood, and Jonathan reached out for Justin's hands before closing his eyes to pray. Justin watched him, eyes open. It struck Justin then how different Jonathan really was from his father—as different as Justin was from his own—and perhaps it was this realization that made him consent to the wake.

He was scheduled to turn himself in on a Monday—November 2—and he agreed to submit to the ceremony the day before. That morning he found the sidewalk outside his building deserted. He felt an odd ambivalence about this fact. Two dozen photographers had been staking out the block when he'd first come home from jail wanting only to be left alone. He'd watched with relief as their ranks thinned after he'd made his plea and received his sentence, but their complete absence seemed to suggest that his story was over. For Justin himself the hard part was just beginning, but his role in the great public drama had played out. What happened from here would go unreported.

Tommy gave his usual nod into the rearview mirror before pulling into traffic. It was comforting how little he'd changed. If it weren't for their frequent discussions of logistical matters, Justin might have believed that Tommy was completely unaware of what was happening around him. Justin had asked him to stay on to look after Netta, and he'd promised to keep him on the payroll if anything should happen to her, but Tommy hadn't seemed to need any such guarantee. He would work so long as there was work to do. He drove as always with professional aggression, and they pulled up half an hour later outside the Denison, where Netta waited in the lobby. She came outside at the first sight of them, and Justin got out of the car to meet her.

She'd stopped talking about moving after Justin's arrest, but they'd both known that she'd be going back to Crown Heights as soon as he was gone, and he'd preferred to see her settled before then. He'd also wanted to protect her from the media horde on Fifth Avenue.

"How do you like it?" he asked.

"Just fine," she told him. "It's a nice place you made."

Justin took her hand, and they walked around the corner, down Franklin Avenue toward the Pathway. A large crowd waited outside, probably a hundred people, more than had filled the place in George's heyday. They all turned as Justin and Netta approached and, from the looks of curious anticipation, there could be no question that they'd been waiting for him. Justin recognized some of the people waiting—Mrs. Bradley, who'd lived downstairs in their old building on Park Place; the waitress from the diner where they'd gone for lunch after church when he was growing up. A few closer to his own age looked familiar, though he couldn't say why until he recognized in one face the features of a kid from his class at MS 61, a boy whose name he didn't remember, whom he hadn't seen in almost thirty years.

Justin's only request had been that this thing not be publicized, but he should have known it was too much to ask that Jonathan keep it to himself, that he not use it as an opportunity to fill his church. Justin was less disappointed in Jonathan than in himself for agreeing to this ordeal. His first thought was that all these people were there to watch his humiliation, to see him brought to his proper level. He scanned their faces skeptically, and he was surprised to find their expressions warm and sympathetic, with no hint of triumph or disdain. They all gave way as Justin and Netta approached, clearing a path through the church's front door.

Most of the pews inside were already full, and Justin realized there were even more people there than he'd first thought. There would hardly be room for them all. Two empty spots waited in the front row, and Justin and Netta walked up the center aisle as though in a wedding procession. In Pastor George's time, a full band had played with a choir, but where that had all stood there was only Jonathan's two sisters—Lisa and Linda, but Justin didn't remember which was which—one seated at the organ, the other standing in front of the microphone, gripping her tambourine. The moment that Justin and Netta took their places, the two women began to play. There was a rustling sound as everyone reached in unison for the lyric sheets in front of them, except for Netta and a few other women up front, who knew the words by heart. While the congregation sang, Jonathan emerged from a side door in purple vestments.

After the music, Jonathan welcomed the crowd in the name of the Lord. He acted as though he were used to having such an audience, as though all of these people filled his pews every week. He had a Bible in one hand, which he waved in front of himself while he spoke, in a gesture that might have been meant to ward something off. Eventually he opened the book, but he continued talking without looking down at the page.

"Jesus told this parable," he said. "A woman has ten silver coins, and she loses just one. Does she say, 'Well, I've still got my nine?'"

He paused expectantly, and the congregation called back to him: "No."

"She turns on the lights, and she tears up that house, looking for her one lost coin. And when she finds it, she calls up her friends, and she says, 'Praise God, I found my coin.'"

He put the Bible down still open on the lectern in front of him.

"For a few years now, since I took over as pastor, we've been making little improvements to this building. First it was a new paint job and new carpeting. Not long ago, we got this pulpit I'm standing behind. Just a few months ago, it was the air-conditioning, which we aren't thinking much about now, but it's going to be pretty nice come August again."

A murmur of assent passed through the church.

"After each of these changes, people come to me and say, 'Pastor, the church looks *nice*.' And I tell them, 'The church *does* look nice.'"

He laughed, as though to give the congregation permission to do the same, and they quickly obliged.

"But when I say the church looks nice, I'm not talking about a building with some new paint. I'm talking about all of you God-fearing people standing in front of me. Because the church is all of you."

He waited a moment for these words to make their impression.

"I'm going to tell you something you all probably suspected, though I've never said it before. Every one of these improvements was paid for by Brother Justin Price."

In the pews nearest Justin and Netta, a few people applauded, but Jonathan immediately spoke over them.

"The reason I never said this before is that Brother Justin was never here to listen. He's made a lot of contributions to this building, but that's not the same as giving yourself to the *church*. I don't want to say that we haven't been grateful for his gifts, but I can tell you honestly that I'm more grateful to have him here with us today. He'd given us nine coins, but it was just that one we were looking to find. We would have torn the whole house up to find it. Now here it is, and we're ready to praise God in thanks. To Jesus, what matters is not your presents *to* the church, it's your presence *in* the church."

There was more clapping, and this time Jonathan smiled to encourage it. Lisa or Linda even played a few notes of accompaniment, until most of the congregation was clapping along. Jonathan looked down from the pulpit at Justin as though at an old friend, and for the first time in his life Justin felt that this was just what Jonathan was.

"I'd like to ask my brother to come up here now," Jonathan said.

Justin should have been well prepared for this, having known that something like it was the purpose of their all being there, but he felt frozen in his pew. The entire church was looking at him now, waiting for him to walk up and take his rightful place. They'd all come just for this. He felt embarrassed—but what did he really have to feel embarrassed about? Everyone there knew exactly what he'd done. What would walking up in front of them change? In fact it was something more than embarrassment he felt. He felt fear. What had been up to now an abstraction struck him with great force: they were all there because in another day, he would be gone.

"Brother Justin," Jonathan called out, as though Justin's hesitance was a necessary part of the proceedings, "I know it's hard to take this step. But we are all here because of our love for you. And the love we have isn't a pin drop in the ocean compared to the love that God has for you. All you need to do to feel that love is to stand up here and accept it."

Justin had thought there'd been an understanding, that there wouldn't be any talk about accepting God's love or anything of the sort, that the only love he needed to accept was that of the community, but he could hardly do anything about that now. He turned away from Jonathan and saw his mother, who wasn't looking at him or at the pulpit, but straight up at the ceiling, as though she could see God sitting up there waiting for what came next. Through a great force of will, Justin moved himself out of the pew and into the aisle. As he did, the entire congregation applauded in support. He walked up the altar steps, and Jonathan came down from the pulpit to place his hands on Justin's shoulders. Justin felt a great buzzing in his ears, which wasn't the sound of the congregation or even the sound of his beating heart but something that combined the two and was also other than them.

"The King said unto them on his right hand, Come, ye blessed of my Father, inherit the kingdom prepared for you, for when I was imprisoned, you came unto me. And the righteous answered, saying, Lord, when did we see you imprisoned, and come unto you? And the King answered, as much as you have done it unto one of the least of my brothers, you have done it unto me."

Jonathan held him for another moment, before turning him toward the congregation. Lisa and Linda started to play, and the whole church sang to Justin, a song whose words he couldn't make out above the sound in his ears, though it was a song he remembered from his childhood. When the song was done, Jonathan released him, and Justin hurried back to his seat, where his mother stood smiling.

As they left the church and headed back up Franklin Avenue, Justin spotted a large billboard that he hadn't noticed while coming in the other direction. It showed the face of the man who'd schemed Eddie out of his money, and beside it the words *What would you change if you knew it was all going to end?* Justin had heard about all these billboards Eddie had ordered, but this was the first one he'd seen. Their sudden appearance a few weeks before had sparked a lot of online talk—so Blakeman had said—that Nash had gone into hiding but planned to show himself in time for the apocalypse.

Beside the words was a date: November 1. Today. Justin had forgotten, if he'd ever known it, that Nash had named this day for the end of the world. He laughed at the idea. Certainly for him, something was coming to an end. He wondered whether Netta would notice the billboard and make the connection, perhaps find some significance in it. But she was not looking up anymore. She was looking at her son laughing beside her, and she started to laugh with him, as though they were sharing a private joke.

As they approached the Denison and noticed the small crowd gathering outside, Justin assumed it had something to do with him. The morning after his mother's move, half a dozen websites had reported that Justin Price was giving up his apartment on the Upper East Side and spending his last weeks of freedom in Crown Heights. He'd sent out a press release correcting the record—his only public statement since his arrest—just to keep them from hounding her, and there hadn't been many reporters around after that, but it wouldn't have taken much to figure out that his mother was living there and that he was likely to spend his last day of freedom with her. Surely someone would want a picture. But as they approached, Justin saw just a mixed group of people from the neighborhood, and it didn't look like they'd been there long.

"What's going on?" Netta asked a woman on the outskirts of the crowd.

"Some white girl collapsed," the woman answered.

A few people near them now recognized Justin, and they instinctively made way for him, as though he commanded a natural authority. Perhaps they knew that he was the building's owner. He had no desire to get himself involved in whatever had happened, but he felt himself urged on. If he hadn't seen Lucy Waxworth in the neighborhood in recent weeks, he might not have recognized her. She didn't look much like the girl he'd met in Bridgehampton months before. She wore a thick mask of makeup and clothes that she must have put on the night before. She might have been a drunk laid out on the street. She was conscious but obviously confused.

"Don't just watch her," Netta told the crowd. "Someone call an ambulance."

"The ambulance will take ten minutes. We can get her there faster."

This came from Tommy, who had joined them on the sidewalk without Justin's noticing it. After a moment of thought, Justin agreed.

"We'll take her," he told Netta. "I'll come get you as soon as I can."

Netta nodded, in full agreement with the plan. They were eating a last dinner that night, and he would be free in plenty of time.

After they'd loaded Lucy into the back of the Range Rover, Tommy punched "Brooklyn Hospital" into the GPS. Reading the words from the back seat, Justin knew that he didn't want to take Lucy there. He didn't even want to see the place.

"Take us to New York General."

"Are you sure?"

It was part of Tommy's job to question Justin's judgment once in a while, but Justin waved him on. Though Lucy was disoriented, she was still awake, and she wasn't in any obvious pain. Given the waiting times at the Brooklyn Hospital emergency room, she might well see a doctor sooner if they headed straight into Manhattan.

As they did, it occurred to Justin that he ought to let her husband know where they were taking her, though he had a sense that they weren't together anymore. He'd never seen Waxworth in the neighborhood, and he couldn't imagine him letting this become of her. Every few minutes she opened her eyes and muttered something. Once, she looked at Justin with what seemed an expression of recognition before turning her head and closing her eyes again. Was she on drugs? She hadn't seemed that sort in the brief time they'd spent together, given her penchant for early morning runs.

Eventually he hit on the idea of calling Blakeman.

"Still a free man," Blakeman said when he answered the phone. They already had plans to spend the night drinking together after Netta went to bed.

"Are you in touch with Sam Waxworth since you fired him?" Justin asked.

"I can't say that I've spoken to him recently," Blakeman responded. "But I've got his number if you'd like it. You want to spend your last night of freedom talking sample variance?"

"Tell him that his wife is on her way to the New York General emergency room."

"You're going to have to give me more than that to work on," Blakeman told him. When Justin briefly explained what was going on, Blakeman laughed. "One day this Good Samaritan routine is going to get you into trouble."

They got lucky with the traffic, and Tommy pulled the car in front of the ER less than half an hour after they'd gotten Lucy into it. They brought her inside, and Tommy sat with her while Justin explained the situation to a woman at reception.

"My friend collapsed. I think she may have taken something."

The woman didn't seem overly impressed. There were probably a couple of ODs on every shift, and there was a drunk man with a bloody lip being walked in by a cop right behind them. Still, it didn't take long for an orderly to appear and help Lucy onto a rolling bed, which he pushed through a pair of automatic double doors that read "Authorized Personnel."

When Lucy was gone, Justin sent Tommy back to Crown Heights to pick up Netta and bring her to the apartment.

"I'm going to wait until her husband shows up," he said. "But I'll be home in plenty of time."

He'd been waiting about ten minutes when a nurse appeared with a clipboard and handed Justin a form to fill out.

"I'm not sure how much I can tell you," he said. "I don't know her very well. I just happened to be there when she collapsed."

"Anything you give us would be a help."

He worked his way quickly through the form, leaving most of it blank. He put in Sam Waxworth's name as a contact, though he had no further information to give. When he got to a part about recent traveling, he wrote down that she'd made a weekend trip to eastern Long Island. He wasn't sure this really qualified, but writing something made him feel useful.

After handing back the form, he sat in the waiting room for another forty-five minutes, reading a magazine and wondering when Waxworth would arrive. He was acutely aware that his last hours with his mother were ticking away. Every time the automatic doors opened, he looked up attentively, as did nearly everyone else— hoping either to be called inside or for news about someone already there. Because of this, he was watching carefully when Eddie emerged in his EMT uniform. It seemed strange that he would come out this door while on the job. Maybe his shift had just ended. He seemed, in his way, more troubled than the civilians in the waiting room. They had not seen each other since that afternoon at Eddie's apartment, and though they had spoken several times on the phone, Justin realized now how badly he'd wanted to see him in the flesh before he went away. When Eddie finally spotted him, he nodded in recognition, as though completely unsurprised. By his manner, he might have come out into the waiting room looking for him.

Justin put down the magazine, stood up, and instinctively wrapped his arms around Eddie.

"It's Frank," Eddie said. After a moment, as though explaining himself to a stranger, he said, "My father."

Justin held him closer, and Eddie tucked his head between Justin's shoulder and his neck. How many times over the years had Justin wished for this closeness? Eddie started to let out great sobs, and Justin wondered what the other people in the waiting room were making of the sight—a uniformed EMT, presumably still on duty, weeping into the arms of another man. Some people turned their heads in a show of discretion, but others showed no such compunction, and the drunk man with the bleeding lip started to laugh at them.

What happened to Frank, Justin wanted to ask, but it didn't seem that Eddie was capable of telling him.

"It's going to be all right," he said instead, though this was one thing Justin knew by now could not possibly be true.

5.

Margo was reading in her room when she heard a knock on her door. She ignored it, and a moment later, her mother appeared.

Since Justin's arrest, they'd occupied the same house, taken their turns looking after Frank, but Margo had avoided being alone with her mother or speaking to her more than their shared responsibilities required. She'd learned most of the details of the situation by talking with Eddie or reading the paper or listening to Kit try to explain things to her father. This last Kit had done once in great detail, as though honesty required it, though she must have understood how little Frank would absorb, and that what he did absorb he wouldn't remember. By now it was clear that he wasn't getting better.

"Can we talk?" Kit asked.

"Do we have to?"

"I know you're angry with me. But we need to work through some things."

One might almost have thought that she wanted to air her feelings—regret over what she'd done, fear about what she had now to do—but Margo knew her mother well enough to know that there must be some practicality to discuss. Still, this represented a kind of overture. Logistics were an intimate matter to Kit. They struck to the heart of her. If one

could find a way into her mother's *sanctum sanctorum*, Margo sometimes thought, one would see atop the altar a date book, a flight schedule, a balance sheet.

"I'll be going away very soon," she continued, as though she were
traveling for work or spending a week in Vail. Margo remembered
all the euphemisms they'd used while Eddie was in the army. That
seemed like a dress rehearsal for what they needed to talk around
now. "I've got to make arrangements for your father."

Margo wasn't sure what needed to be arranged. She would stay
with Frank until her mother's release, after which she would figure
out what to do next.

"It's just a few months," she said. "I can handle it."

"You don't need to take all this on yourself."

"What's the alternative?"

"There's a place for him at Mary Manning Walsh."

Margo couldn't believe what she was hearing. Once she'd learned
the real reason for the visit from the men in suits, she'd given up the
idea that her mother might put her father away.

"We don't need to send him to a nursing home. If he gets to be too
much, I'll hire help."

"Don't you want to get on with your life?"

For the first time since coming into Margo's room, Kit sounded
like her old self.

"I can go back to school in January, after you get out."

She could, but she knew that she would not. She imagined herself
in forty years being like her father—a distinguished figure in her
field who was nonetheless haunted by the realization that she had
not done her real work, that she had wasted all her time. She didn't
even know what her real work was, but she knew it wasn't teaching
Byron to undergraduates. She already had so many things that she
regretted. She didn't want to become one of those people who relived
decisions made decades before.

"The house is going on the market," Kit said.

"We already talked about this."

"Not in January. Right away. The government is seizing it to pay off my fine. Both houses, actually, but they've got to sell this one first because—well, because if they don't, the bank will foreclose on it anyway. If there's money left over after Bridgehampton sells, it will mostly go to attorneys' fees. You have to find your own place to stay, and I need to put your father somewhere. Medicare will pay for Mary Manning Walsh." After a moment, she added, "Just until I get back."

This was utter bullshit. If Frank went into a facility, he would never come out. He might not survive until Kit's release. If he did, she'd find a reason to leave him there. It would probably even be a good reason. He's happier where he is, she'd say. He belongs in a place that can give him the help he needs. She might actually be right about these things, but was it really the kind of decision you made by carefully weighing the alternatives?

"Let me think about it," Margo said.

Never had she responded in such a way when faced with Kit's plans. It had never before seemed that she had any say in the matter. She waited for Kit to tell her as much now.

"All right," Kit said. "But we don't have much time to decide."

Margo made an appointment to see Ted Grable the next day. She wasn't sure exactly what to tell him, but she was confident they could work something out. He'd always been accommodating, and there would be a fair amount of money freed up now that she wasn't going back to school. Somehow she convinced herself that he would be happy with the news—after all, she meant to get a real job—but when she explained her plans he nodded grimly, and she realized that seven years of living expenses was now showing itself to be a dead loss investment. He listened politely while she described the family's situation, though he must have known nearly all of it already.

She finished, and she waited for him to respond, though she hadn't asked any question or even proposed a way ahead.

"This money was not intended for your parents," he told her. "Your grandfather gave them plenty. The point of establishing a trust was to make sure there was something left for you and Edward when you became adults."

He said this rather sharply, as though to indicate that recent events had proven the wisdom of such precaution.

"I'm an adult now," Margo replied. "I'm twenty-nine years old."

"Your grandfather wanted to be sure that you got your start in life on your own steam. He didn't want you dependent."

"That's all fine in theory, but my family—*his* family—is dependent on me right now."

"This is an unusual situation," Grable acknowledged. "I don't want you to think I'm unsympathetic. Your mother and I have known each other for a very long time. But I wouldn't be doing my duty as a trustee if I let that affect my decision. Spending income from the trust on your parents' day-to-day expenses runs completely counter to your grandfather's intentions. If circumstances were different, I might advance a loan, but their financial picture isn't likely to change in the near future. I know you don't want to hear this, but I think your mother is right about finding someplace for your father until she can get them on sustainable footing herself."

"So there's nothing you can do?"

Grable let out a long sigh.

"In a few years, the principle will turn over to you, and you'll be free of me. You can spend all the money on your parents. You can spend it on yourself. You can throw it away if the spirit moves you."

He added this as a kind of flourish, and it wasn't clear whether he meant such a pointed allusion to Eddie, but the possibility set something off in Margo.

"My father is going to be in the ground by then."

She said it only because it seemed the most powerful rhetorical weapon at hand, but once it was out of her mouth, she knew it was true, and she thought she might cry in front of this man she'd known her entire life but had never seen express the slightest emotion. She fought the impulse violently. Tears would have somehow confirmed that she was a child who couldn't be allowed to have her way.

"The income from the trust will cover your rent on a one-bedroom apartment, plus reasonable living expenses," Grable said after giving her a moment to calm herself. He spoke like a judge rendering a verdict, and Margo understood that their meeting was coming to an end. "If you want to live with your parents, the trust will pay your share on a two-bedroom apartment, but it won't pay for all of it."

As she left the office, Margo wasn't sure what she was going to do next, except that she still wasn't going to let her mother put her father away. She walked crosstown from Seventh Avenue, and she headed uptown on Madison. She wanted to ask someone for advice. Usually when she felt this need, she called Amy, but they'd never spoken about money before. There had never been any need. It wasn't that she was embarrassed, just that she couldn't imagine Amy being able to help. For the first time since walking out of that room at the Cue, she thought it would be nice to speak with Sam Waxworth. Certainly he'd have an opinion on the matter, and he'd work it out dispassionately, which is what she happened to need right now.

She considered calling Eddie, but she didn't know how he'd take it. She was not without resentment toward him, but also not without sympathy. While Kit seemed to blame him for the whole situation, Margo mostly blamed Kit, and she didn't want to remind Eddie of their hardship for no good reason. She thought of Grable's remark about giving her money away. In the past, he'd always held Eddie up as an example of fiscal discipline because he hadn't spent any income from the trust. Now he was barely making rent on the Lower East Side, and he'd shown little interest in helping their parents. She'd spoken to him a few times since Justin's arrest, and she was sure that he'd help her, but she wasn't the one who needed the help. There ought to be some transitive property by which help could be passed along.

And maybe there was.

By the time she got home, she'd worked it all out. With a bit of online searching that afternoon, she found several acceptable one bedrooms within Grable's price range. That evening, while Frank dozed in the library with a book in his lap, she told Kit what she meant to do.

"I'm going to rent an apartment and move Dad in. Grable said he'll pay for one bedroom, but he didn't say anything about who sleeps there. I can crash on the couch and look after Dad until you get out. Then the place will be all yours."

"Where will you live?" Kit asked.

"With Eddie," Margo said, as though it were obvious. She hadn't asked him yet, but she was sure that he'd agree. "He's got a bedroom sitting empty. I'll just stay for a few months while I find a job and save enough to get my own place. Once I'm making some money of my own, I can use the income from the trust to help you with Dad."

Though neither of them said it, they both understood the offer being made—Margo would support Kit and Frank together, but if Frank was sent away, Kit would be on her own. Kit took some time with the idea, as her pride seemed to demand, but Margo was sure she'd agree.

The place was on Second Avenue in the upper nineties, and the lease started at the beginning of November. The movers came early on the morning of the first, and Margo told them to get started downstairs, so that they wouldn't disturb Frank. Before they made their way up, she would wake him and remind him what was happening that day. She'd spoken to him about the new apartment several times, and he'd always taken it well enough, but days or hours later he would say something that made clear he had no idea they were leaving the house. For him the move was an abstraction, one that would not alter his daily life.

Standing in the doorway of the library, watching the men pack up her father's books, Margo realized that she too had treated this day as an abstraction. She couldn't believe that she would not spend another afternoon reading in this room. Most of her parents' possessions would be sold at auction, and the auction house was paying for storage until Kit could go through them all. Margo's job had been to set aside a few things to bring with them. She'd marked off several pieces of furniture and some of her parents' clothes, but she wished now that she'd gone through these books. She had consigned them all to storage because she didn't think Frank would have any use for them. It hadn't occurred to her that she might take them for herself. She had nowhere to put them now, but after all they represented his legacy to her. She felt a loss that seemed to stand in for the greater loss that could not possibly be reckoned.

She didn't have time to stand there watching. She had to face her own room, decide what she was bringing along. She'd been so busy with the rest of the house that she'd managed to put this task off, as though she were only incidentally involved in this change. Whatever she didn't take would be sold as well—or, more likely, just thrown away.

When she got back to her room, she walked to the window and looked down at the street. No view on earth was more familiar to her, and in a matter of hours it would be lost forever. She imagined walking down this block someday, looking up at this window, and seeing a girl like the girl she once was, looking back down at her. She imagined the vertigo she would feel as she was propelled into the past. Even now she felt that vertigo, compounded by the fact that she was racing into the future in order to experience it. She tried to remain in this feeling. Perhaps this day would come to stand in her life as the Dodgers' departure from Brooklyn stood in her father's, as the moment she came to understand that some losses were irrevocable. Such sharp dividing lines were rare. She felt almost lucky to have one.

Would she try to hold on to all of this when it was gone? Would she turn into someone like her father, who spent half his life pining over a lost childhood? She didn't want to be that kind of person. She wanted to look to the future. She wanted to live the life she'd been given.

After she finally turned away from the window, she started going slowly through her closet, where she took her clothes one at a time off their hangers, putting them either into a large duffel for the movers or a pile for Goodwill. She'd just about finished when she heard her father yelling downstairs. He'd gotten by her while she was staring out the window. She hurried down and found him facing off with one of the movers.

It hadn't seemed necessary to warn the men about her father's condition. Managing him since Kit went away hadn't been as difficult as she'd anticipated. Even the strangest things he said had an odd logic to them. He sounded not as though he'd lost his grip on reality but as though he had access to that distant star from which we'd all come and must one day return. Listening to him, she felt as Yeats must have felt while shuffling his tarot deck, as Merrill felt beside the Ouija board. Of course it helped that she had to do it only for a fixed time, not the rest of her life.

It occasionally depressed her when he talked about the big book as though he had no idea that it was never going to get finished, or when he asked where Kit had gone. The first few times, she'd just told him the truth, but a few hours later, he was asking again, and she got tired of speaking the facts out loud, so she began to put his questions off. This agitated him, as he was agitated now, fighting with the moving man. She tried at such moments not to sound like an exasperated parent, which only made him more agitated. This time she was able to get him upstairs and into his office, where she sat him down in front of some baseball highlights. She thought she could safely leave him there while she went back to her room.

As she finished emptying her closet, she realized that she was the only one left to say goodbye to the house. It came to her then that she had been wrong to think of this day as a great dividing line. You couldn't plan your endings out in advance. Often you couldn't even recognize them when they happened. If her family was indeed over, it had ended some time ago, when Kit went off to prison, or when Frank fell down in the backwoods, or on the day of the Ballpark Incident, when Margo lost faith in her father. It had ended when Eddie went off to war. Herman Nash's great mistake was not to believe that the world would come to an end, but to think that it wasn't ending every day. Everything was always ending, and nothing simply ended outright.

After the closet, she turned to her dresser, and she worked her way down its three drawers. In the bottom one, she found the fortune cookie fortune she'd saved from her Chinese lunch with Sam. *You are about to embark on a great adventure.* She'd hardly thought about him since Justin's arrest. She'd been surprised to read of his firing from the *Interviewer*—surprised not so much by what he'd been doing as by his continued existence. She tossed the fortune into a garbage bag. She did the same with a layer of movie tickets and theater programs and class handouts before arriving at her poetry notebooks.

There were about a dozen of them, and nearly every page of every one was full. For six or seven years, from around when she'd started reading poetry until she left for college, she'd written in one of these books every day. Sometimes she'd just written stray lines, not poems or even the beginnings of poems but signposts that might point the way to some place where a real poem might one day get written. As she got older, she got more systematic. She set formal goals for herself. She imitated poets she was reading.

She pulled the first book off the top and opened it. This was the last one she'd worked in, the one she'd put away when she'd left for Yale, so it was only half-full at most. She turned to a page at random, and she read.

> We came this far, in part, for this:
> To sing availability of thought
> Long wished available; to wish
> A name upon the passing moment caught
>
> Within our thinking's web; to rush
> The moment, yet unnamed, along; to leave
> Our names unwatched, their letters brushed
> By whispers of analphabetic breeze;
>
> To grieve the moment's loss not overmuch—
> As if the whispers were a kind of name;
> To sing our silence song; to touch
> Our tongues against the sacerdotal flame;
> To touch our tongues against the flaming star:
> For this, in part, we came this far.

For a period she'd been reading a lot of Richard Wilbur, which had sent her in a formalist direction. She's experimented with sonnets, alternating tetrameter and pentameter. She found the result now a bit willfully obscure, maybe even precious, but she wasn't embarrassed, as she'd expected that she would be. Why had she ever given this up? How could she have thought that she didn't actually love poetry? She read through more of the pages, and with each one she became more convinced that this was what she was supposed to be doing with her life.

She would have to start almost entirely over. It would take a long time, maybe years, before anything really worthwhile came of it. Perhaps that day would never come. But she needed to take that risk. She would leap without knowing what lay on the other side. She'd get a job in a bookstore or waiting tables somewhere, and she'd write. Not for her father's sake, not for Richard's, but for her own.

She looked up from this reverie to find one of the movers—the largest one, who seemed to be in charge—standing in the hall outside her door, slightly out of breath, waiting for her to take notice of him.

"We're pretty much done downstairs," he said. "What would you like us to start on next?"

"You can do that room," Margo told him, pointing in the direction of her father's office. "Just give me a second."

As she walked down the hall to get Frank and take him upstairs, she imagined that she'd have to explain everything over again. She was starting to realize how hard the transition would be. He'd wake up every morning in the new apartment and ask her where they were, when they were going home. Before she opened the door, she heard the TV playing World Series highlights for probably the fourth or fifth time since she'd placed him in front of them, and when she walked in she looked instinctively at the screen, so she didn't immediately register the condition of the room. Dozens of books had been taken down from the shelves and left on the floor. Some were in neat piles, others just thrown about. He might have been trying to pack his things. She found the idea oddly moving, though on further consideration it seemed more likely that he'd been pulling things down in a kind of tantrum.

She went upstairs to her parents' bedroom, which was also a mess. Her father's clothes had been taken out of the closet and tossed onto the bed, along with more books. There was still no sign of him.

On her way downstairs, she ran into the men bringing boxes and packing paper into Frank's office.

"Have any of you seen my father?" she asked.

"Not since he went out," one of them said.

"Went out? When was that?"

"I'd say an hour ago. He went out with a bag in his hand."

"Why didn't you tell me?"

This was a stupid question. Frank was a grown man, and Margo hadn't asked them to look after him. She hadn't thought to worry that he might run off.

Plenty of times over the past month she'd put him in front of a ball game. He'd happily spent entire evenings that way. But all the packing had obviously upset him. This development annoyed more than worried her. He'd lived here for forty years, and his long-term memory was still intact. He'd find his way back. If anything, she'd have to worry about his finding his way here for months to come. What bothered her was what the mover had said about Frank carrying a bag when he left, as though he meant to run away somewhere.

Before heading out, she gave the movers her number and asked them to call if her father showed up. She turned uptown at Madison, retracing one of the walks they often took. She walked for a few blocks before she admitted that she was wasting her time. He'd already been gone more than an hour, and he could have gone anywhere. She wasn't going to find him. She considered calling the police, but that seemed a bit dramatic under the circumstances. He didn't have dementia, exactly. He didn't have a history of getting lost. He wasn't a danger to himself or anyone else. He'd just gone out without telling her. Was that something you were supposed to call 911 about?

He'd work his way back to the house before long, having forgotten why he'd ever left, and it would only make things more difficult if she wasn't there when he arrived. All she was doing was wasting time that she needed to spend packing.

She returned to the house, where the men were still at their work. She didn't ask, but she could tell from their chastened expressions that Frank had not returned. She went back to her room. She had plenty more packing to do, but she found herself picking up the notebook she'd left on the bed. She turned to the first empty page, as though she might convert the anxiety she was feeling now into something there. She was so out of practice. She didn't know how to begin. She was still looking at the blank page when her phone buzzed with a call from Eddie, probably checking in to see how the move had gone. She should have called him herself, but she hadn't wanted to make too much of the thing. She was relieved to have an excuse to tell him what had happened.

"I've got Dad," he said abruptly before she could start.

Had Frank wandered his way down to the Lower East Side looking for his son? It didn't seem possible. She didn't think he had any idea where Eddie lived.

"Where is he?"

"New York General."

"What happened?"

"He walked in front of a cab. He was fine in the ambulance, but then his oxygen levels started to drop."

Eddie's voice trailed off. He sounded like he was crying, something he didn't do in the way that she and Frank did, so she knew it was serious. Right away she started crying, too. It was her fault. She'd said that she could take care of him. She'd insisted on it. And she'd let him walk into traffic.

"Is he all right?"

"I don't know," Eddie said. "I don't think so. You need to get over here."

She ran straight out the door, this time without telling the movers anything. She didn't pack a bag; she didn't even put down the notebook or throw on a coat. She got lucky finding a cab, but the traffic going crosstown was excruciating. Several times she decided to get out and run, but right before she did, it picked up for half a block.

In the hospital lobby Eddie waited in his EMT uniform, which she'd never seen before. She didn't recognize him right away.

"Where is he?" she asked when he stood to greet her.

"Still in the emergency room." He sounded much calmer than he had on the phone. "He has a pulmonary embolism. His hip and his leg are both shattered, and something got into his bloodstream and his lungs. They're intubating now. Once they're done they'll bring him up to the ICU."

He led Margo into a staff elevator, up to intensive care, where the receptionist looked through a file and told them it would be at least an hour before they could see the patient. They sat together in the reception area for about ten minutes, neither saying anything. Margo was still in shock, and Eddie looked completely exhausted.

"Why don't you get some sleep?" Margo said. "I imagine you've got a nook somewhere in this place? This will probably be a long process, and we'll need to take turns."

Eddie hesitated before nodding and standing up.

"Call me if there's any news," he said.

Alone, Margo wished that she'd thought to bring a book—a real book, not her high school poetry. She'd have a lot of hours to get through here. She began reciting to herself. *I felt a Funeral, in my Brain, / And Mourners to and fro / Kept treading - treading - till it seemed / That Sense was breaking through.* This—not those books that the men had packed up today—was her father's legacy to her. She wanted to think that he was reciting something, too, whatever he was going through right now.

She'd been waiting for about an hour when she checked back at reception, where they told her that it would still be a while.

"If you want to go out for some air," the nurse said, "you've certainly got time for that."

Margo decided to get a cup of coffee—a real cup, not the sludge at reception. Maybe also something to eat. While she was at it, she would call the movers and tell them to go ahead without her.

At the shop in the hospital's lobby, she ordered a large coffee and picked out a muffin. She was nearing the front of the line for the register when Sam Waxworth walked through the hospital doors with a bouquet of bodega flowers in his hand. He seemed to have wandered in from an entirely different story.

"What are you doing here?" she asked.

He was startled into silence before saying, "Lucy was just admitted."

"What happened?"

"She's got Lyme disease," Sam said. "They're going to give her an antibiotic drip, and the doctors think she'll be all right."

"That's good to hear," Margo said.

"She hasn't been feeling well for a long time," Sam said, looking curiously pleased. "The truth is that she hasn't been herself for months."

He said it almost as though Margo had pulled some kind of trick, taken advantage of him by making him compare her to Lucy when she wasn't at her best. Margo could see the narrative he was already putting together, in which his wife's illness had made her throw him out, and he had sought solace in the arms of another woman, before rushing back to her side. If this was the story that he and Lucy needed to tell about these months in New York, that was just fine with her.

"Well, I'm glad she's on the mend."

"We're going back to Madison," Sam added, as though the news might be painful for Margo to hear. "I'm going to write a book." He seemed almost ready to walk away when something occurred to him. "What brings you here?"

Margo felt very strongly that she didn't want to stand in the hospital lobby talking with Sam Waxworth about her father. She wanted to bring her coffee and her muffin back upstairs and wait.

"I'm visiting Eddie," she said. "He works here now, as an EMT."

They stood in silence, both aware that they had nothing left to say to each other.

"Tell Frank I said hello," Sam told her before they parted ways.

Back in the ICU, the nurse at reception said that her father had a room and she could see him now. She felt a surge of relief, followed by guilt. She should have stayed. She didn't want to think that he'd been alone even for a moment when she could have been with him. She followed a nurse around the corner and down a long hallway.

"It might be a little jarring to see his condition," the nurse said before opening the door to his room. "The important thing to know is that he's not in any pain."

Inside Margo saw only a curtain that was pulled around the bed, but she could hear all the noises—the beep of some machine measuring something, a pumping sound that she imagined was the oxygen being sent into his lungs. Rather than pulling the curtain back, the nurse walked Margo around it, so that they were all wrapped inside.

"Mr. Doyle," the nurse said, "your daughter Margo is here to visit you."

She said it loudly, but in a friendly conversational tone, as though he were sitting up, awake and responsive, but a bit hard of hearing. Perhaps it was just what nurses were trained to do when they came into a room, because he was clearly unconscious, and he made no movement in response to her words. He was laid out with his eyes closed, the tube that ran down his throat keeping his mouth open in a surprised O. Tape around his cheeks and chin held the tube in place. The light marks on his neck seemed to be something internal, perhaps caused by the tube going down, but there were more serious bruises on his face. The lower half of his body, which was where Margo had been made to understand the real damage had been done, was covered in blankets, and the mound underneath them did not look like a human form. It snaked around in stomach-churning ways. At least the feet sticking up at the bottom of the bed in their hospital-issue socks with the traction on the bottom—as though he were going to be walking anywhere in them—looked like human appendages. His arms rested lightly beside him and his chest, visible beneath the half-open hospital gown, moved up and down in rhythm with the oxygen machine. He looked so thin. Her father had always been a thick man, almost Falstaffian. It was the only appropriate shape for someone of his voraciousness. She didn't know when he'd gotten so small.

There was a light knock on the door, and a woman not much older than Margo walked in, pulling the curtain from around the bed.

"I'm Dr. Drezler," she said.

"Nice to meet you," Margo answered. "I'm Frank's daughter."

The doctor repeated much of what Eddie had told her about the broken bones and the embolism.

"We've got this tube in to help with his breathing, and we're dripping a lot of morphine now, which should keep him knocked out. He won't be in any pain. Unfortunately, there isn't much we can do beyond that, besides wait to see if he can clear this thing out. That could be tough at his age, in his condition."

"And what if he can't clear it out?" Margo asked.

"It's hard to say how long he can go on like this. Maybe days, maybe weeks."

She didn't say months, Margo noted. It certainly seemed unlikely that he would make it until her mother got home. Kit would probably get some kind of compassion leave, but that would take a day or two, and it didn't seem certain that Frank would last even that long.

The doctor pulled a chart from the foot of the bed and made a few notes in it.

"Keep talking to him," she told Margo before leaving the room. "It makes a difference."

When she was gone, Margo sat in the chair beside the bed and took her father's hand. She wanted to talk to him, but she didn't know what to say. Mostly she wanted him to know that she didn't want him to die. She'd spoken with Eddie about taking shifts, but she was not going anywhere. The moment she got up, even for the bathroom, he would go—she was sure of it. For now she would stay right where she was. Tomorrow or the next day or the day after that, she would begin her new life, the life in which she became whatever she was supposed to be without him, but for now she needed him to know that he wasn't alone.

"I'm here," she said. "I'm here."

After another half hour, she opened the book and started to write. She knew what she was putting on the page wasn't any good, but that didn't matter. There was a brief stirring beside her, and she thought she saw Frank's head turn slightly toward her. His eyes fluttered as though he was coming awake, though she knew this wasn't likely.

"I'm here," she said again. "I'm here."

She sat still with the pen in her hand, poised over the page. There was so much she wanted to say, but it would all have to wait. It could get written down someday, if she had the strength for it. For the time being she could only bring out the same two words.

"I'm here," she said. "I'm here. I'm here."

6.

The week after Waxworth submitted his proposal, he got a text from Matthew Penty, the *Reverberator*'s reporter, who had a few last questions for his piece. Waxworth was happy to get the thing moving. Craig didn't want to send the proposal to publishers until after the profile landed, and Waxworth wanted his book sold as soon as possible.

He went out for a walk while they spoke. Leaving the apartment, he felt almost wistful about the smell. He couldn't say he was going to miss it, but he imagined he'd think of it often in the years to come. As he escaped his block, he felt himself slowly unwinding. He remembered getting lost in these streets in his first days in New York, before he'd met the Doyles, before he'd taken his life off track. It felt like a very long time ago. He'd been filled with all of the possibility that comes from being in a new place, with a new job. He felt this again now, but in reverse—he was on the verge of going back home, having somehow achieved his goals after all.

"Thanks for taking the time to talk with me this morning," Penty said when Waxworth called. "This should only take a couple of minutes. I was finishing up my draft when I got an email from a reader who raised some issues. I was hoping you might be able to respond."

Waxworth laughed.

"Some of my readers are pretty tough. But I'm happy to give it a try."

"To begin with, he's identified about two dozen instances of self-plagiarism on *Quantified World*."

Waxworth stopped in the middle of the block.

"What does that mean?"

"Quoting previously published work without proper attribution."

He made it sound like a grave offense.

"It's possible that I've repeated myself a few times," Waxworth allowed. "How many truly original thoughts do any of us have?"

"These accusations go a little ways beyond that. My source claims that you habitually present items from your personal blog as new work."

Waxworth knew he had to tread carefully.

"That seems like an exaggeration."

"So you admit that you did some repurposing?"

"No, I don't admit anything. I'm just saying that—Can we go off the record for a moment?"

"If you think that's necessary."

"I wasn't really prepared for an interrogation this morning. I didn't want to get into it, but I've got a family emergency going on."

"I'm sorry the timing is bad for you, but I'm working against a tight deadline here. If you've got anything to say, I'd like to hear it now. Otherwise I'm going to have to run with what I've got."

Waxworth couldn't decide how much trouble he was actually in. Penty's source noted two dozen instances, which seemed about right. He'd written around a hundred posts for the *Interviewer*, which made this an error rate of almost one in four. Put that way, it sounded pretty bad. It would be embarrassing to have this included in the profile, but he didn't think it would be fatal. He hadn't known the rules. No one had told him he couldn't borrow from himself. They'd add proper attribution to the posts, or else just take them down. His best bet was to go at things head-on, acknowledge some mistakes, and try to get the conversation back to the rest of his work.

"I can talk a little bit."

"So what do you have to say?"

"There probably are some places where I relied on previously published work, and I should have made that clear. The truth is that I'm still pretty new at all of this. I'm going to talk with my editors about fixing the problem."

"My source suggests it was a little more systematic than that, and I have to say I find his evidence compelling. He sent me cached versions of the original posts—all of which you took down—and he's highlighted the overlaps. It's quite substantial."

"Who is this source?"

"He'd like to remain anonymous."

"How am I supposed to respond if I can't even face my accuser? The guy's probably just angry because I didn't like one of his Teeses."

"I see your point," Penty said calmly. "It's tough to know what motivates whistleblowers. But in this case, he's given me a good deal of objective evidence, and I think the story has news value for my readers."

"What news value? I stole from *myself*? That's newsworthy? My old blog had a few dozen followers. I wanted to share some of it with a bigger audience. Who exactly is the victim here?"

"My source also identified about a dozen instances of outright plagiarism."

"That I absolutely deny."

Penty paused as though reading over some notes.

"A post from May 15 used two lines substantially similar to a May 14 article in the *Herald*. A post from June 23 used three lines that were substantially similar to a June 21 article, also in the *Herald*. A post from July 1 used two lines substantially similar to a June 30 article, that one from the *Post*. I can run through the others if you want."

Waxworth didn't know exactly which articles he was talking about, but it sounded true. He relied so much on the *Herald*'s reporting—he'd always been clear about that—and it had sometimes seemed easier just to use their words. The underlying story was a kind of foundation on which his real work was built. What was the point of doctoring sentences to give the superficial appearance of originality?

"'Plagiarism' seems a little harsh as a description in these cases. It's just a few lines."

"So you do admit to lifting work without attribution?"

"I admit that it's possible that over the course of writing a hundred posts in a very short time I failed to cite some sources adequately. I do a lot of reading for these posts, and I take a lot of notes, and it's possible that a quote just got separated from its source. I'm glad to have these examples, so I can fix them. If you send me the details, I can check them against my work."

"I appreciate your openness to resolving this."

"No problem at all. Really, you're doing me a favor by bringing this to my attention. I'm just not sure how interesting all this sausage-making is going to be to your readers. There's nothing nefarious here."

As soon as he was off the phone, Waxworth headed for the train. He needed to get into the office. Blakeman would have a plan for damage control. The important thing was to explain the problem to him properly. Waxworth spent the ride into Manhattan practicing his presentation. But when he walked off the elevator and saw the look on Emily's face, he knew that word had already spread, and he knew he was in trouble.

"Blakeman's waiting for you in the Cube," she said.

The Cube was the *Interviewer*'s conference room, the office's only enclosed space. In keeping with the principle of open design, its walls were transparent glass, so anyone in the office could see what was happening within. As Waxworth approached, Blakeman looked through papers on the table, studiously avoiding eye contact. Even when Waxworth knocked on the door, Blakeman barely looked up to wave him inside.

"Have a seat," he said, more seriously than Waxworth had heard him say anything in the six months they'd known each other.

Waxworth sat down across the table from him. Over Blakeman's shoulder he could see some staff members moving their laptops closer to the Cube to get a better look.

"I guess I don't have to run through the whole bill of goods," Blakeman said. "I'll just ask whether you have anything to say in your defense."

Couldn't the apportioning of blame be done some other time? He was perfectly willing to take responsibility, but right now they needed a plan for how to proceed.

"The stuff he's calling plagiarism is about ten sentences. I linked to the articles I was quoting. It's not like I was trying to pull one over on anyone. You knew I was using the *Herald* to come up with ideas. You suggested it. Sometimes I would cut and paste the article into my file, just so I wouldn't have to stare at a blank screen. No question I should have been more careful about rewording things. It was sloppy, but it wasn't malicious. I'll be much more careful in the future."

Blakeman nodded, and Waxworth thought he might be convinced.

"You've got a point about all that. It wouldn't look so bad if it weren't for all this shit from your website."

"That was a mistake," Waxworth said. "I was overwhelmed by the workload, and I didn't realize how big a deal that was. But I know what I'm doing now."

"Is that it?" Blakeman asked. "That's the entirety of your defense?"

"I guess so."

Blakeman looked down at the paper in front of him. He seemed embarrassed—an emotional state of which Waxworth would have thought him incapable. Waxworth hoped whatever tongue-lashing Blakeman was obliged to give could be accomplished quickly, so the old familiar Blakeman could come back.

"In that case, you're fired."

Waxworth was distracted briefly by more movement outside the Cube, and part of him didn't register what Blakeman had said. There was now something approaching a crowd near the back wall. Waxworth realized that they were there for a show, and this realization brought Blakeman's words to him.

"I have a contract."

"The contract calls for original work. You've been violating it for months. Our lawyers have recommended that we cancel it effective immediately."

Waxworth couldn't believe they'd already gotten lawyers involved. He'd only learned of the situation himself an hour earlier. Had Penty called Blakeman before calling him?

"There's got to be some way to work this out," he said. "I know I fucked up. But I moved my whole life to New York because you told me we were going to do great things. Don't you owe me anything?"

Blakeman looked down at the paper again, and when he looked back up his expression had softened slightly.

"This isn't really up to me."

"You wanted Teeses and comments and shares, and I got you all that. I've done a lot of good work, and I've got a lot of readers. Do you really think it's such a good idea to give in to pressure from some random anonymous reader? Don't you think there might be a backlash?"

"I'll be honest with you," Blakeman said. "Adrian's thrilled to have an excuse to cancel your contract. Ad sales are in the shitter right now. All those Teeses and shares have not turned into revenue. Most potential bidders, they just want the magazine's name, with as few liabilities as possible, and right now your contract is a liability. Whoever buys this thing will probably turn it into a content farm, outsource all the writing. For all I know, Adrian's the one who tipped Penty off."

"Are you serious?"

Blakeman shrugged.

"I've got no idea. I wouldn't put it past him. Either way, he's not changing his mind. We actually talked about clawing back some of the money you already got. I had to convince him that the bad press wouldn't be worth it."

"So that's it?"

"I'm afraid so," Blakeman said. As they stood and walked to the door, the onlookers outside scurried away, as though they could not be seen through the glass. Blakeman put an arm lightly around Waxworth's shoulder. "Listen, the next little patch is going to be pretty rough for you. But there's something you need to remember."

"What's that?" Waxworth asked.

For the first time that day, Blakeman's old smile came back. As angry as Waxworth was, he found the sight of it comforting.

"Everyone loves a redemption story."

When he got outside, Waxworth called John Craig. He needed to warn him what was coming. That was what he should have done right away. Maybe they could stall the *Reverberator*, keep the news under wraps and rush the proposal out. What happened with the *Interviewer* hardly mattered. It was a sinking ship.

"What the fuck," Craig said after his assistant transferred through the call.

"You've heard?"

"Of course, I've heard. It's been up for an hour."

"What do we do now?"

"We don't do anything. It's over."

"I need to sell this book," Waxworth said. "I can live with a little less money. We'll wait a few weeks for this to blow over, and we go out with it then."

"We're not going out with this proposal. You want to write a book about decision-making, and the one thing everyone now knows is that you made some colossally bad choices."

"The book doesn't have to be about decision-making. I can change things around if that will help."

"You know that you're completely toxic now, right?" Craig explained, not unpolitely. "You and Mario Adrian—the men who brought down the *Interviewer.*"

"You're saying that a one-hundred-and-sixty-year-old magazine—an American institution since the time of the Civil War—is going to fold up shop because I smuggled some old blog posts onto their site?"

"I'm not saying it, but some people will. They won't even know what you did wrong. They'll just know it was dishonest. The number one thing people want in a nonfiction writer is someone they can trust."

"So we build back that trust. Isn't it your job as my agent to help me with that?"

"I'm not your agent anymore. I've got my own reputation to consider."

He should have been mad, but he couldn't blame Craig. He'd hired him only because of his numbers, and he'd understood that Craig had taken him on for the same reason. Now those numbers had changed. For the moment, he had no one on his side. He wanted to call Lucy, but he couldn't do that until he had everything straightened out. He'd promised himself that.

The last time they'd spoken had been the day after his debacle with Margo in the hotel. He'd texted her as soon as he'd gotten home. Before that, his messages had been carefully calibrated, in a way he could now admit to himself, to be conciliatory and sympathetic without actually including anything that encouraged her to come back right away. He'd wanted this time to maneuver. But no longer. *We need to talk*, he'd written. *I want to figure this out. I'm sorry for everything.*

She hadn't responded, so he'd called the next morning. When she answered, she said she was on her way to work—he'd forgotten that her school year had started—but she seemed happy enough to hear from him. She'd told him that she accepted his apology, but that she wasn't yet ready to come back. This "yet" seemed to signify that she knew she'd be coming back eventually. So what was she waiting for?

Waxworth had spent a long time thinking the problem over. She'd picked up everything to follow him to New York. She'd trusted in his picture of the future: a year from now, he'd told her, they would be back in Madison, his writing career would be launched, and they could start a family. He had to regain her trust, and this meant that he had to make his prediction come true. He had to get a contract and bring her home. That's when he'd promised himself he wouldn't call again until he had everything in place.

It still seemed possible to him. Craig had talked about a half-million-dollar advance. Even if his brand had lost eighty percent of its worth, that meant six figures, a round number he could proudly present to Lucy. Whatever ethical lapses he'd committed—he wasn't a hundred percent prepared to admit that he'd committed any, since he'd never been made to understand that the field in which he was working *had* any ethical standards, but just assuming that there had been lapses—they didn't suggest that he'd lost the ability to write things that people wanted to read. He had a proven track record—most of the copying he'd done had been from his own work!—and Bayesian theory told you not to overcorrect in response to one bad data point.

If he could sell the book before she finished her semester, they could go back to Madison for Christmas and stay. That was a quick turnaround, but he didn't want to wait until the school year ended in the spring. He no longer had any reason to stay in New York, and she had no desire to be there. The sooner they got out, the better off they'd be.

There was another reason for his urgency: he was nearly broke. This was perhaps more surprising than anything else that had happened to him over the past month. He'd always been so diligent about financial planning. He'd gotten his first job in high school, tutoring younger kids in math and computer science, and he'd worked his way through college. There had never been money around when he was growing up, and he'd never taken it for granted as an adult. His family had not been rich like the Doyles, or even comfortably middle class like the Kellehers—whom, with their two-income household and front and back lawns, he'd always viewed as rich. The moment he'd sold YOUNT, he'd paid off his loans. The single extravagance of his life thus far had been Lucy's engagement ring.

Before the move he'd put together a detailed budget, one that would have allowed them to finish the year having added to their savings. They had three sources of income: Lucy's salary, his own, and the rent (minus carrying costs) on their place in Madison. If for some reason they lost one of these, they would break even for the year. If they lost two—an unlikely worst-case scenario, perhaps involving some catastrophic event in New York—they would probably be back in Madison, where they could rely on the Kellehers' help. But it turned out there was a worse worst case than this. He'd lost his salary, and Lucy was spending hers on whatever living arrangements she'd worked up. Their tenants handed the monthly check directly over to the Kellehers, and Waxworth could hardly ask them to pass it along now. He wasn't sure he was even entitled to it, given the fact that they'd provided the down payment for the place. What little he'd saved from his first six months at the *Interviewer* would be gone by the end of the year.

If he couldn't sell a book, he'd need to get another job, and it wouldn't involve writing for a national magazine. Likely it wouldn't involve writing at all, except maybe code for some start-up. He couldn't return to spending all day in a cubicle, punching lines of Python into an IDE, writing blog posts at night, trying to build up some kind of following, all in hopes of one day earning himself a third chance.

How had he fucked it all up so badly? It was an important part of his ethos to admit mistakes and analyze them. Getting things wrong had always been central to his method. If he'd now gotten things catastrophically wrong, that only meant there were greater lessons to be learned.

But why? he suddenly asked himself. That is, why do we have to *keep* getting things wrong? If we really learned from our mistakes, shouldn't we make fewer all the time? We weren't just occasionally irrational. Something in us *wanted* to be irrational. Something wanted, perhaps, to be wrong. We hated nothing more than indisputable evidence, because we wanted to dispute. We wanted to take sides. We had more and more information, which ought to make our decisions better, but all we did with this information was find new ways to fuck up.

He realized what he had to do next. This would be his new proposal. He wouldn't avoid what had happened to him; he would use it as a launching point for what he wanted to say.

That afternoon, Sam went to the public library, where he found a dozen relevant books on evolutionary psychology, economic modeling, even military history. He spent the next two days and a sleepless night in between writing a summary. He even gave it a kind of epigraph, from Talleyrand: *It's worse than a crime; it's a blunder.*

He knew he had a winning idea. He needed to get someone on the phone to whom he could explain it, someone who would listen and understand. He'd received countless offers of representation over the past six months. He was locked out of his *Interviewer* email account, so he didn't have any of those correspondences, but he could remember most of the names. He found an online database of literary agents, and he started making calls. Over the course of the morning, he called a dozen agencies, where a dozen assistants took down his name and number. By the afternoon he'd gotten no calls back.

The only person left was the junior agent who'd claimed to know about analytics. Eliot something. He'd worked for an agency that began with a *B*. Waxworth went back through the agency database, and he called all the *B*s, asking each time to speak with Eliot. The very last one was the Buckley Agency, where the young man on the other end paused for a moment before answering.

"Do you mean Eli Elliott?"

"That's right," Waxworth said. "Eli, not Eliot."

There was another pause before the young man said, "Speaking."

Eli Elliott was still answering the agency's main line, and based on the sound of his voice, he was about fifteen years old.

"This is Sam Waxworth."

They spent the next half hour talking about the idea.

"I know people don't think I'm the most trustworthy narrator, but if we make my mistakes the hook for the whole project, use them as a launching pad for what I want to say, it will neutralize the critics. It will give me a kind of credibility."

"It's brilliant," Eli said. "I'm going to email you an agreement the moment we get off the phone."

"There's one more thing," Waxworth told him. "I need to have it sold by the end of the year."

Eli laughed.

"It takes time for people to read things, and everything pretty much shuts down for the holidays in mid-November. If you want an offer by then, we'd need to have a proposal in people's hands within the week. This process usually takes months to get right. The better bet would be to wait a little bit, catch people when they're coming back to their desks in the new year."

"I can't wait that long," Waxworth said. "I already have something written."

"You're prepared to write about what happened at the *Interviewer*?"

"Why not?"

"In that case, I can sell it. Have you thought about a title?"

Waxworth answered immediately.

"The Index of Self-Destructive Acts."

Waxworth sent over the signed agreement along with the pages he'd written, and Eli called back within an hour.

"To be honest," he said, "it feels a little dry. I thought you were going to write about your experience at the *Interviewer*."

"That's just a jumping-off point."

"The more personal you can make it, the better chance we've got, especially if you want to do this quickly."

"I'm not really interested in writing a memoir."

"Think of the proposal as a blueprint. Once construction is underway, you can build whatever you want."

The most important thing, Waxworth knew, was getting something sold. He set aside all his volumes from the library and simply tried to write down what had happened. He'd never written about his own life before, but it seemed to pour out of him. He knew that he needed to keep going, which made it all easier. He included things that he would never have mentioned in conversation, things he could certainly never put in a book. He wrote that Max Blakeman had told

him that the quality of his writing didn't matter. He wrote that
Mario Adrian never read the magazine. He wrote that he'd been
fired because it would make it easier for Adrian to find a buyer.
Though he didn't know it to be true, he wrote that Adrian had been
the *Reverberator*'s source.

Once he'd written all this, he wrote that he'd brought everything
on himself. This was what editors wanted to hear, and it was also—
he realized once he'd written it—the truth. The *Interviewer* had
given him the biggest opportunity of his life, and he'd thrown it
away because he'd fallen in love with a girl he hardly knew, the
daughter of someone he'd written an article about. He'd acted irrationally, he'd fucked up his life in the process. This book, he wrote,
would be his attempt to reckon with these facts.

"I can sell this," Eli said.

Thought you'd want to see, read the text that Eli sent him on the day
the proposal went out. Beneath it was a link, which Waxworth followed to an article in the *Reverberator* with the headline "She Had
His Number." The piece began, *"I did it for love," serial word thief
Samuel Waxworth plans to say in new book*. There followed an article
built entirely out of quotes from his proposal, which seemed to have
no other purpose than his embarrassment. He read through the
whole thing and then turned to the comments section.

Someone's got to dox this femme fatale, read the first comment,
from *Lord of the Files*. There followed a string of guesses, most of
them people he didn't even know, until someone wrote, *Does Doyle
have a daughter?* Two comments down, there appeared a photo of
Margo, from some fund-raising gala. *Gotta admit I'd rip off the
herald for a piece of this.*

Nah way her face is flat, wrote *Naughty by Nate*.

*Every time we talk about a hot chick Nate thinks her face is flat.
Not. That. Hot.*

"How did this happen?" Waxworth asked when he got Eli on the phone.

"Probably some editor's assistant is friends with someone at the *Reverberator.*"

He seemed surprisingly calm about the whole thing.

"What can we do about it?"

"We don't have to do anything. This is great for us. You're still news. If the *Reverberator* can make a story out of your proposal, imagine what they'll do with the book. This is exactly what we want."

"There's a lot of personal stuff in there," Waxworth said, as though they'd published his journals, rather than things he supposedly planned to put in a book.

"Go take a long walk," Eli said, in a counselor's tone that didn't fit his pubescent demeanor. "In a few more days, you're going to have an offer."

But he was still sitting in front of his computer, reading the comments, when his phone rang an hour later. The call was from Max Blakeman. He assumed that Blakeman had seen what he'd written. Maybe he'd explain that Waxworth had violated some non-disparagement clause and owed them all money. Waxworth didn't pick up, but when he saw that Blakeman had left a voice mail, he couldn't resist listening to it.

"Hi Sam, this is Max Blakeman," the message began. His tone was surprisingly friendly, even concerned. "This will sound strange, but Justin Price is taking your wife to New York General. I don't have much more information. I don't think it's anything life-threatening, but you'll probably want to get over there."

There was no sign of Justin Price at the emergency room, but a woman at the desk said that Lucy had been admitted to the hospital a few hours earlier.

"She's on the seventh floor," the woman said, after looking up the name. "That's the general ward," she added with a smile, "which means she's probably stable and on the mend."

Upstairs, a nurse took him into the room, where Lucy was asleep. She had an IV in her arm and a pulse monitor on her finger, but otherwise she looked perfectly comfortable. Sam sat next to her, watching her breathe, and felt his heart lift. It had been only a few weeks—a shorter period than they'd been apart after he moved—but he'd missed her so much more this time.

He'd been sitting for a few minutes when a doctor came in to look over her chart and waved Sam outside.

"We believe your wife has acute Lyme disease," the doctor said. "We're still waiting to get some tests back, but it seems she got infected several months ago, and she's been quite affected by it. She says she's had some cognitive problems, besides the usual fatigue and joint pain."

"She hasn't been well for a while now," Sam answered, feeling suddenly like an irresponsible husband. Had she told the doctor that she wasn't living with him?

"Based on her numbers, that doesn't surprise me a bit. The good news is that she should make a full recovery. We're going to keep her here for a few days, on an IV antibiotic. It's a heavy dose, and it will probably wear her out a bit, but it should do the trick. Right now, I'd like to let her sleep. Why don't you go get yourself a cup of coffee or something to eat, come back in an hour or so?"

He walked outside to York Avenue with the feeling of a great worry lifted—not just the worry of the hour since he'd gotten Blakeman's voice mail, but something much larger than this. All that craziness about a psychic, Lucy's decision to walk out on him, her refusal to come back—it hadn't even been her. It had been some kind of bacteria. She'd been infected with something. They were going to get it fixed, and she would be her old self.

He had a slice at a pizzeria on the corner, and he stopped on his way back to buy flowers outside a grocery store. He'd never been good at these things, so he asked the man to pick something and wrap it up. As he walked back into the hospital, he passed a pregnant woman in a wheelchair, apparently in labor, and he imagined someone thinking he was a new father, returning to his wife with a bouquet. The idea pleased him. Perhaps it wouldn't be too long before he was walking into a hospital with flowers again. He was still enjoying this thought when he ran right into Margo Doyle.

It was shocking to see her in the flesh, as though she'd ceased to exist, become just a character in his book proposal. He worried that she'd already heard about the thing, but she gave no sign of it. Ever since he'd left the hotel, the idea of seeing her had filled him with embarrassment, but he didn't feel that now. He understood what had happened. He hadn't wanted to be with her after all. If he had, why had he not been able to do it? While he was still in that room, this inability had felt shameful. Worse than shameful: irrational. There had been no good explanation for it. He could almost have believed that Lucy's psychic really had put some spell on him. But now it all seemed clear. He was just lucky that this clarity had returned before things went too far. The step he'd nearly taken would have been irreversible. Now it was not too late to go back.

They spoke briefly while Sam held the flowers dumbly between them, as though presenting them to her. More than anything, he found himself eager to get upstairs. He wanted to be there the moment Lucy woke up. How strange it would have seemed two months ago to be hurrying away from Margo for a chance to see his wife. He didn't exactly regret getting tangled up with her, despite all the pain that had come out of it. This was the funny thing about causality. If you were happy where you'd wound up—and Waxworth thought that he was, or that he would be in a matter of days—you had to accept that everything that had come before had played some part in determining it. You could not pull out one thread and wish it away.

Upstairs, a nurse said that Lucy was still asleep and directed him to a small waiting area. A television mounted on the wall was playing the World Series. The Yankees were playing the Phillies, and Buck and McCarver—the agents of Frank Doyle's downfall—were calling it. Waxworth had been too busy with his proposal to watch much of the first few games. It was the top of the first, and Jeter led off with single against Blanton. He moved to third on a Johnny Damon double, and he was just scoring on a Teixeira ground out when a nurse arrived to say that Lucy was awake.

Waxworth walked into her room almost shyly, presenting the flowers as though arriving for a first date. She smiled but made no move to take the bouquet from him.

"Thanks for being here," she said.

"Of course," he told her. "I came as soon as I got the call."

"I'm glad someone found you. Things were so crazy. I guess it just didn't occur to me."

He'd assumed that she knew he'd been contacted, that she had asked for him. Perhaps she was just a little confused.

"How are you feeling?"

She paused as though taking an internal inventory.

"Better, I think. I guess it will be a little while before the antibiotics have any effect, but just getting some rest made a big difference. And it's nice to finally know what's wrong."

He was still holding the flowers out, but now he pulled them back, and placed them on the table beside the bed, on top of a tray of finished food.

"I'm selling my book," he told her.

"That's great," she said, and she smiled again, a bit distantly, he thought. He'd built this news up in his mind as the decisive point in their reconciliation. He had to remind himself how tired she must be.

"Eli—that's my new agent—he thinks we can get a pretty good price."

"No one's bothered by what happened at the *Interviewer*?"

"That's the beauty of my new idea. It's about making mistakes and learning from them. It's going to be about all the things I did wrong." He laughed. "I did a lot wrong, Lucy. I know that."

"Isn't it a little soon?"

"What do you mean?"

"I mean, isn't it soon for your redemption? Do you really think you've learned whatever lessons you have to learn from all this? Doesn't it take a little more time than that?"

He didn't know what to say. She sounded like one of those guys in the comments section.

"There will be plenty of time for reflection back in Madison, while I'm writing the book, but I can't do that until I get the contract."

"In Madison? I always assumed that if you sold a book you'd want to stay here."

"I want to go home," he said. "Right away. I mean, after you're feeling better and get released from the hospital, of course. But as soon as possible after that. We could be home by Thanksgiving if you want. Christmas at the latest."

"I can't just walk out on my job."

"You're not walking out. You're sick. They'll understand that. It's going to take a little while to get you back on your feet. You can start teaching again in Madison, in the fall."

"I need to speak with the school before I make any decisions about taking leave."

She still wasn't thinking straight. He knew he shouldn't be getting frustrated—*cognitive problems*, the doctor had said—but he couldn't help it.

"I thought you would be thrilled by this plan," he said, trying to keep the exasperation out of his voice. "You've been desperate to get back home the whole time we've been here."

"Two months ago I was desperate to get home. We've barely spoken since then, so I don't think you should assume that you know what I've been feeling."

The sharpness of her tone surprised him.

"The only reason I haven't called is because I wanted to have everything in place first. I wanted to plan everything out for us."

"Isn't that something we ought to be doing together?"

Of course she was right.

"Fair enough," he said. "We can take our time. Talk things over. If you want to try to finish out the semester at school, that's fine. You can finish out the whole year if you want. I'm in no rush. I just thought that you wanted to get home."

"I'm not coming back," she said.

She wasn't listening at all, he thought.

"I just said we don't have to go back. That's what I'm trying to tell you."

"Not coming back to *you*, Sam."

What struck him most was the clarity of it. Her expression wasn't that of someone in a mental fog.

"I'm sorry for springing all of this on you. I should have waited until you felt better. I thought it would be good news, but of course you've got a lot of other things to think about. Let's just get you out of the hospital and we can go from there."

Her expression softened now, and somehow this was even worse.

"I've been doing a lot of thinking since I've been gone," she said. "Maybe I'm confused about some things right now, but I know I'm right about this. I'm going to stay in New York, and I'm going to live on my own. If you want to go back to Wisconsin, that's great. If you want to stay here, that's fine, too. I'm happy you're selling your book, and I want you to succeed. I'm proud of you. But we're not getting back together."

"What about starting a family?"

"Do you even want to do that?"

"I'm not really sure," he admitted.

"Go write your book. It will be a big hit, and you'll meet someone right for you."

It seemed pointless to try to change her mind in that moment, to hector her while she lay in a hospital bed.

"I'm sorry I dragged you here against your will. I should have just listened to you in the first place."

"It was the best thing that ever happened to me."

"What now? I don't want to leave you alone."

"My parents are in the air. They'll be here in a couple of hours. Mostly I just want to sleep."

She closed her eyes, and he walked back out to the waiting area, where the game was still on. He wouldn't leave his wife alone. He would wait until the Kellehers got there, explain the situation to them.

After another inning, he checked on the story at the *Reverberator.* The headline had already changed. "Did Samuel Waxworth Plagiarize His Book Proposal?" It was irresponsible, he thought. What could he have possibly plagiarized? He'd only really written about himself. He forced himself to continue on: *Just hours after we posted Samuel Waxworth's book proposal, an eagle-eyed* Reverberator *reader has spotted yet another example of plagiarism. "The things that can't be proven are the only things worth talking about in the first place," Waxworth writes. The only problem being that this line comes unattributed from a five-year-old column by none other than racist columnist and Waxworth-profile-subject Frank Doyle. We are in the process of reaching out to Waxworth's agent.*

On the phone, Eli sounded shell-shocked.

"This is bad," he said.

"It was one line that Frank said to me in conversation. I had no idea he'd ever written it down. I wasn't plagiarizing him. He was plagiarizing himself."

"We've already lost half the houses," Eli said. "We need to pull the proposal."

"The proposal was never supposed to be made public."

"I'm as disappointed as you are. This was going to be my first big sale. But we can't do it right now. We'll pull it, we'll rework it, and we'll go back out in a few months. We'll be selective. We won't be getting you much money, but you'll have a contract. You just have to write a great book. That will solve everything."

Waxworth hung up the phone, and he sat unmoving in front of the TV. The Phillies were at bat in the bottom of the fourth. Ryan Howard scored to tie the game at two. A few minutes later, the inning ended, and the TV cut to commercial. The ad that followed shook Waxworth from his stunned stupor, mostly because of its poor production values. It belonged on a local late-night broadcast, not a World Series game. Waxworth thought for a minute that it might be some kind of joke, an ironic ad by a beer or car company, but once he saw the face on the screen, he knew it was something else.

He had spent a lot of time looking at this face and listening to this voice at the start of his time in New York. He'd written his very first post about Herman Nash. Now here Nash was on the screen, proclaiming the end of the world. And it was just a few hours away. How did something like this make it to national television? For some reason, Sam imagined his mother watching it, though he was sure she wasn't tuned in to a baseball game. If she were, she might take a moment to pray, to clear her conscience just in case the man was right.

Sam almost never thought of his mother without feeling a great surge of anger, but now he felt empty. So much of what was wrong with him was her fault, he thought, but no doubt whatever was wrong with her had come from somewhere, too. How far back did it all go? At what point could we just start everything from scratch? Self—or circumstance?

When he got back to Wisconsin, he would go to see her. For he knew now that he was going back. Lucy could stay and have whatever sort of life she wanted, but his time here was done.

Once he realized this, he realized too that he didn't want to face Mitch and Joan Kelleher. They weren't, after all, his parents. They were hers, and if the marriage was over, they had nothing to do with him. He didn't want their sympathy, and he certainly didn't want their genial insistence that Lucy would change her mind somehow. Better that they think he'd just left her here.

Now the game was back on, and he wanted to watch a bit more. The season would be over in another day or two. He'd stay for a few more pitches, then take the train back to Brooklyn. Swisher walked to lead off the inning. He'd just watch another at bat. When he got home, he'd start packing his things. Now Cabrera singled to move Swisher into scoring position. They had a rally going. He would just watch the rest of the inning. Might as well stay to see it through. But when the inning ended, he couldn't get up. The Kellehers were still in the air. They wouldn't arrive for hours. It was going to be a long off-season. He had time to watch the rest of the game. When it ended, everything would start back at zero.

7.

It was all going to end.

The afternoon light was fading, the street lamps had come on. The boys who lived in the neighborhood's outer reaches had already headed home. You could play a decent game with two in the outfield, but things got tougher after that. With six on a side, everything that cleared second base on a fly got called a home run, everything that skipped through on the ground was a double. But someone still had to run the ball down. The game slowed, departures took on their own momentum. The Bonner twins left together, then Kowalski and Novak, cousins who shared a room above their grandfather's butcher shop. In a sense it was done when the first boy went. You could play pepper with three; with two, you could still have a catch. Alone—as he was now, he understood— you could throw a ball against a stoop, aiming for the edge of a step so that it caromed off in an unpredictable direction, forcing you to set yourself quickly and react as Jackie reacted to the ball coming off the bat. But to throw the ball you needed to move your arm, which he couldn't do. To set yourself, you needed to move your legs, and so far as he could tell his legs did not exist.

I'm here, a voice said, as though in answer to a question he didn't know he'd asked. Not alone, then. But where was he? Floating just above the pain. He might have escaped it entirely, but something held his hand, pinning him back to the world. All of the pain was still there, but beside him, like a stranger's bag he'd been asked, in a station, to watch. *Agonies are one of my changes of garments.*

He was glad to be pulled back. He didn't want to go yet. The voice spoke again, and he thought it might be Kit. *I'm here*, it said, and he knew it wasn't her. It sounded like her, but he could tell the difference after all these years. Where was she? He'd asked them already. Why wouldn't they say? If it was going to end, she needed to be there.

Now he'd found her, standing on the altar at St. Patrick's, a bridesmaid perched behind the Communion rail in a purple dress with bulbous sleeves. Her red-blonde hair was cut in bangs that framed wide eyes, long lashes, cheeks supported by that almost taunting smile. She'd spotted him looking at her. He was a second cousin to the groom, more friend than relation, seated in a pew most of the way back, but he'd taken a place on the aisle. Across that distance they eyed each other while bride and groom exchanged vows and the rest of the wedding party looked on solemnly. He returned the smile, and she widened hers.

Now was the time for one or both to look away and blush, but neither did. He could tell she'd recognized him. She might have seen his picture, maybe watched him on TV. Of course he knew exactly who she was. Surprising that they hadn't met sooner. Tommy Quinn was one of the mayor's great supporters. About her family Frank knew almost everything: her great-grandfather had himself been mayor for a term, her grandfather had funded Tammany after starting the Irish Catholic answer to the WASPs at Morgan Stanley and the Jews at Lazard, her mother had died when she was small, her father brought her everywhere. There was a joke in certain circles. Because she was so beautiful, people said Tommy kept her around to distract you while he picked your pocket. None of this prepared him for the way she looked at him from up on the altar, while a sacrament was conducted just over her head.

The mass was over now, and while they processed the organ played "Take Me Out to the Ball Game." The organist's name was Gladys Goodding. Famous for once playing "Three Blind Mice" when the umpires stepped onto the field. Between innings now she played "Thanks for the Memory," played "Que Sera, Sera," played "Auld Lang Syne." The game was like a funeral, the place nearly empty, a few thousand people at the most. Everyone knew it was going to end, though it hadn't yet been announced. O'Malley had been trying for years to get out of Ebbets Field. He wanted a new stadium on Atlantic Avenue, had enlisted Buckminster Fuller to design a geodesic dome for the site, but Moses would only offer him space in Queens. The team had played eight games that year in Jersey City as a kind of threat, and the *Herald* had already reported the offer from LA. Frank was seventeen years old, a senior in high school.

He bought the cheapest ticket on offer, top of the upper deck on the third-base line, and moved down twenty rows to where the seats nearly hung over the field. There was barely any foul territory at the park, he was on top of everything, and he would remember it all. The Schaefer Beer sign above the scoreboard, whose *h* lit up for a hit, *e* for an error. Below the scoreboard: HIT SIGN, WIN SUIT. ABE STARK, BROOKLYN'S LEADING CLOTHIER. In the bottom of the first, Jim Gilliam walked, and Elmer Valo doubled to drive him in. Frank marked it all on his scorecard. That run was all the team needed. McDevitt pitched a shutout, and the Dodgers won. For the first time in years, they weren't in the pennant race, and as the fans all filed out into the street, some joker in front of Frank said, *We'll get 'em next year*, then spat on the ground disgustedly, for there would be no next year.

So why wasn't Frank entirely sad? It seemed somehow appropriate that this day should forever separate an adolescence spent haunting

Flatbush Avenue from the great thing he would soon become. In a way it had already ended for him. This was how it always went: if you thought the end was coming, that meant it had already passed. You just hadn't noticed yet. It had when the Dodgers finally beat the Yankees in the series, the event he'd been awaiting all his life. It had ended the year after that, when O'Malley sold Jackie to the Giants—the Giants, of all teams, for whom he refused to play. He quit the game to shill for Chock full o'Nuts. It had ended when Frank read *The Adventures of Augie March* and decided that instead of being a sports-writer he'd write a novel that would do for the Irish in Brooklyn what Bellow was doing for Chicago Jews. It had ended the semester he studied Riesman's *The Lonely Crowd* in his intro sociology class, and the novel became instead a grand treatise that would explain the world to itself. By the time he finished Fordham, there was an Irish Catholic in the White House, and Frank had decided on politics.

Why had he not become great? He'd had so much time. When Lindsay was voted out and the *Herald* offered Frank a job on their opinion page, he told Kit that he'd do it a couple of years while he figured out what came next. He might run for office, or write the kind of book that had more influence on policy than any elected official. She said the job sounded like the perfect transition to bigger things.

They were six months married then. For a year, she'd taken the Metro-North down from campus to see him once a week, and they'd married the month she finished school, on the same altar where he'd seen her first. Everyone said she'd been looking for a personality as large as her father's, but there was nothing paternal in his feelings for her, nothing of Dorothea and Casaubon about them. He didn't aim to instruct her. She knew the world they occupied far better than he. Trudging east to Sutton Place to ask Tommy Quinn for her hand, waiting to be announced by the doorman, he'd felt like the young man from the provinces.

Near the end of Frank's first year at the *Herald*, John Rooney retired from the 14th, and a few people in the party talked with him about running for the seat. Of course he'd need Tommy's support to do it, would need to return as supplicant to Sutton Place. Kit was just getting settled at Q&M, eager to have a child, didn't want him spending half his life in DC. She quoted back a favorite line of Frank's— Keynes on ideas: "The world is ruled by little else"—and told him that six square inches three days a week was as good a perch as any from which to rule the world.

So the column stopped being a step on the way to the big thing, became the big thing itself. He couldn't blame Kit for this. Everyone knew that Frank did what Frank wanted in the end. There had been other opportunities over the years, but their life was so comfortable. He traveled with Brzezinski to Beijing, with Baker to Berlin. The great men of the world wanted his ear and eagerly offered him theirs. How easy to think of himself as great, rather than just a spectator to greatness.

There was nothing shameful in watching. You needed observers to make meaning, which was Frank's stock-in-trade. *The sense of the world must lie outside the world.* If no one wrote it down, it was gone the moment it happened. Words were the only way to pin things into place, to stop the flow of time. But time itself had to be spent on them, and life was wasted in a chair. One wanted to be a man of action and a man of contemplation both, to live the story and to tell it at once, to look up at the jumbotron and see one's own face staring back. If only you could know it was all being written in the book, that you didn't need to take it down yourself. If only there was a recording angel. But there was not. Nothing would be returned to us in the fullness of time, because time had no fullness. It was a constant emptying.

I'm here, the voice said. It might almost have been Margo's voice, but Margo wasn't speaking to him anymore. She thought he didn't notice, but of course he did. She was angry about a stupid thing he'd said.

Worse than stupid, he could say, now that it was past mattering. Why had he not admitted as much at the time? The rules of the game as he'd been taught them didn't allow for retreat. Apparently those rules had changed, but what was that to him? They were telling him that his day was past. Maybe so, but was he supposed to like it, too? Was he supposed to accept a buyout from life? He'd always enjoyed the fight for its own sake—he supposed it was another way of feeling like a man of action instead of a spectator—and he'd meant to battle on.

Silly to put it that way, he knew, when he'd never been in a real battle, as Eddie had. But Edward wouldn't even go to a ball game with him. What kind of boy didn't want to go to the game with his dad? That was all that Frank had ever wanted as a child. Edward wouldn't go, Margo wasn't talking to him, and Kit had disappeared. He had to sit alone, and they wouldn't put him up on the scoreboard. No one would know he was there.

If only he had written something great. They couldn't have taken that away from him now, no matter what he'd said. The great made their own rules. It wasn't a double standard, just a simple fact about what would last. Who was it who said your contemporaries judged you by your worst work, posterity by your best? Kind of thing he used to remember. He would not be judged at all, because nothing of his would last. It had already not lasted. Thirteen books over forty years, and only the three about baseball still in print. These would disappear soon enough, since no one cared about the game anymore. *Writ in water*, everything he'd done.

He had to finish the big book. If he could do that, he would live forever. They would remember him. But how could he finish it, when he couldn't move his arms? *My hurts turn livid upon me.* He needed some kind of help.

I'm here, the voice said, and he could see her, seated across the room from him, at a table full of younger guests. Despite his tenuous relation, he'd been given a seat of honor near the center of the room, and he moved his place card so that he could watch her eat. Beside her sat a boy her own age with a thick brown mustache and shoulder-length hair he would certainly cut off the moment he got a job offer. Frank watched him striking his cynical poses, laughing at the whole spectacle, as if his contempt for her world would impress her somehow. He watched her pretend to listen, until she looked up and again caught him watching. This time she didn't smile, but she didn't look away.

After dinner came dancing. He crossed the room and wordlessly reached out a hand for her. The boy beside her smirked but she stood immediately. Lester Lanin played "I'm Beginning to See the Light," and Frank sang under his breath as he took her into his arms. *Used to ramble through the park / shadow boxing in the dark / Then you came and caused a spark / that's a four-alarm fire now.* When the song ended, he didn't ask whether she was up for another. He just didn't let her go. They still hadn't introduced themselves. At the end of the next song, he looked her straight in the eye and said, "Katherine Quinn, I'd like to marry you."

She could have laughed, but she did not.

"Why don't you take me to dinner first?"

At every party they still danced to it, lived it over again, but there would be no more parties, because it was all going to end. Once he was gone, she would be the only one left who remembered it. There were so many things that needed to be remembered. Who else knew the smell of her when he held her in his arms for the first time? Who else knew the particular play of colors that struck the eye when you stepped through the tunnel and the grass came into view on a sunny August afternoon in the middle of a pennant race? Who remembered the sound that a Spaldeen made when hit squarely with a broomstick, the shiver that contact sent up your arms while you ran toward whatever parked Packard or Plymouth had been designated that day as first base? How many people alive still carried that feeling in their bones?

He wasn't ready to go yet. He had to write it all down. He still had so many things that he wanted to say. He wanted to talk. He wanted to argue. He wanted to disagree. He didn't want to be alone. *I'm here*, the voice said again. He turned his head toward it, but he saw only darkness. He fought to open his eyes. Far above him was a woman's face. She was beautiful. She might almost have been Kit, but she was not. She had a bit of him in her face. Perhaps this was what he found so beautiful. *I'm here*, she said. He saw the book on her lap. He saw the pen, poised to write. She was the great recording angel, and she was calling to him: *I'm here*. He could relax now. Everything was going to be written in the book. Every thought would be saved. Nothing would ever be lost. Each moment would last forever. Even this one. Even this one. Even

ACKNOWLEDGMENTS

The two great engines of this project—my love of baseball and my love of argument—were cultivated in a childhood bedroom (and, for that matter, a childhood) shared with my twin brother, Jim. He was the reader I kept foremost in mind while writing this novel, and I am honored to dedicate it to him.

I'd further like to acknowledge the love and support of Alice and Len Teti, Jim (again) and Alyson Beha, Lindsey and Charlie Schilling, and all of the nieces and nephews attendant to the aforementioned; Lynn, Bob, and Palmer Ducommun; and, especially, my parents, Jim and Nancy Beha, for providing the best parts of the family life depicted in these pages—particularly their sense of excitement about books and ideas—and none of the worst.

The generosity of my late grandmother, Sanny Beha, gave me much needed breathing room during the long years of this book's composition.

My friend Rick Zappala gave freely of his time and his stories. I could not have written Eddie Doyle's chapters without him. Needless to say, any errors of judgment or fact are Eddie's or my own.

Thank you to Bret Asbury, John Carr, John Crowley, Brian DeLeeuw, and Matthew Hunte for valuable early reads. (Various people mentioned elsewhere on this page also read drafts of the book, in some cases many times over.)

Bill James inspired this book in ways that should be obvious to readers; he also generously gave his blessing to my use of his ingenious statistic as my title.

I remain grateful for the hard work and dedication of Sarah Burnes and her colleagues at the Gernert Company.

It has been a great boon to return to Tin House Books and the familiar intelligence, warmth, and enthusiasm of Tony Perez and Nanci McCloskey. Thank you also to Win McCormack, for making it all possible; to Meg Storey, who saved me some considerable embarrassments; to Diane Chonette, for the best cover I've ever had; to Elizabeth DeMeo, for her sensitive editorial eye; and to Molly Templeton and Yashwina Canter, for getting the word out.

My wife, Alexandra, was seven months pregnant with our daughter, Olive, when I announced my desire to leave my job and spend a few months putting the finishing touches on this book. As I apply those touches now, Olive is three years old and Ally is once again seven months pregnant. (She also started, finished, and sold a novel of her own in that time.) Throughout this process, she has never wavered in her support. There is no way I could adequately express how much she has brought to my life. Olive's help has been of a slightly different kind. Without her, this book would certainly have been finished somewhat sooner, but it would have been finished with much less joy. I share her excitement about the arrival of her baby brother, who should beat *Index* into the world by just a few weeks. And, no, Olive, you still can't eat him.

.

The others gave no sign that they'd noticed Frank at all. He remembered that he was still in his bathrobe, which embarrassed him, though he was standing in his own house.

Kit would know what was going on. She'd taken to reading the paper in the garden while she waited for him to get up. He continued down the hall to the back door, but it was closed and locked. He looked out the window, at the cover of fallen leaves. Of course it was too cold to sit outside. Why had he been thinking of summer this morning? Kit would be in the kitchen, then. He walked back up the hall, passing again the open library door. The kitchen was empty, the lights still off, even the coffee maker untouched. Did Marinela have the day off? Had Kit mentioned something about going out that morning? Frank didn't think so, but he couldn't remember the last time they'd spoken. He'd been having trouble with his memory lately, just the usual problems of getting old, but this was unnerving. When had he last seen his wife? She hadn't been in bed when he woke up, but she always got up before him. Forcing himself now to think about it, he had a memory of sleeping alone the night before. But that might have been some other night, some other time. The harder he tried to pin things down, the more trouble he had. It seemed possible that he hadn't seen her in several days, maybe even weeks.

Back in the hall, the skinny one was walking toward the front door with a box in his arms. Emboldened perhaps by finding him alone, Frank called out.

"What are you doing with that?"

The young man continued along as though he hadn't heard anything, and Frank noticed the headphones tucked into his ears.

"What are you doing?" he asked again, more loudly this time, as he stepped into the man's path.

Moving with almost exaggerated care, the man put down the box, removed the little things from his ears, and looked up expectantly. In his hand, the tiny knobs blared what seemed to Frank